# WHITE SILENCE

## JODI TAYLOR

Published by Accent Press Ltd 2017
Octavo House
West Bute Street
Cardiff
CF10 5LJ

www.accentpress.co.uk

ISBN 9781786155658
eISBN 9781786155665

Printed and bound in Great Britain by Clays Ltd, St Ives plc

## Also by Jodi Taylor

### The Chronicles of St Mary's
Just One Damned Thing After Another
A Symphony of Echoes
A Second Chance
A Trail Through Time
No Time Like the Past
What Could Possibly Go Wrong?
Lies, Damned Lies, And History
And the Rest is History

### The Chronicles of St Mary's short stories
When a Child is Born
Roman Holiday
Christmas Present
Ships, Stings and Wedding Rings
The Great St Mary's Day Out
My Name is Markham
The Very First Damned Thing
A Perfect Storm
The Long and Short of It – a St Mary's collection

### The Frogmorton Farm Series
The Nothing Girl

Little Donkey

The Something Girl

A Bachelor Establishment (as Isabella Barclay)

This book is dedicated to the Boldurmaz Family.

This book is dedicated to those who make it safe.

# *Prologue*

People say, 'Silence is golden'
They're wrong.
Silence is white. White and deadly.

My name is Elizabeth Cage. I'm a widow. My husband, Ted, died suddenly.

They took me after the funeral. It was quick and it was quiet. No one knew where I was. There wasn't a soul in the world who knew what was happening to me. There was no one I could call on for help.

I knew what they wanted but they haven't got it yet and they never will. There's more to me than meets the eye. I haven't spent years cultivating the dowdy housewife appearance for nothing. To look at me – I'm a drab, insignificant, anxious, twenty-something housewife with unfashionable hair and no make-up. Unfortunately, my appearance is the only thing I can tell you about me. Because I don't know who I am. I don't know what I am.

Give me ten minutes with a total stranger and I can tell you things about them they don't even know themselves. I can look at someone and I know. It's not voices in my head, or visions, or anything like that, but I know. I know when you're lying. I know when you're frightened. I know when you're bluffing. You don't have to say a word, but you're telling me, just the same.

Everyone has one. Some people call it an aura. Before I'd ever heard the term, when I was a child, I called it their colour. Everyone has one. A shimmering, shifting web of colours, constantly weaving itself around them, changing from moment to moment as they react to what's going on around them. They're all different. Some people's colour has a defined shape, thick and even. Some colours are rich and strong and vibrant. Others are pale and insubstantial. Sometimes – and I hate this – there's an ominous dark patch over their head or their heart, and I know that's never good.

Sometimes, friends or family members have similar colours. Colours that are related in the spectrum. You may have noticed there are those for whom you feel a natural affinity. That will be because your colours are similar. Some people repulse you and you never know why, but it's usually because your colours won't merge.

When I was a child, there were three dustmen. One man, the noisy one, was a deep, royal blue; the older one was turquoise, and the young one a soft green. They came every Thursday morning. They ran up and down the street, shedding rubbish and shouting insults in equal measure, and yet their colours reached out towards each other, blending softly. I used to stand at the window, watching their colours swirl about them, a thing of wonder to a small girl. Sometimes, I can see the same thing with a mother and child. That gentle merging of colours as one shades into another.

But with good, comes bad.

2

I think I was about twelve years old. I was in the High Street in Rushford. The paper boy had missed us again and my father had sent me to pick one up. I stepped out of the newsagent's with his paper wedged under one arm while I carefully peeled the wrapper off my ice cream.

The sun went in. That's the only way I can describe it. The day grew dark and cold. The sounds of people and of traffic became distorted and ugly.

I looked up. Everything looked completely normal. I stared up and down the street. Cars passed backwards and forwards. People scurried about, in and out of the shops. But there was something. I knew there was something.

I stood stock still on the pavement, the stream of pedestrians parting around me.

And there it was. A woman. She strolled serenely towards me. There was nothing unusual in her appearance. On the contrary, she was well-dressed and made up and her white-blonde hair was beautiful. I felt my heart stop with fear and the thing that lives in my head said, 'Hide.'

People are blind. They never see what's really there. She walked slowly and I could see that although no one seemed to notice her, no one touched her. No one made eye contact. No one got in her way. They might not know why they were doing it – they might not even be aware they were doing it at all – but everyone was giving her a wide berth.

I stood, rooted to the spot. Terrified. Terrified of what was approaching and doubly so because no one seemed able to see it but me.

Yes, she had a colour, but it was the energy

3

emanating from her that frightened me. Most people's colours swirl a little bit, especially if they're emotional at the time, but this one ... it was as if she was encased in a thick black grease. I saw oily colours that made me feel sick. But the worst part was the movement. Her colour didn't swirl – it spiked. Like a conker case. I'd never seen anything like it before. And the spikes moved, stabbing in and out. Fast and vicious. Never stopping. In and out. Some of them extended a good eighteen inches from her body.

I was only twelve. I had no idea if the spikes constituted defence or attack but I do know that, as I saw her – she became aware of me.

My ice cream fell to the ground, unheeded. It was suddenly very, very important that she shouldn't see me. Or even know I was there. I slipped behind an advertising hoarding, easing my way around it as she drew nearer, and when she was level with me, she stopped.

I stopped too and held my breath.

She looked down at the ice cream splattered across the pavement and then she lifted her head, turning from side to side. I knew, I just knew, that she was seeking me out.

The two of us both stood motionless while everyone else, for whom this was just a normal day, streamed past us, intent on their Saturday morning business.

I still wasn't breathing. I knew with certainty that to make even the slightest sound, the smallest movement would be a very, very bad thing. For me, anyway.

My chest and head were pounding and the

pavement swam beneath me. And then, finally, she lifted her head on that graceful neck and began to walk away. I edged my way around the hoarding, watching her disappear into the crowd. She was so tall that her blonde head was easily visible. I watched her until I couldn't see her any longer and then I turned and ran as hard as I could in the opposite direction.

I was only a child. I thought all monsters were ugly. That's why they were called 'monsters'. That was the day I discovered I was wrong.

I don't know who she was or what she was. I'm sorry there's no neat ending to that story, but I never saw her again. It was, however, the first time I realised that, as well as beauty, there was ugliness in this world. Evil, as well as good. And there were things out there that, for some reason, only I could see.

And they could see me.

# *Chapter One*

All my life I've worked really hard at being really average. Exam results – good, but not brilliant. Achievements – respectable but not world-shattering. I used to spend hours carefully plotting how to come fourth at our school Sports' Day. Not a winner, but the best of the rest. Good, but not quite good enough. I was quiet, well-behaved and – ironically – as colourless as I could make myself. Instinctively, I knew I must never expose myself, or something terrible would happen. Whether to me or to others was never clear.

I'd learned the hard way. I remember a playground quarrel when I told Rowena Platt that if she didn't stop lying about who took the money from Suzanna Blake's purse, I'd send the bogeyman to hide under her bed and eat her as soon as she fell asleep. She fled crying and there was a lot of whispering which stopped whenever I turned around.

There was a similar incident when I told another girl – whose name I forget – to lay off Sharon Tucker's boyfriend. There was a bit of a punch- up after that and we were all dragged into our Year Head's office.

My dad took me aside that evening and we sat in his little shed at the bottom of the garden.

'It wasn't my fault,' I said, quietly. 'I was just

trying to help.'

'I know, love.'

'I can't help it.'

'You can't, no.'

'Sometimes, I just know things.'

'You do, pet. Me and your mother, we've noticed that. The thing is, though, knowing things is all very well and good, but keeping them to yourself is better.'

'But she was the one stealing Sharon's boyfriend,' I said, the memory of the injustice still fresh within me. 'Why did I get the blame?'

'Well, lass, was Sharon any happier when she knew?'

I had a brief memory of two girls rolling across the grass, tearing at each other's hair as their friends egged them on.

'No, I don't think so.'

'You see, pet, some people think that somehow, saying something makes it come true.'

'You mean they thought I'd somehow made her steal Sharon's boyfriend?'

I remembered, in yet another flash, after they'd been hauled to their feet, the way everyone had stared at me ...

'And you, Elizabeth? How did you feel afterwards?'

I remembered Sharon Tucker, sobbing bitterly and declaring her life was over, and how I wished I'd kept my mouth shut.

I hung my head.

'The thing is, lass, once something has been said, it can never be unsaid. You can't unsay something any more than you can unhear it, either. You might want to think about that.'

'What's wrong with me?'

'There's nothing wrong with you, pet. Nothing at all. You just have a set of skills – unusual skills. Some people can sing. Some people can cook. Some people can play an instrument.'

'And what can I do?'

He looked straight at me.

'You know things. That's all. All sorts of things. At the moment, you can't control it – a bit like falling off a bike when you're trying to learn – but one day you'll get it under control. I think it's important you control it and not the other way around.'

'How do I control it? I don't know how?'

'Well, if you don't practice the piano then you can't play the piano, can you? Why not just try ignoring it? You know how it is – ignore something for long enough, and eventually it gives up and goes away. You think about it.'

I nodded. I'd hung around the outside of giggling groups often enough, waiting to be noticed, and it was true. When you find yourself ignored, sooner or later, with as much dignity as you can muster, you go away.

I took his advice. As best I could, I ignored it, and gradually the thing in my head … subsided. Not completely – it was rather like having a TV on in the background. I always knew it was there, but I didn't have to listen.

And from that moment on, I kept my mouth shut at school and aimed at average. I think my school teachers thought that initially, I'd been attention seeking. Now I stayed apart and my classmates thought I was a snooty cow. But I'd learned my lesson. To keep quiet. And slowly, over time, the thing inside my head relaxed, closed its eyes and went to sleep.

As I grew up, I became better at filtering out the stuff I really didn't want to know. I couldn't turn it off completely, but I could relegate it to the back of my mind where it lurked quietly. Waiting.

'Why me?' I said to my dad, one day.

We were in his shed again. A magical place that smelled of wood and creosote into which he disappeared whenever, according to Mum, she had something important to say to him. I used to spend hours in there. I always remember it as being warm and golden, even in winter, and full of fascinating odds and ends. When I was small, I was allowed to hold his pencils and the tape measure. Later, I hammered the occasional nail, and even, once or twice, and with a great deal of apprehension on both our parts, my dad allowed me to saw something.

He shrugged.

'Why can't everyone else do this?'

'Because me and your mum, we think you're special. We chose you, you know. Picked you out from all the others. Your mum, soon as she saw you, said you were the prettiest baby in the room.'

He picked up his pencil.

I'm sure I wasn't, but it was just like him to say so. He's been gone a long time now, and my mum even longer, but the memories they left behind are full of happiness and kindness, and a sense of security.

'Did you know my parents at all?'

He shook his head. 'I know what you're thinking. Could one or both of them do what you can, and the answer is that I don't know.'

He marked off his piece of wood and tucked his pencil behind his ear.

'I never knew them or anything about them.' He looked at me. 'You could have a go at finding them. The law says you can do that now.'

Silence fell in the dusty little shed. He busied himself looking for screws in one of his many drawers, but I wasn't deceived. I could see his colour, swirling around his head. My dad was a deep golden colour, rather like the pieces of wood he loved to work with, and when he became anxious or upset, a dark brown stain would begin to superimpose itself. Like ink in water. He was agitated now, although you'd never know it to look at him. Only I could see it.

'No,' I said, as casually as I could. 'I know who my real parents have always been.'

He closed the drawer and gave me a hug. 'That's my girl. Now – can you hold this piece of wood for me?'

We worked together quietly for a while. Actually, I mean that he worked and I held things for him. It took a while to pluck up the courage to say it.

'Daddy, we could be rich.'

'We already are, lass, but I think I know what you mean.'

'But perhaps, if I tried, we could win the lottery.'

'Aye lass, maybe we could, but I reckon you've never heard the story of The Monkey's Paw.'

10

I shook my head.

'Well, there was a family – a mother, a father and their child. The man and the woman were very old. Their child came to them late in life.'

'Just like us.'

'Well, theirs was a son, but yes, just like us. Anyway, they weren't very well off and one day, there came into their possession a monkey's paw, and the story goes that if you made three wishes, then the monkey's paw would make them come true.'

'Really?' I said, excited.

'Ah, but – and it's a pretty big but, lass – the wishes were granted in such a way that you wished you'd never made them in the first place.'

'But …' I said.

'Ah, that's what the mother said. "But …"'

'What happened?'

'Well, she reckoned she'd wish for a bit of money. Not a lot. She reckoned no good ever came of being greedy, so she wished for fifty pounds. A respectable sum in them days. She took hold of the paw …' he clutched his Phillips screwdriver dramatically, '… and said, "I wish for fifty pounds."'

'What happened?'

'Nothing. To begin with. Next day, their son went off to work. He didn't come home.'

I could see what was coming.

'A man from the company came around that evening. There'd been an accident at work, he said. Their son had been caught in some machinery. He was dead. He was very sorry. It wasn't the company's fault, he said, but here was a sum of money as a gesture of goodwill.'

11

I whispered, 'How much?'

'Fifty quid.'

I shivered.

'That's not the end of the story though. The old lady, she thought she saw a way to make things right. Grabbing the monkey's paw again, she wished they could have their son back.'

I went cold. 'What happened?'

'Nothing. To begin with. And then, faintly, in the far distance, they could hear footsteps. As if something was coming from a long way away.'

I held my breath.

'And they weren't normal footsteps, either. These dragged along the ground, as if whoever was approaching couldn't walk properly. And the old man remembered what had been said about their son being caught in the machinery.'

He paused to rummage for something in a drawer.

I swallowed hard. 'What ... happened?'

'The old woman was running to the door. To let whatever it was into the house. He tried to stop her but she was too strong for him. I suppose she was a mother and she just wanted to see her son again. She pushed the old man away and he fell to the floor. He saw a dreadful dark shape pass the window. He could only guess at what their son looked like after falling into all that machinery. All the time, the old lady was scrabbling to get the door open and any minute now ...'

'What did he do?'

'He saw the monkey's paw, lying on the ground where the old lady had thrown it. He picked it up, and just as she dragged open the door, he made the third and final wish.'

I couldn't speak.

'And when she finally got the door open, there was no one there.'

'He wished their son to go away?'

'No, lass, he wished they'd never had the monkey's paw in the first place. Now, let's go and see if your mum's got the tea ready, shall we?'

I tried not to think about it, but I couldn't leave it alone, so the next day I went to the library and read the story for myself. It frightened me so much I could hardly move. I had a vivid flash of my daddy, lurching through the front door with his limbs hanging off and his innards ripped out and his ribs so shattered that I could see his still beating heart. He was looking at me with a mixture of hatred and despair and love, even as he reached out for me. I slammed the book shut and ran from the library. I had nightmares for weeks afterwards.

And I became very, very careful about what I did and said.

My mum died first. I was about twelve. She went into hospital and never came out. Dad was quiet and sad for a long time afterwards. His colour was almost all brown. Especially around his heart.

Life went on, though, and we learned to do without her. I studied cookery at school, and we always had a special Sunday lunch, followed by watching football in front of the telly. Then I had chess classes after school on Thursday, and on Friday nights Dad went to his working man's club. On Saturdays, we had fish and chips, and got a DVD in.

It wasn't a bad life. Dad was a retired council worker who was now able to indulge his passion for joinery. He was sweet and plump and grey-haired and I loved him very much.

And then, two days before my twentieth birthday, he died too. Quietly, in his sleep, at home. I was devastated, but I wouldn't have had it any other way. Everyone was very kind to me. I thanked everyone politely and just carried on. I would have been lonely if I'd known how.

I had a job in the council records office where they'd known my dad. After a few months, they'd sent me down to the basement to begin digitising the records stored there. It was a lonely little room, miles from the toilets and with no windows. No one else wanted to do it, but it suited me down to the ground. It became my own little kingdom down there. I set myself a daily target, had little races with myself, listened to music and was as happy as I knew how. I honestly thought that would be my life. That I was all set for the uneventful existence of an unmarried woman in a dead-end job in one of the most sedate market towns in the country. But the universe had other plans for me.

One day, about eighteen months after my dad died, I met Ted. Not straight away – I met the flasher and his puppy first, but Ted came along shortly afterwards.

I'd taken my lunch to Archdeacon's Park, because it's pretty there. The gardens slope down to the river and there's a small lake with ducks and a few swans. I chose my usual bench, laid out my lunch beside me, and sat back to enjoy the sunshine. People were strolling around, throwing sticks for their dogs or feeding the ducks. It was all very pleasant and quiet. There were people around, but not too close. Close enough for me to feel as if I belonged, but not close enough to impact on me, which was just the way I liked it.

I ate my egg sandwiches, drank half my drink, nibbled my apple and cheese, and finished the rest of my drink. Just as I always did. I liked the unvarying routine of my life. It made me feel safe. Today was Friday and after lunch, I would return to my basement office, tot up the number of completed records for the week, enter the figures into the file management system, and send them off. I have no idea whatever happened to them after that, but that's local government. You just keep doing something until someone tells you to stop.

The rest of my afternoon would be spent shelving the old files, pulling out the new ones ready for next week and tidying my desk. Once that was done, I was all set for the weekend. Clean the house on Saturday morning, go shopping in the afternoon, read the papers in the garden on Sunday morning, have a bit of lunch and then watch a film on TV. I like routine. It makes me feel safe. That afternoon, however, my life was about to change for ever.

I was just packing up my lunch box when a man plonked himself on the other end of the bench. I hardly noticed him because my attention was all on his puppy – which was exactly as cute as all puppies are. He snuffled around my ankles, not just his tail but his whole bottom wagging with excitement.

I smiled at them both. The man's colour was a

15

yellowy-brown – almost the same colour as his puppy. There was nothing to show he had any hostile intentions of any kind. He smiled back and said, 'Would you like to stroke my puppy?'

I nodded. He stood up and it was suddenly very clear to me that it wasn't his puppy he wanted me to stroke.

I remember, I felt no fear. More puzzlement as to what he thought he was playing at. I could see he meant me no harm. I put him down as a bit of an exhibitionist – no more than that, but there were children in the park, so I walloped him around the head with my plastic lunch box and walked briskly away. I didn't look behind me, so I've no idea what he did next, but I called in at the police station to report him. I spoke to a very kind policeman whose colour was almost the same blue as his uniform, signed a statement and went back to work. I was a little late, but no one seemed to notice.

Because of my lateness, I had to bustle about to get everything done, which served to take my mind off what had happened. I did occasionally wonder whether I should be more upset than I actually was, but he'd never meant me any harm, I was sure of it. Mostly, I think, I just felt sorry for the puppy.

Anyway, that evening, there was a knock at the door and there stood Ted, although obviously, I didn't know that at the time.

I saw a sturdy man of medium height, with a thick head of brown hair, eyes that were almost exactly the same colour, and the world's most unflattering moustache. His colour was brown too, fitting neatly and tightly around him.

'Miss Ford?'

'Yes?'

'Good evening. My name is Cage.' He held up some ID. 'I've come about the incident in the park this afternoon. May I come in?'

'Yes, of course.'

I led him into the kitchen and offered him a seat at the table. 'Would you like some tea?'

'Very much,' he said, looking around. 'It's been a long day.'

It was only a very long time afterwards that I realised he never once claimed to be a policeman. I just assumed …

'Well,' he said, stirring in two neat spoonfuls of sugar, 'I have some good news for you. We've got him.'

'Really? So soon?'

'Yes, the silly ass tried something similar about an hour later. In exactly the same place, would you believe? We had a presence in the park at the time – more as a precaution than anything because we never thought he'd be stupid enough to come back again, but he did, complete with his puppy, and we arrested the pair of them. They both came quietly.'

His brown eyes twinkled at me over his cup and I couldn't help smiling back.

'The even better news is that you won't have to testify in court. He's confessed. Quite willingly. We're not even sure he knows what's going on around him most of the time. Quite harmless, but he should be in secure accommodation and from today he will be.' He twinkled at me again. 'We've even found a home for the puppy.'

17

'So it's true – our policemen are wonderful.'

'Well, I certainly like to think so. Anyway, the important thing is that you're quite safe, Miss Ford, and you can consider the incident closed.'

'Well, that's amazing. Thank you so much. And thank you for taking the trouble to call this evening to tell me.'

'My pleasure. I have to say, it is nice to be the bearer of good news occasionally.'

'I don't suppose that happens very often.'

'Not as often as I would like, no.'

There was an awkward pause. I watched his colour suddenly stream towards me, as brown and shiny as a new conker.

He cleared his throat.

'Would you like another cup of tea,' I asked, almost certain I knew the answer to that one.

He accepted the offer.

An hour later he offered to take me to dinner.

Six months later he offered me his hand in marriage.

Seven months later we were married.

# *Chapter Two*

My life changed. Everything changed.

Ted had his own house and so, after a lot of discussion, we sold mine and put the money away.

'For a rainy day,' said Ted, which was typical of him. I sometimes think he was born in the wrong century. He would have fitted so neatly into the time between the wars. The 1930s were made for him. Or *vice versa*. He was a kind, gentle, paternal, family man. He loved to come home to his wife, so I gave up my job and became a housewife. I'm certain they laughed at me at work, but I didn't care. I loved being a housewife. I loved being Ted's wife. I would see him off in the morning and welcome him home at night. His house was small and easily kept clean – it wasn't all vacuuming and dusting. I had time to sit with a coffee in the afternoons and read for a few hours.

In his spare time, he would work in his garden. There was a small lawn outside the back door with flower borders running around three sides. He grew roses and geraniums and dahlias and chrysanthemums – which he would tease me about because I can't say the word. Behind the lawn, he grew his precious fruit and vegetables. Onions, peas, beans, marrows and raspberry canes. I would take him out a beer on hot afternoons, sitting on the garden roller and watching him work. He would cut the grass with an old-fashioned push mower because he liked the stripes. Every weekend he brought me in a big bunch of cut flowers for the house. He went out occasionally with his friends from work, but most of his spare time was spent quietly at home with me.

I was happy. Not the glorious, head-bursting happiness of a romantic heroine, but deeply, richly, quietly happy. I loved Ted very much and I think – I know – that he loved me.

A little while later, he came home one night to tell me he'd been offered a new job. In the private sector.

'There's a place the other side of Rushford,' he said. 'The Sorensen Clinic. They have some pretty important people staying there sometimes and they've offered me a position as head of security. The money's good. What do you think?'

'I think it sounds very exciting. Will I see more or less of you?'

'Hard to say,' he said, grinning. 'Which would you prefer?'

He took the job, of course, and as far as I could see, nothing changed at all. His working hours remained the same. He still had the occasional call-out in the middle of the night, and he still didn't talk about his work.

'I have two worlds,' he said once. 'I like to keep them separate. I leave my work behind me when I drive out the gates.' He smiled down at me. 'This is my home.'

I snuggled against him on the sofa as he sipped the one beer he allowed himself on weekday nights.

'Steady on there, lass, I nearly spilled me beer.'

I blew gently down his ear and he suddenly

decided he had other things to think about than his beer.

Yes, we were happy. I often wondered if his colleagues sneered at him behind his back. Whether they called him 'Steady Teddy' out of contempt or affection, but I wouldn't have changed a single part of my life.

That summer, the clinic held an Open Day.

'We've never done this before,' said Ted, pushing a shiny leaflet across the kitchen table.

I picked it up. 'Why are you doing it now? You surely don't need the publicity?'

'It's more of a PR thing. There are always all sorts of rumours flying around about us.'

'What sort of "rumours"?'

'Well, everything really. From brainwashing to baby sacrificing. Apparently, we experiment on human brains. When we're not eating them, of course, and turning our patients into zombies. Or dancing naked around an old stone altar to raise the devil.'

I poured another cup of tea. 'So what exactly *do* you do up there?'

'Believe it or not, it's actually quite dull. We're a small, very discreet private hospital with a high-security clearance. We take in people who, for the good of the country, daren't let it be known they're a little ...' he paused.

'Unstable?' I suggested.

'Well, madder than a fish, actually,' he said. 'We glue them back together and send them out to rule the world again.'

'Surely these world rulers won't want the public peering at them through the bars of their cages.'

He sighed, 'Bars are very *passé* these days, Elizabeth. Do try and keep up with current developments in modern mind-management.'

'Sorry.'

'Anyway, the main building will be closed to the public. Only the gardens are open and there are tents and marquees with examples of staff and patients' work. We have a great arts and crafts facility. So, do you want to come? It'll be worth it just for the gardens and cream teas.'

'And you'll have to be there anyway.'

'In my capacity as head of security, yes. I'll be the one alternately glaring at people or trying to think of a good reason to frisk the pretty girls.'

'I think I had definitely better come. It strikes me you're not safe alone.'

'Good,' he said. 'Dr Sorensen says he's looking forward to meeting you.'

I smiled. 'It will be fun. I just hope the weather holds.'

It did. We had a glorious June day and it was an excellent excuse to wear a pretty summer frock. Out of respect to the lawns, I put on a pair of ballet flats. I don't like to carry handbags, so I handed Ted my lipstick to put in his pocket. As I always did. He grumbled, but tucked it away. As he always did.

The Open Day was already in full swing when we arrived.

We pulled in at the main gate and the scanner read the security badge on his windscreen. The barrier came up automatically. The two guards didn't quite salute but they came very close.

The clinic was housed in a lovely Georgian building, built of cream-coloured stone, complete with ancient lead gutters and pipes. An unreadable crest, weathered by time, was carved over the front door.

The front gardens were very formal, with flower beds in geometric shapes bordered by neat little box hedges. Hanging baskets on stands lined the gravel drive. To the sides and rear, the style was more informal. A beautiful grass walk led down to the river, with terraced beds on either side, backed by tall yew hedges. On either side of that, grass stretched away to almost as far as I could see, with groves of silver birch, oak and beech at nicely picturesque intervals.

There were quite a few people here already, strolling around the gardens pointing at plants, or wandering in and out of various large tents scattered around the lawns. They even had a small brass band on the terrace, playing hits from various musicals.

'What do you think?' said Ted.

'It's beautiful,' I said, gazing around. 'You're so lucky to work here.'

His colour wavered for a moment, flickering almost to nothingness at the edges.

'What's wrong?'

'What? Nothing. Nothing at all. It's just that I don't get to see very much of it, that's all. I'm usually inside.'

'Down in the dungeons,' I said.

I knew at once I'd said the wrong thing. Ted's face

never changed, but his colour curdled slightly. Something cold touched my skin. There was the smell of snow. And then it was all gone. Ted was himself and the sun was shining.

I really didn't like Dr Philip Sorensen.

We found him outside the refreshment tent, talking to a bunch of local dignitaries, who seemed to have turned out in force.

'Back in a minute,' said Ted, and went to join them.

I drew back under the shade of a tree and watched.

For all that Sorensen's head was attentively bent as he listened to what was being said around him, I could see that all his attention was on me. Even as I watched, his colour, a weak and weedy thing of insipid blue-white, suddenly flared up – like one of those geysers in a national park – and roared out towards me. Like a tidal wave of dirty milk.

I stepped back in alarm, seeking shelter behind the tree. Every instinct warned me to keep my distance because I really didn't want that thing touching me.

In a flash, he had himself back under control again. His colour reeled itself in and settled about him. I watched him greet Ted, introduce him to those present, and then politely excuse them both. The two of them trod across the grass towards me. I made myself step out from the tree as if I'd just been enjoying the shade, and smile politely.

He didn't wait for introductions. 'Mrs Cage. This is such a pleasure. I've been wanting to meet you for some time now.'

Yes, he had. I could see he was telling the truth.

He *had* wanted to meet me for some time now. His colour flickered around the edges and, despite his outward polite calm, occasionally a tendril would reach hungrily towards me. I made sure to keep Ted between him and me.

'Good afternoon, Dr Sorensen. I've been enjoying your beautiful gardens.'

'How kind of you to say so. They are lovely, aren't they? Now that you've finally met us, Mrs Cage, we'd be delighted if you'd visit us more often. Ted can easily arrange a pass for you, and you can enjoy our gardens any time you like.'

'That's very kind, thank you,' I said, deciding never to take him up on his offer.

Pleasantries over, I hoped he would make his excuses – it was his Open Day after all and there had to be loads of people to meet and greet – but he showed no intention of moving away. Ted had stepped back a little and was watching something going on elsewhere. Even as I moved towards him, intending to put a little much needed distance between me and Dr Sorensen, he said suddenly, 'Would you excuse me a moment please, Elizabeth?' and strode away, leaving me alone with a man I really didn't like, and who was showing far too much interest in me. And not in the usual way.

I hadn't been this frightened since I'd seen that blonde woman, all those years ago. There was something in the way he looked at me. The thought flashed into my head. He knows something. He might not know the specifics, but somehow, he knows about me. How could that be? No one knew. I'd kept it quiet and buried it deep. I'd never spoken of it to anyone. Not even Ted. Sorensen might not know what I was – *I* didn't know what I was – but somehow, he knew there was something about me. I felt a little twist of fear, deep inside. Suddenly, the afternoon was not so pleasant after all. I really, really wished Ted would come back.

I stared down at the grass, determined not to meet his eye, and still keeping a good distance between us. We stood in silence, and I knew he was watching me. I should say something. I should start some innocuous conversation about the weather. Anything to prevent him saying what he was obviously gearing himself up to.

I assembled a remark about the lack of rain. From there I intended to move on to Ted's vegetable garden and his complaints about said lack of rain. I really didn't care if he thought me the most boring woman in creation – a persona I worked hard at projecting, by the way – I just didn't want to have any sort of conversation with this man. Sadly, he was Ted's boss so I couldn't follow my first instinct which was to turn around and run away.

I was just about to embark on the rain conversation, when, from behind me, Ted said, 'Look who I've found lurking in the shrubbery.'

Dr Sorensen looked past me. 'Now if you'd said lurking in the beer tent, I would have found that much more believable.'

The words had an edge. It wasn't quite a joke.

The newcomer clapped him on the shoulder, making him stagger slightly. I warmed to him at once. 'Sorensen, you old bugger. I can't believe you're still alive.' He saw me. 'Hello, who are you?'

26

He wasn't very drunk, but he'd had a few.

Ted said, 'Elizabeth, this is a colleague, Michael Jones.'

I said politely, 'How do you do?' and drew a little closer to Ted.

Michael Jones was damaged. There's no other way to put it. I could see it everywhere. His colour was subdued and still. Small patches of a vibrant mix of gold and red still swirled faintly, but there was a nasty dead patch over his heart. I suspected he'd suffered a loss, and very recently, too. I didn't need any special powers to see he wasn't handling it well. The rather large drink in his hand was a bit of a giveaway as well. I wondered if he was a patient here. If he was drinking, then that didn't seem very likely.

Dr Sorensen wasn't pleased to see him. Not pleased at all. I watched them face each other. Normally, when two people stand together, their colours intermingle for a while. That's when you get that feeling of attraction. Or not, of course. Sometimes you can really take a dislike to a person without knowing why. You might not know why, but your colour does and stays quiet and close to you. There's no mingling. I sometimes wonder if it's to avoid contamination. There are a lot of things in this world you don't want to touch and you certainly don't want them touching you.

Attention had moved away from me, enabling me to study the dynamics of what was going on here. There was Dr Sorensen, the smallest man present, but somehow dominating everything around him. His thin grey hair was brushed back from his forehead. His eyes were the colour of a wet pebble. I would

27

never want to be alone with him.

Then there was Ted, medium height, neatly turned out in his second-best suit, his moustache trimmed for the occasion – and no, even though he often swore he'd die for me, getting rid of the moustache was, apparently, a sacrifice too far. His lovely brown colour swirled gently around him.

And finally, the newcomer. This Michael Jones. A big man who had once been even bigger. A man who had regularly worked out and now couldn't be bothered. Something bad had happened to him and he had withdrawn into himself. His blondish hair was close cropped with just a little fleck of grey at the temples. Tired eyes regarded the world from underneath heavy lids.

Sorensen was talking.

'You should check into the clinic for a few days, Mr Jones. The rest would do you good.'

Jones shook his head. 'I want to go back. Someone should keep looking.'

Ted shifted uneasily. 'Gentlemen, it's too lovely a day to talk shop.'

There was obviously some sort of security issue here. I seized the excuse.

'If you'll excuse me for one moment, I'll leave you to talk business,' and turned away before anyone could stop me.

Sorensen's colour flared towards me again, but I had stepped behind Ted and was moving off towards the grass walk.

'I'll come with you,' said Ted. He too seemed to want to leave and so we walked slowly away. I could feel Sorensen's eyes burning into my back, but neither he nor Jones followed us.

Just as we were moving out of earshot, I heard Jones say, 'So that's her, is it?' I assumed he was referring to me as Ted's wife and thought no more about it. I just knew I wanted to go home. To get away from this place and never come back.

I didn't make the mistake of dramatically demanding to be taken home. Besides, Ted was enjoying himself, so we strolled from group to group, greeting and being greeted. There's safety in numbers. By now, the lawns were so crowded that everyone's colours merged into one indeterminate hue, with just the occasional flash as someone somewhere registered a deep emotion. The faint Sorensen-induced nausea faded soon enough.

Of course, Ted had to give me the full tour of the gardens, which was no hardship at all. We strolled across the grass and down shady paths, ending at the gardens' centrepiece, a large rectangular pool with a rather well-built Atlas, cheerfully shouldering the world as the fountains cascaded around him. The whole thing was surrounded by high yew hedges and the air was soft and warm. I could hear bees zipping past. Ted was walking around the pool, peering into the dark water hoping to spot a fish, when a voice spoke.

'You shouldn't be here. Leave and don't ever come back. And if you want to be really safe, leave your husband behind as well.'

I spun around, which was a stupid thing to do, because, as I've said, there was only a tall hedge behind me and whoever had spoken was on the other side, out of sight. I did try to peer through, but yew is thick and impenetrable.

From over the other side, Ted called, 'Come and look at this one, Elizabeth,' Not taking my eyes off the hedge, I walked slowly around the pool.

Great. I already saw things no one else could see. Now I'd started hearing them as well.

Five months later I was trying really hard to get out of going to the clinic's Christmas Party and Ted was trying very hard to get me to go.

'Why are you so keen for me to go?'

'Well, I have to go and I'd like to have a beautiful woman on my arm.'

'But you're stuck with me.'

'That wasn't what I meant,' he said. 'As you well know.'

'It's too cold, surely,' I said.

'It's inside, silly.'

I definitely didn't want to be inside that house but I could see he really wanted me to go. And after all, I'd survived the summer Open Day.

'What about the patients? How do they feel about all this going on?'

'Most of them go home for Christmas. And, sadly, those who are still there have no idea it's Christmas anyway. It's a bit of a staff knees-up, really. I've already put our names down. Don't you want to go? They're getting in outside caterers, and we've started decorating the place already. It's going to look fantastic.'

'But you won't be able to drink.' I can't drive.

'They're sending a car for us.' His colour deepened with anxiety.

I fell back on the old favourite. 'I don't have anything to wear.'

'Is that all? Go into town and treat yourself.'

'Is it formal? I don't like formal.'

'No, cocktail dresses and lounge suits. Nothing fancy. The whole point is to enjoy ourselves, not stand around looking uncomfortable. Don't you want to go?'

'Of course I do,' I said, praying that something would occur to prevent me. I rather thought I might develop a heavy cold. Nothing too serious. Nothing that would make Ted want to stay with me. I didn't want to spoil his evening. I just didn't want to meet Dr Sorensen again. And above all, I didn't want to enter his house.

I did try the whole 'too ill to go out, but not ill enough for you to have to stay at home and look after me' routine and I was wasting my time. Apparently, an evening out was just what I needed to buck me up. And he looked so much happier once I said I'd go. I told myself that so long as I stayed with Ted then everything would be fine. After all, what could Dr Sorensen actually do to me? And in a government establishment of all places? I was being ridiculous. I'd be perfectly safe.

They did send a car for us. Ted ushered me into the back. I put away the thought that we would have no getaway car, gave myself a stiff talking-to for being silly, and tried to relax.

There couldn't have been a greater contrast to my last visit. Instead of hanging baskets, this time the drive was lit up with fairy lights. White and yellow bulbs glittered and twinkled in the frost. Every window was lit up and the light from the uncurtained windows fell in long rectangles onto the terrace at the front of the building.

Far from being closed and threatening, the front doors stood wide open in welcome, light streaming out across the terrace. Even before our car drew up, we could hear the music and voices coming from within.

'A bit of a busman's holiday for me, I'm afraid,' said Ted helping me out of the car. 'Because the house is open I'm on duty this evening. Not all the time, of course, but I'll have to nip off every now and then just to make sure everything's running smoothly.'

He hadn't mentioned that. I didn't mean to look anxious, but he must have noticed because he squeezed my hand. 'Don't worry, I won't leave you alone. All the people you met last time will be here, so there's no need to fret.'

We entered the house together. I paused briefly on the threshold – expecting that familiar chill of something unpleasant, but there was nothing as we walked into one of the most luxurious entrance halls I'd ever seen.

Ted had been right about the large frosted Christmas tree, smothered with twinkling fairy lights at the foot of the stairs. A rather superfluous log burned in a huge stone hearth with the same heraldic crest cut into the wall above the mantel. Two enormous grey sofas sat on either side of the fireplace and there were any number of comfortable-looking armchairs scattered around. A currently unmanned very smart reception desk was placed just inside the door.

I was surprised at how many people were there. Little knots of people were standing around chatting and obviously enjoying themselves. No one seemed tense or threatened. I felt encouraged. It should be very easy to avoid Sorensen.

Some doors stood open, signifying the rooms could be explored. I could see a string quartet in what looked like a library. A number of doors were firmly shut, but I had no inclination to explore anyway.

Dr Sorensen bustled towards us, every inch the welcoming host. And there it was again – that little frisson of cold.

'Mrs Cage, how delightful to see you again.'

'And Mr Cage,' murmured Ted, and Dr Sorensen laughed merrily. The effect was rather like broken glass hitting a metal surface.

'I was so looking forward to seeing you again. I told Ted I wouldn't accept any excuses. We hardly had the chance for more than a few words back in the summer, did we? I'm rather hoping for an opportunity to show you around later. We're very proud of our facilities here.'

I smiled politely and decided wild horses wouldn't drag me from Ted's side that evening. And if he had to nip off to inspect something then I was heading for the Ladies and not coming out until he returned. We had a taxi booked for midnight, so only another three and a half hours to get through.

I don't drink much. I don't like it. And I particularly don't like getting drunk. Some of the things that prowl around the edges of our subconscious, waiting for that unguarded moment ... waiting for a way in ... no, I don't drink.

Not very often, anyway, and certainly not tonight.

Ted got me an orange juice. 'I'll have a drink later,' he said. 'I just have to nip off a minute. I won't be long,' and off he went.

I couldn't see Dr Sorensen nearby, but it occurred to me that the best way of avoiding him was to keep moving so I flitted from one group to another, watching out for him from the corner of my eye, and always keeping him a whole room width away. He was busy greeting his guests though, and never looked my way once.

One reason I avoid large gatherings is that, sometimes, it's like having a hundred TVs on all at once, and all of them on a different channel. I usually manage to tune most of it out, in much the same way that we all tune out street noises when we're in town, but this evening I had to stay alert, so obviously, I got everyone else as well. Just for the record, there was one couple having a really nasty row – the sort that's no less spectacular for being conducted in a hissing whisper in the corner by the buffet. One couple – not married, I guessed – was trying to sneak off together without their official partners noticing. That one was actually quite funny. A number of people had drunk too much and were already incurring spousal displeasure.

I was just oozing around a huge bookcase filled with ancient leather volumes when someone spoke in my ear.

'Hello there. I see you were stupid enough to come back.'

I jumped a mile and stared up at him.

'Michael Jones,' he said, helpfully.

34

'Yes, I remember. And apparently, I'm not the only one.'

He peered at me. 'The only one what?'

'Stupid enough to come back here.'

'Patient,' he said, flourishing a glass that I suspected had a lot more in it than orange juice. His colour, like his glass, was all over the place. He was drunk enough and rude enough for me not to feel any social obligations.

He swayed a little. 'Still with Steady Teddy?'

'Always,' I said, stung.

'Big mistake.'

He started to move away.

I blocked his path.

'And why is that?'

He appeared to have the short attention span of the more than slightly inebriated. 'What's all the fuss about you anyway?'

'What fuss?'

He leaned forwards and I was enveloped in a cloud of alcohol.

'He wants you for his collection, you know.'

I grew suddenly cold. *In vino veritas* ...

'What collection?'

He regarded me owlishly. 'The one downstairs.'

I tried not to shiver. 'In the basement?' I remembered that slight moment of nausea. That slight smell of something cold. Stay away from the basement.

He tried to look mysterious and succeeded only in staggering slightly.

I stepped forwards so he had to move back, and there we were, snugly ensconced in a corner of the library where no one could see or hear us. I remembered to ask open questions.

'Tell me about his collection.'

'Well,' he said, chattily, swaying even more.

'There you are,' said Ted.

'Bugger,' said Jones. He looked up at a security camera. 'Ah yes, of course. The all-seeing eye of security. Except, of course, when it isn't. Eh, Ted? Shame it wasn't so all-seeing when it needed to be. I said, shame it wasn't ...'

'Yes, I think we need to get you upstairs. If Dr Sorensen sees the state of you ...'

He tailed away, which was unfortunate because I would have liked to have heard what Sorensen would do if he saw him.

Pulling out a bunch of keys, he handed them to me. 'Elizabeth, would you go first, please. Down to the end of the room. Door in the right-hand corner. The big key.'

I unlocked the door and we got Jones through. He could still walk so it was mainly a case of nudging him in the right direction or intercepting him when he attempted to veer off down the wrong passage.

We staggered up a scruffy flight of backstairs that I was certain the paying patients would never see, along a badly lit corridor, through another door, and out into a large reception area with a nurses' station. Ted propped Jones against the wall, said, 'Stay,' much as you would to a very large and unruly dog, and left me alone with him. A bored-looking nurse was flicking through a magazine. She looked up as he approached. 'Mr Cage.'

'Good evening, Cathy,' he said. 'Everything all right up here?'

She sighed. 'Yes, everyone safely in bed and fast asleep.'

Beside me, Jones snorted. I nudged him. 'Shush.'

He nudged me back. 'You shush.'

Back at the nurses' station, Ted was asking to see some sort of rota. She disappeared into a nearby office. As soon as she disappeared, Ted gestured down the corridor. 'Room Twenty-one.'

I pushed Jones in what I hoped was the right direction, counting doors as I went. Odd on the left, even on the right. Room Twenty-one was at the end. I pushed open the door.

'Coming in?' he enquired, pulling me in after him.

'No,' I said, wondering why I was so unafraid of this big, slightly unstable, man who was trying to pull me into a dark room, when I was so utterly terrified of the impeccably behaved Dr Sorensen.

I didn't dare put the light on, but the curtains were open and I could see the dim outline of a bed. I pushed him towards it and he toppled slowly backwards. I yanked off his shoes, avoided his hands and covered him with a blanket. He started to snore almost immediately. I slipped out of the door. Ted was bending over a file with the nurse. Her back was to me. Catching sight of me, he said, 'That's fine, Cathy, everything seems to be in order. I'll send you up some mince pies,' and signed across the bottom of the page. She turned away with the file. I nipped up the corridor and through the door. A second later, Ted joined me, and we returned to the party, giggling like a pair of idiots.

The rest of the evening passed without excitement. Almost as if he were aware of my anxiety, Ted never left me again. We moved from group to group. People were friendly. The food and drink was good. I enjoyed myself more than I thought I would. On the few occasions I encountered him, Dr Sorensen was charming. His colour kept its distance. I had no alarms of any kind.

On the way home I stared out of the window at the dark shadows flashing past and wondered if I'd allowed my imagination to get the better of me.

## Chapter Three

It was a day like any other, except that Ted came home looking cross and tired. That wasn't like him at all, so I served him his dinner on a tray in front of the TV, and went to run him a bath. I was sloshing the water around when I heard the telephone ring, and when I went downstairs, he was pulling on his coat and picking up his car keys.

'Sorry, love, I have to go back.'

'Must you? It's so late.'

'Only for an hour or so. Don't wait up.'

'Are you sure? I can do you some sandwiches.'

'No. I won't be long, I promise, but you go on to bed. I'll try not to wake you when I come in.'

He opened the front door, dropped a kiss on my head and pulled it to behind him.

I never saw him alive again.

There was no clue. No warning of any kind. I spent days afterwards, running over those final moments together, looking for some sort of sign, but there was nothing. I heard the car drive away and then he was gone.

I had a bath myself and decided on an early night. I read for a while, expecting to hear his key in the lock at any moment. Eventually, I switched off the light, turned over, and fell asleep.

* * *

I awoke suddenly. The room was cold and dark.
A half-moon shone through the window. I knew I
was alone. I reached out an arm to switch on the
light and the pain in my chest nearly paralysed
me. I curled into a ball, fists clenched. I couldn't
catch my breath. The moon swam like a
pendulum. I felt an overwhelming sense of fear.
Of mortality. Because I was dying. I knew I was
dying. I was alone and afraid and I was dying. I
tried to call out, forgetting Ted wasn't here. I
tried to call his name and then, suddenly, I
realised it wasn't Ted's name I was calling – it
was my own. I was alone, in the dark, in my car
at the side of the road, afraid, in pain, and using
my last moments to call for my wife. In that
moment, I knew how much Ted had loved me.
And how much I loved him.

And then, suddenly – it was gone. The pain.
The fear. The moon. Everything, and I was alone
in the cold emptiness of death.

And then I was back in my bed again.

I fumbled so badly I knocked the lamp of the
bedside table and had to get up, on legs that
would barely hold me, to switch on the overhead
light. Around me, everything was exactly as it had
been when I went to bed.

Except that Ted was dead. I knew, as certainly
as if I'd been there myself – which in a way I had
been – that Ted was dead. Kind, gentle, patient,
unspectacular, dear, sweet Ted. I curled up on the
pillows and pulled the covers up around me, and
let the tidal wave of emotions wash over me. Not

just grief, but disbelief, anger, and, underpinning everything, fear. Fear that began as the faintest flicker and grew to an overwhelming flame.

I sat in the dark and waited for them. I thought it would either be the police doing some sort of official notification, or perhaps one or two of Ted's colleagues from the clinic, subdued and sad, but it was Dr Sorensen himself who pulled up in his car, just as dawn was breaking.

I wished I could get dressed, but it struck me that being awake, dressed, and already aware of what had happened would not be a wise move. I had to be seen to be normal, but it was hard. There was so much going on in my head. All I wanted to do was curl into a ball and think of Ted, and now I had to deal with Sorensen instead. The occasional tear trickled down my cheek. I brushed it away. There would be time for tears later. All the time in the world, in fact, as I faced the rest of my life without Ted, but now, at this moment, I couldn't afford to be a grieving widow. I had to be the woken at dawn, slightly confused, still sleepy little housewife, wondering what was going on.

He had brought someone with him. I could just make out two blurry shapes through the glass as I went to open the front door. The porch light had come on automatically, but I didn't switch on the hall light behind me. They were illuminated and I was in shadow.

I clutched my dressing gown in a timid gesture that wasn't entirely assumed.

'Dr Sorensen?'

'Mrs Cage, I'm so sorry to call at this hour ...'

'Where's Ted? Oh my God, has there been an accident? Is he all right?' My voice was rising in panic. I'm not an actress. I knew what he was here to tell me and the urge to give way and burst into tears was becoming overwhelming.

He said quietly, 'May we come in?'

'Of course.' I stepped back to let them in, gesturing them into the sitting room. I still didn't put the lights on, but I did draw back the curtains so that a dim grey light filtered sullenly through the windows. I couldn't see his face very clearly, but he wouldn't be able to see mine, either.

He sat. I didn't, standing with my back to the window. 'What's happened? Why are you here?'

He did it very well. If I hadn't see his nasty, dirty colour reaching hungrily towards me, then I would have found comfort and support from his words.

'Mrs Cage, please believe me when I say how sorry I am to have to break this news to you. As you know, your husband was called in for a few hours yesterday evening. Nothing major, but we both know what a conscientious man he was.'

I said, 'Was?' Because I was sure that with this man, everything was a trap. And I was angry because Ted was dead and all I wanted to do was think about him and instead, I had to confront this man and lie and conceal the truth. I wished he would just go away and leave me. It occurred to me, suddenly, that with Ted gone, there was no one to protect me from this man. This ... monster.

42

With that thought, however, came a new strength. Ted was gone, but I could think about him later. Right now, there were other priorities. He would have understood. My eye fell on the framed photograph of the two of us, taken last year when we visited London. We were at the Tower of London, posed against an ancient stone wall. Ted had his arm around me. Our heads were close together. We were both smiling. It had been such a happy day. Looking at the photo now, I felt a small warmth inside. I lifted my head and prepared to get Dr Sorensen out of my house as quickly as possible.

'I'm afraid I have some bad news. A few minutes after he left us, your husband suffered a heart attack. He was able to pull in to the side of the road, but it came on so suddenly, he was unable to telephone for help. I'm sorry to say he died almost immediately. He was discovered an hour or so later by a member of staff coming in early for the midnight shift. I don't know if this helps at all, Mrs Cage, but even had the attack happened while he was at the clinic, I don't think the outcome would have been any different. I tell you this so you don't torture yourself by wondering if he might have survived had he still been on the premises. The answer is no, I don't think he would.'

I could say it at last. 'Ted is dead?'

'I'm afraid so, yes. I cannot say how distressed I am. We all are. Your husband was highly regarded by everyone at the clinic. He was popular and respected. In short, Mrs Cage, Ted was a good man. He will be sadly missed.'

I bowed my head and let the tears fall at last.

'Please,' he said gently, 'won't you sit down? This is Dr Lewis, whom I don't think you have met before.'

She had a faint, soft Irish accent and her colour was a lovely soft jade, shot through with flecks of red because she was anxious. 'Would you like a cup of tea, Mrs Cage? No, don't you bother yourself. I'll make it.'

She disappeared into the kitchen and I sat down, choosing an armchair so he couldn't sit close to me. I was vulnerable and alone and instead of the luxury of giving way, I had to deal with a man I sensed would take every advantage of my weakness. I think I hated him more in that moment than I ever had before. All I wanted to do was nurse my grief and think of Ted.

I could hear the sounds of cupboards opening and closing in the kitchen. All the tea stuff was out on the worktop. Apart from the milk in the fridge, there was no need for her to go opening cupboards. She was snooping. I had no idea what she could possibly be looking for, but she wasn't going to find anything in the kitchen, so I closed my mind to it and focused on Dr Sorensen instead.

'Mrs Cage, this will be a very difficult time for you. I know it's customary in these circumstances to say, "If there's anything I can do to help ..." Well, I would like to help if I may. I can certainly offer practical assistance and take some of the load off your shoulders at this sad time.'

I wondered if he knew how practiced this

sounded and then pushed the thought from my mind because I needed to concentrate.

'The first thing ...' he paused delicately. 'Are you all right for money? I know you don't work ...' He paused again, because these days, if you're a woman and you don't work then there must be something wrong with you. Fifty years ago, no women worked. Now all women work. Except me, apparently.

I shook my head. We had joint bank accounts. I had the money from the sale of my house. Ted's 'rainy day' appeared to have arrived more quickly than we had anticipated.

'The second thing ...' Looking around he said, 'I can see you have a lovely home here, Mrs Cage, but sometimes, people find it almost too painful to continue in a place they've shared with a loved one. Should you feel this way I shall be more than happy to take you into my clinic for a few days, until you feel more able to cope. As our guest, of course.'

*And take the opportunity to have a good look around the house in my absence.* I wondered again what he was looking for. We both knew Ted never brought work home so did he think I would have some sort of a private journal, or a written confession, perhaps – as if I'd be stupid enough to write down my private thoughts, or commit secrets to paper.

He was wasting his time anyway. There was no way I would leave Ted's house empty for him to rummage through. There was nothing, absolutely nothing here that could possibly interest him in any way, but just the thought of him – or more likely a member of Ted's security staff – pawing away at our private possessions, rummaging through our memories …

I shook my head. 'Thank you, but I prefer to remain here.'

He took it very well. If he was disappointed, it didn't show. 'As you wish. However, there is one thing I can do to help at this sad time. Ted belonged to our pension scheme, as you probably know. I can handle all those formalities for you and, if you will permit me, I will organise the funeral as well. I do know that neither of you have family members, but there are many at the clinic who will wish to pay their last respects. Would you allow me to offer Sorensen House as a venue for after the funeral? I think it would take a great weight off your shoulders and we can convey you home afterwards.'

I considered this offer. He would certainly take advantage of my absence at the funeral to send his people in. It was beginning to dawn on me that there really wasn't much I could do about that. Go with the flow, as my dad would have said.

I nodded. 'Thank you.' I straightened my back. 'You will, of course, send all the bills to me.'

'There is no need,' he said calmly. 'Ted subscribed to our scheme. The costs will all be covered.'

That was news to me, but should I argue? The sun was coming up – or rather, the room was less grey, and what I could see of his face was sympathetic and concerned. Even his colour seemed restrained, rippling quietly around him like greasy milk. There were none of the flares I'd seen from him the first time we'd met.

'Thank you. I accept your offer.'

Dr Lewis came back in with the tea on a tray she'd apparently had to open every door in the kitchen to locate. She poured me a cup and passed it over. I looked down at the steaming liquid. To anyone else it would have looked perfectly normal, but it was bad. I could see it. The colour was wrong. I could see swirling dark streaks of whatever she had put in it. Were they trying to drug me? Would I wake up in Sorensen's clinic? A quick and easy solution for him. On the other hand, it might only be a sedative. Are doctors allowed to drug people without their knowledge? I was certain this one was.

They were both looking at me. On the surface, it was just a cup of tea. The sort of thing anyone with a kind heart would offer a grieving widow. How could I not drink it without giving myself away? I was strongly tempted to say, 'I'm not drinking this – it's drugged,' just to see what would happen. Old habits die hard, however. My dad would always say, 'Softly, softly, catchee monkey.'

I smiled politely, took the tea, set it down beside me and let the silence gather.

'Don't forget your tea,' she said, and the red flecks deepened. I wondered how much trouble she would be in if I didn't drink it.

'I won't,' I said.

Silence fell again. They watched me. I would

have to be more positive.

'If you don't mind, I'd like to be alone now.'

There was a brief pause, and then he rose to his feet. 'Of course you would, Mrs Cage.' He pulled out his wallet and took out a card. 'I'm sure you already have the clinic's number, but here's my private line. Call me at any time.'

I took it. 'Thank you.'

He began to move towards the door. I followed hard on his heels because I couldn't hold on much longer.

'And I'll be in touch about the funeral.'

'Thank you.'

*Just go. For God's sake, go.*

He made one last effort. 'I don't suppose – do you know – did Ted ever bring anything home? Might there be some files or keys ...?'

Once again, his colour reached out to me.

I shook my head. 'Never. As you know, he was very particular about keeping his work life separate.'

'Of course,' he said. 'I hope you don't mind me asking.'

'No.'

Another brief silence. Neither of them looked at the tea. They really were very good.

I moved to the front door and they followed me. Yes, I wanted them out of my home, but that was a perfectly normal reaction under the circumstances. I didn't bother being polite. I opened the door and stood waiting, clutching at my dressing gown so neither of them could shake hands.

48

They filed out. I practically shut the door on their heels. Returning to the living room, I watched them drive away.

Then I went into the kitchen and tipped the tea down the sink.

## Chapter Four

The service was at St Stephen's in Rushford. Most of the people attending it were from the clinic. I remember being surprised there was no one from the police force there, but not taking the thought any further. I was too busy saying nothing.

Dr Sorensen escorted me through the funeral and afterwards. Having him so close set my teeth on edge, but I have to say, his behaviour was impeccable. He touched me only once when we were walking along the side of the road and he took my elbow to draw me aside as a van went past. My arm did not drop off with the contact.

Back at Sorensen House they'd opened up one of the smaller rooms leading off the hall. I sat in an armchair as various people filed past to pay their respects. Most showed genuine regret – one or two of the nurses were quite tearful – and I was grateful. I had been married to a wonderful man and I had no idea how I was going to live without him.

After about half an hour, people began to drift away and I think that was the worst moment. That was the moment when I realised how truly alone I was, sitting in my armchair watching other people leaving me to get on with their own lives. Life does indeed go on. Just not for Ted.

I became aware someone was watching me.

Looking across the room, I could see Michael Jones, clutching a teacup just for once, staring at me. On the outside, he was smartly dressed in a dark blue jacket and black tie. His hair, longer than when I last saw him, was neatly combed. On the inside, however, he was falling apart. His whole colour had darkened. The swirling gold and red had almost completely disappeared, overwhelmed by the dark patch over his heart which had grown larger and was spreading tentacles everywhere, contaminating everything it touched.

Not looking at me, he walked across the room, depositing his teacup on a nearby table. As he straightened up, still without looking at me, he said quietly, 'Leave. Just walk out now. Don't look back.' Then someone stepped between us and when they'd gone, he had disappeared.

There had been something in his voice …

I got up to go and Dr Lewis was there immediately.

'I can call your car whenever you need it, Mrs Cage, but before you go, Dr Sorensen has a few papers for you to sign. He's in his office.'

It occurred to me afterwards that sending Dr Lewis was a stroke of genius on his part. I studied her colour, now back to normal – a pretty jade with flecks of turquoise. She showed no signs of her former anxiety. She gave her message in all good faith. I followed her to Dr Sorensen's office.

It was the first time I'd ever been in here. Everything was quietly expensive – from the Turkish carpet on the gleaming floor to the very good art on the walls. His desk was huge and highly polished. The blotter and his pens were precisely lined up. He sat with his back to the window, his face in shadow.

'Ah, Mrs Cage, do come in and sit down. I have some documents here for signature, if you feel up to it.'

It was very quiet in his room. I remember only the paper crackling as I took the papers and the occasional tick of his radiator.

I read everything very carefully. I don't know if I expected some sort of trick on his part, but everything was quite straightforward, just paperwork relating to Ted's pension and one or two other minor things. His colour was very restrained and under control. Had I misjudged him after all? He could not have been kinder.

And then – having lulled me, I suppose – he abruptly pulled out a small cardboard box and literally plonked it down in front of me. Everything changed. The box contained personal effects taken from Ted's locker. A spare pair of shoes. A few ties, one black. One or two paperbacks. Even an old t-shirt and pair of shorts for when he joined the staff/patient kickabout in the gym. And worst of all, one of my lipsticks, which Ted must have discovered in one of his pockets and tucked away in his desk drawer. The suddenness of it took my breath away. The very worst moment was when I opened what I thought was a small leather book to find it was a framed photo of me on our wedding day.

'It sat on his desk,' said Sorensen quietly and with those words, the tears just poured down my cheeks. I closed it carefully and held it close.

I heard him get up and open the door. He spoke

quietly to someone and then returned. He stood looking out of the window, staring at the frosty garden outside while I wiped my eyes and blew my nose.

The door opened behind me. 'Mrs Cage, I think you remember Dr Lewis.'

The red flecks were back. 'Mrs Cage, can I be of any assistance?'

Something snapped. 'What a stupid question. Of course you can be of some assistance. You can wave your magic wand and bring back my husband so that the two of us can live happily ever after, that's what you can do.'

I regretted the words as soon as they were out, but it was too late. Dr Sorensen turned from the window. His colour surged towards me.

'I think today has placed too great a strain on you, Mrs Cage. You're understandably overwrought. My colleague and I feel it might be in your own best interest to spend a few days here, recovering quietly from what has been a terrible shock for you.'

I stood up and said, as firmly as I could, 'That's most kind of you, Dr Sorensen and I appreciate your concern, but I would like to go home now.'

Too late, I remembered Jones's words. 'Leave. Just walk out now. Don't look back.' Why hadn't I listened? Why hadn't I just walked straight out of the door?

I suddenly realised that if Sorensen said no – if he refused to let me go – what could I actually do? This was a secure mental facility. There were any number of people on the other side of that door who could prevent me leaving with one hand tied behind their backs. How stupid I had been to come here.

I was suddenly hot and cold all over. A small bead of sweat trickled down my spine. The door seemed a very long way away, and there were two of them.

'I'm sorry, Elizabeth, but as a doctor and your friend ...'

'Friend? When did that happen?'

I didn't need his nasty, sickly colour streaming towards me to know I could be in real trouble here. I put the picture back in the box, picked it up and went to move towards the door. I don't think he even noticed.

'As a concerned friend, I really feel it would be unwise of me to let you return home – alone, and to an empty house – when you are so very obviously unwell.'

'I'm grieving for my husband,' I said shortly, 'not going down with flu,' and headed towards the door.

Dr Lewis was suddenly there. She wasn't happy – I could see that – but she would do as she was told. I wondered what he had told her. That I was unbalanced? Or ill? Or that I had a drink problem? What was the euphemism? Oh yes, 'tired and emotional'. Because no one who has just attended their husband's funeral would be 'tired and emotional', would they?

It was vital I didn't give way to the overwhelming fear that was welling up inside me. I said to her, 'I'd like to go home now, Dr Lewis. If there's no car for me then I'll call a taxi.'

She shot him a look, but didn't move.

He moved forwards, saying smoothly, 'You're really not well, Mrs Cage. It would be most remiss of me to let you leave us. You've been under a great strain over the last few days. I really think you should rest here for a while. Take things easy. And then when you're feeling better, we'll take you home.'

I said, 'No,' and left it at that. No ambiguity. No room for misinterpretation. Just say 'no'.

'I'm afraid I really can't allow that.'

'I'm afraid you really can't stop me.'

He said, 'Actually ...' and let the words hang in the air.

My heart was hammering fit to burst. What had I got myself into here? How did I go from grieving widow on one side of the door to possible prisoner on the other? This was ridiculous. This was England. You couldn't just lock people away because you felt like it. There's *habeas corpus* and ... civil rights ... and ... other things.

I pulled myself together, clutching my little box of Ted like a talisman.

'I am leaving now, Dr Sorensen. If no transportation is available, then I shall walk.'

'You must see how impossible that is, Mrs Cage.' He gestured outside. The afternoon, never sunny to begin with, had clouded over. It would be dark in half an hour. 'And I have to tell you that these wild statements of yours do not lead me to believe that you are capable of acting in your own best interests, at the moment.'

I kept my voice calm. There's nothing as counter-productive as hysterically trying to prove your own sanity.

'I appreciate your concern. It is unfounded. I am leaving now.'

'As a doctor, Mrs Cage, I cannot possibly let you leave in your current condition.'

'I shall telephone ...' I stopped.

He smiled. 'Precisely. No one knows you're here. At present, you are our guest, but I am a doctor. All it will take is a couple of signatures on a form and you couldn't leave here even if you wanted to. We are very concerned about your mental health – and, after all, we *are* the experts.'

'You can't keep me here.'

'My dear Mrs Cage, three signatures and it's done. Especially when one of them is from a Section Twelve-approved doctor. That would be me of course, which is very convenient. You have no relatives or carers who could look after you during this trying time and this leaves us very little choice. I beg you to reconsider this intransigent attitude. Life will be so much easier for all of us if you remain here voluntarily.'

'You can't keep me here against my will.'

'Under the terms of Section Two of the Act, we can hold you for twenty-eight days.'

'I can appeal.'

'Of course, you can. I look forward to seeing you try. I don't believe you have a mobile phone, do you? Perhaps I should mention that failure to cooperate would almost certainly result in you being detained under Section Three of the Mental Health Act, and that's for up to six months, with the option of a further twelve on top of that. You decide.'

I sat slowly, trying to ignore the clamouring panic inside and tried to think clearly. Cooperation meant being a voluntary patient. Theoretically I would be able to leave at any time. All I had to do was pick a moment and climb over the wall. Or snatch an opportunity to make a telephone call for help. Clearly, I wasn't going to be able to leave now, but if I shut up, cooperated, and bided my time, I might be able to leave tomorrow. Or the next day. Once again, I remembered my dad. 'Softly, softly, catchee monkey.'

I had a sudden vision of embedding an axe in Sorensen's head, which was both surprising and horrifying. I'd never had a vicious impulse in my life. It was also strangely satisfying. I might put it on my list of possible escape strategies.

He was talking again. I waited until he'd finished and then said, 'I'm sorry. I didn't listen to any of that. If you want any cooperation from me you're going to have to say it all again.'

He compressed his lips. His colour darkened and I had a sudden clue. He rather enjoyed inspiring shock and awe. He was less at home with ridicule. I bet he took himself very seriously.

He said, 'I shall require your keys, Mrs Cage. We'll send someone to pack a few things for you.'

I looked him in the eye. 'No need, surely. I shall be completely recovered by this time tomorrow. A toothbrush will be all that I need.'

'I don't think we should be making any assumptions at this stage.'

I felt a sudden spurt of anger. I didn't know what he wanted from me, but whatever it was he wasn't going to get it. Remembering where I was, I hastily amended that to – he wasn't going to get it easily.

I said very softly, 'I think not making assumptions

could work both ways, don't you?'

His head jerked up, but I didn't give him a chance. Wheeling about, I said to Dr Lewis, 'Well, why are you standing there? I'm assuming you have a room already prepared. If you haven't then that certainly shows poor planning on your part. Take me there at once.'

She looked over my shoulder and he must have nodded because she opened the door. 'This way please, Mrs Cage.'

## Chapter Five

I was escorted to Room Eleven – a room I guessed was something of a halfway house. Not the sumptuous comfort set aside for the rich and famous suffering a temporary disconnection from reality, but not the basement torture chambers of my imaginings either. The sort of room set aside for those who actually needed treatment but couldn't pay for it, rather than those who didn't but could. His *pro bono* work.

It was a pretty room, feminine in pink and cream. My room was L-shaped, because of the bathroom, with two long, narrow windows overlooking the gardens sloping down to the river. There was a hospital bed – even Sorensen's clinic had ordinary hospital beds, but the linen was high quality and the colour scheme pleasantly calming. I had a dressing table-cum-desk, a wardrobe, a comfortable armchair from which to look out of the window, and a bedside table. Innocuous prints lined the walls. I had several views of Derwentwater. There was a pleasant smell of lemons, but the windows didn't open and there was nothing sharp anywhere in sight.

While Dr Lewis checked over the towels in the glittering white and chrome bathroom, I was examining the outer door.

'Can I help you, Mrs Cage? What are you looking for?'

'The lock.'

'We don't lock our guests in,' she said, rather as if I'd suggested they water-boarded patients for fun.

'So I can leave at any time?'

'Well, you'll have to get past the continually manned nurses' station, down the stairs, past the consulting rooms and offices, past reception, down the drive and through our heavily manned front gate, of course.'

Which told me what I wanted to know. It would have to be the back door for me. I thought perhaps I could tunnel to freedom and then remembered I was on the first floor. Today was obviously not a day for thinking clearly. I abandoned any hope of escaping today.

'I shall want a pot of tea,' I said, deciding to make as much trouble as possible. 'And a biscuit would be nice. Is there a TV? Where's the remote? Do you have Sky? Where's the library? And I'd like a copy of today's paper. Could you have one sent up, please.'

The door was on one of those special hinges so she couldn't slam it behind her, but she did try.

I sat in the armchair and looked out over the darkening garden and wished with all my heart that Ted was here.

The tea arrived, much to my surprise. The downside was that it was accompanied by Dr Sorensen and another request for my keys. I handed them over. There was no point in fighting a battle I couldn't win. They had only to wait until I was asleep and take them. Besides, I needed a few things – toiletries and stuff. I had a little fun detailing precisely what I wanted, and where they would find it, and in which suitcase they were to put it. Then I enquired whether he would be emptying the fridge.

He stared at me. I'd been right. He really didn't enjoy not being taken seriously.

'Well, since I'm a prisoner here for an indefinite period of time, it's all going to go off, isn't it? It will stink to high heaven and that will bring my neighbours around, and then someone will realise they haven't seen me for a long time, and someone else will remember I haven't been seen since the funeral, which will bring them here and, although by that time I'm sure you'll have me buried in your deepest dungeon, trust me, I'll find some way of attracting their attention. Or, of course, you could drug me to the eyebrows and present a dribbling mumbling idiot whose claims couldn't possibly be taken seriously. Or, you could have a word with your boss, who could certainly attempt to stifle any police enquiry at birth, but we've both watched enough TV to know that some maverick police officer with drink problems and a broken marriage will refuse to give up despite official disapproval, follow it through to the end, and uncover a whole raft of illegal government activities in the process. I expect you'll get the blame for that.'

He stared at me. 'The drugging part has a certain appeal.'

He was bluffing. As soon as I'd mentioned his boss, his colour had wavered quite considerably. There was something wrong there. It dawned on me that he wasn't the only one who could extract information. Even if he didn't speak, I could see his

61

reaction to everything I said. Perhaps I wasn't as helpless as I thought I was.

I pressed home my advantage. 'And I don't suppose your boss will be happy about that, will he? Or these days, of course, she.'

His whole colour jumped.

Result!

They left me alone all the next day. They didn't starve me – rather nice meals turned up at regular intervals, but no one came anywhere near me. If it was a ploy, then it was working. Being ignored is rather disconcerting. My attempts to explore were politely thwarted by the nurses at the station. I gathered I could have anything I wanted, but they would bring it to me.

I returned to my room, picked up my book and sat down to see what would happen next.

Nothing happened next. I wondered if they were all too busy tossing our house to attend to me. I could imagine Sorensen standing in the middle of our living room, pulling Ted's books onto the floor, rummaging through our drawers, our papers, our clothes. Of his people lying on our bed while they read our bank statements. Crashing around in my clean kitchen, getting grease and dirt everywhere. A sudden flash of revulsion ran through me. I would never live happily in that house again.

For two days, nothing happened. The weather was dark and dirty. I took what I needed from my small suitcase, very pointedly not unpacking and placed our photograph on the bedside table where I could see it. Every time I felt overwhelmed by what was happening – which was quite often – I looked at Ted and thought about what he would advise me to do. How angry he would be on my behalf. How he would rescue me somehow. How no one would even dare to treat me like this if he was still alive. I thought of Ted a lot.

It began on the third day. Everything happened on the third day.

For a start, the sun came out. One or two people went out walking in the gardens. For the first time, I could hear voices under my window. I know people passed along the corridor outside my room, but the corridors were so heavily carpeted that there was never any noise. I wondered if that was deliberate. To induce feelings of isolation. If so, it wasn't working today. Today there were definitely signs of life.

Too many signs of life, because Dr Sorensen sent for me. I considered remaining where I was and telling the nurse he knew where I was if he wanted me, but on second thoughts, I was sick of this room and I wanted to get the layout of the place, and his office was on the ground floor, so off I went.

I thought there might be a bewildering number of identical corridors, all with closed doors giving no clue as to what was going on behind, but it wasn't like that at all. Each corridor was carpeted and painted in a different colour, making navigation easy even for the more challenged amongst us. Most doors were propped open. Some rooms were empty, but others were occupied. Because they were L-shaped, most of the interiors weren't visible from the corridor, but I could see personal belongings scattered on dressing tables, or vases of flowers, or the occasional dressing gown thrown over a chair.

The lift was at the top of the stairs, but I opted for the stairs themselves, which were wide and shallow and swept around in a graceful curve to the hall where we'd had the Christmas 'do'. Which seemed quite a long time ago now.

I swept into his office, channelling indignant, innocent, recent widow.

'Well? Now what ridiculous reason have you come up with for keeping me here against my will?'

'My dear Elizabeth ...'

'I am not your "dear Elizabeth". I am the recent widow of a member of your staff being kept here for some sinister and almost certainly illegal reason.'

'How on earth have you come to that conclusion?'

'You obviously want something. You're too cowardly to come out with it so it must be sinister and illegal, mustn't it. You'd hardly have imprisoned me for three days if all you wanted was a donation to the widows' and orphans' fund. So what do you want, Sorensen? Out with it?'

'I think I might dispute your use of the word "imprison".'

'I'm so sorry. I can see now that I chose poorly. How about "detain"? Incarcerate? Intern? Confine? Bang up?'

'Mrs Cage, it was never my intention to ...'

'Never mind what you didn't intend to do – what do you intend to do?'

'I just want to talk.'

'About?'

'Well, let's begin with you. How are you feeling today?'

'Well enough to go home. So no change there.'

'I don't remember Ted mentioning you were this spiky.'

'I think if Ted were here today and found you holding his wife against her will, you'd have more than my spikiness to worry about.'

His colour flared towards me. Somehow, without meaning to, I'd given him an opening.

'Yes,' he said pensively. 'Ted.'

I was making lots of mistakes, but I was learning from them. I remained silent.

'You were very fond of Ted, weren't you?'

I carefully arranged myself into a neutral position. Upright in the chair, legs neatly crossed at the ankles, hands resting lightly in my lap. No clues there, Sorensen.

He continued thoughtfully. 'Yes, he did a good job there, don't you think, Elizabeth?'

I know my face said nothing, but I couldn't do anything about my heart knocking so violently against my ribs that it hurt. Or about the huge lump in the back of my throat.

'As soon as I read your file I knew he was the man for you.'

I could physically feel the words, 'What file?' forcing their way to the surface and I was determined – absolutely determined to give him nothing. I was at a disadvantage with the low winter sun streaming in through the French windows behind him, but apart from giving him an excellent view of my less-than-perfect complexion, he wasn't getting anything from me.

'I know you have a high opinion of yourself,

65

Elizabeth, but even I never thought it would be that easy. You never questioned any of it, did you? The man with the appealing puppy? He worked for me. The *policeman*,' he hooked his fingers, 'who called around that evening to tell you everything was settled. He worked for me. His instructions were simple. Arrange a dinner date, make you fall in love with him, and marry you, and you fell hook, line, and sinker, didn't you? Your husband worked for me, Mrs Cage. Ted has always worked for me. His "new" job here was simply his old job here. I must admit I thought you'd query the lack of former colleagues from the police force paying their respects, or the lack of a police pension, but no – nothing. Too easy.'

No. He was wrong. Ted had loved me. I knew it. Men can lie and deceive – and this one certainly did – but Ted had loved me. It was there in the way his colour streamed towards me whenever he saw me. The rich, strong colours. Ted had loved me.

I opened my mouth to shout that he was wrong. Completely wrong. That I knew something that he didn't. That he was the one who wasn't as clever as he thought he was – and stopped. Because he was *exactly* as clever as he thought he was. Classic tactics. Unsettle your opponent, rock her world – and not in a good way – and then wait for her to trap herself with unwise words.

I said nothing.

He waited a moment, and then realising nothing was forthcoming, leaned back and smiled.

'His weekly reports were entertaining enough to begin with, although I must admit he was flagging a little towards the end. What was it he called you?

"The most boring woman in the universe." Day in, day out, everything exactly the same. You don't even work, do you? We often used to speculate as to what you actually did in his absence. My favourite theory was that you simply stood in a cupboard until you heard his car pull up and then, out you'd pop, cup of tea in hand, another boring meal in the oven, another night in front of the TV. On and on and on ... he was bored to tears even before he married you. I had to order him to do it. In writing, no less. And even then, he was so drunk the night before I thought we'd never get him through the ceremony.'

His words were like razor blades, slicing through whatever protective layers I had built up over the years, and carving their way straight into my heart. Every word he uttered diminished me further. There was just enough truth in his words to open the floodgates of self-doubt. Had I been wrong every day of our marriage? Had the whole thing been a massive, monstrous lie? So massive and so monstrous that I'd missed it completely?

He wouldn't shut up. If I could only have a minute to think calmly. To find some rock of truth to cling to while I tried to weigh his words. But he just wouldn't stop talking. His colour enveloped me, curling with malice. I began to feel sick.

'He always said Wednesday and Saturday nights were the worst. You lying there in your sensible nightie while he hung around in the bathroom trying to get himself into the mood. To force himself to lie, nose to nose, with someone whose idea of uncontrollable passion was to leave the light on. He was a good boy, was Ted, but as I said, he was beginning to fray at the edges a little towards the end. I don't normally permit inter-staff relationships, but I have to say that when he took up with that very pretty nurse on Dr Lewis's team, even I didn't have the heart to say no. He always used to say it was so good to be with someone who actually moved during ...'

Someone tapped at the door and entered.

He leaped to his feet shouting, 'Get out. Get out,' but it was too late. I was up and away. I ducked under someone's arm; I have no idea whose, and was out into the hall. Normally it was quite crowded with medical staff or patients, and there was always someone on reception, night and day, but today, just for one moment, one precious moment, not only was reception empty, but the front door was open. They must be admitting a new patient.

I raced through the hall, my shoes skidding on the ancient tiles and out through the door. The steps were shallow and I took them two at a time. Someone shouted somewhere. I heard Sorensen behind me, bellowing something. I had a faint impression of a big car and startled faces, and then I was off.

I hadn't run properly since I left school, but I was on wings of fear that day. My instinct was to run down the drive to the gate, but I knew they would never let me through. Someone would already be on the phone to them, telling them to watch out for me. I veered around the side of the building, across the grass, lengthened my stride and ran. Blindly. I had no idea where I was going. I just had to get away from Sorensen and his voice. The voice that dripped poison every time he opened his mouth.

I ran through a shrubbery. Branches whipped at my face and caught at my clothing. Emerging the other side, the ground was rougher. This was more like pastureland. I could hear shouts behind me.

Panic gave me strength. I set off again, running for dear life and all of a sudden, the ground gave way beneath me and I was falling. I tumbled down a short bank, and hit something hard which fell on me, blaspheming horribly. I lay, tangled in something or other, and crushed underneath the quite considerable weight of Michael Jones.

## Chapter Six

He sat up, nearly caving in my ribs with his elbow.

'Bloody hell, woman ...'

I kicked out. 'Get off me.'

There was a certain amount of thrashing around as we sorted ourselves out. I could hear voices drawing ever nearer and struggled to get free.

'Wait, wait,' he said. 'Just wait a minute.'

'I can't. I have to get away.'

'Far too late for that,' he said. 'You should have gone when you had the chance.'

'I'd go now if you would get off me.'

The shouting was very close.

'Stay still.'

'What?'

'Just do as you're told, will you?'

He tossed an old smelly blanket over me and, from the feel of things, began to bury me alive.

'What are you ...?'

'Just lie still and shut up.'

I had no idea whether he was helping me or just keeping me here until whoever was chasing me turned up, but I didn't have a lot of choice. The initial surge of adrenalin was draining away and I was aware my legs were trembling and I couldn't catch my breath.

'And breathe more quietly. You sound like a wind tunnel.'

I did my best and, in the sudden silence, I could hear people approaching. Very, very carefully, I peered through a tiny chink in the blanket.

I could see Jones, some ten feet away, holding a fishing rod and staring upriver.

Two orderlies – at least I could only see two – slid down the bank towards him.

He turned his head. 'What's going on?'

'Did you see her?'

'Of course I did. I'm not blind.'

'Which way did she go?'

He nodded up the path. 'You'll never catch her. She went past me like a rocket.'

'How long ago?'

He shrugged. 'Two minutes. Three minutes.'

They looked at each other, panting, and then set off again.

Jones watched them out of sight. I began to disentangle myself.

'Stay where you are.'

I did as I was told. Minutes passed and nothing happened. Jones carried on with his fishing, standing on the bank, staring at the water. I was just about to ignore him and emerge from my hiding place, when, without warning, one of the orderlies emerged from the trees, and the other from the river path. If I'd shown myself, they'd have caught me in a neat trap.

Jones spoke without turning his head. 'No luck?'

'Did she come back this way?'

'Are you kidding? At the speed she was going, she's probably in Ireland by now.'

They glared at him and stamped off.

'I think they've finally gone,' he said, tweaking

something on his rod, 'but give it a minute or two just to be on the safe side.'

I did. He obviously knew what he was talking about.

After another five minutes, he laid down his rod and began lifting things off me. As far as I could see, I'd been buried under a musty old blanket, some sort of wicker hamper, an unassembled keep net, a backpack apparently full of chinking bottles which neither of us mentioned, and a plastic container full of things that wriggled. My day was not getting any better.

'Well,' he said, pulling the blanket off me and hauling me to my feet. 'What was that all about?'

A legitimate question, I suppose.

'Your precious Dr Sorensen was being his usual self.'

'He's not *my* Dr Sorensen and he's certainly not my *precious*. You're making him sound like The One Ring, although now I come to think of it, that's quite apt. One of a kind. Dangerous. Twists in your hand and bites you. Yeah, well done – you've nailed it. *Did* he bite you?'

I nodded, suddenly unwilling to talk about it. I started another topic.

'Why am I here?'

'Well, you fell down the bank and ...'

'God, does no one ever answer a simple question around here? Why am I in this clinic. Against my will.'

'Well, obviously, you've got something Dr Sorensen wants.'

'What?'

'How should I know? We've barely exchanged three words. Don't you?'

'Don't I what?'

'Know what he wants?'

I said slowly, 'I'm not sure. He said he had a file on me. What does it say?'

'Again, how should I know?'

'Why would he have a file on me?'

'Well, it's a kind of chicken and egg thing, isn't it? Either he has a file on you because you have something he wants, or you have something he wants and so he's started a file on you.'

'He said he told Ted to marry me.'

Silence.

'Well, nothing clever to say this time? No smart answer that really isn't an answer at all?'

Apparently not.

'Is it true?'

He looked at me. 'Look I'll tell you if you want to know but don't go all hysterical on me if you don't like what you're hearing.'

I nodded. 'OK.'

'Yes, you were Ted's assignment.'

My world swam before my eyes.

'And before you go all girlie and faint, he loved you.'

I said in a small voice, 'I don't believe you.'

'Oh for God's sake, Cage, of course he did. Have you forgotten what Ted was like? Honest as the day's long, our Ted. Of course he loved you. He couldn't have done it otherwise.'

'You think so?'

'I know so. He was always talking about you. I'm

not going to pander to your vanity by going on and on, but you made him happy. Couldn't you see that?'

I sighed. 'Of course I can. God, I'm useless. One morning with Sorensen and my world is in pieces.'

'Well, ten minutes with Michael Jones and it's all superglued back together again,' he said modestly.

'All right, answer me this. How did Sorensen know about me? What does he know about me?'

He shrugged. 'He has people everywhere. Occasionally, they report back on something they've seen or heard that they think he might find interesting.'

'Interesting enough to marry one of his people to me?'

'Well, yes, obviously.' He stared at me. 'I wonder what it is.'

I changed the subject. That wasn't a road I wanted to go down. 'So how do I get out of here?'

'You can't.'

'Yes, I can.'

'There are walls, fences, gates, cameras, laser beams, alarms. Face it, Cage, anything that can keep out the paparazzi is way beyond anything you can cope with.'

I looked around. 'I made it this far, didn't I?'

'No cameras here. Bit of a blind spot. That's why I'm here. Some peace and quiet. Do you want to share my sandwiches?'

'You've just told me you want to be alone.'

'I don't count Ted's wife. Besides, anyone who can ruin Sorensen's day is entitled to as many sandwiches as she can eat. Egg and cress, or ham and tomato?'

I was hungry. 'Both.'

He dropped the old blanket over my shoulders because now the adrenalin was fading, I'd begun to shiver, and I stayed. Partly because I had no idea what to do next. Running away from something is all very well. Running to is even better. I didn't have a 'to'. And partly because I was curious about this man, Jones. His colour was dreadful. I had no idea what was wrong with him and I certainly wasn't going to ask. However, in the half hour or so that I'd been here, a small patch of golden peach colour had appeared over his head, swirling quietly. A tiny bright spot in all the cloudy murk that was his colour. A tiny spark of interest.

'Do you want to have a go?'

I started back to the present. 'What?'

'I've got a spare rod. Do you want to have a go?'

'OK. Can you do the wiggly bait thing?'

He sighed. 'You slay a giant one moment and the next you can't pick up a maggot. Women!'

'That's what men are for. They're the experts on small wiggly things.'

We sat, side by side, staring at our rods, watching the River Rush go by on its journey to the sea, until the light started to go.

'Why haven't we caught anything?'

'Oh, there's no fish in this part of the river. Haven't been for fifty years.'

'Then what's the point?'

'Well, we both have had a day away from the clinic. Lots of fresh air and exercise. Sorensen will be in overdrive by now. His head might have exploded if we're really lucky. Where's the downside?'

I remembered the chinking bottles. Had he come

here to drink? Or maybe dispose of the empties? I shouldn't ask. I had my secrets. The least I could do was respect his.

'I have to go back, don't I?'

'Yeah, you do, but why is that a problem?'

'The whole walk of shame ...'

'What are you ashamed about? He's the one who lost you. You've won this round. Underline your victory by kicking the front door open and shouting, "Sorensen, you wanker, I'm back."'

'Appealing, but I'm not sure that's quite my style.'

'OK, how about I get you back in and no one notices. You sit quietly in your room watching the telly, and when they eventually do discover you, you have your "what's all the fuss been about" expression.'

'I like that one.'

'Then that's what we'll do. You pick up the maggots.'

We walked back in the gathering dusk. I was still apprehensive about going in.

'Stop it,' he said. 'You haven't done anything wrong. Have you?'

'Not as far as I know.'

'There you are then.'

'There I am where?'

'Stop worrying. I myself should have signed back in more than two hours ago, and I don't care. They'll be so busy shouting at me that you can just slip past.'

And, as it happened, that's exactly how it went.

He stood in the hall being as disruptive and difficult as he could manage – which was a very great deal – and the ensuing arguments enabled me to get upstairs with no difficulty at all.

I looked back once. He was surrounded by a miscellaneous group of nurses, orderlies and security people, all talking at once, his fishing gear slung over one shoulder and slowly dripping muddy water all over their immaculate floor, and as far as I could tell from the slowly expanding patch of light over his head, thoroughly enjoying himself. I left him offering to show them his maggots.

They found me in my room, feet up on the windowsill, reading. Dr Lewis stopped dead. 'Mrs Cage?'

'Yes?'

'When did you get back?'

'I don't know.'

'Where have you been?'

I gestured vaguely. 'Outside.'

She compressed her lips. She was anxious, I could tell. The red was flickering everywhere.

I turned back to my book and after a moment, she went away.

# Chapter Seven

I was hungry after my day's fishing and when no one came with the evening menu I did wonder if they were going to punish me with starvation, but I was wrong.

Dr Lewis put her head around my door and told me Dr Sorensen had decreed I could eat in the dining room that evening.

'With the other inmates,' I said, brightly.

'With the other *guests*,' she said reprovingly. 'Dinner is served between seven and eight.' She stared at my still muddy jeans. 'Dress is smart casual.'

'Or, in my case, funereal.'

She went away.

I took a book with me in case anyone mistakenly thought I was feeling sociable and was careful to choose a small table by the wall. I sat down, opened my book and refused to catch anyone's eye.

The dining room was very pleasant, done out in shades red and cream. Four long windows down one side would look out over the gardens during the day. The curtains were cream and red patterned and the same colours were picked up in the tablecloths.

A number of small tables were arranged in rows, and I noticed that despite being able to seat two or four people, most people sat alone. The fresh flowers on each table were a nice touch, as were the larger floor arrangements between the windows, but there was no getting away from the fact that this was a hospital. Sorry – *clinic*. There were knives on the tables and so several people had a member of staff sitting with them. Within arm's reach. Just in case.

Michael Jones came in just as I was ordering the chicken. His eyes passed vaguely over me. The message was obvious. We were near-strangers to each other. He too chose a small table against the wall, but on the other side of the room.

The food was good, but the atmosphere subdued. Most people ate alone. I was informed that coffee was served afterwards in the library. I was in two minds, but I was so sick of my room and there wasn't anything else to do, so off I went.

This was not the sort of establishment that had anything as mundane as a TV lounge. There was no big, bleak room with chairs around the walls, all pointing towards a speckled TV, screwed high up on the wall, with its blurred picture and blaring sound. No heavily drugged, blank-faced occupants sitting quietly, waiting to be instructed to be somewhere else. For a start, we all had a TV in our own nicely appointed rooms. Videos, CDs satellite TV, interactive whatnots – everything was provided – so the library was the nearest thing to a communal lounge, with its groups of tables and chairs, its comfortable armchairs, magazines, and of course, books. A large table stood against the far wall with flasks of coffee, cups and saucers and after-dinner mints. I poured myself a cup, snaffled a mint, paused, and then took another. Perhaps I could destroy Sorensen by bankrupting him.

One or two people sat together, talking quietly and another two sat at a table doing a crossword puzzle, otherwise we were determinedly unsociable. Jones came in just after me, settled himself in an armchair and read his newspaper while I concentrated on my book. A lot of people just stared into space, lost in their own unhappy thoughts.

There were no staff present. I gathered there was a kind of gentlemen's agreement. We would sit quietly and behave ourselves while they had their evening meal and wrote up their notes.

I finished my coffee and sat quietly, holding up my book as a shield against the world. I was reading *Three Men in a Boat*, normally a source of comfort and enjoyment to me. I was just thinking it had never seemed less funny, when it happened. One minute, everything was perfectly normal, and then, without any sort of warning, the page darkened in front of my eyes, and for a moment, the world swam away from me.

My first thought was that I was having some sort of neural event. The second, that Sorensen had drugged the coffee and somehow, I hadn't noticed. The third was that I was going to be horribly sick.

I felt the blood drain from my face, leaving my skin cold and tight. My book fell from my hands, bounced in my lap and fell to the floor. Instinctively, I bent to pick it up, and as I did so, a head appeared through the wall at the far end of the room.

I was still leaning down and we were on the same level. The lighting was good. My eyesight is good. There was no mistake. A head was slowly emerging from the wall. At floor level.

I picked up the book and shot a swift glance around the room. No one was taking any notice at all. Everything was perfectly normal. People were drinking coffee and sitting quietly, and all the time, a head was coming through the wall. It was obvious no one else could see it because there was no screaming and running, which there certainly would have been if it had been visible to anyone else, because it was hideously ugly. Frighteningly so. The head was hairless and eyeless, its skin burned black in places. And it was coming through the wall.

Shoulders followed, and then first one bony stick that turned out to be an arm, and then another, pulling itself silently through the wall and into the room.

Around me I could hear the gentle murmur of voices as the crossword puzzlers got into their stride, while ahead of me, the creature was nearly through, dragging itself with painful slowness across the old parquet floor.

The smell was awful and I felt my stomach heave. Burned meat. Not in itself an offensive smell, but this was burned human. A badly burned human. A few scorched rags of clothing were visible on its upper body, apparently seared into its flesh by a fire.

From the waist down, everything was burned, black and twisted. There were no legs. Wherever and whenever this person had burned, the fire had started at the legs which were completely burned away. Only two blackened stumps remained, terminating just below the knee. The feet were completely gone.

Slowly and with great determination, it pulled itself across the floor. I could hear the scrape of bone on wood. I could see the strain as it raised itself on stick like forearms, dragged itself another inch or so, rested a moment, and then did it again. And again. And again.

I glanced around again. Everyone was completely immersed in their own world, completely oblivious to this creature ... this monster ... which would surely send them all screaming from the room if they had any idea it was here.

And what did I do? I was an unwilling inmate in a secure mental establishment, and the last thing I needed to do was to run to a member of staff and tell them an invisible monster had just crawled through the wall. That sort of thing does not get you released the next morning.

Actually, I was wrong. Someone *was* watching, but he was watching me, not the thing on the floor. Jones had lowered his newspaper and was staring at me. I didn't have time for him right now, because the creature had stopped. Now, almost in the centre of the room, it paused and looked around. An eyeless skull it might be, but it could see. I was certain of it. For what or whom it was looking, I had no idea. I remember offering up a fervent prayer that it wasn't me.

Apparently, it wasn't. It shifted slightly on its elbows and set off in a new direction. It had located its prey.

A man sat some twelve or fifteen feet away from me, alone in an armchair pulled well away from everyone else. His coffee sat untasted at his elbow as he stared, sightlessly, at something only he could see. Occasionally, his right hand would twitch with a life of its own.

His colour was dreadful. What had, I suspected, been a soft, gentle blue, had deteriorated to a thin, muddy yellow. Occasionally, it gave a little flutter that reminded me of a dying bird. A black patch sat over his heart, tenuously connected to another black patch around his head. Even as I watched, his whole colour grew darker and thinner. There wasn't much of it left.

I jerked my eyes back to the creature which now, apparently with great pain and effort, was crawling towards him. As I watched, it reached out a blackened claw and seized the man's ankle. He gave no sign that he knew what was going on, but the sad remains of his colour swirled downwards towards the creature and enveloped it.

With an abrupt movement, he thrust back his chair and got up. He stood for a moment, as if, having got this far, he was unsure what to do next, then he turned and slowly walked towards the door, seemingly unaware of the thing he was dragging behind him.

They had to pass me to get to the door. Instinctively, I drew my feet back well out of the way, and as I did so the creature turned its head and looked at me. For a long second, we stared at each other. It had no eyes, but I knew that somehow it could see, and it was seeing me now. I clutched my book as if my life depended upon it, and then it was gone, dragged towards the door by a man who had no idea it was there.

I didn't know what to do. I really didn't know what to do. My dad used to say I saw things for a reason and that reason would become clear one day.

It hadn't yet. Was this that day? But what could I say? What could I do? I had to do something. No matter what sort of trouble it got me into, I couldn't do nothing. My dad wouldn't have liked that.

I made my way to the door and looked out. The man was already half way up the stairs, moving slowly and heavily, leaning on the bannisters. His colour had almost completely disappeared.

I ran to the reception desk. The man looked up in surprise. I wasn't famed for chatting to the staff.

'Mrs Cage? What can I do for you?'

'That man.' I pointed.

'Yes?'

'I don't think he's very well.'

'Really, in what way.'

What could I say?

'He seemed ... agitated. Distressed even. And he left very suddenly. His behaviour made me ... uneasy.'

He stared after the man, now disappearing around the landing, but made no move to get up or pick up a phone.

'I think someone should check it out,' I said.

'I'll certainly mention it to the duty nurse.'

That was no good. I sought for something to say. Something that would galvanise them into action.

'I thought I saw him slip something into his pocket.'

Suicide was a big fear here. There were people here on suicide watch who never had a member of staff further than three feet away from them. We were all checked hourly at night, a torch appearing briefly through the dark. There would be a pause as someone

84

made the appropriate annotation on a clipboard and then the torch would move away again.

'Oh? Did you see what it was?'

Now what did I say? I was spared the trouble. Michael Jones stood behind me. 'Is there a problem here?'

'Mrs Cage has some concerns about a patient, sir.'

'Which one?'

'Mr Johnson.'

'Then I suggest you check it out.'

'The duty nurse ...'

'Now.'

I jumped at the tone in his voice and the receptionist reluctantly reached for the telephone. I moved away. I'd done my duty. They could all sort it out among themselves. I wanted to be alone to think about what I'd just seen. And have a quiet cup of tea and wait for my heart rate to return to normal, as well.

I was worried they'd confine me to my room again, but no one tried to stop me leaving the next morning. I made my way to the dining room, only to be intercepted by Michael Jones who didn't seem in any way to be familiar with conventional behaviour, grabbing my arm and whirling me at top speed into the library.

'Come on, Cage, out with it.'

'Out with what? Let go of me.'

'I saw your face last night.'

I'd been an idiot. I should have kept quiet, but I'd had to do something. I tried to undo some of the damage. 'I don't understand.'

'Yes, you do. I saw your face and I wasn't the only one. You saw something. You couldn't hide it. By now, Dr Sorensen will know you saw something. You need to be very careful.'

'I suspect it's too late for that.'

'It's never too late.'

I went to move away and he pulled me back.

I was angry. 'Will you stop doing that?'

'Aren't you the slightest bit curious?'

'About?'

'About what you saw. Last night. In the library. When you had your *I've just seen something horrible* face on. When you watched something move across the room. Something only you could see.'

I stared at him. 'Why should I trust you?'

He let go of my arm. 'I let someone down once. Let's say I'm returning the favour. Even if it isn't to the right person. Now tell me so I can help. You can trust me.'

I stared at him. The golden peachy red of his colour was beginning to reassert itself. The dark areas were shrinking and his whole colour had more movement and move vigour. More life. Could I trust him? I felt I could. On the other hand …

I said bitterly, 'I trusted Ted.'

'Listen to me. Ted had your best interests at heart. And he wasn't stupid. You can't live with someone for years and not know all about them. He knew there was something different about you. He could have turned you over to Sorensen at any time and he didn't. For God's sake, Cage, who do you think has been protecting you from Sorensen all this time?'

'Ted …? He did that?'

'Yes, he did. He's been quietly lying to Sorensen for years, and he got away with it because everyone always believed him. Trusty Ted.'

'Why would he do that?'

'Because he loved you, you idiot.'

'Why would you help me?'

'Because I'm Ted's friend. Because you're an idiot who doesn't know what she's got herself into. Because I've lost someone and I know it's no fun being the one left behind. Do I have to go on with this sickeningly sentimental conversation? Tell me what you saw.'

I couldn't. The words wouldn't come out.

He shifted impatiently. 'Someone will have seen us come in here and I want my breakfast. Tell me.'

'Fine. I'll tell you. I saw something come through the wall and take hold of Mr Johnson's ankle. When he left, he was dragging it behind him.'

There was a long silence and then he said quietly, 'Johnson died last night. He hanged himself with his own dressing gown cord.'

Everything suddenly flew away from me. Shards of darkness shattered in all directions. He grabbed my arm. 'For God's sake, sit down. You're a bit girlie, aren't you?'

I snatched my arm back. 'Yes, I am. And I'm the girlie who lost her husband last week. And you didn't have to fling it at me like that.'

He paused. 'No.' He paused again. 'No, I didn't.' His colour flowed towards me. 'Sorry.'

I nodded. He *was* sorry. I could see it.

'So, do you think the thing I saw attached to Mr Johnson was connected with his death?'

'I'll go further. I think it was the cause of it.'

I nodded. That made sense.

He was frowning. 'There's something …'

'What?'

'I can't remember. Something I heard once. Nurses' gossip. Let me see what I can find out.'

'What can you do?'

'I can talk to people.'

'Will they let you?'

'Oh yes, they'll be so pleased I'm rejoining the human race that they'll tell me anything. Besides, nurses like to gossip. And they always know far more than the doctors do. And the orderlies know most of all. Leave this to me. Now, we shouldn't leave together. I'll go first, because I'm hungry. Give it a minute or two and then you leave. And don't not look at me in the dining room. That's a dead giveaway.'

I don't know what made me say it. 'Are you a spy?'

He made his mouth prim and said nothing.

I stood in front of him. Between him and the door. Or between him and breakfast would have been a better threat. 'I told you my secret. Now you tell me yours.'

He sighed. 'I wish I'd never met you.'

'You and me both, buster.'

'Yes.'

I was bewildered. 'Yes what?'

'Yes, to your question. I'm a sort of spy.'

'Oh.'

'You sound disappointed.'

'Well … do you have an Aston Martin?'

'What? No!'

'A watch that doubles as a nuclear bomb?'

'I've changed my mind. You leave first. Now would be a good time.'

I looked around the library. 'Could you kill someone with a brochure?'

'Hand me a brochure and we'll see.'

I left. Before I killed him with a brochure.

# Chapter Eight

I honestly thought he wouldn't get anywhere. I've seen one or two things in my life, and believe me, it's not like the story books where there's always a neat explanation for everything and a satisfactory resolution at the end. I see something – usually a piece of someone else's story – and that's the end of it. I don't know the beginning and I certainly don't know the end, so I really didn't expect Jones to discover anything.

I spent the morning in my room, thinking about what I'd seen. And thinking about Ted. Who had loved me. I was sure of it.

Just before lunch, someone scratched on my door. Before I could say or do anything, Jones slid into the room. There was a regulation about patients not being in each other's rooms. It was pasted on the back of the door, along with the fire instructions. I'd never before met anyone with such a blatant disregard for the rules.

'You're not supposed to be in here.'

He grinned at me.

'I suppose you think that because you're a spy you don't have to follow the rules like lesser people.'

'If it makes you feel any better, I never followed them before I was a spy, either. I would, however, be grateful if you could lower your voice when discussing my spyness. If Sorensen knows, you know neither of us will ever leave.'

I didn't know if he was joking. His colour was ambiguous, but surely spies shouldn't be so light-hearted about what he referred to as their 'spyness'.

'Are you here for a reason or am I just on your quota of Rules to Break Today?'

'Ted never said anything about you being so sarky. I'm beginning to feel quite sorry for the poor bloke. Living with you must have been a nightmare.'

'You sound like Sorensen.'

'What's he been saying now?'

'Oh, nothing important. Ted had to be plied with alcohol before he'd marry me. He was having an affair with a nurse … you know, little things.'

He regarded me with exasperation. 'Again. Ted loved you. Only you. Would you like me to write it down?'

'Sorry,' I said meekly. And then remembered. 'Why are you here?'

'I just came to say – I'll meet you after lunch. Something to tell you,' and he whisked himself out of the room.

We met again after lunch. When I say met, I mean he was hiding in my bathroom when I returned to my room and nearly gave me a heart attack.

'I thought *my* nerves were bad,' he remarked, making himself comfortable in the only chair.

I sat on the bed. 'There's nothing wrong with my nerves. The problem lies with the company I'm keeping these days.'

His colour was rippling with excitement. 'Do you

91

want to waste more time discussing whose fault everything is, or do you want to hear what I've found out?'

'That was quick.'

'Nurses,' he said complacently. 'Offer them a chocolate biscuit with their tea and they'll tell you anything.'

'So what did they tell you?'

'Long story short – legend says there's a ghost which appears whenever someone is about to die. Comes to claim them, so to speak.'

I shivered, remembering that poor doomed man dragging that thing around with him. Dead already and he just didn't know it. 'Do we have any details?'

'A whole biscuit tin's worth. Although it wasn't really needed. Everyone is full of it. They all have theories of course, and there was a lot of argument and disagreements, but the gist seems to be that during World War Two, this building was used as a hospital and convalescent home. At some point, it was bombed. Casualties weren't high – the main damage was to the area where the kitchens are now – but everyone says say there was a nursing sister trapped in the burning building. They said, piling on the narrative excitement, that her screams could be heard from miles away. The firefighters and every available person tried their utmost, but they couldn't get to her. She had a terrible death. She burned from the legs up. They could see her trying to beat out the flames with her hands, and all the time she was screaming, "Don't let me burn. Don't let me burn." It wasn't their fault – they did what they could but it just wasn't enough. Now, the legend says, she appears, to claim others out of a spirit of revenge because they didn't save her.'

I shivered, remembering that dreadful dead thing clasping Mr Johnson's ankle. The sound of bones being dragged across the floor.

'Has Sorensen sent for you yet?' he said, getting up.

'No.'

'He will.'

Of course he would. I'd rather given myself away by running to the reception desk. Try as I would, though, I couldn't regret it. I don't think I could have lived with myself if I'd done nothing. The result would have been the same, but at least I had tried.

I was sitting in the gardens, actually on the very seat from where I'd watched Ted look for fish in the ornamental pool. The day was chilly, but the surrounding yew hedges made it a bit of a sun trap. I sat quietly, enjoying the winter sunshine. Atlas still held the world on his shoulders, but today, the fountains were silent.

'Good afternoon, Elizabeth. May I join you for a moment?'

I sighed, opened my eyes and squinted up at Dr Sorensen. 'I really would rather you didn't, but since you seem impervious to polite hints, I don't see any way of stopping you.'

'I understand you had some conversation with Mr Johnson before he died.'

'No.'

'I beg your pardon, the reception staff said ...'

'I had a conversation with the receptionist before Mr Johnson died.'

'Yes, in his report he describes you as being quite agitated.'

'Really? How easily alarmed he must be. Poor boy. He's not going to do well here, is he?'

'Do you deny speaking to him?'

'Who? Johnson or the receptionist.'

He sighed. 'Perhaps you could just tell me what happened.'

'Mr Johnson was sitting quite close to me. I had some concerns about him which I reported to your staff. Later, Mr Johnson died.'

'May I ask what caused you this concern?'

'He seemed depressed.'

'Can you describe the way in which this depression manifested itself?'

'I don't think so. It was just an impression.'

'Just an impression,' he repeated. 'And yet no words were spoken.' I watched his nasty sour milk colour curl towards me and shifted my position away from him.

'Isn't eighty per cent of communication supposed to be non-verbal? I'm surprised none of your staff picked up on it. Isn't the importance of body language included in their training? The truth is that Mr Johnson was displaying clear signs of distress, a patient reported her concerns to a member of staff, and despite all that, he still died on your watch. A pretty poor performance, Sorensen. And it's not as if this place is cheap, either.'

He cast me a very unloving look.

I surged on. 'I really don't feel the level of care

here is quite what I would like to be accustomed to, and surely your people have had more than enough time to ransack my home. Kindly organise my discharge from this establishment immediately.'

He sat back on the bench and regarded me with some hostility. 'I wouldn't be in too much of a hurry to leave this establishment, if I were you, Mrs Cage. If you don't respond to ... treatment ... here, there is every possibility of you being transferred to some other sort of establishment. The sort of establishment in which you will be only too eager to cooperate.'

I snorted, but only because I couldn't think of anything to say. This was a legitimate threat. I could see it. It struck me suddenly that yes, there probably were many, many places worse than this one and I didn't want to end up in even one of them.

'You should take some time to think about the alternatives, Elizabeth.'

I resumed my gaze out over the pool. 'I don't think I can be bothered.'

He still didn't move.

Without looking at him, I said, 'That will be all, Sorensen.'

He waited a moment longer and then got up and left.

I watched him walk away.

'"That will be all, Sorensen."?' said a voice behind the hedge. 'What sort of a death wish do you have?'

I shrugged. 'He wasn't going to go away.'

'We need to get you out of here. Preferably before he murders you in justifiable exasperation.'

'How can he get away with this? I'm being held here against my will. I need to contact the authorities.'

There was a sigh from behind the hedge. 'Haven't you grasped it yet, Cage. We *are* the authorities.'

# Chapter Nine

Dinner that evening was very subdued. No one sat with anyone else. Even the crossword puzzlers kept to themselves. No formal announcement had been made about Mr Johnson, but these things always get about and everyone knew something had happened. A heavy silence hung over the room. The only sound was the chink of cutlery on crockery, or the doors swinging as the serving staff went in and out. No one ate very much.

I kept my eyes firmly on my book, not even looking around the room for Michael Jones. Excusing myself as soon as possible, I made my way back to my room. In my absence, someone had, as usual, pulled the curtains and turned back the bed. A long bath and an early night suddenly seemed a very good idea.

I tossed my book onto the bed and pushed open the bathroom door. I was immersed in the preliminaries for using the loo when a voice spoke behind the shower curtain.

'Good evening, Cage.'

I shrieked and jumped a mile. I'm certain my feet left the ground. I reassembled myself as quickly as possible and wrenched the curtain back with such vigour that some of it came off the rings.

'Jesus Christ, Jones. What the hell are you doing in my bath?'

'You scared me,' he said reproachfully. 'I thought you were the housekeeping staff.'

'Get out of my bath.'

'All right. Keep your hair on. It's not as if I saw anything ...'

I marched back into my bedroom and turned to face him. 'What are you doing here?'

'I came to see you. Although, as I say it, I can see you might be getting the wrong idea.'

'Why?'

'Well, you know, "see you" – in this case meaning to talk to you, rather than "see you" – meaning literally to see you as you undressed, and ...'

That wasn't what I'd meant and he knew it.

'Get out.'

'No,' he said calmly, helping himself to my fruit. 'No dessert,' he said, waving an apple around. 'I skipped a course so I could be sure of getting to your room first.'

'Why?'

He picked up the armchair with no effort at all and carried it into the bathroom.

'To keep an eye on things.'

'Why?'

He sighed. 'You said it saw you. That whatever it was turned its head and looked at you. It knows you, Cage.'

I felt suddenly very cold. I hadn't thought of that, but he was right. It knew me. 'Do you think it will come back?'

'I don't know. Do you?'

I shook my head.

'In that case, I'm spending the night here. I'm

almost certain you won't allow me to join you in bed ...' he paused hopefully. I maintained a discouraging silence. '... so that just leaves the armchair, which, in its previous position, was visible from the window in the door. I'm sure you don't want me ruining your reputation by being spotted during bed-checks, so I'm moving it into the bathroom. A simple yet effective solution to our dilemma.'

It was becoming apparent I wasn't going to get a long hot bath and an early night. 'You can fix the shower curtain while you're in there.'

I could hear him grumbling to himself as he snapped the rings back into place.

I did eventually consent to getting into bed, albeit fully clothed and with my shoes only an arm's reach away.

Jones manoeuvred his armchair into what he claimed was the optimum position – in the doorway between the bedroom and bathroom, ignoring all my protests. He did make some remarks about both of us exercising increased bladder control during the night, but these I ignored, because I could see he was genuinely anxious. His lighter, golden patch was a little larger today, which was good news, but occasionally, a nasty red colour swirled unpleasantly. Like blood in water.

There was a lot of tossing and turning, but eventually we both settled down and silence fell. I'd pulled the curtains back and although there was no moon, enough light came in through the windows to identify the outlines of furniture and doors. Jones left the bathroom light off because a member of staff would certainly investigate someone supposedly in the bathroom all night long.

Silence fell. Somewhere outside, a long way off, a dog barked. The house creaked. We waited in the darkness.

It came on so slowly that at first, I didn't notice. I lay on my back, watching the darkness swirl with colours only I could see, when I swear the bed moved. Just slightly and then, slowly, very slowly, my cover began to slide off the bottom of the bed. Without thinking, I seized it and tried to pull it up again.

Something pulled back.

The shock caused the world to swim away from me. Just as it had before. I swallowed down the sudden nausea, but I couldn't do anything about the overwhelming cold that left my skin feeling stretched and tight.

It's everyone's nightmare. It's the reason why, as a child, I would never stick any part of my body out from under the covers. Because of whatever lurked underneath the bed. Something that was always awake and always waiting for an unwary child to hang a leg or an arm over the side. Waiting to seize that child, drag it down to the nightmare realms under the bed, and devour it. My monster was called The Red James. I thought I'd grown out of that particular fantasy, and now I was discovering I'd been wrong.

Whatever was pulling the covers off me was very, very strong. I abandoned the tug-of-war and sat up, hissing, 'Jones.'

I half suspected he was asleep – or even that he might have returned to his own bed, the silence from the dark bathroom was so complete, but I was wrong. The response came immediately.

'What?'

'It's here.'

A torch beam stabbed through the darkness, alighting first on me – I blinked in the sudden brightness – and then on the bed.

There she was – if it was a her – at the foot of my bed, sightless eyes fixed on me, pulling herself towards me. Two hands that were really nothing more than burned bones had each seized a handful of duvet which was slowly being dragged off the bed. Whether she was trying to pull herself up onto the bed, or whether she was pulling off the covers to make it easier to get to me was unclear. I only knew that tonight she'd come for me. I'd seen her. She'd seen me. And now she'd come for me. My skin felt cold and oily. Another wave of sickness rolled over me.

I scrambled to the very top of the bed, drawing my legs up underneath me.

Something grabbed my arm and I shrieked.

'Shut up,' he hissed, 'or we'll have them all in here. Get off the bed, you idiot. Stand in the middle of the room where you have room to move. Where is she?'

'Can't you see?'

'No. That's why I'm asking you.'

'At the foot of the bed.'

I scrambled off the bed and stood where directed, ramming my feet into my shoes. 'Give me the torch.'

As soon as I moved, the thing that was more skull than head turned in my direction. Without a sound, she relinquished her hold on the covers, lowered herself back to the floor, and began to drag herself towards me. Slowly, but inexorably. The thought flashed through my head. There is no escape. She knows me. However long it takes, she will catch me. She will never stop and I can't keep moving for ever.

'You have to tell me where she is,' said Jones. 'I can't keep you safe if I don't know where she is. Talk to me, Cage.'

'About six or seven feet away, heading towards me, but very slowly. Almost inching her way along.'

'Stay in the middle of the room. Don't let her get between you and the door. Describe her.'

I took a deep breath, telling myself I couldn't really smell burning flesh. It was all in my mind.

'Only blackened bones for legs. Nothing below the knee. Twisted body. Bone showing through. Her skin is black and red. Tattered rags of clothing burned into her flesh. Hands like claws. She's reaching for me.'

I moved to my left, pushing Jones with me.

At once, the creature dropped her arm. Inch by painful inch, she began to change direction. Towards our new position. When she was more or less pointing the right way, she lifted her pitifully burned face and looked directly at me. Just as she had done the previous night.

'What's happening?' said Jones.

'She's stopped.'

'Why?'

'I don't know,' I said in exasperation. 'Perhaps it hurts her to move. At the moment, she's just looking at me.'

'Do we have a clear path to the door?'

'Yes.'

'Then let's get out of here.'

'Where to?'

'In this case, as in so many others, Cage, the journey is more important than the destination.'

He began to nudge me towards the door.

The creature made no attempt to follow. In fact, it let its head hang down in what I would have called a moment of despair. Even as I turned away, she looked up and at the same time, raised an arm in what could have been a gesture almost of appeal.

'Wait,' I said, pulling my arm free from Jones.

'What are you doing?'

'I don't know.'

'Has it gone?'

'No. I think she wants something.'

'Yes. You.'

I looked down at the creature, still illuminated by Jones's torch. She lifted her arm again. And now I really *could* smell the charcoal smell of burned flesh. I would never eat a barbecue again.

'What do you want from me?'

She made a tiny movement. As if she could do no more. As if she was saying, 'Please.'

I didn't want to die. I was young. I had a whole life ahead of me. I didn't want to be touched by that … thing … and die.

I said again, 'What do you want?'

Again she reached out her hand to me.

'I know that if you touch me then I will die. I know that you come in the night and anyone you touch is dead by morning. I don't want to die.'

'Cage, what are you doing?'

'Can you nod your head?'

She nodded her head. I had an impression of appeal.

'Ask it why it's here.'

'Do you mean me harm?'

Nothing.

'Have you come to kill me?'

Nothing.

'Do you mean harm to anyone tonight?'

Nothing.

I had a sudden thought. 'Have you ever meant anyone harm?'

Nothing.

There was no point in asking what she wanted; she couldn't tell me.

'Do you want something from me?'

A tiny dip of her head.

'Can I do something to help you?'

Again, a tiny dip.

'What?'

She lifted her hand to me.

'You want to touch me?'

A nod.

'Will it hurt me?'

Nothing.

'What about him?' I nodded towards Jones.

'What about me?' said Jones, drawing back slightly.

Nothing.

'Will you hurt him?'

Nothing.

'If you touch him, will he die?'

Nothing.

'Ask it ...'

'Ask *her*,' I said angrily.

'Ask *her* ... if she touches me, will I see her?'

A very good question. One I should have asked myself.

I didn't need to. She was already nodding.

'Yes, you will.'

'So why didn't Johnson see her?'

'I don't know and she can't say.'

That wasn't quite true. I think that was the moment when I had a faint glimmer of her true purpose, but there was no time to stop and think.

Jones was uneasy. I didn't blame him. 'What do you think, Cage? Do we risk it?'

'I don't know,' I said doubtfully. 'I really don't. Somehow, she's not so frightening now. I don't think she means to harm us.'

'Are you sure this isn't wishful thinking on your part? I tell you now, if I'm dead in the morning then you and I will be having words.'

'I'm going to take that as a go-ahead.'

There was a sound outside the door.

'Quick,' he said. 'Bed-check.'

I scrambled back into bed and pulled the covers up to my chin. Jones melted away into the shadows. I saw the torch flash and closed my eyes. There I was, a good little mental patient, fast asleep in her bed. I don't know if it was my imagination, but I had the impression whoever was on the other side of the door was being more than normally thorough. I watched through my eyelashes as the beam jerked around the room. Finally, it disappeared and we were back in the dark.

'What about you?' I whispered, sitting up. 'What about your bed-check?'

'I'm on the other side. It'll take them a minute or two to get to me. This is up to you, Cage. What do you want to do?'

I heard my father's voice again. 'We don't know what you can do, pet. Or why you can do it, but maybe you'll find out one day. One day perhaps, everything will become clear.'

I looked at the poor, burned creature in front of me. Suppose I was here to help people. People just like this. People with no voice, who couldn't make themselves heard, who couldn't speak for themselves, and needed someone like me. Once I would have quailed, but tonight – tonight I had help. I looked at Jones, a massive shadow in the darkness. 'I'm game if you are.'

He nodded. 'Where is ... she?'

I switched on the torch. 'Still here. She hasn't moved.'

'All right then.'

She lifted herself up on bony forearms so frail and so thin that I was almost expecting them to snap under the strain, and prepared to drag herself towards us, inch by painful inch.

'No,' I said, full of last minute doubts. 'Wait a moment.' I turned to Jones. 'Are you sure about this?'

'Just hang on to me, Cage.'

'You're not scared, are you?'

'I'm bloody terrified, but I don't want you disappearing off somewhere without me and then me having to explain to Sorensen where you've gone and what I was doing in your bedroom at the time.'

'Somehow I think that might be the least of your problems.'

'Can we just do this, please?'

I took a deep breath. 'All right.'

## Chapter Ten

I was, literally, stepping into the unknown. Whatever was lying in front of me had no colour for me to read. I had no idea whether she meant us harm or not. Suppose she was lying? I kept remembering Mr Johnson, walking slowly out of the room, dragging his death behind him. Were we about to do the same thing? Was I taking Michael Jones to his death?

'What's the problem?' said Jones, as I stood stock-still. 'Second thoughts?'

'I was thinking it's all right for me to do something stupid, but I'm worried about you.'

His voice came out of the dark. 'Live or die, Cage – it makes very little difference to me.' He wasn't joking.

'If you're sure ...'

He took my hand. 'Yes, I'm sure. Let's do it.'

I turned back to her. 'We're ready.'

She began to inch herself forwards.

'No,' I said, certain that every movement gave her pain. 'You stay there. We'll come to you.'

Jones stepped back. 'What?'

'It's still not too late to stay behind.'

He said nothing, in that way that men do.

Still holding on tightly to Jones, I crouched and reached out to her. 'Here.'

She hesitated for a moment and then, slowly she took my hand.

I felt nothing. Her clasp was feather-light. Nothing happened to me – but everything changed. Suddenly there was light – lots of it – shouting, explosions, sirens, screaming and the sound of engines. The sharp tang of smoke seared my nostrils and made me cough. Cold night air bit through my thin clothing. Before I had time to take in any more, Jones had his arm around my waist in a grip of iron. 'What the f ...?'

An enormous explosion nearby made us both flinch.

'For God's sake, Cage. Where are we?'

'I don't know.' I said, panicking and looking wildly around. 'How should I know?'

My first thought was that we could be anywhere, but as Jones flashed his torch about, I could see we hadn't moved at all. We were still in my room. Or rather, my room before it was my room. There were differences. My bed was gone, to be replaced by two plain hospital beds separated by an old wooden cupboard. A tall narrow wardrobe, chipped and scratched, stood against one wall. One of the windows had been blown out and thick black curtains flapped in the draught. Blackout curtains. Avoiding the broken glass, I cautiously peered outside. The view was almost the same as I remembered, except that now the smooth lawns had been cut up into allotments. I could see neat rows of vegetables. Beans growing up canes. Small sheds were scattered around. A huge moon hung brightly in the sky, throwing a silver light over everything.

I could hear an ancient siren, rising and falling, but

not masking the drone of engines overhead.

'A bomber's moon,' said Jones, beside me, pulling me away from the window.

'What?'

'A bomber's moon. That's what they called it.'

'That's what who called it?'

'Fighter pilots in the Second World War.'

That made sense. Blackout curtains. Droning aircraft engines. What sounded to me like an air raid siren. Second World War.

He was still talking. 'They must be heading for the old aircraft factory in Rushford. They're following the river. It's reflecting the moonlight. Better than a signpost.'

'But they're bombing a hospital. Why would they do that?'

He shrugged. 'Accident? Engine failure perhaps? He'd want to dump his bombs and get home as quickly as possible.'

'But ...'

There was high-pitched whistle, getting louder all the time, then silence for a very nasty moment or two. I opened my mouth to speak and Jones pushed me to the floor. 'Roll under the bed.'

There was a sound best described as a 'crump' and the whole building shook. Plaster fell from the ceiling onto the wooden floor. More glass tinkled from the broken windows.

'I need to get you out of here,' he said. 'There must be shelters somewhere. Come on.'

'But what about ...?'

'You can't do anything if you're dead. Priorities, Cage.'

He seized my hand. Through the shattered window, I caught a glimpse of people fleeing the building. Old fashioned ambulances and fire engines were racing through the neat vegetable patches, scattering plants and tearing up the soil, their headlights cutting through the night. I wondered briefly about the blackout, but there seemed little point now.

Another explosion rocked the building. The shouting intensified.

'We need to get out of here,' said Jones, and just for once I agreed with him.

He eased open the door and we emerged into a smoke-filled corridor.

'Hold on to my jacket,' he said. 'Do not let go. If you can't breathe then drop to the floor and crawl. Where is she now?'

I looked down. Nothing. I stared around. No one.

'Not here. She's gone.'

'Bloody brilliant. So she has brought us here to die after all. Bloody marvellous. We're going to be talking about this later, Cage.'

Our corridor was deserted, all the doors standing open. If they were evacuating the building, then this upper part had already been cleared. Downstairs, however, was a different matter.

Gone was the gracious furniture, the expensive carpets, all the artwork. The hall was jam packed with people. It was chaos, but controlled chaos. Some patients were being wheeled out in their beds. Some were being helped by the nursing staff. Those who could walk on their own were helping those who couldn't. There was shouting, lots of shouting, but no panic. The hall was clear of smoke and I couldn't see any flames yet. It was an orderly evacuation. I remembered Jones saying there had been few casualties this night.

I turned back and said quietly, 'Something's wrong.'

'In what way?'

'I don't know.' I looked over the bannisters again. 'I don't think she's there.'

'No offence, Cage, but how do you know what she looks like?'

'Well, you said she was a nursing sister. They wore blue, didn't they, and there's no blue nurses down there.'

He took my arm. 'Cage, I'm having strong second thoughts about this.'

I didn't blame him in the slightest. What had I got us into here? 'Off you go then.'

'What?'

'Go home.'

'How?'

'Exactly.'

'You're a witch, aren't you?' At least, I think he said 'witch'.

'If she's not here,' I said, leaning over the bannisters and scanning the crowd again. 'Where would she be?'

He pulled me back against the wall just as a man dressed as a fireman appeared on the other side of the stairs shouting, 'All clear.' The cry was echoed somewhere else.

'Well,' he said, 'we know where she's not. All these upper rooms have been cleared. There's no problem

112

with the ground floor, which leaves ...'

'The basement,' I said with a sinking heart. I really didn't want to go down there. I'd had bad feelings about that place right from my very first visit. Was this why? Was there something awful waiting for me down there?

He looked down at me. 'Problem?'

'No,' I said stoutly. 'Do you know the way?'

''Course I do.' He nudged me back the way we'd come. 'Do not let go of my jacket.'

'Your concern for my safety is touching.'

'Of course it is.'

'And you might not be able to get back without me.'

'And that. This way.'

There was an unobtrusive door at the end of the corridor. He ran his hands over it like a blind man.

'It's not hot. We should be OK.'

The door was unlocked. A flight of wooden stairs ran both up and down.

'Down,' he said, flashing his torch and setting off. I hung on to his jacket and followed him down. He was directing the beam downwards so we could see. I told him he'd make a wonderful usherette.

There was no smoke here, but occasionally, in the distance, we would feel the vibrations of something heavy falling. Once, in the far distance, I heard voices shouting a warning and then something shattered.

'They've been bombed,' he said. 'I can't hear any more explosions, so perhaps the enemy planes have cleared off, and now all we have to worry about is fire, smoke and the building collapsing on top of us.'

'If the planes have gone then why aren't they

sounding the all-clear?'

'Bombing raids come in waves. The second wave will be here soon. They'll see the flames, assume this was a legitimate target and perhaps drop a few more.'

I shivered. 'Should we be here?'

'Absolutely not.' He stopped dead and I bounced off him. 'Actually, that's a good question.'

'Is it?'

'Well, yes. Think about it. We know that most of the building is still standing in our time. The only bit that was destroyed was what is now the kitchen block at the back. That's where she'll be.'

'Why would a nurse be in the kitchens?'

'Well obviously they weren't kitchens then. Perhaps they were wards.'

'Or operating theatres,' I said slowly, thinking about oxygen tanks and explosions and wishing I'd kept my mouth shut about all of this and could just go home. All I'd ever wanted to do was live quietly at home with Ted.

Jones was irritatingly calm about everything. I remembered his comment, 'Live or die, Cage – it's all the same to me.'

There was a similar door at the bottom of the stairs, opening into a long, empty corridor. At the end, an orange glow flickered.

'Oh good,' he said cheerfully. 'We've found the fire. I think the kitchens would be more or less above us now so the chances are that our nursing friend is around here somewhere. Stay behind me, Cage.'

I was very happy to do so.

These were all the working bits of the hospital. Big fat pipes ran along the walls. Some were lagged, some were not. Some had large valves attached with 'Do not turn off' labels attached. Piles and piles of files and folders were packed along the walls. Some were in boxes but most were loose, their contents spilling across the corridor. Wooden chairs and trestle tables were stacked all along one section and beyond them, for some reason which escaped me, old mattresses were piled nearly to the ceiling. I know it was wartime and no one ever threw anything away, but this was ridiculous. All of it was horribly inflammable. I began to see how easily this place would burn. With us in it.

We inched our way along, Jones opening doors and flashing his torch around empty storerooms. I mean that they were packed with what I assumed were medical supplies, but empty of people. I think we were both hoping that somehow, she was in one of them, injured, but unburned and we could just scoop her up and gallop away. We were both wrong.

At the end of the corridor was an open area, with two doors leading off. One was marked Theatre One, the other, Theatre Two. The door to Theatre One was open and the room was ablaze. Flames roared around the door. If she was in there then she was already dead. Jones hesitated for a moment, then ripped off his jacket, wrapped it around his arm, jumped forward, kicked away the wedge holding the door open, and pulled it closed. The sound of roaring flames died away.

'That's bought us a little time,' he said.

I looked down at the floor. Brown lino, polished to a high shine. There were layers of polish on that floor. Generations, even. The walls were the sickly green always considered so appropriate for hospitals. Everything here was liable to go up at any moment. We really should get out of here while we still could. We should retrace our steps and get out and at that moment, with an enormous crash, part of the ceiling came down at the other end of the passage, and a great tangled mass of burning timbers, plaster and furniture blocked our way back. I jumped a mile, grabbing hold of Jones. I could feel the heat from here. Now we had no choice but to go forwards.

The door to Theatre Two was closed but unlocked.

'This door's hot,' he said. 'Careful.'

I had no intention of being anything else.

He inched it open. This theatre was on fire as well and the heat was immense. I could feel sweat running down my back. Flames ran along the floor, licked the walls and ran across the ceiling. Part of the ceiling had already come down. I could see up into the floor above. The rest of the floor hung at a sharp angle and would surely come down at any moment.

She had been a theatre sister. That's why she was here. She was dressed in a theatre gown, although her head was bare. Whether she had been prepping for surgery or clearing up afterwards, we would never know.

She lay at the far end of the room, flat on her back, her legs buried under a tangle of beams and wires and broken equipment. Her face was black with smoke and contorted with fear and pain. She was much, much younger than I had thought she would be, and her tears had tracked through her dirty face.

116

Even from here I could see both her legs were broken and shattered. There was a lot of blood. The upper half of her body had been protected by the twisted remains of some sort of medical trolley, but this was also pinning her down. Beneath it, she was half sitting, half lying, and struggling to free herself. As we looked, a large piece of burning plaster dropped down on top of her and she screamed, frantically trying to brush it off and beat out the flames with her bare hands. At the same time, she was shouting, 'Help me. Don't let me burn. For God's sake, please don't let me burn.'

Another burning timber fell through the ceiling and crashed to the floor nearby, sending a shower of sparks all over her.

She screamed again. 'Help me. Please help me. I'm burning.'

Jones pushed me back against the wall. 'Stay there.'

I ignored him. He would need help.

He rolled his jacket around his hands again.

Another shower of burning plaster fell. She screamed again. I could smell scorched clothing and burning meat. We didn't have very long.

Jones was a strong man. He grunted and heaved at one end of a timber and the whole mass of stuff lifted slightly, sending more sparks flying. 'Can you pull her out, Cage?'

I tried. I really tried. Jones would have made a much better job of it, but only I could do this. I wasn't anywhere near strong enough to lift those timbers. But she was so heavy. Much heavier than I thought she would be, and her legs were broken. She couldn't help me and I couldn't move her. I was hurting her for nothing. I stifled a frightened sob and tried again.

'Grab her collar and yank.'

I did as I was told and she moved fractionally, screaming with pain.

'Again,' yelled Jones.

I did it again and she moved. Jerking was the answer. It hurt her, I know, but she was burning. We had no time.

'Just get her clear,' he shouted. 'I can do the rest.'

The smoke was making my head swim and the heat was intense. I didn't dare think about oxygen tanks. The smell was awful. Burning wood. Burning clothes. Burning people. We struggled on, Jones straining to hold the tangled burning mess clear of her legs, and me, sweat pouring down my face and back, labouring to pull her away.

'Keep going,' he said, teeth clenched. 'I think we're nearly there.' And at that moment, the rest of the ceiling came down.

Something pushed me clear. I sprawled on the hot floor.

He shouted, 'Get the door.' I struggled to my feet and raced to open the door. He was heaving burning debris clear like a madman and the next moment, he had scooped her up in his arms. I heard her scream with pain, but she was clear.

I remembered to close the door behind us and then we were retracing our steps back down the corridor. The blocked corridor.

'Never mind trying to get back to the stairs,' he yelled. 'We can't get back that way. Look for an outside door. There's got to be one somewhere. For deliveries.'

There was, but we would never have found it in time. The corridor was filling with smoke and I couldn't see where I was going. I could hear flames roaring everywhere. I was coughing and choking. We were never going to get out. We would die here. We'd come to save her and we would die with her. I had a sudden mad vision of three burned and twisted bodies dragging themselves down the long corridors of the Sorensen Clinic ... until the end of time ...

And then, suddenly, behind us, there was an almighty crash and a door spun off its hinges and fell into the passage. Two dark indistinguishable figures shouted. We ran towards them. One seized my arm and almost threw me through the doorway. Someone caught me on the other side and I was dragged up a flight of stone steps and out into the suddenly cold night air. Someone else seized me and I was flung from one person to another until I was clear of the building. It was rough, but it was fast. Seconds only from start to finish.

Behind me, I heard the crash of falling masonry. I tried to call out for Jones but the words caught in my chest and I was overcome with a fit of coughing. Someone laid me out on the cold ground. I pushed myself up on my elbows, trying to see and cough at the same time.

The fire wasn't too bad. The flames seemed confined to only the back of the building where we'd been. It certainly wasn't widespread. Looking at the snake of people being led away, I wasn't sure there were even any major casualties. Just our nursing sister. Without us, they would never have got to her in time to pull her out. She would have been buried alive beneath the burning ceiling. We had saved her from a terrible death.

They had laid her on the grass beside me and I crawled to her side.

No, we hadn't. Yes, we'd saved her from burning, but death had come for her tonight, regardless of anything we had done. Somewhere not too far away, a man was shouting for a doctor. With some surprise, I realised it was Michael Jones.

I bent over her. She lay on her back, not moving. Her gown was covered in dark bloody patches. A lot of it had burned away. Her face was blistered and red. A fireman, his own face black and streaked with his sweat and her blood, was shaking his head at me.

Even I could see she didn't have very long. The last seconds of her life were flying away like swallows swooping in the sunlight. We hadn't saved her at all. I felt the anger of impotence. This wasn't right. There should be a happy ending. She couldn't die. She had brought us here to save her. She should have lived. I felt an enormous sob well up inside of me. We'd failed. We'd been just those few minutes too late. Ten minutes earlier and we could have got her out. We could have got her out before the ceiling came down. We'd been in the right place at the wrong time.

She was trying to speak, blindly holding out a burned and bloody hand in my direction. Very carefully, because I didn't want to cause her any more hurt, I took her poor, blackened hand in mine.

She whispered, 'Thank you.'

I was crying. 'I'm sorry. I'm so sorry. We were too late.'

'No,' she said and her voice was just a sigh in the night. 'You saved me.'

I shook my head, tears stinging my eyes.

'Please ... I want to see ... before I go ... help me ...'

Her voice failed. She was leaving us but I knew what she wanted. She slipped softly away, but not before I gently lifted her head and showed her the stars.

## Chapter Eleven

I sat holding her hand as people milled around us. I didn't know what else to do. I was desperate for a drink. Someone large loomed over me. 'We should go,' he said, pulling me to my feet. 'While we still can.'

Yes, we should, but where to? How would we get back? What if we were trapped here for ever? Well, at least it would get Sorensen off my back.

He looked down at her lying on the crushed grass and sighed. 'I thought we were here to save her.'

'We did,' I said. 'Well, you did.'

He shook his head. 'If we had found her earlier ...' Even in the dark I could see his colour curdle. His face was expressionless but there was emotion there. 'Another woman I failed to save.'

'What did you say?'

'I said, time to go, Cage.'

'How? Where?'

'Well, away from here to begin with. There's a war on and we don't have any papers or identification.' He looked down at the body on the grass. 'Rest in peace, sweetheart. Now then, Cage, can you run?'

I looked down at my shoes. 'Low-heeled courts. Smart yet practical.'

'I don't believe you. Here we are, about to be arrested as spies, lost in time, more than slightly scorched around the edges, and you're talking about shoes.'

He was hustling me away into the darkness. Shouts behind us slowly faded away.

We reached some shrubbery. I took a final look behind me. Flames billowed from one side of the building. I could see small black figures running to and fro, silhouetted against the fire. Whistles blew and men shouted. A score or more of ambulances, tradesman's vans and farm vehicles were parked at a safe distance. Patients were being helped towards them. Shouts indicated they'd found our nursing sister.

'We never even knew her name,' I said.

'Evelyn,' said a voice behind us. 'My name is Evelyn Mary Cross and I'm from Bournemouth.'

And with those words, we were back in my room.

Nothing had changed. Although, as Jones said, 'Why would anything have changed? One minute you're outside on the cold, wet grass a safe distance away from a burning building seventy-something years ago, and the next minute you're in a well-appointed bedroom in a secure government establishment. Happens all the time.'

Actually, I think even he was a little fazed by recent events. He, however, was handling things much better than me. I was again fighting back nausea and disorientation. I hung on to the bedhead and waited for the world to stop spinning.

We kept the lights off because I was supposed to be asleep and Jones wasn't supposed to be here at all. Neither was the shadow figure standing by the window. My first thought was – why is she still here? My second thought was – she can stand up. My third thought was that I was going to be horribly sick any moment now.

Jones crossed the room to stand by the door, occasionally peering out through the viewing window and keeping watch.

I swallowed hard and said, 'We couldn't save your life. I'm so sorry.'

She was just a whisper in the dark. 'I didn't burn. I can't thank you enough.'

'There's no need.'

'So what now?' said Jones from over by the door. Presumably you'll … cross over.'

'No.'

'Well, that's good because I felt really stupid saying that, but what will you do?'

'Nothing. Nothing has changed.'

He seemed confused. 'But we saved you. You can … move on. Or whatever it is dead people do.'

'I don't want to move on. This is my home. You were all mistaken about me. I don't kill people. I don't take life. I simply go to those who would have died anyway and I ease their passage from this world into the next. I'm a nurse. I don't harm. I try to help. There is so much unhappiness in this place. I cannot stop death but I can try to take away the pain.'

She stepped towards the door and by the dim light of the moon, I saw her face. Young and serious. 'You should leave this place. You should not stay. You will die here. This place is not good for you.'

She was already drifting away, becoming less substantial every moment, and with those final words, she was gone and we were left alone.

Now what? Jones was still staring out of the viewing window into the corridor beyond. 'I can't believe any of that just happened.' He looked down at his hands. 'But apparently, it did.'

'How are your hands?'

'Hurting.'

'How will you account for the burns?'

'Smoking in bed. Fell asleep and set fire to the sheets. Burned myself beating out the flames. Not the first time.'

'Won't you get into trouble?'

'I'm always in trouble, Cage. It's only the depth that varies. With a bit of luck, they'll chuck me out.'

'How is that lucky?'

'Because, once I'm outside, I can get you out too.'

'You mean you'll go to the authorities.'

He sighed. 'Will you stop with this touching faith in authority to solve all your problems? Again – it's the authorities who have put you in here. If you want to get out, then you'll have to do it yourself. With my help, of course.'

'Why would you do that?'

He shuffled his feet. 'Ted's wife deserves better.'

'What if they don't chuck you out?'

'Then we'll break out together.'

Twenty-four hours ago, I wouldn't even have considered it. Now however …

Jones looked at his watch. 'Bed-check due. I'd better push off.'

I was jolted. I don't know why. I thought he would want to stay and discuss what had happened. 'Oh … yes … of course. You'll have some explaining to do.'

He smirked. 'Nurses. Putty in my hands.'

Personally, I thought he was kidding himself, but he seemed confident and I didn't want to burst his bubble.

'We'll talk tomorrow,' he said, easing the door open. 'Meet me in the garden.'

The door closed behind him.

Typical Michael Jones. Meet me in the garden, he said. There was the Summer Border Garden, the Sunken Garden, the Rose Garden, and the Water Garden. To say nothing of four acres of lawns and garden walks. I covered every single inch looking for him, finding him eventually, sitting on a bench in the middle of a vast space, miles from anywhere.

'Why here? Everyone can see us.'

'Very true, but no one can hear us.'

'Ah.'

'Well,' he said as I joined him on the mossy bench. 'Any fallout from last night?'

'No, none. Although I had to hang my clothes out of the window to get rid of the smell of smoke. You?'

'Oh God, yes. I was up before Sorensen at the crack of nine o'clock this morning.'

'What did you say?'

'Not a lot. He, on the other hand, burbled on for hours about my desire to escape my past. My unwillingness to face the future. My lack of co-operation. My disregard for the rules. How difficult I was making life for nearly everyone on the planet. You know how he goes on.'

'Doesn't he ... worry you at all?'

'Not really. I'm just an uncooperative patient. He takes people like me in his stride.'

'He worries me.'

'Not as much as you worry him, I suspect.'

'Is that supposed to make me feel better?'

'No, Cage, it's supposed to galvanize you into getting out of here while you still can.'

'How?' I demanded. 'All I have is what I stand up in. More or less. Where would I go? Who would I go to?'

'You don't need possessions. A couple of changes of clothes is all you need. And a toothbrush of course. Never neglect dental hygiene, Cage. Leads to all sorts of problems in later years. As to where you would go – you can go anywhere you like. You don't answer to anyone but yourself. There must be somewhere you've always wanted to live. Go and live there.'

'But,' I said, bewildered by what he was saying. In my world, people were anchored by houses, and possessions, and relations, and jobs, and … things.

He turned to me. 'If I could get you out, would you come?'

'How could you do that?'

'Leave that to me. Would you come?'

Would I? I wasn't safe here, but at least I knew where the danger was coming from. Out there – on the other side of the wall – was a whole new world of which I knew very little. A world without Ted. And then I thought – why not? I wasn't destitute or penniless. People made new starts all the time. I could find a little house in a little town and … make a new start. I could live quietly. On my own, obviously, but I wouldn't have to watch what I said or what I did.

127

And the things I could see would be my own business and no one else's.

'Oh ho,' he said softly, watching me. 'Have I started a new train of thought?'

I looked at him. Big, blond and capable. 'How would you get me out?'

'Successfully. And I'll help you get established, if that's what's worrying you. For God's sake, Cage, I'm not going to just drop you off at the railway station and drive away. You're Ted's wife. Of course I'll help you.'

I was thinking about his when he took his hands out of his pockets and I saw they were bandaged. I'd been so busy thinking about the future, I'd forgotten the past. And it was only last night.

'What did they say about your hands?'

'I had a thirty-minute lecture on Smoking Kills, although I suspect that if I set fire to my bedclothes again, it will be the nursing staff who do for me, never mind nicotine. And do I know what a nuisance I am? And do I know I could have burned down the hospital? Quite honestly, at that point it was hard not to make some smart comment about been there, done that, but I didn't think that would be helpful, so, Cage, hard to believe it may be, I held my tongue, allowed myself to be bandaged up and went meekly to bed. Although one of them did bring me a mug of cocoa later on, so I haven't completely lost my touch.'

He stared complacently at his feet.

No – he hadn't lost his touch. The soft golden patch was growing larger all the time, and now golden tendrils suffused the dirty patch over his heart, instead of the other way around. He was good-looking in an unconventional way, and he did possess a kind of careless charm – none the less effective because he really didn't try very hard – and now that he was lost and sad I could imagine nurses tumbling for him by the bucketload.

'So,' he said. 'Any thoughts on last night.'

'Not really. I saw what you saw.'

'Actually, I was meaning your ... unique contribution ... to the night's events.'

I shook my head, staring at the ground.

'You can trust me, you know.'

I nodded my head, staring at the ground.

There was a long pause.

'OK,' he said, getting up. 'Another day, perhaps. Although you're going to have to learn to trust me sometime. However,' he thrust out his chin, looking noble. 'I can wait.'

I smiled reluctantly.

'That's better. I wonder, would you care to be my guest for dinner this evening.'

'Me?'

'Is there anyone else here? Really, Cage, you do have moments of complete lunacy, don't you? I'm beginning to wonder if this might not be the best place for you after all.'

'I meant, you've just gone to all this trouble to ensure we're alone and not disturbed and now you want to ... flaunt me in front of everyone this evening.'

I didn't think *flaunt* was quite the word I wanted, but I was still tired from the previous night.

His lip twitched, but he let it go. 'I was simply thinking that you and I need to be seen together occasionally so that when we do eventually get around to tunnelling out of this place, our togetherness will not attract attention.'

'Oh I see. I'm camouflage.'

'Yes, of course you are. What did you think?'

'Nothing,' I said hastily, before he got the wrong idea.

'Besides if I don't ask you then that idiot Jenkins in Room Two will and I tell you now, Cage, you don't want to have anything to do with him. Man's got more personality disorders than you can shake a stick at.'

I appreciated his efforts to distract me. Doubts, fear and grief were all nibbling away at the edges of my mind. I sometime felt as if I was holding shut a door behind which all sorts of dark things waited.

I managed a small smile. 'And how do you know that?'

'We've worked together for years. Close friends. All right, yes, I'm slightly odd, but he's well over the event horizon.'

'So,' I said, filing this away to be thought about later. 'It's not just the rich and famous who are patients here.'

'God no. They're just the window dressing. There are all sorts here. Some are like me, poor overworked sods in need of a bit of TLC. Some have seen too much and have to be enticed out of the warm fuzzy worlds in which they've taken refuge. Some need to be induced to talk. Some need shutting up. Some need to be induced to cooperate. You must have guessed, Cage. There's a very dark underbelly to the Sorensen Clinic.'

I suddenly realised that, yes, I had guessed. I'd just never admitted it to myself. This was a very dark place. My fears about the basement had been more than founded. Would my fear and dislike of Sorensen turn out to be justified as well? Or was I confusing dislike with fear? After all, Ted had worked here.

I said to Jones, 'What about Ted? What was his role here?'

'Ted was Head of Security. Nothing more – nothing less. Relax.'

'This is why I'm here, isn't it? I'm one of those to be induced to cooperate.'

'And after last night's little party ...'

My heart stopped. I couldn't believe it. 'You've told him?'

'Of course not, Cage. What do you take me for? But you can't carry on like this. He knows there's something dodgy about you and he's determined to find out.'

'How? How can he know?'

He shrugged. 'As I said before – I don't know. But you don't want to hang around here while Sorensen dusts off his cooperation-inducing techniques, do you?'

I shivered. 'No.'

# Chapter Twelve

I wore my black dress for dinner.

'You smell like a bonfire drenched in Chanel,' said Jones, amused.

'Hush,' I said, looking around. 'We're in enough trouble as it is.'

'Not you,' he said easily, opening the dining room door for me. 'I think it's the injustice that's so galling. You're the cause of all the trouble and you come out smelling like a bed of roses. Figuratively speaking, of course.'

We were in trouble from the off. A member of staff approached us. 'Mr Jones – a jacket, please.'

'I've lost it,' he said cheerfully. 'But I am wearing a tie. See.' He flourished his tie.

I was stricken with guilt. I'd left his jacket behind in the burning hospital. And his torch, now I came to think of it.

'Sir, the rules state ...'

'I know,' he said, pulling out a chair for me. 'I'll pop into town tomorrow and get another. In fact, I'll go now, if you like.'

'That won't be necessary, sir. But tomorrow ...'

'Tell Sorensen not to get his knickers in a twist – I'll sort something out,' he said, seating himself and picking up the menu. 'Oh good, you've got the sea bass tonight. Mrs Cage, I do recommend the sea bass here. It's excellent.'

It was. In fact, it was a pleasant dinner all round. The food was excellent. And the service. 'In fact,' he said to the server who stopped at our table to enquire if everything was all right, 'if we weren't being held in a secret government establishment, against our will, and for unknown but almost certainly sinister reasons, we'd be having a lovely time, wouldn't we?'

The waiter, obviously accustomed to comments like this from him, sighed heavily and moved on to the next table.

I had wondered what on earth we would say to each other that didn't involve mysteriously vanishing medical staff, WWII bombing raids and nearly burning to death seventy-something years ago, but Jones chatted easily throughout the meal. I smiled and nodded as appropriate and tried not to notice the stares from everyone around us.

At the end of the meal, he stood up and pulled out my chair again. 'May I offer you coffee in the library, Mrs Cage?'

I smiled and politely declined. 'I'm very tired today, but thank you for a lovely meal.'

'My pleasure. May I escort you to your room?'

'That won't be necessary, but thank you.'

He did walk with me to the staircase, however. 'I have enjoyed your company, Mrs Cage. I do hope you will join me again one evening.'

'Thank you,' I said gravely, even though I could see he was laughing at me. 'That would be very pleasant. Good night, Mr Jones.'

Half of me was convinced that this wild talk about

breaking us both out of the clinic was just that. Wild talk. I was wrong.

Two days later, he appeared alongside me as I was pouring myself a coffee after lunch. 'Please allow me, Mrs Cage.'

'Thank you.'

Under cover of handing me the cup, he said, 'Tomorrow.'

'Tomorrow what?'

He sighed. 'I wonder why I bother sometimes, I really do. Tomorrow, Cage. Don't pack. Don't do anything to alert them. Wear something warm. It's going to rain. Which is good.'

'Why is it good?'

'Tell you later. Do you want this coffee or not?'

Irritatingly, he was right. I awoke the next morning to the sound of rain lashing against the windows. It made me feel cold just to look at it, but it was an excellent excuse to wear jeans, a thick sweater and a jacket over the top. And trainers.

I caught Jones's eye as I entered the dining room and he nodded slightly in approval. Just to be on the safe side, however, I had stuffed my toothbrush into an inside pocket. I still couldn't quite believe he could get me out, but just in case ...

His plate was piled high, and given my own uncertain plans for the day, I did the same. The staff commented on my improved appetite and I smiled, channelling Michael Jones, and asked if they could bring me some more hot water, please.

He joined me, bringing his newspaper folded back to the crossword page.

'Good morning, Mrs Cage. What's a six-letter word for a fruity relative?'

'Damson,' I said, without thinking, and had the satisfaction of seeing him startled. Just for once.

'Ah. Which makes that one 'deed,' and that one 'munificent.' Thank you very much. Meet me in the library in five minutes.'

'Why?'

'I want to finish this first.' And was gone before I could tell him that wasn't what I had meant.

I sat and watched the clock, finishing my last piece of toast. Five minutes passed very slowly, and then, without knowing why, I topped up my tea and made him wait another two minutes. Just a small and very inadequate bid for independence, but I felt better for it.

He was leafing through a magazine as I entered. 'Go down to the end.'

I walked straight past him and he joined me a moment later. I could see the door through which Ted and I had smuggled him back to his room at the Christmas party.

'Quick. It's unlocked. We need to hurry. I'm not sure how vigilantly they'll be watching the CCTV at this hour of the morning, but we can't take any chances. Along to the end and wait for me there.'

I hastened down the dusty corridor and stopped at yet another locked door. With a keypad and I didn't know the code.

I turned in a panic, but he was already there, reaching over my shoulder and tapping it in. The door opened silently and we were looking out over the rain-lashed car park. The car nearest us was big

135

and black. I don't know what he did, but I heard the double chirp of the alarm system being disabled. Lights flashed briefly.

'Come on,' he said, propelling me across the car park. 'Into the back. Lie down.'

'But – what's happening?'

'We're tunnelling to freedom, Cage. Pull the blanket over you and keep quiet.'

I heard the door slam with that gentle clunk that denotes a very expensive car indeed.

'Whose car is this?'

'Oh, I think we both know the answer to that one, don't we?'

*'What?'*

'Shush.' The engine purred into life. 'Quiet now.'

It's hard to shriek in a whisper. *'This is Dr Sorensen's car.'*

'Correct.'

'Why?'

'What better car to get us past the gate unchallenged?'

'But ...'

'That's why I had to wait for a rainy day.'

'What? Why?'

'Because the scanner will read his security clearance and the barrier will rise automatically.'

'But the guards?'

'Are not going to be standing about in the rain when they can see it's only the boss's car. That's why I waited for a rainy day.'

'Oh. That's quite clever.'

'Could you sound a little more impressed and a little less surprised?'

Rather to my surprise, everything went exactly according to plan. We slowed for the barrier, which rose automatically. I heard him give a cheery toot to the guards. I heard the indicator blink on – we turned left and increased speed. And that was it. We were out.

'Stay where you are,' he said softly. 'There's tinted windows in the back but staff use this road a lot. It's not for long. We'll be there in ten minutes.'

He was right. I heard the engine slow, felt a sharp turn to the right, and then the car stopped. I heard an up-and-over garage door open. He drove in and switched off the engine. 'You can sit up now.'

We were in someone's garage. An old workbench piled high with what looked to me like junk ran along one wall. Bits of cars lay everywhere. I had long since given up being surprised by anything that was happening today. I folded up the blanket and laid it neatly on the back seat and climbed out.

'Why are we here?'

'I'm changing the number plates.'

I didn't know you could actually do that, although I wasn't about to say so. It was beginning to dawn on me that I was very much out of my depth.

He disappeared around the back of the car, whistling to himself.

I stared around the garage. 'Don't just stand about,' he called. 'Grab those two suitcases and put them in the boot.'

Two smart black suitcases stood in the corner. I wheeled them to the back of the car and struggled to lift them in.

He laughed at me and lifted them, one handed, into the boot and slammed the lid. 'Clothes,' he said. 'You didn't think I was going to make you live for ever in what you're wearing at the moment, did you? Clothes, toiletries, everything we'll need.'

I didn't know where to begin with questions. We? Everything *we* would need? Where had it all come from? Where were we going? No. Enough was enough. I stepped back and folded my arms.

'No.'

He was fishing for the car keys. 'What?'

'No. I'm not going anywhere with you. I don't know you. I don't know why you're doing this. I don't know where we're going. I don't know what's going on, and I'm fed up with being shunted around like luggage while various men lie to me. So ... no.'

I thought he would be angry, but he laughed. 'Well thank God, Cage, you're finally developing some sort of instinct for self-preservation. And not before time. I was seriously concerned about the rapidity with which you jumped into a strange car and allowed me to kidnap you. Yes, I will explain everything, but we need to be on our way. Sooner or later Sorensen's going to look out of his window and see his car's missing. And me. And you. And then the shit will really hit the fan so we need to be as far away as possible.'

He set off for the driver's door.

I stayed still.

He stopped. 'I understand,' he said quietly, resting his arm on the car roof. 'Believe me, I really do. All I ask is you put aside your concerns for half an hour or so. Just give me the time to get us out of here.'

I still didn't move.

'Do you really think I'd do anything to hurt Ted's wife?'

No, he wouldn't. I could see it. He wouldn't do anything to hurt Ted's wife.

He held open the door. I waited a moment, just so he wouldn't think I was too easy, and then climbed in. I didn't really have a lot of choice.

We backed out of the garage and he pulled the door down behind us.

'Off we go,' he said cheerfully.

Thirty minutes later we'd left Rushford and were heading north.

'Well, isn't this nice?' he said, settling himself more comfortably in his seat and slowly increasing speed. 'We've been a bit busy these last few days – me organising our successful gaolbreak and you saving the universe or whatever it is you do.'

'I don't save anything. Or anyone,' I added, remembering Evelyn Cross dying on the grass.

'So what *do* you do, Cage? And before you deny everything, remember I'm asking with all the curiosity of a bloke who suddenly finds himself in the middle of a burning hospital during an air raid seventy-something years ago, and still hasn't quite recovered. And I should add that attempts to tell me I was drunk, drugged or imagining things will not go down well. I have proof.' He flexed a bandaged hand at me.

There was a long pause. The car purred along. He didn't speak.

Eventually I said, 'I'm sorry, this is quite hard for me. My father warned me to keep quiet and never

139

mention it to anyone. And that was just minor stuff. I've never done anything like ... like ... you know, what we did the other night.'

'Start with the minor stuff then. What did your dad tell you not to tell anyone?'

I said with great reluctance, 'I see things.'

'Oh, go on. Say it. *I see dead people.*'

I couldn't help a reluctant smile. 'And living people. And the sort of people they are. And what they know. Whether they're lying. Or happy. Or ill. Or hiding something. I see connections. I see a web of light around people and how that reacts to other people or events. I see things and I just ... know.'

'Are you kidding me? No wonder Sorensen wants you in his collection. My God, Cage, we could sit you down in a room full of world leaders and you could tell us who's lying, who's bluffing, who's afraid, who's deadly serious, how they're reacting to each other. It would be amazing. And it wouldn't stop there. Politicians, bankers and other major criminals would be an open book to you.'

He became aware of my silence. 'Sorry. Sorry, but you have to admit – for someone hearing all this for the first time ...'

'I've lived with it all my life,' I said. 'Believe me, it's no fun. Do you really want to know what people think of you? The boss who's spinning you a tale about there being no better positions available because you've been groomed for a crap, dead-end job that you'll never leave. Or your girlfriend whom you adore and she's only with you until someone better comes along. Or your best mate who actually can't stand you and is only ...'

140

'Yes, yes,' he said, 'but you must be aware of the value of …'

I shrugged. 'I'm only aware of the cost, And I don't want to pay it. I married Ted and tried to forget it.'

We drove for a while in silence. I waited for the inevitable question. 'So what do you know about me?'

Well, he did ask.

'You've lost her,' I said. 'Or rather, she was taken from you. She was ripped away without warning. You feel responsible. It's ruining your life. Pervading your every moment. It's becoming an obsession and you lack the will or the strength to break free. You alleviate feelings of guilt and failure with too much alcohol. Recently you have become interested in me. Whether professionally or personally I'm not yet able to tell. Your usual colour is a golden peach, shading towards red, and it should stream behind you like a comet's tail, but at the moment it's a poor, sad, frail thing, enveloped in guilt and regret from which I would have to say, if asked, it looks unlikely you will ever recover.'

There was a very long silence after that little lot.

'Way to kill a conversation,' he said eventually, negotiating a ring road.

'Well,' I said, 'did I tell you anything you didn't actually know?'

'No, but you told me a lot of things I didn't want to face.'

I waited again.

'So what's your colour, Cage?'

'I don't know. I can't see it.'

141

'What, not at all? Why not?'

I shrugged.

'But if you looked in a mirror ...'

'I can't see anyone's in a mirror.'

'So you're saying ...'

'I'm saying I know everything about everyone I meet and nothing about myself.'

'Your parents ...?'

'Adopted.'

'And that thing that happened the other night ...?'

'No idea. I've never had that happen before.'

'But you saw her?'

'And she saw me. I was lucky. She was benign. Suppose she hadn't been. Suppose she really did turn up to take a life. How long do you think I would have lasted in that place? I couldn't get out and I couldn't keep moving for ever. Sooner or later she'd have got me. I'd have been dragging my death around behind me just like poor Mr Johnson, only I'd have known I was doing it. There's some nasty stuff out there,' I said, remembering the beige spiky woman I'd seen all those years ago, 'and I don't want it coming after me.'

'No,' he said. And then again, 'No.'

I waited for his next question.

'What colour is Sorensen?'

'Pin-striped,' I said shortly.

He gave a crack of laughter and put his foot down.

'Where are we going?'

'Northumberland.'

Three hours later, we were still going to Northumberland. It's a very long way away. Especially if you're not travelling on motorways

142

because of all the CCTV cameras. I slept a lot of the way. I hadn't been kidding when I'd told Jones I was very tired.

When I awoke, the landscape had completely changed and I was looking at sweeping moors with steep, tree-filled valleys. White waterfalls tumbled everywhere. There were even patches of snow on the very high ground.

'Where are we?' I said, struggling to sit up and surreptitiously checking my chin for drool.

'Nearly there,' he said. 'Wipes in the dash. We're going somewhere quite smart so try and tidy yourself up a bit.'

I did what I could, which wasn't much. I didn't even have a handbag with me.

We were climbing now. The occasional grey cottage flashed past. A fast stream tumbled over a rocky bed and was gone. We entered a village, grey and neat, with a large, triangular village green.

'Two pubs,' said Jones, slowing down to let a tractor past. 'Promising.'

I wondered again about his drinking.

He nodded ahead. 'And here we are.'

'It's a castle,' I said in delight. And it was: a genuine, *bona fide* castle. With towers and battlements and two huge wooden gates, grey with age and studded with nails. They stood open, but Jones swept around the side of the tower, following the sign which said, 'Car Park'. There were two other cars there. An ancient Land Rover and a smart SUV. He pulled into a space and turned off the engine. There was that sudden strange silence you get after a long journey. When you're about to leave the safety and security of the car and step out into the unknown. Personally, I liked the car. It was warm and comfortable. I would stay here and Jones could bring me food.

'Come on,' he said, climbing out. 'I haven't driven for hours to have you refuse to walk the last twenty feet.'

The air was biting. Even though a weak sun was shining, the air had an edge like a knife. I pulled my jacket around me. The view was fantastic. The castle stood, four-square, at the head of the valley. Nothing got past this place unless they wanted it to.

'Brilliant, eh?' said Jones, modestly. 'Where better to defend yourself than a genuine castle? Shame they don't have a moat and a drawbridge, but they close the gates every night, so you'll be quite safe. Unless Sorensen turns up with a tank regiment and a squad of attack helicopters, of course, in which case we will be in trouble, but we'll deal with that when it happens.'

Strangely, I felt quite cheered. Nothing ever seemed to bother Michael Jones and I rather thought some of that was beginning to rub off on me.

He was pulling the suitcases from the car.

I heard a shout and turned around.

A short stocky man was striding towards us, almost completely engulfed in what seemed like a sea of Labradors. Two black, two golden, and a brown one. Five dogs. No, seven! Scampering at his heels were two Jack Russells as well.

They loved Jones, fawning and dribbling all over him. He forgot both the suitcases and me, and stroked and patted them and pulled their ears and generally made himself their best friend. I couldn't see any of them being any use in a crisis. Jones included.

'Good afternoon,' said the man, somewhat breathlessly. His colour was full of soft greys and greens – the colours of the landscape around him. Even the outline of him, all straight lines and sharp angles was the shape of the craggy cliffs from which the castle was hewn.

'Welcome. Welcome. Get down, Juno. Sorry. They won't hurt you, although you may be trampled under their affectionate feet. Get off. Get off.'

The dogs subsided.

'Hello there,' said Jones.

'Nice to meet you,' he said. 'Thomas Rookwood at your service. You must be Mr and Mrs Jones.'

'We are,' said Mr Jones, while Mrs Jones resolved to have a number of words with her husband later on. 'Michael and Elizabeth. I wonder, could I take my wife inside. She's not been too well recently.'

'Of course, of course. Sorry to hear that, Mrs Jones, but I'm sure our good Northumberland air will soon buck you up.'

I smiled weakly, mentally doubling the number of words I would be having later on.

They seized a case each, the dogs galloped ahead to clear the way, and I entered my first castle, through the enormous gates and into a long, low-roofed stone passage.

'Do you have a portcullis?' asked Jones, castle enthusiast.

He pointed upwards. 'We have two. One at this end of the passage and one at the other. And murder holes. Look.'

145

I dutifully stared upwards at the holes in the roof above our heads.

'Boiling oil,' said Jones knowledgeably.

'Sometimes,' he said, 'but hot sand is more effective. Or even just large rocks of course.' His colour surged to and fro with his enthusiasm. He loved his castle.

We left the passage and emerged into a large open courtyard, irregularly paved with ankle-turning cobbles. To the right was an enormous wooden door, heavily studded with nails and with hinges the size of my arm.

Thomas Rookwood turned left. 'Your rooms are here, in the south-west tower. Here's your front door key. He handed Jones a small Yale key. I think Jones had been expecting something made of solid iron and six inches long – however, he concealed his disappointment well.

'We'll get Mrs Jones inside,' continued Mr Rookwood, 'and I'll give you an idea of the layout and the grand tour tomorrow morning, if you like. The fridge is stocked, the fires lit and everything working. Including the telephone. We're a bit remote here and you'll find the wi-fi's a bit dodgy and the mobile signal is dreadful, I'm afraid.'

'Excellent,' said Jones. 'We really want to get away from it all.'

'Well, you've come to the right place for that. I'll leave you now. I hope you'll be comfortable. If you need anything, just pick up the phone and dial zero. Someone will pick it up. Good day to you.'

He strode off across the courtyard, surrounded by a frothing sea of Labrador tails and entered a corresponding door in the opposite tower. There was a small amount of turbulence as seven dogs all tried to get through the door together, and then the door closed and I was alone with my 'husband'.

He inserted the key and opened the door.

'You go in first,' he said. 'Get out of the cold. I'll bring in the suitcases.'

I found myself in a small stone passage, obviously used as some sort of cloakroom. There was a row of pegs on one wall and two enormous wicker baskets filled with logs. A disappointingly unimposing door in the right-hand wall led into a large square room, comfortably warm with a bright fire burning in a large fireplace. Two sofas sat either side of the fire with a coffee table in between. The surface was covered in magazines and brochures detailing local attractions, which I thought was rather optimistic in this weather. There was a bookcase against one wall, bright with paperbacks, packs of cards and board games. The walls were roughly plastered and painted cream. Wall lights made it cosy. The floor was wooden and slightly uneven. Despite Jones shoving folded card under different legs of the table every time we sat down, we were never able to stop it wobbling.

A small alcove contained a tiny kitchen. I could hear Jones opening the fridge to investigate the contents. A small door over in the corner revealed a stone staircase excitingly spiralling up into the gloom. I groped for the light switch and set off to explore.

Only just around the first bend was another room – a small bedroom with a view over the courtyard and a very comfortable bathroom. In this bedroom, the floor was of stone, but covered in

147

brightly coloured rugs. The curtains and bedspread were in dark red and green geometric pattern and there was a wardrobe and large chest of drawers. Fresh, fluffy towels were piled on the bed. The whole atmosphere was one of cosy comfort.

'Nice,' said Jones, sticking his head around the door. 'You can have this one, Cage.'

I hadn't given any thought to the sleeping arrangements.

I could hear him stamping on up the stairs. 'Oh, cool. Come and look at this.'

I followed him up the stairs and around the next bend to a rather grand bedroom. A four-poster bed was hung in thick crimson cloth that matched the cover. Windows on two walls gave a panoramic view over the countryside and a neat *en suite* nestled in the corner.

'Bags this one,' said Jones, tossing his suitcase on the bed. 'You go and unpack and I'll get us something to eat.'

I trailed back down the stairs and disobeyed his instructions. I sat on the bed in my room and wondered what on earth had happened to my life. This time last month, Ted had been alive and now ... I curled up on the bed and cried. I forgot everything. I forgot Sorensen and Jones and Northumberland and burning hospitals and everything. I lost all track of time. I just cried.

I think it must have been quite some time later when Jones turned up. He scratched at the door. 'Cage? Are you in there?' The door opened quietly. The afternoon had turned dark and he had to switch the light on.

He took one look, said, 'Oh dearie, dearie me,' and returned a few minutes later with a steaming mug of tea and helped me sit up. Out came the wipes again. He made a big thing of staring out of the window while I dealt with the devastation. I was actually quite touched by his kindness.

'Thank you.'

'You're welcome,' he said. 'Isn't it lucky that I've reduced so many women to tears during the course of my life that I know exactly what to do. Are you hungry?'

I shook my head.

'Well, I suggest you finish your tea, have a hot bath and go to bed. I promise you things will look better in the morning.'

## *Chapter Thirteen*

He was right. Things looked much better the next morning.

I awoke, warm and comfortable after a good night's sleep. I could hear snow and/or sleet pattering against the windows. My suitcase stood against the far wall and even as I contemplated getting up, Jones knocked at the door.

'You still alive in there, Cage? Or are you dead?'

'I'm dead,' I shouted back. 'Go away.'

'I've brought tea.'

'In that case come in.'

'Shitty day out there,' he said, dumping a mug of tea on the bedside table. 'I hope you weren't contemplating a healthy trek across the moors.'

'God no,' I said, curling my hands around my mug.

'Well, I thought I'd make you some breakfast and then you could unpack – you know, like a normal person would.'

His words touched a nerve and for a second I was back in the past, when I had to watch my every move, every word, always thinking, what would a normal person do?

He was watching me. 'What did I say?'

'Nothing.'

'I'm a good cook, you know,' he said, and I

couldn't decide if he was deliberately misunderstanding me. He too seemed more relaxed this morning. His golden colour was growing and deepening. Definitely less fragile than a week ago.

'Are you?' I said, slightly disbelieving.

'I am. And if you can drag yourself out of bed then you'll find out. Twenty minutes, Cage. Don't be late.'

'I've just swapped one tyranny for another, haven't I?'

He laughed and took himself off. I swung my legs out of bed and went to investigate the contents of my suitcase.

They were my clothes. They were my clothes from my house. Someone had been to my house, sorted through my possessions and carefully packed them in this suitcase. They'd even picked up the book I'd been reading off my bedside cabinet. Everything I could possibly need was here, immaculately packed. There was even tissue paper between the layers!

I went downstairs.

'How did you do that?'

He didn't pretend to misunderstand me this time. 'Sorensen is not the only one who can indulge in a bit of surreptitious breaking and entering, you know.'

'You broke into my house?'

'Of course not. That would be illegal.'

'Oh.'

'I got someone else to do it.'

'Who?'

'The bloke whose garage we used yesterday. When we swapped number plates.'

'And where are they now?'

'The plates or the bloke?'

151

'Either. Or both.'

He shrugged. 'Bottom of the river, I expect. The plates, I mean. Don't know where old Jerry will be.'

'You are beginning to lose the power to surprise me.'

'Sorry to hear that. You don't want breakfast then?'

'You cooked breakfast?'

'Well, we both know you didn't, so that just leaves me. Sit down.'

I expected burned toast. I got delicious creamy scrambled eggs and crispy bacon on wholemeal muffins, washed down with fragrant coffee.

'You *can* cook!'

He sighed. 'I like cooking.'

'You're just full of surprises, aren't you?'

'And I'm not the only one.'

I grinned reluctantly and felt some of the tension I hadn't known I'd been carrying just melt away.

I cleared away the breakfast things and Jones laid and lit the fire. Cheerful flames pushed back the horrible day outside. We took a sofa each and stretched out. Jones worked his way through the pamphlets and brochures, occasionally reading out bits he thought might interest me. I read my book. The snow fell, the fire crackled and it was all very peaceful. I was just beginning to relax when someone knocked at the door and I sat up in a hurry.

'Stay calm,' said Jones, getting up. 'One of the reasons I chose this place is because you can see everyone approaching from about forty miles away. This will be our host come to give us the guided tour.'

It wasn't our host. It was our host's children. 'We were told not to disturb you too early,' said the oldest, 'but it's nearly lunchtime so we thought you wouldn't mind.'

'I suspect you were told not to disturb us at all,' said Jones.

They shuffled their feet.

'Come in.' He held the door open and in they came.

He closed the door behind them and then immediately had to open it again to let in an aged Labrador who shoved everything else aside and dropped heavily in front of the fire. The smell of hot dog began to pervade the room. He closed it and reopened it again to let in another one, younger this time, who immediately began to bustle around the room, investigating everything.

'That's Juno,' said the oldest boy, indicating the sleeping dog.

'And that's Harry,' said the youngest, indicating the other who appeared to be checking the waste bin for anything edible. 'He's her son.'

'And you are ...?' said Jones, getting up to shoo Harry out of the kitchen and close the door.

'I'm Alex,' said the older one.

'And I'm Leo,' chirped the younger.

They didn't look like each other at all. I would never have taken them for brothers. Alex was tall and fair and slender. His colour was an unusual bluey purple, shot through with pale blue and gold. Leo, on the other hand, not only had his father's build – short, stocky and brown haired – but his father's colour as well. His was more green than grey though,

153

and bubbling with excitement and enthusiasm for life.

'We thought we'd come and welcome you,' they said.

'How kind,' said Jones. 'Can I offer you any refreshment and do your parents know you're here?'

'Yes and no, but they won't mind.'

Something else scratched at the door.

'I'll go,' offered Alex. 'That's probably Benjy.'

Another dog trotted in, heaved itself onto Jones's sofa and went to sleep.

'Are there likely to be any more of you?' enquired Jones. 'Should I leave the door open?'

They grinned at him. Great. Dogs and small boys loved him.

'I am Mr Jones,' said Mr Jones. 'And this is Mrs Jones.'

I did my best to look like Mrs Jones. 'Hello.'

I was subjected to intense scrutiny. 'Daddy said you were ill,' said Leo.

'She's getting better,' said Jones, straight-faced.

'I've just had chickenpox,' said Alex.

'I had it first,' said Leo.

'Yes, but I had it best.'

'I suspect you mean worst,' said Jones.

'I'm sure you both had beautiful chickenpox,' I said, in the interests of world peace.

'My spots were huge,' said Leo, dramatically. 'I looked like a spotted hyena.'

'You do anyway,' said his brother and a potential scuffle was only averted by a knock at the door.

Thomas Rookwood was there, accompanied by all the other dogs who weren't already fast asleep in our room. He took in the situation at a glance. 'I'm so sorry. What can I say?'

I was still curled up on the sofa, facing the door and saw everything. I saw Alex's colour dim and then retreat, wrapping itself around him as if for protection. Little red flecks of anxiety began to appear. Leo's on the other hand, roared out towards his father. Their two colours were very similar. They touched briefly and then curled back again. So, Alex was afraid of his father and his father didn't seem to like Alex very much. Interesting. But nothing to do with me. I struggled to stand up.

'No, please, Mrs Jones, don't get up. Things were so quiet in our wing that I suspected the boys were here, together with any dogs they had managed to scoop up on the way. I do apologise. Boys, what did I tell you?'

'It was my fault,' said Leo, quickly. 'I made him come and once we were here it would have been rude not to come in when they asked us. Mummy says we mustn't be rude.'

Thomas Rookwood stared around. 'Did you have to bring all the dogs?'

'We didn't,' pointed out Leo. 'We only brought a few. You brought the rest, Daddy.'

'I'm here to guide Mr and Mrs Jones around the castle. Why are you here?'

'To welcome them,' said Alex quietly.

'Well, you've done that, so off you go now. Take this lot with you.'

'But I wanted to show them round,' wailed Leo.

Again, his father's colour streamed towards him.

'Actually,' said Jones, 'we were about to have elevenses if you'd like to join us.'

'Not just at the moment,' he said. 'I have rather a lot on today.'

'In that case,' I said, 'please let the boys show us around. I'm sure they'll make an excellent job of it. And neither of us minds the dogs at all.'

It occurred to me as I said it that I should possibly have consulted Jones, but consoled myself with the fact that if he didn't like it then he shouldn't have married me.

Thomas Rookwood shuffled. 'I feel rather guilty.'

'No need,' said Jones. 'You have two very able deputies here.'

'Well, in that case, let me ask you to dinner sometime this week. I know my wife would love to meet you.'

'Thank you. We'd like to.'

'Can we come?' asked Leo. I rather had the impression that they'd worked out they would always have more chance of success if Leo always did the asking.

'It's rather late for you, boys ...'

'Oh, Daddy, please.'

'Oh very well. If you're good. And no dogs.'

They both nodded.

He smiled at us. 'I'll leave you with these two terrors then, shall I?'

We all explored the castle together. Jones, me, the boys, the dogs – with the exception of Juno, who sensibly couldn't be budged from the fire, so we left her behind.

We started in the courtyard.

'That's our tower and wing over there,' said Leo.

He pointed to the enormous door I'd noticed yesterday. 'That's the Banqueting Hall through there. It's got armour and a minstrel's gallery and everything. Do you want to see?'

'Yes, please,' I said.

'This way.' He began to walk away.

Jones wandered over to the very imposing wooden door that had to lead to the Hall. 'Can't we go this way?'

'No. That door is always locked. We have to go this way.'

Jones lingered a while, peering closely at the massive iron hinges and lock. 'Bet you need a key the length of your arm for this one.'

'Nearly,' said Leo. 'I put my arm in the keyhole once to see how big it was and my arm got stuck.'

'I got my head stuck in some railings when I was a kid,' said Jones.

'Did they have to use butter? They used butter on me.'

'Butter is for wimps,' said Jones. 'I had the Fire Brigade.'

He was regarded as a god.

We saw it all. Starting with the Banqueting Hall, a great cavernous place with a massive fireplace and faded and probably very old heraldic banners hanging from the roof beams. And yes, they had three suits of armour lining the walls.

Jones walked from one to the other, rapping on the breastplates.

'Just checking they're empty,' he explained.

I rolled my eyes.

157

'People get married here sometimes,' said Alex, his tone of voice clearly indicating his bewilderment that people would choose to do any such thing. Whether it was the ceremony or the location of the ceremony that was causing his disapproval remained unclear. 'They come through there' – he indicated a door beside a faded tapestry depicting, in gruesome detail, a pack of hounds bringing down a stag – 'and then they go out that way to have a lot to drink.' He indicated an arched door at the other end. 'Do you want to see?'

'Is there any drink there now?' said Jones.

They shook their heads.

'Then no. What else have you got?'

They'd got the lot. We saw the Long Gallery. 'We used to play cricket in here,' said Alex, surveying the pock marked walls, 'but Daddy said we were bringing the walls down and to stop.'

We saw the library with shelves of musty leather volumes that I doubted anyone had ever read. Leading out of that was a picture gallery with portraits of long dead ancestors.

'Rookwoods on this wall,' said Alex pointing. 'Crofts on that one. Before the Crofts were the Scrotes, but they were Norman so we don't talk about them and they hadn't invented painting then anyway.'

'Do you know who's who?' asked Jones and, not to my surprise, they did.

'We have to,' announced Leo. 'Daddy asks us questions.'

He led us slowly down the room. I didn't look much at the faces. In my experience, all portraits tend to look like the monarch reigning at the time they were painted. I always think it's astonishing how many men look like Queen Anne.

I pointed to a small portrait of an unexpectedly lively-looking lady by the empty fireplace. 'Who's that?'

'That's Arabella Croft. She was a special friend of Charles II,' said Leo, innocently.

'Ah,' said Jones, grinning at me.

'Daddy says we should be earls because King Charles always made his special friends' children earls or dukes, but we think he forgot us, so we're not earls.'

They seemed quite cheerful about not being earls.

We walked around while the boys gave us a potted history of each portrait. A depressing number of them seemed to have been either on their way to a battle from which they never returned or if they did, only to head for the scaffold shortly afterwards.

'We never pick the right side,' said Leo cheerfully. 'That's why we're poor.'

'That's a shame,' said Jones, gravely. 'Can we see the dungeons? Are there any bodies left over from the Middle Ages? Do you have a torture chamber here?'

Their eyes sparkled. 'Come and see.'

We descended some death-trap steps and along a narrow corridor to what I suspected had been nothing more than a perfectly ordinary cellar in its time, with a perfectly ordinary grating in the floor.

'Just a minute,' said Alex. There was some fumbling in a box on the wall and a lot of whispering. 'Usually it's operated by sensors,' he explained. 'but we switch it off in the winter because we only have visitors in the summer,' he said over his shoulder, 'but

159

it's really good.'

'You have to stand exactly here,' said Leo.

Jones grinned at me and we stood exactly there.

'Ready?' said Alex.

Leo plucked my sleeve. 'You might want to hold Mr Jones's hand. It's very scary. Ladies scream sometimes.'

'Thank you for the warning,' said Jones gravely, and put his arm around me. 'Don't worry, dear. I'll look after you.'

Alex flicked a switch and we were enveloped in a spooky green light.

'Look,' shouted Leo and we peered through the grating in the floor. Down below, a skeleton sat up suddenly, a rat ran across the body and an eldritch scream echoed around the cellar.

'Pretty cool, eh?' said Leo, proudly.

'Amazing,' I said. 'I was terrified.'

'The rat's electric,' confided Alex.

'Really?' said Jones. 'I would never have guessed.'

We visited the old kitchen tower, complete with spits and cauldrons. It was miles from the Banqueting Hall. God knows how they ever got a hot meal.

We saw the bedroom where, said the boys, Queen Elizabeth had slept. The original hangings were still there – they said – all in faded purple and gold.

And then there was Lady Croft's Sitting Room, furnished in early 18th-century style, and looking, I thought, extremely uncomfortable, with dark wooden chairs and tables. More gloomy portraits hung on the walls. 'That's Lady Croft,' said Alex, pointing at the picture over the fireplace.

'She doesn't look very happy,' I said.

They looked at each other. 'She wasn't,' said Alex, simply. He took a deep breath. 'There's more to see. Come on.'

Everything was up twisty stairs, through tiny doors, along dark, narrow passages and then back down twisty stairs again. I became quite bewildered. And cold.

'Enough,' said Jones, when they showed signs of wanting to go outside and show us the deer park, the herb garden, the maze – 'It's not very tall yet but it's going to be great!' – and the stocks. 'We'll take Mrs Jones back for her afternoon nap, you can collect your dog, and we'll see you tomorrow.'

I spent the rest of the day back in our warm room, watching the rain come down.

# Chapter Fourteen

I awoke next morning to a weak and watery sun.

'Great,' said Jones, buttering toast. 'Spring is here.'

I scowled at him and poured myself some coffee.

He pushed a paper and pen towards me. 'Shopping list. Add anything you think we might need.'

Without even looking, I scribbled 'Sunshine and Warmth' at the bottom.

He looked at me in some concern. 'Are you cold? Do you think you're going down with something?'

The fire was blazing away in the living room and we had somehow acquired Juno and an anonymous Jack Russell, both of whom were stretched out in front of the fire and trying to present as much of themselves as possible to the flames.

'No,' I said, reluctantly. 'I'm just ...' and stopped because I didn't know what I was just ...

'Talk to me, Cage.'

I stared at him helplessly.' I don't even know where to begin.'

He sat back and sipped his coffee. 'Could you at least indicate your areas of concern? You know, give me something to work with.'

'Well, to begin with – you.'

He smirked complacently. 'Top of yet another list. What about me?'

'Well, who are you?'

'I told you. Michael Jones. Really, Cage, I think a lot of your problems stem from the fact you don't listen properly.'

I ignored this. 'All right, since that's too difficult for you, 'Who's Sorensen? And don't say Head of the Sorensen Clinic. You know that's not what I mean.'

He nodded. 'OK.' He twirled his mug around on the table, moving the handle first to the right, then to the left. I waited.

'Ever heard the phrase, "Psychological Warfare"?'

I shook my head.

'Well, I'm not going into any great detail because then I'd have to kill you, but basically it involves devising ways of misleading, deceiving and intimidating people.'

'What sort of people? Enemies?'

'Yes, but allies too, of course, because sometimes they're even more dangerous than our enemies. Basically, anyone he's told to. You know what he's like. His masters just wind him up and let him go.'

'But what does he do?'

He sighed. 'He's an expert on behaviour. That's what makes him so dangerous. He can predict how people will behave under certain conditions and how to manipulate them accordingly. He can tailor-make propaganda tools. He can advise on how to mislead, deceive or even intimidate anyone he's instructed to. He seeks out other people's vulnerabilities.'

'Why?'

'Blackmail, usually. A little pressure at the right time in the right place.'

'But ...' I said, struggling with my lifelong view of

'us' as the good guys.

'And that's just the socially acceptable side of what he does. He supervises interrogations – which means he tells people like me which questions to ask. Which buttons to press to get results.'

'What sort of results?'

He smiled slightly. 'The right ones.'

I looked at him. He was telling the truth, but not all of the truth. I could tell by the way his colour was wrapped so defensively around him.

I had to ask. 'Do you work for Sorensen?'

'Well, strictly speaking, at this precise moment, I'm just a patient. Like you. I was at the clinic for assessment, prior to returning to work. When I get my clearance back I'll work for a department that frequently avails itself of his services. And *vice versa*, of course.'

I shivered. 'He's a bad man.'

'No,' he said seriously. 'He's not. No, he's not likeable, in that he does tend to regard the human race as his own personal chess set, but he has a job to do and he does it. It's not his responsibility what others do with the information he provides.'

'Yes, I know the argument,' I said bitterly. 'Guns aren't bad – it's the people who pull the trigger who are bad.'

He shrugged. 'He stands behind those who do, but no, he doesn't give the orders. He's one of those invisible people who are always careful to remain out of sight.'

'And he wants me.'

'He does, Cage. He wants you very badly. But not to the extent of harming you. You have the potential to be a valuable asset.'

I remembered suddenly that I'd told Jones what I could do. About people's colours … about seeing things … what had I been thinking?

As if he could read my mind, he said, 'Relax, will you. You'd already shown me what you could do long before you told me, but I'd guessed some of it anyway. You probably can't help it but you do have a certain look. I can't describe it. Clear-eyed. Direct. As if you could see straight into my brain and know what I'm thinking.'

I think I was probably staring at him like a small and terrified rabbit caught in car headlights.

'Look, he's not going to hurt you. He'll want you willing and cooperative. I know you're frightened and you don't know what's going on, or how this could be happening to you, but I told you – I'll help you get away. I'll help you with anything you need. You just have to work out what you do need, which is why I've brought you here. Safe, remote and comfortable. You can take all the time you need to think and then we'll put together a plan and sort everything out. OK?'

I nodded – not much comforted.

'Good. Get your coat,' he said, getting to his feet and picking up the list. 'Fresh air will do you good.'

I braced myself as we stepped out of the door into the courtyard but the knife-edged wind had gone. Standing in the sun waiting for Jones to pull on his gloves was rather pleasant in this sheltered place. We walked through the tunnel and out into the sunshine, surveying the village laid out before us.

'Satisfied?' he said, gesturing around. 'No black

helicopters. No armed SWAT teams waiting to shoot you because you looked at them wrong. No sinister limousines with tinted windows – well, other than the one you made me steal, of course.'

'*I* made you steal? Excuse me …'

'Apology accepted. This way I think,' he said, taking my arm.

'The shop is that way.'

'I thought we could have a look around the place. You know, since we're supposed to be on holiday. Really, Cage, you could at least try and act the part of wife and tourist.'

I heaved a martyred sigh but in fact the village was lovely, with neat-as-new-pin stone cottages around two sides of the triangular village green. The tiny church was set back a little, the grey stone tower peeping out from behind skeletal trees.

'Excellent village planning,' said Jones. 'Shop and pubs side by side.'

We wandered around the green, admiring people's gardens. I have to say the view from this high up was superb, with fields, hedgerows, woodlands all spread out beneath us, and the towering moors behind us. Right through the valley, a small river cut a glittering path as it meandered its gentle way to wherever it was going. The sky was that weak and washed-out turquoise blue you often get on cold days. And Jones was right. You could see anything coming from miles and miles away.

I watched my breath puff in front of me.

'Shopping first or lunch first?' he asked.

'We've only just had breakfast.'

'No, *you've* only just had breakfast. Not that a cup

'I'll just have a snack,' I said.

'You'll have a proper meal,' he said sternly.

'You're very considerate for a kidnapper.'

'It is the duty of every kidnapper to ensure his victim eats a properly balanced diet. Or in your case, Cage, anything at all. Now, order.'

In the end, we both went for Yorkshire puddings filled with sausages and covered in gravy. It was delicious. I ate every last mouthful. Jones said nothing but in a very meaningful manner. And afterwards, apparently, it was my round.

I thought the place would have filled up by now, and a few people had come in, but mostly, it was just us.

'Agricultural community,' said Jones. 'They'll all be out in the fields doing ...'

I waited expectantly.

'... agricultural things. But I bet you can't move in here in the evenings.'

'When they've finished doing agricultural things.'

'You can't do agricultural things in the dark.'

'Aren't they a band?'

'That's Orchestral Manoeuvres in the Dark. Really. Cage, do try and keep up.'

'You know a lot about this sort of thing. Are you a country boy?'

He shook his head. 'I've listened to more episodes of *The Archers* than you can possibly imagine.'

'Why? Was it some sort of punishment?'

'I shall pass over your insult to a fine programme and just say – surveillance.'

I was bewildered. 'You surveilled *The Archers*?'

He shook his head. 'Have you ever wished you'd

never started a conversation?'

'I've met *people* I wished I hadn't.'

'And to think I used to envy Ted his comfortable domestic life. I had no idea you were so ...'

'Yes?'

'Now I'm really wishing I hadn't started this conversation.'

Silence fell.

'So,' I said, in an effort to pick it back up again, 'you yearn for domestic happiness.'

'Well, I don't think that was quite what I said, but ... well ... yes, sometimes. Then, of course, I listen to other people moaning about their other halves and realise I've never had it so good.'

He wasn't quite telling the truth. His colour was saying otherwise.

I drained my glass. 'No, you don't.'

'God, Cage, will you stop doing that.'

'I can't help it, so you might as well just tell me the truth. Do you want another pint?'

'Any man stuck with you would want another pint.'

As the barmaid pulled his pint, I leaned casually against the bar and watched Jones stare into the fire. To all intents and purposes, he was a man enjoying a warm fire after a good lunch. I knew differently, however.

I paid for the drinks and returned to the table. He was warm, well fed and mellow so I decided to take a chance.

'So, tell me about this domestic bliss that you have such mixed feelings about.'

He looked around the bar, but we were alone.

Even the barmaid had taken herself off somewhere. I could faintly hear crates being stacked. He took a long pull on his pint and then said, 'Do you remember, on the way up here, you said I'd lost someone?'

This wasn't what I'd expected at all, so I just nodded.

'Her name was Clare. Is Clare. Is ... Clare.'

I nodded again.

'We worked several assignments together. On our last one we were posing as man and wife. I won't say where. It's not yet a terrorist hot-spot and we want it to stay that way. So in we went. Me and Mrs Jones. We were a nice couple. Quiet. No kids. No loud music. Happy to pass the time if you met us in the street or at the market. You know the sort of thing. I was a freelance computer programmer so I could work at home and Clare got a brilliant job helping the old woman who ran the corner shop. Long hours and awful pay, but you hear everything about everyone in places like that. She used to come home absolutely knackered, so I learned to cook and clean. Well, I had to or we'd have drowned in an ocean of dust, dirt and disease, just prior to starving to death, because not only did she not have a clue about that sort of thing, she really didn't care, either.'

He stopped for a while, staring at his memories. I said nothing, seeing it through his eyes. Dark narrow streets. Suspicious eyes everywhere. One wrong move ... one wrong word ...

'It was a long-term assignment. We were about nine months in and expected to be there for at least another six months. As far as I could see, we'd fitted in, no problems at all. I was in the local backgammon team. Clare was supposedly learning to drive, which was actually a wonderful cover for us driving up and down streets, stopping outside suspect properties where she'd screw up another three-point turn while I pretended to shout at her and got photos instead. If asked – which I was, afterwards – I would have said it was going well.'

He sighed. 'I don't know where it all went wrong. Whether it was something we said or did – or something we didn't say or do – I don't know. Don't suppose I ever will now. No one does.'

I still said nothing. His colour was darkening. Dirty black tendrils twisted their way around him, drilling inwards. Nothing pointed towards me. I think he'd forgotten I was there. He was talking to himself.

'Something went badly wrong because they came for us at three in the morning. No warning. We were both asleep. I opened my eyes and they were standing at the foot of the bed. I tried to break free. I'm a big man and I know what I'm doing but there were six of them and they were professionals. Someone dropped something over my head and they dragged me onto the floor. They started with baseball bats and then went on to boots. And all the time, I could hear Clare screaming. She screamed until she was hoarse. I could hear her voice breaking. God knows what they were doing to her. It seemed to go on for hours, but it couldn't have. It just seemed that way.'

His colour was now almost completely dark and folded in upon itself. I sat very still, hardly daring to breathe. The contrast between this warm, sunny, *normal* room with its cheerful fire and the dark story unfolding in front of me was almost beyond imagining.

'They pushed me down the stairs. I suspect I already had a fair number of broken bones so that hurt, I can tell you. The next thing I remember is being in a car. In the boot, I think, bumping over some rough ground. That hurt as well, but I suspected it was going to hurt a lot more when we eventually arrived at our destination.'

He seemed to become aware of me. 'Sorry. Boring on. Shouldn't do it. Not your world. Sorry.'

I shook my head. 'What happened?'

'Well, to cut a long story short they tied a brick around my neck and dropped me into some disused waterway. It smelled and tasted foul. I still can't believe I didn't go down with cholera.'

'How did you escape?'

He laughed bitterly. 'I didn't. I didn't do anything. They hadn't tied the knot very well and the brick came loose. I just floated to the surface. I remember lying on my back, squinting at the sky because my eyes wouldn't open properly, waiting to go down for the third time, when some kids who shouldn't have been there, busy building a raft they shouldn't have been, saw me, jumped in, which they really shouldn't have done, and dragged me to the side. They couldn't get me out and I was in no state to assist and after a long discussion based mostly on what someone's mother was going to say about all this, they telephoned for help. I think they were disappointed I wasn't dead. I think everyone was. I know I was.'

He stared at his beer.

'And Clare?'

'No trace.'

'Nothing?'

'Nothing. Not from that moment to this.'

I had to say it. 'Do you think she's dead?'

'My brain knows she is. Long dead. Long buried. Long gone.'

'And your heart?'

'Is convinced that somewhere out there she's still alive. And I shouldn't.'

'Why not? What's wrong with hope?'

'Because if she's where I think she is then she's better off dead. Much better off. When I think of what they could be doing to her. Right now. Right this minute ...'

I could hear the bitterness in his voice.

'Were you very close?'

'We lived as man and wife. In addition, we'd worked together before. We were a good team. She had my back so many times.'

'And you think she's dead?'

'I hope so.'

'How were you discovered?'

'No idea. Such surveillance as we could muster showed nothing unusual. I've been over and over it in my mind and there have been any number of departmental post-mortems. It could have been anything. We'll never know.'

I didn't know what to say.

'Yes, a bit of a conversation stopper, aren't I? Every now and then I put in a request to go back and dig around but they won't let me. I'd probably never even get out of the airport alive. Anyway, a month or so in hospital, some intensive counselling and a month's light duties, and here I am – as right as rain.'

I looked at his swirling colour – that dreadful dead patch over his heart had returned. No, he wasn't as right as rain. Nothing like.

Actually, neither of us were. For me, the excitement of our escape and new surroundings wore off to be replaced by frequent panic when I would ask myself what on earth I thought I was doing. What had happened to my life? How did I arrive here? Hiding in a remote Northumberland castle with a damaged spy and a stolen car. In fear of a man who apparently wielded powers wider than I could comprehend.

Jones kept me busy. The weather took a turn for the better. The temperature rose and we walked. We explored the countryside, hiking up and down paths, jumping small streams and standing breathless on tall crags, admiring the view as the wind buffeted us from every direction. It wasn't unpleasant. It was certainly better than the Sorensen clinic. I was occasionally quite surprised to find I was enjoying myself. On other occasions, I would catch myself thinking how much Ted would have enjoyed this. Or something would happen and I would think, I must tell Ted that, followed by the realisation I would never tell Ted anything again.

Sometimes, especially as I was preparing for bed, I would find myself crying for no reason at all. Out of consideration for Jones I would try to keep it in, because he wouldn't want me blubbering all over the place, but one evening the panic and the loneliness and the grief were all too much for me to hold things back any longer. He said nothing, made up the fire, presented me with a mug of tea and we sat up all night playing cards. I lost a fortune to him, finally falling asleep on the sofa just before dawn.

I awoke to the smell of bacon and a piece of paper on the table he claimed was a legal document giving details of how and when I was to repay my colossal debt. Apparently if I committed all my income to him for the next thirty-five years then I might just have paid off one third. He'd let me off the rest. I made a rude noise and accused him of usury – I had no idea what that was but I was certain he wouldn't either – and threw the paper into the fire.

We drove into the nearest town, did a little shopping, and, because the weather was very bad that day, spent the afternoon at the cinema. Offered a choice of films, I opted for a romantic comedy and made the mistake of letting Jones buy the tickets. We ended up watching a SciFi blockbuster in 3D. I lost the plot after about ten minutes, and Jones's attempts to explain things didn't help at all, but an impressive number of planets exploded and Jones ate a whole tub of popcorn.

The sun came out more often and the snowdrops came up. Lambs appeared. Life went on.

Complaining loudly, the boys went back to school. They both attended the local comprehensive. Alex looked very smart in his black sweater and white shirt. Leo was dirty even before he got on the school bus. Thomas Rookwood renewed his invitation to dinner yet again. I still didn't like him much and we'd put him off several times, citing my supposed ill health, but, in the end, it seemed best to go ahead and accept, so we did. He said he'd send the boys for us at seven that evening.

They turned up at ten to seven. We could hear them whispering outside the door, counting down the time until seven o'clock. Jones relented and let them inside to wait because it was cold out in the passage. They looked considerably cleaner and smarter than usual.

Jones peered down the corridor. 'Where are the dogs?'

'Mummy makes Daddy shut them up at night. Except for Juno. She sleeps in front of the fire because she's old.'

'Just like Mrs Jones,' said Jones brightly, and, all right, that *was* how I had spent the afternoon, but there was no need to tell everyone.

The family lived in the tower and wing opposite us. The boys took us into their sitting room which was larger than ours. It was typical of the castle, slightly shabby, but comfortable. They had central heating so there was no coal fire and the room smelled of a mixture of pot pourri and Labrador. Juno sprawled on the rug, jowls quivering as she snored. That dog could sleep for England.

They had better pictures on the walls than in the rest of the castle – well, they were certainly more cheerful than the ones in the gallery. Some of them were quite modern and I suspected owed their presence to Mrs rather than Mr Rookwood. There were family photographs scattered around as well. This was obviously their family room. Mrs Rookwood's embroidery lay on the arm of a chair. I was pleased they hadn't made any special attempt to tidy up for us. A family dinner was nice.

Except for the atmosphere around the table.

'So,' said Jones chattily as we seated ourselves. 'You're a bit out of the way up here, aren't you? Do you ever get cut off?'

'Occasionally,' said Rookwood, 'but we don't feel cut off. This castle has been the centre of social life in this part of the country for hundreds of years and I intend it should always be so. We provide employment, especially in the summer when we're open to the public. We cash cheques for the elderly who can't get out. We're a designated point for parcel delivery and collection. I personally petitioned for the mobile library to call every fortnight, to keep the post office open and for a more frequent bus service. I like us to be involved in everything that's going on around here. Don't I, boys?'

Leo nodded vigorously, his mouth full.

Jones turned to Alex and said chattily, 'So, what's it like living in a castle?'

'Great,' said Leo, answering for him. 'Masses of room to play hide-and-seek and no one can hear us if we make a noise.'

'Keep telling yourself that,' said his father dryly, 'and pass the bread to our guests, please.'

I thought I'd sensed a bit of an atmosphere around the table and it seemed Leo had had an accident that afternoon. Nothing serious, obviously, since he was sitting opposite me, apparently unharmed, and shovelling down his chicken as if he hadn't seen food for a fortnight.

'What happened?' asked Jones, passing me the bread.

'I wanted to see if the ice on the pond was thick

enough to walk on.'

'And was it?'

He grinned. 'No.'

'Fortunately,' said his mother, with very great restraint, 'the pond is only about eighteen inches deep. If that.'

Leo, remarkably unabashed for someone who had had, in his own words, a near-death experience that afternoon, was describing his adventure when his mother interrupted him.

'That is enough, Leo. You have been very naughty. You were warned to stay away from the pond in any weather. It was very fortunate for you that the water was shallow enough for you to be able to wade to safety.'

Leo grinned unrepentantly, correctly assuming his transgression had been forgiven. 'I wasn't in any danger. Alex pulled me out.'

I watched Alex's colour curdle away under his father's gaze.

That was interesting. It wasn't Alex who had fallen through the ice, but I could see it was Alex with whom his father was more annoyed. Was Thomas Rookwood one of those fathers who takes secret pride in his son's misadventures? Because that's what boys do, isn't it? If they're not falling out of trees, or skateboarding their way into A&E, or blowing up their bedrooms, then they're not real boys. Was it possible that Thomas Rookwood would value Alex, a quiet and uncomplaining child, much less than he would the cheerfully mischievous Leo? Or perhaps he was simply annoyed with Alex for not taking better care of his brother. Or was there something else here?

I wasn't alone in my concern. It seemed to me that his mother, Helene, who spoke with the faintest French accent, seemed perpetually poised to intervene – to stand as a shield between her husband and her eldest son. Her colour was closer to Alex's than Leo's. Her soft lavender frequently merged with Alex's deeper purple, although tonight, in the presence of his father, Alex's colour was shading more towards red, so flooded with anxiety was he.

He sat quietly, however, eating his dinner, rarely speaking. Unlike Leo who was waving his fork around and scattering his peas.

'Leo,' said his mother, reprovingly, and he subsided. 'And what of you, *mon cher*?' she said to Alex, obviously changing the subject. 'What else did you do this afternoon?'

Alex said nothing His colour curled even more tightly around himself. I suspected he had probably spent his afternoon trying to dissuade Leo from playing on the ice and getting no thanks for it. He was a sensible and sensitive boy who was always going to come second to noisy, boisterous Leo. I felt quite sorry for him.

'I wrote some more of my story,' he said, defensively. He looked at Jones, obviously expecting ridicule, and said somewhat defiantly, 'I'm writing a book.'

'I'm impressed,' said Jones. 'What's it about?'

'I wrote about our ghost.'

'You have a ghost?' said Jones. 'Awesome.'

'We don't have a ghost,' said his father impatiently. 'We have a legend.'

'Yes,' said Leo, dramatically. 'The Legend of The

180

Widow. Daddy found it in an old book and told us the story.'

'Really?' I said. 'Can you tell us about the legend, Alex?'

He looked at his father, who nodded briefly.

'It was before us Rookwoods. It was when the Crofts lived here. There was a rebellion in 1745 and the son of the house, James, wanted to go and fight. His mother, Lady Croft, didn't want him to because her husband had been killed in another rebellion.'

'Was that the one in 1715?' asked Jones, surprising me. 'The Jacobites?'

Alex nodded, pleased to find someone who shared his interest.

'Yes. She said she'd lost her husband in that one and didn't want to lose her son as well. She didn't want him to go.'

'Understandable,' said Jones.

'But he said it was his duty to support the rightful king.'

'Ah, duty,' murmured Jones, and drained his wine.

'So he put on his armour and said goodbye to his mother who was waiting for him in the Banqueting Hall. All the household was there to say goodbye to him. All the men were cheering and all the ladies were crying.'

He paused, obviously picturing the scene.

'Anyway, the big door was open and everyone could see his horse in the courtyard, all saddled up, and his men with their weapons and their pack horses. Once again, his mother begged him not to go but he said he had to. He kissed her goodbye. Everyone was crying. Then he strode out of the Hall, mounted his horse, waved to his mother and galloped away.'

We paid him the compliment of silence as he paused for effect. His colour was boiling with excitement now, the purple enriched with blue and gold. He was enjoying himself.

'His mother locked the door to the Hall behind him and gave orders that it wasn't to be unlocked again until he returned home safely. He had been the last person to leave through them, she said and so he must be the first person to return through them.'

'And did he?' asked Jones. 'Return home safely, I mean?'

He shook his head. 'No, he was killed. We don't know how. We think he must have been blown to bits by a cannon because they never found his body. Anyway, he never came home again and so the doors have never been unlocked.'

'What a sad story,' I said. 'Poor Lady Croft. To lose her husband and then her son.'

'Good for us though,' said Thomas Rookwood. 'The castle changed hands after her son's death and came to us.'

Leo's eyes were sparkling. 'And we've never unlocked the door since.'

'Why not?' said Jones. 'Yes, I'd love some chocolate mousse, please.'

'Because,' said Alex, obviously determined not to be elbowed out of his own story, 'Daddy's legend says that if the door is opened for anyone other than Jamie Croft, then the eldest son of the family will die before sunset the next day. The door has been locked ever since.'

Jones looked at Helene. 'That must make things awkward.'

She laughed. 'It's a major inconvenience not having a working front door but I'm afraid we have to live with it.'

'That's why we have our own entrance,' said Leo, hoovering up the last of his chocolate mousse. 'Grandad Rookwood built it hundreds of years ago. It's round the back.'

'Not *quite* hundreds,' said his father.

Jones was persevering. 'What would happen if you did? Open the doors, I mean.'

Thomas Rookwood sipped his wine. 'According to the story I read, someone did, once. Francis Rookwood, in eighteen hundred and something or other, and after a long night of cards and wine, declared the whole thing to be stuff and nonsense. He was fed up with walking the long way around, he said, and to much laughter and encouragement, he unlocked the door. No one had oiled the hinges or the lock in years, so they had to put their shoulders to it, but they got it open in the end.'

'What happened?' I said, enthralled.

'His eldest son, William, died in a riding accident the very next day. Broke his neck. The story says The Widow took him.'

'Tom, 'said his wife, warningly. Alex was looking a little pale and his colour was all over the place. Leo continued eating, completely unperturbed.

'So, obviously, we don't open the door,' said Helene. 'Leo, if you have finished, please put your fork and spoon together tidily, as Alex has done.'

'So, if we open the door,' said Leo eagerly, 'will

Alex die?'

'No,' said Helene firmly. 'It is just a legend that we tell our visitors. And no one can ever open the door again after so long, so Alex and all of us are quite safe. And will we not talk of this any longer.'

I changed the subject. 'So how is school after the chickenpox?'

'I'm in the football team,' bragged Leo.

'Congratulations. What about you, Alex?'

'Captain of the chess team.'

'Well done, you.'

'Yes,' said Rookwood. 'Football for Leo and chess for Alex.'

Alex flushed. I guessed chess didn't rate very highly in this household.

'Chess is a game of skill and strategy,' said Jones.

'I don't like football,' said Alex.

'You didn't even try for the team,' said his father. 'You never do. I'm sick of telling you, Alex, you should take a chance occasionally. Challenge yourself. Do something daring. You gain nothing by always playing safe.'

Alex stared at his plate and once again, his colour wrapped protectively around himself. Jones threw Rookwood a look and for a moment I thought the rules of hospitality might go straight out of the window.

Helene intervened. 'If you have both finished, you may go to your room and watch television for half an hour before bed. I shall come up to see you shortly. Please say goodnight to our guests.'

They both said goodnight politely. They had very good manners. We stayed for one coffee, and then we too politely said goodnight.

The courtyard was well lit and I could easily see our little tower door. The air was crisp and clear and there were a multitude of stars overhead. I shivered, pulled my coat around me, and headed off across the courtyard.

'Just a minute,' said Jones, pulling at my arm and handing me the key.

'Where are you going?'

'There's something I want to check. You go on in.'

It was too cold to hang around so I let myself in and went to put the kettle on. The fire had died down and the room was chilly. I was tired; I disliked Thomas Rookwood more than ever, but mostly, I just wanted to take my tea and go to bed.

I was pouring it out when I heard Jones stamping in the passage and locking the outer door. 'What were you doing out there?'

'Looking at the stars,' he said thoughtfully, taking his mug off me. 'Did anything strike you as odd about our evening?'

'Apart from the fact that Thomas Rookwood doesn't like his eldest son, that his wife is frightened, and that Alex is emotionally desperate, no, nothing really. You?'

'I, for once, am in the unique position of knowing something you don't, but you look worn out, Cage. Go to bed and we'll talk about it tomorrow over breakfast.'

We never did talk about it tomorrow over breakfast. Because that night, Alex opened the door.

## Chapter Fifteen

I was asleep. Very deeply asleep. I can't say I was troubled by bad dreams, because I wasn't, but one moment I was asleep and the next moment I was awake. Wide awake.

I lay for a moment, staring into the darkness, wondering what had woken me. My first thought, despite almost daily reassurances from Jones, was that Sorensen had found us somehow and that even at this moment, black helicopters were disgorging hundreds of men, all of whom would be looking for me.

My second thought was not to be so silly.

I lay back on the pillows and let my mind drift away. There was something. Something elusive. I couldn't pin it down at all. Something ... I couldn't quite grasp. The heating had shut down but the thick walls retained the heat. I pulled on my dressing gown and drew back the curtains.

There – in the courtyard. The outside lights were off, but a tiny beam of light darted to and fro. The sort of tiny beam that might possibly be some malevolent will-o'-the-wisp, haunting an ancient building since time out of mind and seeking souls to dismay and torment, but was much more likely to be a small boy dodging about with his Junior Spaceman torch and very definitely up to no good.

It was far too cold to undress, so I dragged on

jeans, a T-shirt, sweater and a thick coat over my pyjamas. Shoving my feet into trainers, I opened the door, switched on the stair light and set off up the twisting stair to Jones's room.

He met me half way and very nearly frightened me to death.

'Did you see?' he demanded as I pulled myself together.

'I did. What's going on? Why are you awake?'

'Because I suspected those two young buggers were up to no good. Didn't you see the freshly oiled hinges, Cage? Smell the WD 40 they'd been spraying into the lock? And then that idiot Rookwood goes and tells Alex to take a risk occasionally. To do something daring, and surprise, surprise, Alex takes him up on it. They're going to open the door.'

All the strange vague feelings that had been swirling around me suddenly coalesced into one very strong feeling of danger. Of dread.

I clutched his arm. 'They mustn't do that. Bad things will happen. You must stop them, Jones.'

He stared at me. 'Well, I was only worrying about them bringing that old wooden thing crashing down on top of themselves, but I can see you're worrying about more than that.'

He pushed past me. 'We can't get into the castle from here. You rouse Rookwood. Tell him what's happening. I'll try and shout some sense into them through the door.'

We unbolted our own front door and ran out. Jones flashed the torch which he'd thought to bring with him and I hadn't. The beam alighted on Leo, white-faced, standing outside the door. I suspected he

187

was there to push while Alex pulled from inside.

Jones seized his arm and pulled him away. 'Leo, take Mrs Jones to your father. Go and wake him now.'

Leo was cold and crying. His eyes and nose were streaming. Suddenly the big adventure wasn't as exciting as he had thought.

I said quietly, 'Come on, Leo. We need to find your dad.'

He put his cold hand in mine and we set off towards the Rookwoods' private wing. He opened the door and I switched on the light.

'Leo, go and wake your parents.' He still looked too frightened to move, so I shouted, 'Mr Rookwood. Mr Rookwood. Wake up.'

The sound of my voice seemed to rouse Leo. He ran off shouting, 'Daddy. Daddy. Help.'

Behind me, through the open door, I could hear Jones pounding on the doors shouting, 'Stop. Stop it. Stop what you're doing, Alex. Stop it now.'

At the end of the corridor, another light flicked on and Thomas Rookwood stood in the doorway, tying his dressing gown. He looked sleepy and dishevelled and his colour was flitting about in agitation.

'Mrs Jones? Whatever is the matter? Is there a fire?'

I stifled my dislike and said, 'Alex is opening the door to the Banqueting Hall.'

He smiled patronisingly. 'I doubt that, Mrs Jones. That door hasn't been opened in a hundred years. It will take more than feeble Alex to open it.'

I stopped trying to stifle my dislike. 'They've been oiling the hinges and the lock for some time now, Mr

Rookwood. Alex intends to get that door open.'

His mouth dropped. 'Is he mad? That door hasn't been opened in a hundred years. It'll fall off its hinges. They might even bring down part of the wall with them. How could he be so stupid?'

I refrained from pointing out that only a couple of hours ago, he'd been urging Alex to challenge himself and take a few risks.

He seized his keys and we raced through the castle, switching on the lights as we went. I soon lost my bearings, and it seemed to take for ever before we were unlocking the heavy oak door beside the tapestry and emerging into the Hall.

The lights were on, but it was such a cavernous space that the corners of the room were still lost in the gloom. Alex had arranged three or four torches to shine on the keyhole. A backpack lay nearby, with cans of WD40, oil, grease, a bottle of cola, two bars of chocolate and a Bible. I couldn't help but feel admiration for him. He was obviously a meticulous planner. Lubricant for the lock and hinges. Cola and chocolate for him and Leo. And a Bible for whatever came through the doors after he'd opened them.

Eerily lit by the torchlight, he was holding a long key.

Thomas Rookwood switched on more lights and shouted something, his colour jumping from green through grey to red and back again, coiling around him in excitement. I could feel his tension.

Alex glanced over his shoulder for the briefest second and then turned his attention back to the key. His own colour purple flared out around him, spiking defiance and determination. 'You told me to do it.'

'I did no such thing.' The echoes of Rookwood's voice boomed around the hall. I was trying to get past him but he was standing in the doorway, one hand still holding the heavy metal door ring and there wasn't enough room for me to squeeze through.

'You said I had to be brave. And do things that made me scared. So I am. You said we don't have a ghost. So I'll be safe. Because it's only a legend.' His voice sounded shrill and defiant.

Holding the long iron key with both hands, he worked it into the lock and began to turn. I remember thinking that surely the lock couldn't work after all this time. There was never any danger of him getting the door open.

I was wrong. The clunk of the wards falling into place echoed around the hall. Leaving the key in the lock, he seized the door ring with both hands.

I pushed at Rookwood, but at that moment, Helene appeared behind us, wearing a puffa coat over her dressing gown and with a sobbing Leo in tow. She screamed when she saw what was happening. 'Alex, what are you doing?'

Rookwood and I both looked around at her and by the time we looked back again, Alex was heaving at the door.

Thomas Rookwood shouted, 'Alex, stop. I forbid you to open that door,' which I thought was a particularly useless thing to say.

It was all too late anyway. Alex heaved with all his might and with a monstrous groan, slowly, ponderously, the door opened about twelve inches or so and then stopped. It was a dramatic moment – worthy of a television drama. The great, grey, wooden door slowly creaking open. The poor lighting. The jumping shadows.

As Jones said afterwards, he really didn't think anything would happen. He thought that the door would open onto an empty courtyard, that there would be a few moments of embarrassed silence, then there would be sheepish goodnights from everyone and then we'd all slope off to bed with the younger generation expecting to get a good talking to in the morning.

He was partly right. Nothing happened. No tall black-shrouded figures materialised, pointing dramatically at Alex. No banshee wails of revenge and retribution. We all stood, frozen to the spot, and absolutely nothing happened. I let my mind drift a little, and still there was nothing. I heard someone – Helene, I think – give a huge sigh of relief, just before the hinges creaked loudly and the door moved again. Just an inch or so, but this door was far too heavy to move all by itself. No wind would ever blow this door shut. The hinges creaked again. The door opened wider.

I couldn't sense a thing. There was nothing there. I would have bet my life there was nothing there, but some unseen hand was opening the doors. From the other side. Or, to be properly dramatic – The Other Side.

I heard Helene stifle a gasp of fear. I tried again to get past Thomas Rookwood because Alex was there alone and exposed to whatever was coming through.

And then Michael Jones strolled into the hall saying calmly, 'Everything all right in here?' and the huge sighs of relief nearly blew him straight back out into the courtyard again. I don't think anyone could think of anything to say. Alex stared up at him, his mouth open. Jones put a hand on his shoulder. 'OK Alex?'

He swallowed hard and nodded.

Jones bent and began to inspect Alex's provisions. 'Excellent forward planning,' he said. 'Every contingency taken into account and the appropriate equipment brought. Well done, young Alex.'

He was defusing the situation nicely; we were all beginning to relax, and I was just beginning to think I might be back in my warm bed soon, when Thomas Rookwood gave a hoarse cry.

'There!'

'Where?' I said, spinning around.

'She was there. Over there. Watching us.'

'Where?' I said again, looking wildly around. I couldn't see anything. In any sense of the word.

'There.' He pointed into the shadows. 'It was her. I saw her. Oh my God, it's all true. I thought it was just a legend. I swear I thought it was just a legend.' His voice was jumping with agitation. Leo redoubled his sobs.

I finally managed to push my way past Rookwood to join Jones in the middle of the room. We stood closely together, with Alex between us.

Jones lowered his head to me, speaking quietly. 'What did you see?'

'Nothing,' I whispered. 'He was blocking my view.'

'No, I mean, what did you *see?*'

I shook my head again. 'Nothing.'

For the first time since I'd met him, he looked

worried. 'Cage, I don't like this.'

'Neither do I.'

'Stay with Alex. Do *not* let him out of your sight. Not for one moment.'

'I won't,' I said, putting my arms around Alex. He was trembling violently.

Thomas Rookwood and his wife joined us. Helena scooped up Alex and held him close. Rookwood seized the handle and forced the door shut again. The boom of its closing reverberated around the Hall causing dust to drop from the ceiling above. He struggled with the key a little, but eventually got the door locked. Silence settled back in the hall again.

We stood in a group with the two boys in the middle, facing outwards and staring about us for the slightest sign of The Widow.

Leo was sobbing violently. Helene, her eyes huge with fear was trying to calm him and hold on to Alex while not far off hysterics herself.

I could see the tension coming off Rookwood. His colour was jumping about, pumping red and purple. The green had disappeared to be replaced by a muddy grey. I didn't like this at all. The man was becoming unbalanced. He pulled Alex from Helene's grasp and shook him hard. 'You stupid, stupid boy. What have you done?'

Jones knocked his hands away. 'Exactly what you told him to do. He's shown a little backbone. Challenged himself.'

His voice cracked. 'I meant on the football pitch. Not – this.'

I stood close to Alex and put my hand on his shoulder. He was shaking, not very far from tears, but holding himself in. I said quietly, 'Good boy, Alex,' almost as if he was a small dog, but I couldn't think of anything else to say.

We stood in our huddle, listening to our own ragged breathing in the silence, staring about us.

'She's gone,' whispered Rookwood.

Jones span around, flashing his torch into every dark corner. 'Has she gone, Cage?'

'Why are you asking her? I'm the one who saw The Widow.'

'No one else saw her,' said Helene, quietly.

'I'm the Rookwood here,' he said, angrily. 'Her blood runs in my veins. If anyone's going to see her then it's me.'

'I thought you said she didn't exist.'

'I just said that to stop everyone having nightmares. And yes, I'll admit I didn't really believe it but now I've actually seen … something … I'm not so sure.'

Jones took me aside, saying very quietly, 'What do you think, Cage?'

'I don't know. He's very definite he saw something. Perhaps I'm losing my touch. I do know I'm very scared. I think something is going to happen – I just don't know what.'

'Welcome to my world, Cage.'

I stared down at the terracotta and black floor tiles and let my mind wander … just a little way … and pulled it back sharply.

'What?' said Jones.

I whispered to him. 'I don't know. It might be. There's something here but it's … ugly. Not nice. I'm sorry – it's faint. I just don't know.'

Rookwood must have overheard. He spun around. 'What would you know about it? I'm telling you – I definitely saw her.'

I felt my insides clench.

'Well,' said Jones cheerfully, 'and you'll laugh at the coincidence, but by enormous good luck Mrs Jones here is one of the very few people in this country – or anywhere in the world probably, although she's very modest and won't talk about it – who is capable of seeing your ghost. She's an accomplished medium and I know for a fact that her talents are in great demand by ... the authorities.'

I scowled at him but he just smiled blandly back at me.

'Really, the best thing we could do would be to leave Mrs Jones to work her magic, while rest of us shoot off to bed and then she can report back to us over breakfast. Seriously, Rookwood, if anyone's going to be able to get to the bottom of what's going on here, it will be Mrs Jones, eh, Lizzie?'

Rookwood stared at us. 'Are you both mad?'

'Actually,' said Jones, 'that's a very good question. Would it help in any way if you knew we'd both just broken out of a secure mental establishment?'

He raced on before Rookwood could say anything.

'So why don't we all go back to bed and Mrs Jones can tell us all about The Widow tomorrow.' He began to make ushering gestures, but Rookwood wasn't having any of it.

'What? What are you talking about? I'm not standing around to listen to this nonsense. I need to save my son.'

He snatched up Leo, who was still crying. I put a

warning hand on Jones's arm. Rookwood was far too unstable to wind up. His colour was jumping in all directions, flashing from one shade to another. His agitation was setting my teeth on edge. He was obviously in the grip of some strong emotions. Was it apprehension? No, it was more than that. Anticipation? Was he actually *hoping* to see The Widow?

I whispered to Jones, 'What shall we do?'

'Get you out of here for a start.'

'We can't go off and leave them.'

'I promised I'd keep you safe. I'm not losing another one.'

'I don't think it's me that's at risk.'

A wind rippled the tapestry on the wall, but that might have been just another cold draught in this cold and draughty hall.

Jones turned back to me. 'We should at least get Alex out of here. He's the one at risk.'

'Agreed, but where? Where could he go?'

'Anywhere but here.'

He turned to Rookwood, who was still whirling around as if he expected The Widow to materialise at any moment. What he would have said to him I don't know, because at that moment, Rookwood looked at his wife and said deliberately, 'I think we'll find Alex isn't in any danger, is he, my dear?'

He began to stride up and down the hall, Leo still clinging to him like a monkey to a stick, and shouting at the shadows. 'I'm not afraid of you or what you can do. I'm taking my son out of here. Do you hear? You'll never catch us. You'll never be able to find us.'

He turned back to Helena. 'You and Alex can go

or stay. Your choice.'

Jones blocked his path. 'Don't do this, Rookwood. You'll be making a huge mistake.'

Rookwood ignored him. Looking around the hall, he shouted, 'I defy you, whoever you are.' Carrying Leo in his arms, he disappeared out of the door, leaving Alex standing like a small statue, staring after his father in disbelief. It hurt my heart to look at his face.

Helena put her arm around him. 'It is no matter, *mon cher*, I am here. Your father didn't mean anything. He just thinks it best if we …'

She stopped, unable to go on. After her husband's actions, I could hardly blame her.

Jones crouched beside Alex. 'Your father thinks it best if you and Leo split up. He's taken Leo and you're staying with your mother. It's clever thinking, Alex. If The Widow is here – and I don't think she is – but if she is here, then she can't follow both of you.'

He looked so lost and bewildered. 'I didn't mean this to happen. Daddy said it was just a legend. He said it couldn't happen. She wasn't real. I thought if I did something brave then he would like me. And it was for my book as well.'

'Of course it was,' said Jones, calmly. 'Top marks for dedication to research, by the way. All great writers research their masterpieces. But for the moment it's probably best if you're not here. Your mother will take you to a safe place.'

He looked at her over Alex's head and she nodded.

'Do you have your own car? If not, you can take mine.' He paused briefly while we both wondered what Dr Sorensen would say to that.

This was all getting away from me. I took his arm and said quietly, 'Jones ... if it turns out that *Leo* is the eldest son ...'

'Yes,' he said. 'I know what you're going to say but despite everything Rookwood is trying to persuade us to think, we both know that Alex, not Leo, is the one in danger here. We need to get him and his mother to safety. Helene, can you guide us out?'

She made a huge effort at bright normality. 'Of course.'

A good plan. I wasn't in any danger and getting Alex off the premises seemed an excellent idea.

He looked down at Alex who had his eyes squeezed tight shut. Such a typical child's reaction. If you can't see it then it can't see you. Because he seemed much older than his years, I had forgotten he was still a little boy, vulnerable and afraid.

Without showing any signs of haste or alarm, Jones crouched at his side. 'Alex, look at me, please.'

Reluctantly, he opened his eyes.

'My job is to get you to your car. Yours is to look after your mother. Can you do that?'

Wordlessly, he nodded and reached for her hand.

'Excellent. Off we go then. Just a few minutes, Alex, and everything will be all right again.'

The lights went out. There was no preliminary flicker. No sort of warning. The lights went out and the darkness was complete. Thick and black and pressing down upon us. Alex cried out. Helene screamed and even I might have squeaked slightly.

'No cause for alarm, everyone,' said Jones calmly. 'I have a torch and Alex, I believe, has several.' He picked them up and dished them out. 'Off we go.'

Jones went first, Helene at his shoulder with Alex, each with a torch, and I brought up the rear, remembering to look behind me every now and then. And whether I was watching out for The Widow or something else, I had no idea. Both Alex and his mother knew the castle like the back of their hands, warning us about low doorways, uneven stairs and the like. We were making good progress. In a few minutes, we would be out under the stars and running for the car.

'Not long now,' said Jones cheerily. 'I don't know about anyone else, but I'm starving. I'm thinking we'll head to the nearest motorway services and fill up on burgers and chips. Green vegetables have their place in this world but not tonight, I think. What do you say, Alex?'

'Pizza,' he whispered, gazing up at Jones.

'Excellent choice,' said Jones and at the same moment, I said, 'Stop. What's that?'

'Where?'

'There.'

He focused his torch. We were at the top of a flight of very narrow steps that twisted down into darkness. At the top, curled neatly on his side, lay Leo, quite unconscious. Of Rookwood, there was no sign.

'Damn,' said Jones softly. 'I did warn him not to ...'

He was nearly knocked off his feet as Helene pushed past him.

'Oh my God. Is he dead? Leo? Leo? What happened?' She fell to her knees and shook him. 'Leo wake up.' Looking wildly around, she shouted, 'Thomas? Where are you?'

Deep in the shadows, something moved. Something was here. I flashed my torch around. Just for a moment, I had the briefest glimpse of a small dark shadow standing below us on the stairs, looking up. Helene screamed and threw herself over Leo. I thrust Alex behind me and an arm, black clad and with nails so long they were almost talons came out of the dark.

It was the last thing I saw for quite some time.
I felt a sharp, white, searing pain in my eyes and the next moment I was in agony, hands to my face, clawing at my eyes, fighting for breath. My whole face was on fire. My eyes streamed rivers. And my nose. And I couldn't see. My world was dark. There was nothing. I couldn't see a thing. I was a blind woman in a world of thick, black, impenetrable nothingness. Something I'd never seen before. Even with my eyes closed there was always a constant kaleidoscope of shifting colours. Colours had always filled my life and now they were gone and I was blind in every sense of the word. For the first time in my life I couldn't see anything. My eyes no longer saw what others couldn't see. Now they saw nothing at all. I was in the dark. Adrift and terrified. I had lost my place in the world. I was disoriented. There was nothing to ground me. I wasn't even sure I was the right way up. Someone screamed. Something hit me hard and I staggered to one side. For one terrifying moment, I thought I was about to fall down the stone steps and then something so heavy it could only be Michael Jones

fell on top of me and I sprawled on the cold floor. Helene screamed again. I heard Alex cry out for his mother. His voice seemed a long way off. And then there was silence.

## Chapter Sixteen

I never would have thought that this could happen to me. That I could be attacked and never see it coming. All my life I'd known when things meant me harm and this time – the time it really mattered – I'd sensed nothing. The Widow had got me and I never saw it coming. I felt Jones beside me. I could hear the rustle of his clothes as he pulled my hands away. 'Cage. Let me see.'

I was panicking. 'She's blinded me. I can't see. I can't see anything at all.'

He held my hands in a crushing grip. 'Cage, stop. I'm here. Listen to me. I'm here. Stay as still and quiet as you can. Alex has ... had an accident. I have to see to him. Stay still and *don't touch your face.*'

'You don't understand. I can't see. I can't see *anything.*'

'I *do* understand, but I have to see to Alex. Stay calm for me, Cage.'

I heard him move away. I sat in the dark, gripping my hands together so I wouldn't touch my face. And because I was shaking violently with shock and cold and pain. The last thing I remembered was that arm – reaching out of the dark. Reaching out for me.

Unable to bear it any longer, I called out, 'What's happening? Tell me.'

Helene replied from quite close by. She must still

be with Leo at the top of the stairs. 'It was The Widow. I saw her. She pushed me. I would have fallen if Mr Jones had not caught me. And then she threw Alex down the stairs.'

'Oh my God. Is he all right?'

I could hear the hysteria in her voice. 'I think he has hurt his leg.'

'Broken?'

It was Jones who replied from far away at the bottom of the stairs. 'No, I don't think so, but he can't walk.'

Helene's voice was pitched high with fear. 'What shall we do? Even if you take Alex and I take Leo, who will help Mrs Jones? And where is Thomas? Oh dear God, what is happening?'

Jones was calm and reassuring. 'Is there anywhere near here where you can lock yourselves in? Somewhere with a bolt?'

'A bolt? Wait – yes. Yes, I think so. Just down these stairs and around the corner.'

'Right. Come down here and stay with Alex. Don't leave him for even a second.'

'What about Leo? He won't wake up. What did she do to him?' Her voice trembled on the edge of panic again.

'Leo is perfectly safe, I promise you. Cage, you stay put – I'm coming for Leo and then for you. How's your face?'

'On fire. I still can't see. What did she do to me?'

I could hear him climbing the stairs. When he next spoke, he was close by. 'I'll tell you in a minute. Wait here.'

'No,' I said, panicking at the thought of being left

alone with whatever was here in the dark with us. 'I'll shuffle down on my bottom behind you.'

'Sure?'

Anything was better than being alone. I nodded. 'Yes.'

'Stairs curve to your left. Take it slowly. You'll never be more than a few feet away from me.'

I heard him grunt slightly as he picked up Leo.

'I'll be all right.' And I was. I kept to the outside wall, felt for each step carefully and shuffled down on my behind, bumping my way down until finally I arrived. Jones pulled me gently to my feet.

'Not far to go, Cage. Just another half dozen steps down this passage.'

It's a terrifying thing, not being able to see. I swallowed down thoughts of being lost for ever in this thick, black darkness. Of being stalked by something that could see me while I myself was blind … I tried hard to keep it all together as I clung to his arm. 'Where are we?'

'Do you remember the dungeon? With the skeleton and the rat?'

What a long time ago that seemed. 'I do.'

'Well, guess where we are. One last step, then turn to your right.'

'You're very calm.'

He actually sounded faintly amused. 'Believe it or not, Cage, this is not the worst situation I've ever been in.'

'What are you going to do now?'

'I'm going to leave you …'

I clutched at him. 'No …'

He put his warm hand over mine. 'Hush, don't

frighten the Rookwoods. 'I'm going to leave you, to find the way out. I'll get the lights back on, find the nearest exit, bring the car round and get everyone out safely. Then, as I said, a burgerfest to end all burgerfests. I don't know about you but I'm starving. How's your face? No, don't touch it.'

'My eyes are streaming. And my nose. Everything is running.'

'It certainly is. You're a proper little phlegm phactory, but don't touch it. And don't let Helene try and wipe your eyes either.'

'Why not?'

'It might make them worse. Just leave it. So long as your face doesn't fall off, you'll be fine. Here we are. Turn to your right.' He raised his voice. 'It's me, Mrs Rookwood.'

Someone took my arm. 'Yes, I've got her.'

'Good. I'm going to leave you here. You'll be safe. Cage, keep an eye on them.'

'Very funny. Where are you going?'

He didn't reply directly. 'I'll be gone for about ten minutes. Lock yourselves in and don't open the door to anyone but me. Do you understand, Mrs Rookwood. No one but me.'

There was a pause, and then she said quietly, 'Yes, I do understand.'

'Right. Back in a few minutes. Don't go upsetting the rat. And I'm going to take Alex because he knows the best way.'

'No.'

'He can guide me through the castle. I promise you he'll be quite safe with me, Mrs Rookwood.'

'He will,' I said, heroically not touching my face.

'My husband just *looks* like an idiot.'

'Thank you, Cage. Come on, Alex, up you come.'

I heard Helene close the door and slide the bolts home and no sooner had she done so than something rattled the handle and pushed hard against the door.

A small cold hand crept into mine and we held our breath.

Jones's voice came from the other side of the door. 'It's all right. Only me. Just checking you're safe. See you soon.'

We stood in silence. Occasionally, I heard Helene whisper something encouraging to Leo.

'Is he awake yet?'

'No, but he has just stirred. I thought he might be able to hear me. How are you feeling?'

I said, 'Getting better,' and put my hands in my pockets so I didn't touch my face.

'Do you know … what happened?'

'Yes, I do. So does Mr Jones. And so do you.'

There was a long, long silence and then she said something in French and came to sit alongside me. I waited. She sniffed a couple of times and then said, 'It was Thomas, wasn't it?'

'I'm afraid so, yes, but you don't have to talk about it if you don't want to.'

There was another long silence. I guessed her thoughts were oscillating wildly between the shock of being attacked by her own husband, being locked in a cellar with a possible madwoman who said she could talk to ghosts, and frantic anxiety for her children. I thought she was holding things together very well, all things considered.

Finally, she shifted her position slightly and said,

'At the top of the stairs … just now … Leo …'

'Leo was never in any danger. We were supposed to think The Widow had got him, but I suspect he's been lightly drugged. Just enough to knock him out. Did you not see how carefully he was laid out in the recovery position? Your husband left Leo there as a distraction and waited.'

'To do such a thing to his own son. I thought he loved Leo.'

He does, but …' I gathered myself. 'He hates you more. And Alex most of all.'

I waited.

'He has no cause,' she said bitterly. 'But someone made a remark once – long ago – and it took root. He cannot now rid himself of the suspicion …'

'But there are tests …'

'I think it is something he *wants* to believe.'

'Yes,' I said slowly. 'To give his actions validation. To justify what he tried to do tonight.'

She drew a breath that was almost a sob. I felt very sorry for her. It can't be easy to discover that the person you once loved, the person whom you trusted most in the world, means you harm.

She continued. 'Yes, you are right, I think. And then there is his obsession with this castle, of course. It eats money as you can imagine. It has certainly eaten most of mine and as my money disappeared, so did his affection.'

Another motive. He would rid himself of a troublesome wife and child and begin again with Leo – his true heir.

'Anyway, while we all gathered round Leo – that was his opportunity.'

To throw his wife down the stairs. Only Jones caught her so he pushed Alex instead. The man was far more of a monster than The Widow. She was just a small, sad shadow who was neither vicious nor vindictive, only a mother who wanted her son.

Helene was still struggling to piece events together. 'But surely – it was The Widow – everything went dark.'

'He turned out the lights.'

'Oh.'

She seemed slightly put out. It's obviously much easier to believe in the supernatural than accept your husband has just tried to kill you.

'But you can't see – because The Widow blinded you.'

'No, I'm sorry. Your husband blinded me.'

'But I saw ... that hideous hand.'

I saw again that long black arm and the claw-like hand. 'He put on one of those children's monster gloves so that anyone who saw anything would assume it was The Widow. He had to disable me first.'

'Why?'

'Because Jones had told him I can genuinely see things. That I would be able to see The Widow. Only I didn't because it wasn't The Widow, it was him. If that makes sense.'

I didn't mention that small dark shadow on the stairs.

'But in the Banqueting Hall, it was Thomas who saw ... oh.'

'It was Thomas who pretended to see The Widow. It was Thomas who wound up Alex so that he would

208

open the door. So that if something happened to you or Alex, then everyone would assume it was the legend of The Widow coming true. That she had come for Alex and that you were ... injured ... while trying to protect him. Jones and I were to be independent witnesses to the tragedy.'

'But the legend ... Francis Rookwood ... his eldest son ...'

'I suspect Thomas concocted that story. Did he ever show it to you? Did you see it yourself?'

'No, he just said he had found it in an old book. I believed him. We all believed him.'

She was quiet, thinking through the implications.

'I have to ask,' I said. 'Is there any reason the two of you can't just divorce?'

'Money. Thomas needs money. Thomas always needs money,' she said bitterly. 'Alex *is* his son – a simple paternity test would establish that. Any settlement would certainly be in my favour, so how else could he get rid of me and keep what little money of mine remains?'

How else indeed?

I said slowly, 'So he puts together a plan, utilising the story of The Widow. He goads Alex into opening the doors. He pretends to see her. He knows you will stick with Alex. Jones and I testify to finding Leo unconscious. Obviously, The Widow has already struck. We gather round and somehow, in the dark, you and/or Alex fall down the stairs.'

I could hear the anguish in her voice. 'How could he do such a thing? Alex – both of us – we could have been badly injured'

'You're bigger and heavier. You could have broken

209

your neck.'

She took a deep shuddering breath. 'How could he be sure of that? I might have just sprained an ankle – like Alex.'

'True, but suppose Jones had dashed off for help – which I'm sure was Thomas' plan. I'm lying helpless and blind at the top of the stairs – you and Alex are helpless and hurt at the bottom.

I sat still, imagining Thomas Rookwood, appearing out of the dark with murder on his mind. I'm sure Helene was doing the same.

She sighed. 'The two of you saved our lives.'

'The least we could do. I suspect it was our coming here that triggered events in the first place.'

'How are your eyes?'

'Easing a little, although I still can't see a thing.'

'That might be because we're sitting in the dark.'

'Ah. Yes. Well, that might account for it. But no, they don't sting so much now.'

There was another long silence and then she said in a small voice, 'I have a confession to make.'

I couldn't help it. 'It's not your fault that he used your mace.'

I heard her gasp in the darkness. 'How did you know that? Are you really ...?' She stopped.

'No. Well, yes. Well, perhaps a little bit. But when Jones told me not to touch my face in case I made it worse, I guessed it was mace, and it seemed too much of a coincidence that Thomas just happened to have some on him. I'm guessing you carry it and he simply nipped off and helped himself.'

'In my handbag,' she said bitterly. 'A lipstick spray. Since I was mugged a couple of years ago. Two minutes for him to race back and take it. I'm so sorry.'

'Not your fault, I said. 'I'm just relieved it wasn't anything worse. And actually, I think I'm able to see a little.' I squinted. 'I *can* see my hand in front of my face.'

I heard Leo stir and Helene murmured gently to him again. 'I wish we could leave. Leo will need attention. Did Mr Jones have to put us in the dungeon?'

'Yes, he did. This door has a bolt. On the inside.'

'I do not understand.'

'Don't tell me your husband doesn't have keys to every room in the castle.'

'Oh, yes, of course. Do you think he will be all right?'

'Who?'

'Mr Jones. Thomas is still out there and I think, at the moment, that he is perhaps not very … and his scheme has gone horribly wrong.'

'Oh,' I said cheerfully, 'I think we'll find Mr Jones is not in any particular danger,' and barely had the words left my mouth than there was a movement in the darkness and a long shrieking scream echoed around the cellar, causing the two of us to jump out of our skins.

I said, 'Stay with Leo,' and struggled to my feet, telling myself I was ready for anything and knowing I wasn't.'

'No, no,' she said. 'Please … it is nothing to worry about. It is the tableau in the dungeon, that is all. Do you remember, the skeleton and the rat? And the scream?'

'I do,' I said slowly. 'But I also remember Alex

211

telling us it operates on a sensor.'

'In the passage,' she whispered. 'Something is outside the door. Oh my God, suppose it is The Widow after all.'

The scream came again and now that I knew what it was, I could see a faint green tinge in the darkness as the tableau activated itself again and the light streamed up through the grating in the floor.

She'd worked it out for herself. 'Thomas is out there, isn't he? He's found us.'

I whispered back. 'I'm afraid so.'

'He knows we're in here.'

The green tinge faded. Whatever it was had moved away out of sensor range. There was a minute's silence and then the scream came again. It had come back. I had a sudden vision of something pacing the corridor. Up and down. Up and down. Until hunger and thirst drove us out of here.

And where was Jones? Was it at all possible ...? Had my confidence been misplaced? Had I got it wrong? Was Michael Jones at this moment lying face down somewhere, drowning in a pool of blood?

This is what comes of being locked in a dungeon with an unconscious child, a hysterical mother, a skeleton and a hyperactive electrical rat. Your imagination goes into overdrive. There was no way in a million years that Thomas Rookwood could ever have got the better of Michael Jones.

Unless he had a gun. Or a crossbow. Or some kind of medieval weapon I knew nothing about. A sword perhaps. I saw Jones creeping around the darkened castle while Thomas Rookwood stepped out of the shadows behind him swinging one of those vicious balls with spikes …

The green light flashed on again. The rat … the scream … not frightening in themselves, but quite terrifying when you know that something is waiting on the other side of the door. Waiting for us to come out …

Because we couldn't stay in here for ever. And if something *had* happened to Michael Jones … no one else knew we were in here. Rookwood wouldn't need to do anything. He could just lock the door and leave us here. He could tell everyone Helene had gone to visit relatives in France, taking the boys with her. After a suitable period of time he could tell everyone she wasn't coming back. Very sad, but they'd been having problems … and then, one night, he would open up the door, remove our bodies, and dispose of them somewhere. This was a castle – there would be disused rooms, abandoned wells, miscellaneous holes. Or leave us on top of one of the towers, open to the sky, to have our bones picked clean by the birds. Who would ever know?

And who would miss Jones and me? Would they even bother to look or would they just assume we'd gone to ground somewhere? Somehow, at that moment, Sorensen and his attack helicopters and tank regiments didn't seem so bad.

I could hear a soft, dragging sound, as if someone was running his hands over the door and then a whisper. 'Elizabeth? It's me. Michael. He's gone. Open the door.'

Beside me, Helene made a small sound and moved towards the door. I pulled her back and whispered, 'Quiet.'

'But …'

'Quiet.'

That creepy whisper again. 'Elizabeth. Come on. Open the door.'

We both stood frozen in the darkness.

The scream came again. Helene jumped and sobbed.

I put my arm around her. 'Shush.'

Rookwood abandoned the pretence, kicking at the hefty wooden door. 'Helene. Open the door. It's Alex. He's more badly injured than we thought. Mr Jones is starting the car. We need to get him to the hospital. We'll talk about everything else later. The important thing now is to save Alex.'

I had hold of her arm. 'He's lying. Stay here.'

We sat in silence, not daring to move.

'All right, Mrs Jones, I didn't want to have to say this, but your husband is dead. No one's coming to save you. I have Alex and if you don't open this door right this moment …'

I was struggling with Helene and she was much stronger than me. Fortunately, we both tripped over Leo in the dark and fell to the ground and she was on the bottom. We rolled around, both of us tangled up in Leo who was half awake and crying. I don't know how long I could have held her back – not long, I suspect – when something thudded heavily against the door. And again. And again. And again. Something was hitting the door with massive force, causing it to rattle in its very solid frame. And one last time, as whatever it was finally slithered down the door and everything was silent.

We waited, clutching each other and panting with

exertion, too terrified even to move.

The silence seemed endless and then we heard soft footsteps approaching. There was a pause and then someone hammered on the door. 'Are you still in there, Cage? Get a move on will you. Alex and I are starving.'

I rolled off Helene and began to laugh.

## Chapter Seventeen

One bacon sandwich and two cups of tea later, I was having my eyes bathed again.

'You weren't very gentle with Thomas Rookwood, were you?' I said, as Jones gently sponged my eyes with milk.

We'd both seen the blood-covered casualty as he was stretchered past and taken away.

'Nothing to do with me,' he said cheerfully.

'You're too modest.'

'I'm not modest at all, Cage, you know that. I'd like to take the credit, but alas ... not in this case.'

'But,' I said, bewildered. 'He looked as if ... well, not to put too fine a point on it, he looked as if someone like you had been having a go at him for ten minutes or so.'

'Not me,' he said simply.

'Then who?'

He shrugged. 'Sorry, Cage – I would have liked very much to be your gallant rescuer, but he was a mangled wreck when I arrived. All I did was call for the ambulance. How's that? Better now?'

'Fine,' I said, drying my milky eyes. 'So what's Helene telling everyone?'

'That he fell down the stairs. That the lights went out and he went off in the dark to try and fix the fuse and came the most tremendous cropper down the stairs. Apparently, you and I slept through the whole thing.'

'Who rang for the ambulance?'

'I did.'

'From your bed?'

'Of course not. When he didn't return, a concerned Mrs Rookwood went to look for him, and finding him at the bottom of the stairs, acted with great presence of mind, came to wake me and I phoned for the ambulance. Sadly, we were unable to wake you.'

'And Alex?'

'Tripped in the dark trying to help his mother. Everyone's saying what a brave lad he is and his ankle isn't serious and he'll be up and about in a few days. Tomorrow probably.'

'And Leo?'

'Still snoring in his bed. He may not remember much of what happened when he does wake up.'

I stared at him. 'You did it all, didn't you?'

'All what?'

'Picked people up off the floor, rang for the ambulance, told people what to say, put the boys to bed ...'

'... made you a bacon butty and a cup of tea and bathed your eyes. I've had a busy night, you know. I'm absolutely shattered.'

'So you did everything except actually give Thomas Rookwood the good hiding he so richly deserved?' I said.

He picked up the bowl and the towel. 'So it would seem.'

'Where are you off to now?'

'Just calling in to see how they're doing over there.'

'And not tying up loose ends in any way.'

'Perish the thought. You?'

'I ...' I stopped. 'I thought I'd get some fresh air,'

He grinned at me. 'What a good idea.' He disappeared.

I gave him a few minutes and then slipped out into the courtyard. The infamous door stood wide open now, letting in much-needed sun and fresh air. I wondered if, having been closed for three hundred years, it would now stand open for the next three hundred. I walked slowly into the Banqueting Hall.

She was waiting for me. The same small, dark shadow stood across the room. As if she was afraid to come too close. This was not the vindictive harpy of Rookwood's story, but a faint, frail little woman who had carried the weight of her grief down the long years, and who was lost and alone. Her voice was a whisper at the edge of my mind.

'My Jamie. Do you have him? Is he here?'

'I'm sorry, no,' I said, wondering if perhaps she had no idea of all the time that had elapsed since her son rode off to the wars all those years ago. 'I'm sorry, but he never returned home.'

'But the door was opened and I've waited for so long.'

'Yes, it was opened, but not for him. Another son did it. A very unhappy and confused and frightened little boy. He thought it would make things better with his father but he was wrong.'

She nodded. 'His father saw me on the stairs. I frightened him.'

'You did.'

'I did it to save the little boy.'

'You succeeded. He was not badly injured. His mother would thank you if she was here.'

'He was an evil man.'

'He was, yes.'

'He would have hurt the little boy very badly.'

'If he had had the chance,' I said softly.

'I ...' She stopped, because we both knew what she had done to Thomas Rookwood.

'Again, his mother would thank you if she could.'

'It was wrong, but I was so ... angry.'

'Well,' I said, 'throwing him against the door once or twice might have been sufficient to stop him, but four or five times certainly taught him a lesson.'

She said angrily, 'He used my tragedy to hurt his family,' and I could feel her fury from across the hall. The fury of a woman who would give anything to have her own family back again.

'Yes. He was an evil man. But his son is safe.'

'My own son ...? What of Jamie?'

I said as gently as I could, 'I'm sorry. He's gone. You have waited for so long, but he will never come back here again. Perhaps it is time for you to go as well. Perhaps, somewhere, he is waiting for *you*.'

She looked past me at the open door. 'I am afraid.'

'There is no need to be.'

'That little boy? And his brother?'

'They will both be safe. Their mother will take them far away from here. And thanks to you another mother is not grieving over another lost son.'

She looked out through the doors again. 'Is my son out there?'

'I don't know,' I said gently. 'But you know he's not here.'

'Perhaps,' she said and I could barely hear her. 'Perhaps it is time.'

'Would you like me to come with you?'

She inclined her head. 'Yes. Thank you.'

The sun had risen. Long purple shadows stretched across silvery frosted cobbles. The walls glowed a warm gold in the early morning sunshine.

She paused on the threshold and looked back because this had been her home. I waited.

'I am ready,' she said. 'To feel the sun on my face again ...'

We stepped through together, out into the courtyard. She stood in a patch of weak sunshine, closed her eyes, and lifted her face to the light.

I said, 'Good luck.'

She faded. Right in front of my eyes, she just faded away. I heard a faint whisper, 'Beware the snow ...' and then I was alone in the courtyard.

'And you thought *I* was a bit of a bastard.'

I said indignantly. 'No, I didn't. Well, not very much.'

He frowned and forked his last chip. 'I'm not as nice as you think I am.'

'I don't think you're nice at all.'

'Well, that's a relief.'

'Did you know it was Rookwood all the time?'

'I had an idea. Did you?'

I nodded. 'Yes – his colour was ... wrong.'

'Well, what do you know – we both arrived at the same conclusion – and by completely different routes.'

'How did *you* know?'

'Well, I couldn't understand why he was goading Alex as he did. And then in my job you always check your sources and no one had read the legend but him. No one saw The Widow but him. His haste to get you out of the picture – the one person who could see The Widow. Except you wouldn't see her because she wasn't there and the last thing he needed was you telling everyone she wasn't there. Sorry about that, by the way. I couldn't resist the urge to tell him about you and I do feel his attack with the mace was my fault. Still – no great harm done, eh? And I didn't like the bloke. And I have a suspicious mind. And you said you couldn't see her.'

'You trusted me?'

'Why not?' he said lightly. 'You trusted me.'

'Why did he try something so stupid while we were here?'

'We were to be his witnesses.'

'Was he after Helene or Alex, do you think?'

He shrugged. 'Don't know. Maybe both. Helene's money was fast disappearing and he hated Alex.'

'Because he thought he wasn't his son.'

221

'Man's an idiot. Stick the kettle on, Cage.' He began to clear the table. I waited for him to ask. 'Was he Rookwood's son?'

'How should I know?'

'Well, you know – I thought the colour thing might tell you.'

'What am I? A portable DNA machine.'

'I don't know what you are, Cage. That's the whole point.'

Helene came to visit that afternoon, bringing both boys with her. They huddled together in a tight little group. They all looked tired and Leo had been crying again.

I tried to signal to Jones that she wanted to talk to me alone and astonishingly, he got the message.

'The sun is shining, Cage, so I'm going to leave you for a while. You've eaten all the food in the house so I need to go shopping again.'

'Can we come?' asked Alex, politely. Both of them were very subdued. Their colours were wrapped around themselves and each other.

Jones looked down at him. 'How's your ankle today?'

'It hardly hurts at all.'

'I'll help him,' said Leo, quickly.

'Boys, do not bother Mr Jones today. He is very busy.'

'No, that's all right. Glad to have them. Since your castle inexplicably has no donkeys or other beasts of burden, I shall have to use these two to carry back the heavy stuff.'

He stopped at my side and put his hand on my

arm. 'Can I bring you back anything?'

I shook my head, a little touched by his thoughtfulness. 'No, but thank you.'

He bent his head and said, 'I'm sorry, Cage. I was supposed to take care of you.'

The worlds were light, but I could see he felt badly about this. The grey swirls were seeping back into his colour.

I smiled at him, feeling a tiny warm glow. 'It's good to know there's someone in this world who's looking out for me. Even if he is pretty rubbish at it.'

'Any more from you and you can get your own chocolate.' He moved away. 'Come on, boys.'

The door banged behind them. In front of the fire, Juno snuffled and twitched in her sleep.

Helene declined a cup of tea. 'Mrs Jones. I would not blame you in the slightest if you wished to leave us as soon as possible, but I do beg you will remain at least until the swelling around your eyes has gone down and your sight is completely restored. I can call our doctor to see you if you like. Whichever you choose I will be happy to assist you. And, of course, there is no question of payment for your stay here.'

She wanted us gone. I could see it. She was grateful, but we would always be reminders of what had happened here. I didn't blame her in the slightest.

'No,' I said, 'I think we'll be leaving tomorrow, or possibly the day after. It depends.'

'I understand,' she said.

'And you? What are your plans?'

'I plan to take the boys and be gone before Thomas is discharged from hospital. That won't be for a least a week which will give us time to pack properly and make our arrangements.'

'Where will you go?'

'France. To my family just outside Bordeaux, to begin with. My uncle is an excellent lawyer and will advise me on what to do next. The most important thing is to get the boys to safety, of course.'

'Well, I think if your husband has any sense, he will accept a short sharp divorce with whatever financial provisions your uncle thinks appropriate and count himself fortunate.'

She nodded and stared for some time at her hands. 'It was The Widow, wasn't it?'

We both knew she was referring to Thomas Rookwood's injuries.

'Yes. She did it to save Alex.'

'I wish I could thank her.'

'I did that on your behalf. She has gone now.'

'I shall always be grateful.'

Whether she would 'always be grateful' to us or to The Widow was not clear and I didn't ask.

'I have so many times been on the verge of taking the boys and leaving. If I had done so perhaps none of this would have happened.'

'I doubt you would have been permitted to take Leo.'

'No. It was made very clear to me that Leo would always remain with his father. I didn't want to separate the boys and I certainly didn't want Leo brought up with his father's values, so I stayed. Perhaps it was a mistake.'

'You made what you thought was the right decision at the time. That's all anyone can do. And it's over now. You'll all be safe. And Leo slept through the whole thing and even Alex's memories will fade in time. There will be an exciting new life in an exciting new country. You'll see.'

She smiled. 'Again, thank you. Thank you both.'

## Chapter Eighteen

We left early the next morning. I believe Jones went to pay the bill but none was presented.

I packed with some regret. We hadn't been here very long and now I had to go back and grapple with Sorensen, and Ted's death, and make decisions about my future, and all sorts of things I really didn't want to have to do.

And there was so much to think about. What sort of state would my house be in? Had anyone thought to empty the fridge? And what of Sorensen? Would he be waiting for me? Despite Jones's reassurances, I still wasn't very clear about what he could actually do to me. What legal powers did he possess? And speaking of legal matters, what of the consequences of Ted's death? There would be solicitors, probate and many other things I knew nothing about.

And what of the future? We were cutting our stay short. There hadn't been time to make any plans for my future. There had barely been time to think.

I tried not to feel despondent, but it was hard.

We drove slowly through the village. After recent events, it was a surprise to find nothing much had changed. The grey cottages were still there. The bubbling stream still ran along the side of the road. We drove downhill in silence.

After a mile or so, Michael Jones said, 'I don't

know, I chose the most remote place I could find and you still managed to get us into trouble.'

'Me?'

'Well, you're surely not blaming me.'

I regrouped and attacked from a different position. 'Us?'

'Well yes, we are an "us," aren't we? I don't mean an "us" type of us, but more of an "us" type of us. You know – us rather than *us*.'

'It worries me that I understand what you're saying.'

'That's nothing,' he said. 'It worries me that I'm here alone with you, miles from anywhere and help is very far away.'

'Why would you need help?'

'Sweetheart, I always need help.'

I changed the subject again. 'Won't you get into trouble when you go back to the clinic?'

'No, I was in trouble before I left.'

I couldn't understand this casual disregard for authority. All my life I'd kept my head down and done as I was told. I asked, 'Aren't you worried? Doesn't it bother you at all?'

He shrugged. 'I've been frightened by experts. Takes more than a jumped up little monkey in a good suit to terrify me.'

'He is a bit like a monkey, isn't he? But not one of the nice ones.'

'No, not even like one of the ones who flash their colourful bottoms. I've always had a fondness for those.'

'Do you mean mandrills?'

'I don't know. Do I?'

There was silence for a few miles and then he said, 'So what about you?'

I sighed, returning to the real world. A world full of problems. 'I don't know.'

'Would you take a word of advice?'

'Of course.'

'Sell your house and make a fresh start. You're a bit out in the wilds in Whittington.'

'But where?'

'Come back to Rushford.'

I stared at him in surprise. 'It's a bit close to Sorensen, isn't it?'

'Exactly. You'd be under his radar.'

'He'll find me,' I said, trying not to give way to my mounting fears for the future.

He slowed for a junction. 'He'll find you wherever you go. If you're that close he may be satisfied with simply keeping an eye on you. If you try to hide in the Outer Hebrides, he'll probably have you brought back.'

I shivered. 'I'll go to the authorities.'

'Sweetheart, I keep telling you – we *are* the authorities.'

I said very quietly, 'I wish Ted was here.'

'We all wish Ted was here.'

'I mean, I don't know how I'll manage without him.'

He laughed. 'You've seen off two very unpleasant experiences in as many months. I really don't think Sorensen is going to cause you any grief.'

'I'll think about it.' And I did. I pondered all sorts of futures as Sorensen's big car ate up the miles and we headed south.

With fifty miles still to go, he said, 'Where would you like me to drop you?'

'Well, there's really only one place, isn't there. Ted's house.'

'Your house,' he reminded me.

No, not for much longer. I'd read so many times about people who had been the victims of burglary and no longer felt safe in a home they knew had been violated, and now I was beginning to realise how they felt. The thought of Sorensen's men pawing through our things, laughing, commenting, shoving things back any old how ... if they bothered to shove them back at all.

I'd been thinking about what Jones had said. *There must be somewhere you have always wanted to live. Go and live there.* Such a good idea. I *could* go back to live in Rushford. It's quiet, but big enough to have amenities. I liked the park, and the medieval castle, and the crooked streets, and the nice shops. And what Jones had said about living under his radar made sense. Yes, he'd know where I was. He probably knew where I was now, but if I was so close he could put his hand on me any time he wanted, then he might just leave me alone. Until the day he needed me. That day would come, I knew it, but it hadn't come yet and something inside me felt quite excited at the thought of a fresh start in a new home.

'I have a flat in Rushford,' said Jones, apparently reading my thoughts. 'So it's not as if you won't know anyone.'

'I didn't know your home was in Rushford.'

'It's not. I said I have a flat there.'

'Oh.'

A dark and rainy day was drawing to a dark and rainy close as we pulled up outside my house. From the outside, everything looked perfectly normal. Actually, I'm not sure what I expected. Broken windows, curtains torn down, furniture tossed into the front garden ...

There was none of that. My key slid into the lock and the front door opened. Everything was exactly as I had left it the afternoon I had departed to attend Ted's funeral. Even down to the magazine open on the coffee table. If I hadn't known Sorensen and his men had been here, I wouldn't have known Sorensen and his men had been here – if you catch my drift.

'Yes,' said Jones, running an experienced eye over the place. 'He's very good, isn't he? Shall I take your case upstairs?'

'Thank you. Can I offer you some tea before you go?'

I don't know why I said the bit about him going. I was dreading being alone. Dreading that moment when I closed the door behind him and turned to face an empty house.

'No thanks,' he said, and my heart sank. 'I'd better take his car back. He'll be expecting me.'

'Will he really?'

'Well, if he isn't, he'll say he was, just to perpetuate the legend. Listen, don't worry about anything. I'll telephone you tomorrow. Always supposing he hasn't had me hauled away for stealing his precious car, but I'm betting he won't. My guess is that he'll be thrilled he's actually found someone whom you apparently trust enough to let them kidnap you. He'll wait a while to see what happens. So relax. Don't lie awake at night imagining every sound is Sorensen coming back for you because it won't be. Got it?'

I nodded.

'Right then. I'll call tomorrow and you can treat me to lunch sometime later this week. All right?'

'Yes,' I said, determined not to be a baby.


It seemed strange to be back in our home without Ted. He was everywhere. His books. His clothes. In photos. Furniture we had chosen together. Even his favourite food in the freezer. It would all have to be sorted out. Decisions would have to be made about what to keep and what to dispose of. And how. And to whom. But not yet.

The next morning, I cleaned and tidied the house, changed the sheets, and was just settling down with a cup of tea when Jones rang.

'Hello,' I said, more pleased to hear from him than I cared to admit. 'Are you in prison?'

'Astonishingly, no. He very ostentatiously walked around his car a couple of times, failed to find anything he could legitimately complain about and is now, I believe, making arrangements to have the cost of the petrol deducted from my wages. Oh – and the registration plates will be replaced at my expense.'

'What a miserable bastard.'

'Oh, I don't know, I think I got off quite lightly, all things considered.'

'Does he know where I am?'

'Yes, I told him.'

My voice was high with panic. 'Why? Why would you do that?'

'He asked me,' he said simply.

'But now he knows where I am.'

'Well, he probably knew that before he asked me. He just wanted to see if I would tell him the truth.'

'Oh. Did he say anything?'

'Not really. He's almost certainly got someone watching the house.'

'Oh my God.'

'Yes, and in this weather, too. Stick your head out of the front door, Cage, and see if you can spot some poor bastard in a misted-up car with a radio that doesn't work, slowly going out of his mind with boredom and trying to prevent his bladder exploding. Ask him in, make him a cup of tea, and let him use the bathroom, there's a good girl. Speaking as one who's done more than his fair share of observation details over the years, he will love you for ever. See you Thursday.'

'What for?'

'Lunch. Your treat. Had you forgotten? Or are you one of those people whose people have to contact my people before you can commit yourself?'

'Of course not,' I said, feeling better every moment.

'Pick you up at twelve thirty then. Don't forget the tea and pee break.'

He hung up.

Out of curiosity, because not for one moment did I actually think anyone might be there, I looked out through the net curtains.

Oh my God, there *was* a car parked two doors down on the opposite side of the road. A young man sat behind the wheel. And the windows were misted up.

I don't know what came over me. I suspected I was suffering from 'Contamination by Jones'. I went into the kitchen and made several enormous ham sandwiches, fretted in case he was Jewish, decided I couldn't be expected to think of everything, filled up a thermos with tea and let myself out of the front door.

It was a miserable day, wet and raw. He watched me approach, pretending he wasn't looking. I tapped on the driver's window. For along moment, he stared straight ahead, and then reluctantly lowered the window.

I handed him the sandwiches and thermos. 'There you are. When you've finished, bring the stuff back and I'll let you use the bathroom.'

He stared, appalled. I've never actually had that effect on anyone before. His creamy grey colour streamed away from me as if I had the plague. And then, red-faced, he took the thermos and plate, stammered something, and closed the window again.

I felt better than I had for days.

Jones was punctual to the minute on Thursday, but I was waiting for him. He handed me into the car and then climbed in beside me. 'Don't I get a "hello"?'

'I'm so sorry,' I said. 'I didn't recognise you in an unstolen car.'

He grinned. 'You're feeling better, then.'

We had lunch in a quiet pub down by the river.

He handed me the menu. 'Robbie says thanks for

the sandwiches.'

'Oh, poor boy, I felt so sorry for him.'

'He's not a boy, but he thinks you're a very nice lady.'

'Fat lot of good that will do if Sorensen decides to have me assassinated.'

The couple at the next table turned to look at us.

'Louder, Cage. I think there's a couple of people on the other side of town who didn't quite catch that.'

I could feel myself blushing.

## Chapter Nineteen

I didn't settle well. The house – Ted's house – felt cold and alien. I lost count of the number of times I scrubbed down the kitchen, trying to eradicate any trace of Sorensen's people being there. I ignored Jones's advice and lay awake at night, ears straining for any sound of someone moving around outside ... a quiet footstep on the stair ... the bedroom door slowly opening ...

The stuff I'd left behind at the clinic was couriered to me a couple of days after I arrived at the house I used to think of as home. Everything was neatly packed and it was all there. Even the little box of Ted's possessions. There was no accompanying message. I threw it all away. If I thought Sorensen had touched it – it went. Plain and simple.

I was busy for the first few weeks, sorting through Ted's stuff, dealing with solicitors and the bank, and when I finally had time to lift my head and look about me, spring had arrived. Ted's garden began to push out new green shoots everywhere. For some reason, my sense of loss deepened even further. I didn't think I could bear to look at Ted's garden without Ted in it.

I don't rush into things; I'm not an impulsive person, but Jones's suggestion that I begin again somewhere else had begun to take root. One day, I caught the bus into Rushford. I thought I'd have a look around the shops, have lunch somewhere, cross the bridge and visit the library, and just generally have a nice day out. The sun was shining and the first daffodils were coming through. It was definitely time to get back out into the world.

Actually, I rather enjoyed myself. It was pleasant to browse around the shops. Time passed more quickly than I realised, and I suddenly found I was hungry and I wanted my lunch. There's a nice little café up by the castle and I wanted to call in at the library anyway, so I crossed the bridge and trudged up the hill. It *is* a bit of a trudge, as well. The castle is built on high ground, guarding what was, before they built the bridge, the original crossing point. The River Rush is quite wide and shallow here and a tall stone on either river bank marks the site of the original ford. Some medieval entrepreneur put together the money for a bridge which they built about a hundred yards upstream from the ford. That was the signal for the town to spill over to the other side of the river, taking the commercial centre with it. The market place was built near St Stephen's, the guildhall is there, the town hall, the banks and the best shops. The area around the castle is now almost completely residential and there are some nice properties up there with lovely views across the river.

I strolled up through the narrow streets trying not to puff too much, entering Castle Close through the archway between two fine Tudor houses that have miraculously survived the centuries.

The castle lay to the right and ahead. Built in the twelfth century, I think, modernised in the fifteenth, and again in the seventeenth. It survived the Civil War by siding with whoever seemed appropriate at the time. The outer ward was gone – that was where I was standing now. At some point the wall had been removed and the remaining two sides of the square not part of the castle walls were now occupied by a dogleg of quaint residential houses representing every architectural style known to man. Some of them were quite ancient, others had been built in Victorian and Edwardian times. Nothing was less than a hundred years old. The centre of the square was grassed over and a wide cobbled path ran around the outside. The remains of what had once probably been a dark and dirty moat were now silted up and only two horseshoes of glittering water remained, fringed with willows just coming into leaf. With the castle as a backdrop it really was a very pretty place and the council had placed seats around the green for people to enjoy the view and be mugged by opportunist swans and ducks, keen to investigate their shopping for anything edible.

A wooden bridge led across one of the ponds into the castle proper, which was still well preserved. They hold civic banquets here whenever they want to impress someone. An entire wall is covered in gleaming horseshoes because tradition decrees that every monarch must send a full set of horseshoes as a gift, otherwise they won't reign for long. Next door is the library, which was where I was heading, and the council keeps an information centre there as well. There are people in and out all the time.

I was reminded of Thomas Rookwood telling us his castle had once been the focal point of local life and he was determined to keep it so. It was good to see this old pile still had a place in the community.

After lunch, I found the library, warm and welcoming, joined on the spot, and was issued with a library card.

'Do have a look around,' said the woman behind the desk. Her colour was a gentle fawn, shot through with gold. She loved her job. 'The reference section is upstairs – the stairs are just through that door there. Or there's a lift if you prefer it.'

I said I thought I might as well have a look around while I was there.

'The Local History Society is meeting in there at the moment, but don't worry about disturbing them.' She smiled. 'I think sometimes there's not a lot of local history discussed.'

I strolled around, pulling the occasional book off a shelf to have a closer look and helped myself to some leaflets. I did take a look upstairs. The reference section held a bank of PCs for public use, tables and chairs for quiet study, and the Local History Society, two of whom were knitting, one was laying out cups and saucers, another was cutting a cake and they were all chatting nineteen to the dozen. I left them to it.

Emerging into the sunshine again, I paused to enjoy the scene. People were wandering around, enjoying the day. A little boy and his father were trying, very unsuccessfully, to fly a kite. The swans paddled quietly in water that reflected the blue sky and white clouds. Everything was lovely.

And then I saw it.

Almost directly opposite me, sandwiched between two larger, much more substantial bow-fronted houses, was a tiny, narrow little cottage. What had caught my attention was the red and blue "For Sale" sign in the window.

I stared. What a wonderful place to live. Imagine seeing this, every day. It called to me. I swear it called to me. And who wouldn't want to live next door to a castle?

I started to walk away and then stopped and looked back. It was ridiculous. The location alone must add tens of thousands of pounds to the price.

'You're looking for a new home,' said half of me.

'Yes, but something affordable,' said the other half – the sensible half. 'Not this.'

'How do you know you can't afford it? How much are they asking?'

'More than I can pay.'

'You don't know that. And the estate agent's offices are on the way back to the bus station. You can call in and ask.'

'If I can afford it then so can everyone else. Everyone will want it. And I don't have a job. I'll never get a mortgage.'

'You don't need a mortgage.'

'To buy that I'd probably need six mortgages.'

Silence.

I trudged back down the hill because I had a bus to catch. And the estate agent's office would be full of people clamouring to buy this little gem and I'd miss my bus and be stranded and …

The offices were empty. I could see three people sitting behind their desks and no customers.

I went in.

Twenty minutes later I was back up the hill, in the

company of a charming young man, he trying not to puff in case it put off a prospective buyer, and me trying not to puff as a matter of pride.

I'd thought the little house would be far beyond my means and that would be the end of the matter. The price was surprisingly reasonable and easily within my means. Oh my God – I could actually buy this place. I know I'd thought vaguely about leaving Ted's house, but now, suddenly, I could, and the thought was frightening. I took a deep breath. Perhaps I wouldn't like the inside.

So much for that. The house was a little jewel.

Downstairs was all one room – the kitchen at one end, divided from the living room by a smart breakfast bar. The wooden floors glowed honey in the sunshine. It was perfect. There was even an open fire and built in bookshelves. I stared around in delighted surprise. He was reciting facts and figures and I really tried to look interested because he was doing his best, although if he'd been a little older and more experienced, he'd have shut up and let the house sell itself.

I pointed to a door in the wall. 'What's behind there?'

He opened it with a flourish, revealing a narrow staircase winding up through the wall.

I did still retain some small amount of common sense. 'How do they get furniture upstairs?'

'Beds usually come apart and can go up these stairs. Mattresses bend. Anything else usually goes through the upstairs windows.'

There was another door on the stairs.

'Access to the cellar,' he said before I could ask, and the next thing I was downstairs staring at a large room lit only by a small window up near the ceiling. My mind filled with thoughts of dungeons and secret tunnels to the castle.

'Plumbing for washing machine and dryer,' he said, reminding me why I was here. 'And hooks for overhead washing lines.'

I nodded wisely and tried to look like a prospective homeowner who was interested but would need a considerable amount of favourable negotiating before saying 'yes'.

We went upstairs.

The landing was huge with a door on each side.

'Actually,' he said, you could probably make this space a second bedroom if you didn't mind having to access the bathroom through it. The previous owner kept a bed settee here for guests.'

I nodded. It was a good space – no window, but there was a skylight overhead. I could make a little study here.

'Just the one bedroom,' he said, 'but very large as you can see. Pretty fireplace. Built-in wardrobes.'

Another lovely room, lit by two long sash windows through which the sun flooded, making patterns on the walls. The floors up here were slightly darker in colour. As downstairs, the walls were cream.

The bathroom was clean and modern, all white and chrome. I liked everything. There was nothing I would change. There was no reason in the world not to buy this house.

'Can I look at the kitchen again?'

'Of course.'

The kitchen, like the bathroom, was spotless. The

oven looked as if it had never been used.

'It hasn't,' he said. 'The previous occupant was a single lady. A student.'

'Oh.' I said.

'No, no. Her father had the house fitted up for her, but she just never cooked. She ate out or had a takeaway. I remember, when I came to measure the place up, she was keeping some of her books in the oven.'

There was a pause. I couldn't put it off any longer.

'Why is it so cheap?'

He sighed. 'It's cheap because it's very small, situated at the top of a very steep hill and there's no vehicular access. Not even close. Furniture removers will have you on a blacklist, delivery drivers and refuse collectors will not love you.' He grinned, suddenly looking very young indeed. 'And don't even think about dying here. They'll have to carry your body all the way down the hill and across the bridge before they can get you in the hearse.'

'Not my problem,' I said matter-of-factly. 'I'll be dead.'

I walked slowly around the house. Now he had the sense to shut up.

'Have you had much interest?' I said, watching him closely.

'Some', he said evasively, while his colour said none.

'Well, I quite like it,' I said. 'But this lack of access could be a problem. I'll need to think about it.'

'Of course,' he said, keeping his end up, 'but I have several other viewings scheduled.'

Oh, bless him.

242

I rang Jones two weeks later.

'I think I might be buying a house.'

'What? Where?'

'Rushford – as you suggested.'

'Have you made an offer yet? Do you have a solicitor? What about the valuation? How much did you pay?'

What is it about the British and house buying? We're obsessed. We make TV programmes about it. You can mix together a room full of the most incompatible people in the country and just let someone mention property prices and the next minute they're all rabbiting away like maniacs.

He paused for breath and I enquired if he'd finished.

'Don't tell me you offered the asking price. Cage, you idiot. Why didn't you ask me to negotiate for you? Have you had a survey done?'

'Obviously you haven't finished. I'll just sit down and wait until you're done, shall I?'

He sighed. 'Where is it?'

'Rushford. Up by the castle.'

There was a long silence.

'What?' I said, suddenly unnerved.

'Nothing. Nothing. I was just thinking – good choice.'

'Really?'

'Well, yes. Unless he deploys a squadron of Black Hawk helicopters, there's no way Sorensen's going to get you out of there quietly is there? It's public, there are always people around. And they can't even get emergency vehicles up there so even if he does murder

243

you then he's going to have to carry your body all the way back down to the bridge.'

'Strangely, Sorensen accessibility was rather lower on my list of desirable features than wooden floors, clean kitchen and a modern bathroom. And yes, I've had it surveyed. And valued. And the asking price is fair. And I made them take a couple of thousand off the price to bribe the removal men with. Are there any other aspects of my house-buying technique you'd like to criticise?'

'You know, Ted never mentioned you were such a shrew.'

'Ted thought I was perfect. Anyway, I'm going in tomorrow to measure up. Are you in Rushford?'

'Of course. Where did you think I was?'

'Well, it's you. And this is your mobile, so I was rather thinking Ulan Bator.'

'I'll pick you up at ten, tomorrow.'

'Just let me see if I'm free.'

He laughed and hung up.

## Chapter Twenty

Things go quite smoothly if you're a cash buyer. They go quite quickly, too. Ted's house sold a week after I put it on the market. Six weeks later, I was in my new home.

My last day in Ted's house was sad. Jones, displaying a tact I hadn't known he possessed, waited in the car, surrounded by my last-minute boxes.

I walked slowly around the house, just in case there was one last, faint echo of Ted lingering on somewhere, but he was gone. I closed the front door behind me, posted the keys back through the letter box for the new owners, and never looked back.

Climbing in, I said, 'I've been thinking about a job and what exactly I could do.'

'Is money a problem?' he said, pulling away. 'I knew it. You spent too much on the house, didn't you?'

'No, not at all. There was the money from the sale of Ted's house. Plus the money from my parent's house. Ted had life insurance. And a pension. If Sorensen pays it.'

'It's not up to him. And don't worry. Something will turn up.'

'Do you think so?'

'Oh yes. You're the sort of person things happen to.'

Thinking it over, that might not have been as

comforting as he'd intended.

* * *

Ted's house hadn't been large, but my new one was even smaller. I took some favourite pieces of furniture, but left most behind for the new owners.

It took me a while to settle. It was some years since I'd lived alone. And that had been in my parent's house. Safe and familiar. Now I was striking out on my own.

It was scary at first, getting used to living alone, managing my day with no Ted to give it focus. I missed him very much, but there were some rather nice shelves fitted either side of the chimney breast and on these I put my favourite things, including the picture of Ted and me – the one taken at the Tower of London. I angled it so I could see it from wherever I was in the room and there was always a little vase of fresh flowers alongside. I felt as though I'd brought him with me.

I was still anxious about Sorensen, but Jones said not to fret over it, so I tried not to. It had been some months since my stint as a 'voluntary patient' at the clinic. Yes, he knew where I was but, as Jones pointed out, I knew where he was as well. I wasn't sure how much better that was supposed to make me feel.

I lived a quiet life. Jones disappeared off to somewhere or other. He didn't say where and I knew better than to ask. I shopped daily – I had to. One bag of shopping was about all I could get up the hill. In the afternoon, I would sit on the green opposite, watch the people and feed the swans. If it was raining I sat in the window seat with a book. I wasn't unhappy. I had my picture of Ted, smiling at me and there were always his flowers nearby. When we'd been married, he'd brought me flowers every week and now it was my turn to bring them for him.

And I had neighbours. To my left was a small firm of very upmarket solicitors. There were two elderly men, a middle-aged woman and two young women. I had no idea who was who, but they always smiled and waved when they saw me.

On the other side was Colonel Barton and his wife. They spent much of their day sitting in their bay window watching the world go past. And even up here out of the way, it was amazing how much of it did go past. Tourists, of course, masses of them, to visit the castle. Mothers and pre-school children to play on the grass. Elderly people to sit on the benches and feed the birds. People to use the library, or patrons of the very good little café next to the castle. Some days the place was heaving with people, but all of them a safe distance away. I loved it.

In my ignorance, I thought all this activity was the reason why, like me, Colonel and Mrs Barton spent so much time in their window, but I was wrong.

Mrs Barton had good days, explained the colonel, but these were not as often as he could wish and getting fewer all the time. I watched his colour, already deep red with anxiety deepen even further, shading towards purple and black. Mrs Barton's colour, a delicate shade of robin's egg blue, thin and tenuous, was growing weaker day by day. Sometimes I could almost see straight through it. Those were the days when she didn't know him. Or where she was. Or why their son wasn't here. Or anything at all really. He was devoted to her and the days when she wouldn't even speak to him hurt him deeply. I began to perceive there were people in the world with worse problems than me.

The only time he ever had a few hour's respite was every other Thursday afternoon when, as president of the Local History Society, he went over to the library for what he referred to as one of their 'little sessions'. He did agree there wasn't a lot of local history discussed, but the ladies took it in turn to bring in cakes and the tea was very good. I suspected he was not the only one who enjoyed his few hours' freedom. He offered me membership and I said I'd think about it.

Jones was still away that summer but I had the occasional email from him. Just a few lines, mostly telling me to stay out of trouble. I think he imagined that in his absence I'd wander in front of a bus, or inadvertently board a flight to Sierra Leone.

And then, one morning, I woke early with tears on my cheeks and a jagged sense of loss. The pre-dawn light was filtering through the curtains. I wiped my eyes and sniffed. Even now, at odd moments during the day, I found myself mourning Ted. The unexpectedness of it could be quite disabling sometimes, but this was different. This wasn't the usual gentle surge of sorrowful memories. This was sharp. Painful. Like a knife wound. I was no stranger to grief but there was more to this. There was anger and rage and helplessness and despair and … it just went on and on. Volley after volley of emotion that was too much to cope with. Too much to bear alone …

At first, I didn't know what to do and then I did. I

was experiencing this for a reason. I lay very still and let my mind drift away. It took me a while and several times the emotion was so intense I very nearly had to let it go, but I stuck with it. I lay still and let my mind do the work. I knew from experience that trying to pin something like this down only makes it even more elusive. It's rather like trying to remember something at the back of your mind. You know it's there but you can't quite get to it. You have to tease it out ...

Something to do with Michael Jones. Who was here in Rushford. He was back and something was ... not right.

I wiped the tears off my cheeks again and threw back the bedclothes. I telephoned him and there was no response. I emailed with the same result. He'd never given me his address, only his mobile number and all I knew was that he lived on the other side of the river. Almost opposite me, he'd said once.

I crossed the landing, climbed into the bath, opened the window, stood on tiptoe and peered out across the river. There was St Stephen's. Well, he wasn't there. Next to that stood the old eye hospital now a block of luxury flats, the disused hospital chimney, a multi-storey car park, a corner of the bus station ... this was hopeless. The area was too large. It's not as if I'm a sniffer dog. I couldn't just wander the streets trying to pick up his scent. I had to use what Jones himself would laughingly call my brain.

I didn't know what to do. I stared again. I wasn't looking at a residential area of Rushford, but there was that one single block of flats. A good place to start. Although it was perfectly possible he might have a loft apartment in a warehouse somewhere nearby. I sighed. It was very likely I'd just be aimlessly roaming the pavements either until darkness fell, or until the police picked me up for suspicious behaviour. I thought I'd try the flats first and if he wasn't there then I'd have breakfast somewhere and rethink my strategy.

I grabbed my keys and bag, slammed the door behind me, ran down the front steps, along the cobbled path, through the arch and down the hill towards the bridge.

The old eye hospital was quite an imposing building. They'd kept the old Victorian façade, with its pediment and pillars. I climbed the impressive steps and shoved my weight against the two, heavy wood and glass doors and, of course, they didn't move an inch. I studied the list of names opposite the bells with little hope. He might not even call himself Jones here. Every slot was filled except one and no one was called Jones. I looked thoughtfully at the empty slot, selected four names I thought looked friendly – don't ask me what a friendly name looks like – pressed the bells and held my breath. It was nearly eight o'clock. People would be leaving for work. Someone was bound to be waiting for their lift. Or a taxi. Or something. Someone would buzz me in.

Someone did. I shot through the door before anyone could change their minds, ignored the lift and headed towards the stairs. If the name slots were in flat order, then the blank slot was on the top floor. And if he could see across the river then he was at the back. Flat 4B.

The stairs and passages were well carpeted. I made no noise at all as I made my way upwards, more and more certain I was right with every step. I eased through the heavy fire door and set off down the corridor. 4B was on my left. I rang the bell.

Nothing.

I wasn't going to let that stop me.

I rang again.

Nothing.

More concerned every moment, I kept my finger on the bell. I could hear it through the door, ringing and ringing and ringing and ...

The door was hurled open with some force. It took everything I had not to step back in alarm.

'What?' he demanded. 'What could you want at this time of day? In fact, what could you possibly want at all? Just f ...' he paused and then changed what he had been going to say. 'Just push off out of it will you,' and went to slam the door.

I put my hand on the jamb which didn't turn out to be a smart move. The pain was intense.

'You bloody idiot,' he said, grabbing me and yanking me inside. 'What on earth possessed you ...? What are you doing here anyway? For God's bloody sake ...'

I didn't need any special senses to know he wasn't that pleased to see me.

I stood clutching my hot, throbbing hand and trying not to throw up.

I could hear him crashing around in the kitchen, reappearing with a bowl, a couple of towels and three ice packs.

'Here. Sit down.'

I sat quietly while he wrapped my hand in a tea towel, then the ice packs and covered the whole lot with a towel.

When he'd finished, he sat back with a sigh, saying, 'I'm never going to be able to keep a secret from you, am I? Have you had breakfast?'

'Why do you want to know?'

He passed me a small bottle. 'Very efficient painkillers but you can't take them on an empty stomach.'

'Oh. No.'

'No painkillers?'

'No breakfast.'

He sighed again. 'Toast, I think. God, Cage, you're high maintenance, aren't you?'

Traditionally, a bachelor pad is a wreck, with underwear all over the place, empty lager cans, overflowing ashtrays and a very peculiar smell. The living accommodation of a bachelor who has recently received a severe emotional blow should probably look like a landfill site. Jones's apartment was immaculate. Apart from the bowl and a discarded towel and me, there wasn't anything out of place anywhere.

And it was a nice flat. There was good modern art on the walls, a whole wall of books, a huge and very comfortable sofa, and a state of the art home entertainment system. Everything looked quiet and expensive. Except for the owner himself, currently wearing a crumpled and sweat-stained Grateful Dead T-shirt and the world's most disreputable jeans. He smelled stale and unwashed. He certainly hadn't shaved in a while. A doorway led into a modern kitchen and I could see him slipping bread into a chrome toaster. His colour was wrapped closely around his body, dark and thick. There was no glow about it at all today. I could guess what this was about, but I held my tongue.

He clicked on the kettle and then, probably not realising I was watching, rinsed his face under the tap, buried his face for a long moment in a tea towel, and then turned back to face the world.

'Eat,' he said, bringing in a plate of toast.

Food was the last thing I wanted, but I picked up a piece and nibbled.

'All of it.'

'You too,' I said.

'Not hungry.'

'Neither am I.'

He sighed and we both ate a silent piece of toast. When he considered I'd had enough, he shook out a tablet and handed it to me. I gulped it down with a glass of water.

'How did you know?'

'There's no answer to that question. I just know.'

'That's no answer.'

I shrugged. 'Presumably you know when you're hungry?'

'Yes. My stomach rumbles.'

'Well, my brain rumbled.'

'On your performance to date I'd be surprised to hear you have a brain. Does it still hurt?'

'The pain is subsiding. I probably didn't need the tablet.'

'Put your feet up.'

'Why?'

'You're going to be out like a light in a minute.'

'You *drugged* me?'

'I gave you a strong painkiller, not Rohypnol. Relax, will you.'

'Will you still be here when I wake up?'

'I think we've already established there's no hiding from you. Close your eyes. I'm going to have a shower.'

I did as I was told.

I'd like to think my visit had made a difference but I would have been kidding myself. I blinked myself awake as he emerged back into the living room about half an hour later. Physically, he looked slightly better. He'd changed his clothes, shaved and washed his hair. He was still drunk but less drunk than he had been before. Otherwise, he was unchanged. His colour was still folded in upon itself, tight and defensive.

He seated himself at the other end of the sofa and we looked at each other. He sighed. 'There's no point in pretending is there?'

'No, but if you don't want to talk about it that's your decision. My hand is fine now. I'll just go home.'

I began to unwind the towel.

'No, leave it another thirty minutes or so.'

The silence went on.

Eventually he said, 'How did Ted put up with you for so long?'

'He's obviously a lot tougher than you.'

'Everyone's a lot tougher than me at the moment.'

'I'm assuming, by the state of you, that you've had bad news.'

He nodded.

'Clare.'

He closed his eyes. 'Are you going to make me tell you all about it?'

'No.'

'Do you want a drink.'

I didn't think he meant tea. 'No, thank you, but you go ahead.'

'I don't think there's any left. You would have been my excuse to go out and get some more.'

'I can wait for you to come back.'

'Could you just stop being so bloody reasonable?'

'OK. My hand hurts and it's all your fault.'

'Everything's my fault.'

I waited.

Eventually he said, 'I told you about Clare, didn't I?'

I nodded. 'Have they found her?'

'They have.'

You didn't have to be a genius to see it wasn't good news.

'They told me yesterday. She's dead.'

'Definitely? How do they know?'

He stared out of the window. 'Because they shot her.'

I was confused. 'Who's they? The people who took her?'

'No. Us. We killed her.'

I stared open-mouthed, hardly able to believe what he was saying. 'Why?'

He sighed and turned back to me, his colour a turmoil of scum and filth. 'She's been executed.'

I couldn't believe what I was hearing. We didn't execute people in this country. Did we? 'For what?'

'Treason.'

'But – does that still happen?'

'Sometimes. Oh, the public never gets to hear anything and certainly no one ever talks about it but there's a grim little factory unit in Droitwich with a furnace in the basement. They hold you while they decide whether to let you live or not. No one bothers with a trial on the grounds that if you weren't guilty then you wouldn't be there in the first place. They make sure you tell them everything you know and then they take you down to the cellar and shoot you. And there's none of this blindfold and last cigarette charade either. One to the heart and one to the head and then it's game over.

I was hot and cold at the same time, struggling to make sense of what he was telling me. 'They shot Clare? When?'

'Last week. She didn't die well, apparently. She was hysterical and cursing me and struggling with the guards so they knocked her to the floor and shot her where she lay.'

A hideous picture that made me feel sick. And how much worse must it be for him? I could see anger, grief, despair, guilt, and rage all roiling around him in shades of dirty sludge.

'They've had her since last week?'

'They've had her since January. It's taken them this long to verify her story. She wasn't very cooperative. In the end, she had to write her confession. They'd broken her jaw.'

I still couldn't believe it. I was being given a glimpse of a world I wasn't quite sure I wanted to know about. Like most people, I always assumed 'they' were on 'our' side. But as I'd discovered recently, 'they' were not who or what I thought. And I wasn't sure any longer of what 'our' side constituted either.

Not sure I wanted to know any more, but unable to stop myself, I asked, 'What did she do?'

There was a long silence and then he said heavily, 'She betrayed us. Betrayed me.'

'When?'

'After they broke into our house. The people who took me – they knew I wouldn't talk. That's why they didn't bother with me. They roughed me up, making sure she knew it would much be worse for her. Good psychology. Then they bundled her out of the house back to ... well, somewhere else. Where she gave us up. She gave us all up.'

'How do you know this?'

'She admitted it all.'

'Under interrogation?'

He nodded. 'Eventually.' Remembering the broken jaw, I decided not to pursue that.

'Do they know why she did it? Ideology? Fear? Given what happened to you, I could understand fear.'

'That's what our bosses wanted to know. They needed to know what she'd told them and why. So they sent for a specialist who "interrogated" her.'

My stomach turned over. 'Sorensen.'

'He's very good at what he does.'

It was on the tip of my tongue to ask if that was what he had wanted me to do too. To watch as the questions were asked. To stand, unmoved, as the 'interrogation' proceeded. To say 'Yes, she's telling the truth.' Or 'No, she's lying.' To participate in the breaking of another human being. If they'd had her since January then the timeline was right, but there were other, more important issues here. And I wasn't sure I wanted to know anyway.

'So, why *did* she do it?'

His mouth twisted in a bitter, ugly line. His colour wrapped itself around him once more.

'For me. Apparently, she did it all for me.'

I stared at him.

His lip curled. 'She said she loved me. Had always loved me. Apparently, they – the people who took us – had offered her a chance to get out. You see, not always, but usually the only way you get out of our game is in a box. They offered her – and by implication, me – a second chance. There would be a sum of money, new IDs, a fresh start in the neutral country of our choice. All she had to do was tell them everything they wanted to know. The alternative was too unpleasant to contemplate, they said, so what would it be? A very messy and painful end or a new life with the man she loved. She took the deal. Of course she did.'

'But they tried to drown you.'

'Yes, but she didn't know that. She thought she was buying us both our freedom. The problem was, of course, that having finally got all this out of her in the debrief, attention swung straight back to me. The initial assumption was that I'd been in it with her and they took it from there. I was hauled in front of Sorensen while he established by one means or another whether I was telling the truth. I'm wondering if that's why they'd brought you in. If you'd agreed to do as they wanted, then I would probably have been your first customer. Without you, it's taken them all this time to establish that I'm blameless as well as clueless. Because I really had no idea she was a security risk. None at all. I still don't think they quite believe me. I'm not back on active duty anyway. Probably never will be now.'

'Why not?'

'Because I'm a security risk, too.'

He stopped again. He seemed to be calming down a little. I, on the other hand, was becoming more and more furious on his behalf. They'd had Clare for months. All this time he'd been going out of his mind with worry about her and they'd had her all along. Playing cat and mouse with him. Waiting for him to betray himself with a word or gesture. Did he know this? Was he able to think clearly enough to have worked this out?

I was indignant. 'There's been nothing proved.'

His smile was tired. 'Doesn't matter. Mud sticks.'

'Get another job somewhere else.'

'Chance would be a fine thing.'

'Make a complaint. Kick up a stink.'

'Sweetheart, at the moment I'm only on some sort of unofficial blacklist. If I don't behave myself, they'll stick me on the sex offenders register.'

I was appalled. 'Can they do that?'

'They can do anything they like and if they do that then I'm well and truly buggered. I'll be dead in five years – either through drink or at the hands of half a dozen righteous citizens in a dark alley one night. Either way, problem solved for everyone.'

'I'll see you're all right,' I said, stoutly, not having

the slightest idea how, but it seemed to work because his colour lightened a little and swirled towards me.

'Thank you,' he said gravely. 'I appreciate the offer.'

'It's genuine,' I said, defiantly.

'I know. That's why I'm thanking you, but trust me – I'll never take you up on it. I'll straighten this out, you'll see.'

He stood up. End of conversation.

## Chapter Twenty-one

There was a lot there for me to think about. And I did. I emailed Jones nearly every day, not asking any questions but just so he would know I was here.

My life was very quiet but I wasn't unhappy. I often chatted with Colonel Barton. Occasionally, if he couldn't leave his wife, I did some shopping for him. I was invited to tea with them on one of Mrs Barton's good days. I joined the Local History Society and ate delicious cakes twice a month. I attended an art class at the library and drew an apple. Everyone congratulated me on my realistic interpretation of a pear. Nothing was flashy or exciting, but I was enjoying my new life. I kept my little house clean and Ted had his fresh flowers every week. I had my new start and I was happy.

Autumn was pleasant, mild and windy, with leaves everywhere and the smell of bonfires. I went to the public fireworks display in Archdeacon's Park and ate too many hot dogs. Over there was the bench where I had been sitting when Sorensen's creepy stalker and his puppy had turned up. What a long time ago that seemed now.

Jones occasionally responded to my emails, enquiring after my health. He never said anything about himself or where he was or what he was doing. I was uneasy about him, but the tone of his emails was cheerful. I gathered, more from what he didn't say than from what he did, that he was working again. That he had at least partially regained his security clearance and been accepted back into the fold.

And then one day I opened the front door to find him standing on the top step, his colour curling around him and looking better than I'd seen him for a long time.

'Nice,' he said, stepping back and looking up at the house. 'Bet you're glad you listened to me now.'

I waved to the colonel and his wife sitting in their window and asked if he wanted to come in.

'Will there be room?' he said, doubtfully.

'As long as you don't wave your arms around or stand on tiptoe you should be fine.'

Once inside he was into everything, of course, pulling open cupboards, peering out of the windows and trying out the sofa for comfort. He had to turn his shoulders slightly sideways to get up the stairs, but once on the landing he inspected the bathroom minutely and gave the bedroom his seal of approval from the doorway.

'Not bad,' he pronounced eventually. 'Of course, older properties like this will always have death-watch beetle, wet rot, dry rot, woodworm and subsidence, but other than that it's not a bad little house.'

I told him his approval meant I could now sleep at night and enquired exactly why he was here.

'Christmas,' he said.

I stared at him and he sighed. 'What are you doing for Christmas, Cage?'

'I hadn't actually given the matter any thought.'

He peered closely at me and I couldn't meet his gaze. I hadn't been looking forward to this, my first Christmas without Ted. This time last year he'd still been alive and I'd been trying to get out of going to that stupid Christmas party. I swallowed hard and blinked away my tears.

'Only,' he said, apparently not having noticed, 'I wondered if you wanted to have it at my place.'

'Have what?'

'*Christmas*, Cage. Concentrate.'

'At your place?'

He sighed. 'Obviously, I'm going to have to bring things down to a level easily understood by those with only a very basic comprehension of the world and how it works. I'm inviting you to spend Christmas with me, Cage. Please let me know if there were any words there you didn't understand.'

'But why?'

'Because that's what people do, Cage. They spend Christmas together. Person A – that would be me – trots round to Person B – that would be you – and says, "Hey, Person A. Do you fancy spending Christmas at my place?" And Person B remembers her manners – really, Cage, were you raised by wolves? – and says, "Oh, how kind of you. I'd be delighted. Can I bring anything?" And Person A says "No, of course not, just bring yourself." And then Person B says ...'

'Yes, all right,' I said, because this showed signs of going on for quite some time.

'Well, what do you think? Do you want to come?'

I suddenly realised how much I hadn't wanted to

be alone this Christmas.

'Yes. Yes, I would like to come. Thank you.'

'Usually I'm working over Christmas. Gives the married people a chance to be with their families, but not this year, and I thought it would be great to have someone else to cook for. Can you come on Christmas Eve? We'll get tipsy in front of the fire and then you can sleep it off the next morning while I do busy things with sprouts.'

'Don't do busy things with sprouts on my behalf. I can't stand them.'

'Well that's a relief. Sprout-free zone it is then. So, you're coming?

'Yes, I'd like to. Thank you very much.'

'My pleasure. Pick you up on Christmas Eve afternoon.

His invitation changed everything. Suddenly, far from being something dark on the horizon that I didn't want to think about, Christmas became an event to look forward to.

I bought a big red poinsettia plant for my coffee table, put some fairy lights around the window without electrocuting myself much to Jones's amazement, and even wrapped a little tinsel around Ted's photo.

'That red thing looks nice,' said Jones. 'Very Christmassy.'

'It's a poinsettia.'

'You needed a spot of colour in this room and that does it nicely. How did you get the fairy lights to work? Are they on a two or three pin plug?'

'Two,' I said, winding him up. 'I shoved a

teaspoon in the third hole and everything worked perfectly. By the way, do you have an electric drill?'

He stared at me. 'No.'

'Can I borrow it?'

'No.'

'I want to put up a shelf in the bathroom.'

'No.'

'The shelf is already assembled. I just need to drill a couple of holes. It won't take a minute.'

'No.'

'I'm not asking you to do it.'

'Just as well.'

'Is this some man thing where women aren't actually allowed to handle power tools because it dispels the masculine mystique?'

'Look, it's all we have left. Women are everywhere doing everything better than we can. For God's sake, leave us our power tools.'

'Fine. I'll buy my own drill.'

He sighed. 'Show me.'

I showed him the pre-assembled shelf and indicated its potential position in the bathroom.

'I'll bring my drill round tomorrow, but only so you don't bring the wall down by trying to do it yourself.'

I said demurely, 'Thank you.'

December flew by. Carol singers came and went. And came back again for the TV cameras who wanted to film them against the backdrop of the floodlit castle. I opened the front door to hear them, huddled in my coat and listening to all my childhood favourites.

Colonel and Mrs Barton were in their window as

usual. She looked unusually animated, smiling and waving. I did hope she would be having a few 'good days' around Christmas. I was invited in and the colonel got out his special sloe gin. I'm not entirely clear as to the rest of the evening's events. The colonel later said we'd had a bit of a sing-song, but that didn't sound like me at all. Still, as I said to Jones later after listening to some unkind remarks at my lack of stamina, at least I woke up in my own home.

He came to collect me on the afternoon of Christmas Eve. I was all packed and ready to go. I'd dithered for ages over what to wear. Black didn't seem appropriate, so I pulled out a long thick red tunic to wear over jeggings. If I was going to Christmas lunch, then I was going to need an elasticated waist.

I stacked my suitcase by the door, together with the carrier bag of gifts and my contributions to the festivities, and went to sit in the window seat to wait for him. I didn't normally do that and was quite surprised to find I was more excited than I'd thought I would be.

The last light was going. It would be dark soon. There weren't many people about. By now, most people were either at home or racing, panic-stricken around the shops for all the last-minute things they'd forgotten.

Here he came. I watched him stride through the arch and along the cobbled path. He was muffled up against the cold, his breath clouding around his head and with his colour streaming behind him like a comet's tail. I suddenly thought how much happier he looked these days, compared with when I had first met him. I thought of the black areas and how thin his colour had been. A lot of that had been anxiety over Clare. True, the news had not been good but now at least he knew. Now he could deal with things in whichever way he thought best and move on.

I had the door open as he ran up the steps.

'Did you see the weather forecast this morning?' he said, picking up my suitcase even though I was perfectly capable of carrying it myself. 'It's going to snow. We're going to have a white Christmas. I can't remember the last time that happened in Rushford. Have you got everything?'

I said 'Yes' and pulled the front door to behind me.

'Right,' he said. 'Off we go.'

It was bitterly cold with a heavy sky overhead. I could hear carol music in the background. I think they were having a concert in the castle. All around the square the lighted windows were bright with tiny Christmas trees, even in my neighbours on the other side. They were very jolly for solicitors. There were lights and colour everywhere.

We walked down the hill and across the bridge. I looked at the lights reflected in the water. This side of town was much busier and much more crowded. Very cheerful office workers were spilling in and out of the pubs. Crowds thronged the pavements and the bright lights in the shop windows made the sky seem even darker.

He carried my suitcase for me, although not without complaint, and a few demands to know what I'd got in there. We dodged our way through the crowds until finally we were able to turn into the quieter streets, and eventually to his apartment block.

It seemed very warm after the cold chill outside. We used the lift this time, purring our way up to the fourth floor.

'Enter,' he said, flinging his front door open with a flourish and I stepped past him.

'Seriously, Cage, have I taught you nothing? You jump into stolen cars at the drop of a hat and now here you are strolling into a strange man's house.'

'None stranger,' I agreed, while he stopped to work out what had gone wrong with his last sentence.

I had more time to look around me this time. His flat was small, but well lit. An L-shaped corridor lay before me.

'You're down here,' he said, nodding to the left. At the end was a surprisingly large bedroom. The curtains were drawn and the lights down low, making it look warm and welcoming.

'This is actually the master,' he said, 'with the *en suite* through there, but I prefer the second bedroom. It's smaller, but accesses the family bathroom which is bigger. I could barely get into that little thing.'

It was indeed a small bathroom, but perfectly adequate for the needs of a normal person. As I informed him.

'I'm ignoring the fact you've been here only two minutes yet you've already managed to insult both your host and his bathroom. I'll leave you to unpack. Yell if you need anything. I'll be in the kitchen.'

I unpacked slowly. Everything he had was of very good quality. I was especially impressed by the chest of drawers. In my house, because of the wonky floors, I have to open the drawers in a particular order. The top drawer won't open unless you open the second one first. The third drawer won't open at all unless the second one is open which means you can't access the third one and you can only close the second one if the top one is open. After a while I'd got used to it, whipping drawers in and out without a second thought. Here, drawers one, two, three and four opened perfectly. And in any order. Obviously, there was a certain novelty value in this, but I could see it would soon become quite dull. On the other hand, I wouldn't be cursing because I couldn't access my underwear.

I laid my stuff out in the bathroom. 'Second bathroom' he might call it, but it was still more sophisticated than mine. The shower was one of those multi things with more knobs and dials than a 747 jet. I decided I'd stick to the bath.

The bed was comfortable and the view from the window showed the river, the medieval bridge and the romantically floodlit castle. It was dark now, but I must remember in the morning to check whether he really could see my house from here.

I splashed my face and hands with water, brushed my hair and wandered back into the living room.

'There you are at last,' he said, emerging from the kitchen and turning the light out after himself. 'You were taking so long I wondered if you'd discovered a secret passage or were doing battle with a werewolf.'

'Strangely, none of those things ever happened to me before I met you.'

'I try to bring a little something special to other people's lives. Now – what would you like to drink?' He reeled off a bewildering list. I wondered again about his drinking, but his colour was bright and clear and swirling happily around his head.

'Orange juice, please.'

'Seriously? At Christmas?'

I sighed. 'Wine, please.'

He reeled off another bewildering list. I waited until he'd finished and then said, 'White.'

He sighed. 'I can see there are huge gaps in your education.'

'I don't drink a lot.'

'Nevertheless, it's not in my nature to shirk a challenge. Let's start with … this one. Crisp, cool and fruity. What do you think?' He handed me a glass.

'Mmm. Very nice.'

'You're not exactly the wine whisperer are you?'

I took another sip. 'I'm getting it now. Hairspray, sardines and pomegranates with top notes of creosote.'

'I'm spending Christmas with a savage,' he said, looking remarkably relaxed about it, and seating himself next to me and picking up the TV remote. 'I know it's a bit like a busman's holiday, but do you fancy a Christmas ghost story?'

## Chapter Twenty-two

When I awoke the next morning there was a moment when I couldn't think where I was. Everything was very silent and still. Like a Christmas carol. And then I remembered – it was Christmas and I was in a strange bed. There was the usual visitor uncertainty. Is it rude to get up before your host? Should I stay where I was until I heard movement? If I did get up I might wake him. I haven't stayed in that many unfamiliar houses. Is there proper etiquette for this sort of thing?

I rolled over and sat up at the same moment that Jones knocked at the door. 'Are you awake, Cage?'

'No.'

'I've brought you some tea.'

'In that case ...'

He opened the door and came in, bringing the smell of good things with him. 'Merry Christmas.'

'And to you too.'

'I've been toiling since dawn,' he announced, putting a mug of tea on the bedside table and drawing back the curtains. 'And guess what?'

I reached for the tea. 'You forgot to defrost the turkey. It's fish fingers for lunch with sprouts, stuffing and cranberry jelly.'

He ignored that, turning from the window, his face full of excitement. He looked like a gigantic ten-year-old boy. 'It's snowing.'

I pushed back the bedclothes and joined him. 'Really? On Christmas Day? That's wonderful.'

And it was. It was snowing. On Christmas Day. Not a lot, but a light sprinkling of white covered the roofs below me.

'And there's more to come,' he said. 'Now get back into bed.'

I regarded him suspiciously. 'Why?'

'Because you can't have breakfast in bed if you're standing in the middle of the room, can you?'

I scrambled back into bed and he reappeared a few minutes later with a tray. Scrambled eggs, smoked salmon and Bucks Fizz.

I couldn't believe it. 'I'm drinking champagne in bed at half past eight in the morning?'

'Better than that,' he said smugly. 'You're drinking champagne in bed at half past eight in the morning with me. Move your legs.'

He made himself comfortable at the bottom of the bed and we tucked in together, stopping occasionally to draw each other's attention to the falling snow. I thought about how comfortable we were with each other

We took our time and had two glasses each. He collected the trays. 'I must go. Six course meals don't just cook themselves you know.'

'*Six* courses?'

'Don't panic – it's not a Henry VIII style banquet. Just a series of light courses. We're starting with smoked salmon and cream cheese crostinis, followed by broccoli and almond soup, followed by prawns with mango, mint and tomato. Having warmed ourselves up nicely, we'll move smoothly on to the main event – crispy roast turkey, served with all the trimmings. I don't like Christmas pudding and I know you don't consider anything a proper meal if the word chocolate doesn't figure in it somewhere, so we have chocolate brownies with coffee cream. Followed by cheese and biscuits with grapes and nuts. Followed by mints. Followed by coffee.'

I stared, open-mouthed. 'Wow.'

'Yes, take your time about getting up. I shall be in the kitchen with my arm up a turkey's bottom.'

'How enticing that sounds.'

'Lunch is in five hours, Cage. If you start now you might just manage to look presentable in time to join me.'

He disappeared. I finished my Buck's Fizz and wandered over to the wardrobe.

I showered, dressed, made an effort with my hair, put on a little make-up – not too much – and tidied my room. Finally, I picked up his present and made my way into the lounge. Where the smell of good things was even stronger.

'Hey,' he said, coming in from the kitchen. 'Merry Christmas.' He looked relaxed and happy. His colour swirled gently around him and then reached out for me.

I smiled back because I felt relaxed and happy too. 'Merry Christmas.'

'You look very pretty. I like that red thing. Very festive.'

'Thank you. Something smells good.'

'It all smells good,' he said sternly. 'And just a word of warning – you don't go home until it's all eaten up. No matter how long that takes.'

I smiled up at him. 'Thank you for asking me.'

'Thank you for coming.'

'So, what's the plan?'

'Well, I thought you could open your present. Because I've bought you one. I'll bask in your gratitude and then we'll have a drink, sit in the window and watch the snow and just chat.' He looked suddenly uncertain. 'Unless you think that sounds a bit dull.'

I thought it sounded lovely. 'Well, I'm a little disappointed at the lack of a fly-past, or performing elephants, or an appearance of the Dagenham Girl Pipers, but I'm a guest and must remember my manners, so I'm going to say it sounds very nice.'

'You're such a shrew,' Cage, he said, amiably. 'The thought of spending the next two days in your company makes my heart sink.'

I handed over his present. 'Perhaps this will cheer you up.'

'A present? For me? Cage, you shouldn't have.'

'I know,' I said, 'but the thought of getting rid of you for a week was irresistible, so I consider it money well spent.'

He ripped it open. I'd bought him a fishing holiday in Scotland. His colour soared. He was genuinely delighted; I could see it.

'This is wonderful, thank you.' He looked at me, grinning all over his face, and said, 'Would you like to come?'

There was a small but very important silence. Like the moment just before midnight strikes.

274

I said, 'Fishing?'

'If you like. Or you can walk. Or sit and read a book on the riverbank. No, you're right. It does sound a bit dull.'

I looked down at my hands. 'No, I'd like to come. I really would.'

'Well ... good. I'll arrange it. I hope you won't be bored. Although with our luck, we'll probably stumble over the Loch Ness Monster or the ghosts of the massacre at Glencoe. Here, I've got something for you. Hope you like it. Careful now.'

I unwrapped it very carefully and held it up to the light. He'd bought me a beautiful red lacquered bowl. It glowed in my hands. I loved it.

He was fussing with the wrapping paper, not looking at me. 'It was nearly an electric drill but I'm not sure the world is ready to allow you unfettered access to power tools.'

'It's beautiful.'

'I'm glad you like it. I thought, when I saw that red plant you bought ...'

'The poinsettia.'

'That's the one. I thought how nice it looked, but this will be permanent.'

I smiled. 'Thank you.'

'And thank you for my fishing trip.'

We sat for a while, drinking coffee with something alcoholic in it and nibbling mince pies. In vain did I protest I was saving myself for lunch. Apparently, you have to have mince pies to alert your digestive system that something really major is on the way. He was very determined so I gave in. It seemed the easiest thing to do.

We sipped and watched the world turn slowly white. Jones chatted easily. Accustomed as I was to Ted's long silences, I wondered if he felt he had to entertain me. I told him it wasn't necessary.

'No,' he said. 'I like talking to you, but I can shut up if you prefer.'

'No. I like listening to you.'

Having said that, of course, our conversation immediately fell under a blight. We sat in silence, looking out of the window. From the corner of my eye, I could see his colour swirling and clumping. He was ... hesitating. Something important was coming. I waited.

At last he said, 'Do you miss him?'

I said quietly, 'Yes. Yes, I do. I think I always will. He was my friend as well as my husband.'

'You seem – I'm not going to say better – you seem different these days.'

'Well, I am. My life has moved on. I'm not the person I used to be. None of us are.'

'Does it still hurt?'

'Yes. And I think it always will, but time is blunting the pain. These days I can cope with it more easily.'

He stared out of the window again.

'What about you?' I said. 'What about Clare? Did you love her?'

There was a long silence. I was beginning to think he wasn't going to answer – which was in itself an answer – when he said, 'I don't think I loved her. I think I loved what we had together, which is not the same thing at all. Perhaps if we had had more time – I don't know. But to me she was just a colleague of whom I was fond. We worked together for a long time. Something was bound to develop, but for me at least, it wasn't love.'

Somewhere, something stirred. A cold draught touched my neck and the curtains moved. I shivered.

Jones got to his feet, muttered something about leaving the kitchen window open and disappeared. For something to do – and to dispel the moment – I took another mince pie. They really were delicious. When he re-appeared, I asked if he had made them himself.

He played along. 'Really, Cage, did your parents never teach you not to speak with your mouth full. Look at the mess. Crumbs everywhere.'

I said sorry and we began to talk of other things.

After an hour or so, he got up to go and poke something in the kitchen. 'Can you lay the table, Cage? Everything's all laid out ready.'

I looked around the table-less room. 'Where?'

His head appeared back around the door. 'Well, here on earth, we tend to keep our dining tables in our dining rooms.'

'You have a dining room?'

'You say that in much the same tones as discovering a banker has declined his annual bonus.'

'Sorry – I'm just accustomed to having only one room downstairs. In fact, I've only got three rooms in my entire house.'

'Well, I hope this brief but tantalising glimpse into the way normal people live their lives is inspiring you to become more aspirational in future.'

I shouted after him. 'You do know that, come the revolution, people with dining rooms will be the first against the wall, don't you?'

His head appeared back around the door yet again. 'That sounds rather fun. Will we be against the wall together?' And disappeared again before I could think of anything to say.

His dining room wasn't large and contained only a table with four chairs and another bookcase. By one o'clock the sky was so low it was beginning to get dark again and I had to turn the lights on to read the titles. I drew the curtains, shutting out the snow and the dark, and concentrated on making the table look good.

I threw a red cloth over the white one, laid the cutlery and carefully placed the white side plates. I set out the crystal wine glasses. The centrepiece was a matching bowl of red and green apples all frosted with icing sugar and ringed with holly and a red ribbon. I placed tea lights around the bowl and lit them. Serving utensils went at the end of the table. I folded the napkins the way my mother had taught me and, if I say so myself, the table looked good. When I turned the lights down low the effect was warm and intimate. Candlelight winked off the crystal glasses. Christmassy without being over the top.

I wandered into the kitchen, enquiring if I could help.

'Yes,' he said. 'You can take this, this and … this.'

I staggered slightly. 'What about you?'

'I'm bringing this,' he said, flourishing a peppermill.

Mince pies or not, I was famished. The crostinis came and went.

'Mmmm,' I said, watching my plate go with reluctance. What's next?

'Prawns,' he said, disappearing out of the door.

The prawns were a huge success. I ran my finger around my plate so as not to miss anything. My mum would have frowned at me.

Followed by the acceptable face of broccoli – in a soup – and accompanied by almonds. It was all fabulous. He really was a very good cook. None of it was massive, just a few mouthfuls of each course. And we were in no rush. There were long gaps between the courses during which he would pour the wine and we sat back in our chairs and talked. And then he would disappear only to reappear with something even more delicious and off we would go again.

A very great deal of time passed. The room was warm and soft music played in the background. I got up once to pull back the curtain and have a look out of the window. The snow still fell.

He did talk about what he'd been up to in the summer and autumn, and where he'd been, but only in the most general terms. Eventually, he said, 'Why am I doing all the talking?'

'So I can do all the eating.'

'I like a woman with an appetite but this is like dining with a hoover.'

I grinned at him and held out my glass for a refill. I probably shouldn't have. I remembered I'd forgotten my reservations about getting tipsy. The room was beginning to feel extremely warm and the candlelight was swaying around in a way I hadn't noticed half an hour ago.

'Would you have gone to all this trouble if you were on your own?'

He shook his head. 'Good heavens, no. Egg and chips in front of the TV probably.'

'Nothing wrong with egg and chips,' I said, stoutly. 'Food of the gods.'

He frowned severely. 'Do you eat properly?'

'Of course I do.'

'I mean, do you bother to cook for yourself?'

'Well yes, sometimes. Sometimes it's not worth the effort.'

'Interesting point of view. It's only worth feeding yourself properly if you have a man. Are you saying women without a man don't need to eat?'

'Of course not,' I said indignantly, swaying in my seat to make my point.

'Then why do women feel it's not worth the effort if it's only them?'

'We don't. I don't. I mean … I do, but I don't.'

'I see malnutrition is already affecting your thought processes. I'd better go and get more food. If it's not too late.'

He reappeared with a huge plate of chocolate brownies and a jug of coffee cream. I could feel my arteries giving way just by looking at it. He slipped two onto my plate and covered them with cream.

'There you go, Cage. Get yourself on the outside of that lot.'

I didn't need any urging. The first mouthful was just heaven.

'Mmmmm,' I said again, closing my eyes so it

would taste even better.

Even with my eyes closed I could see his colour streaming towards me. He might, to all intents and purposes, be concentrating on his own brownie, but I knew differently. If we turned out the lights I could probably have read by the light coming off him. He had the strongest colour I'd ever seen.

I put down my fork and thought. Was his colour stronger when he was with me? Because I was stronger when I was with him. Not only could I imagine doing things I'd never dreamed of but I actually had the courage to do them. To help Evelyn Cross. To face The Widow. We were stronger together. We sparked off each other.

I finished my brownies, scraped my plate, wiped my mouth, and cast about hopefully in case I'd missed a mouthful. 'Do you want the rest of your brownie?'

'Yes,' he said.

'What happened to family hold back?'

'What?'

'Family hold back. It's an old saying. If there isn't enough at a dinner party, then family holds back.'

He sighed and stared at me, screwing up his face in mock exasperation.

I smiled in what I thought was a beguiling manner.

'How much have you had to drink, Cage?'

'Well, not as much as you. I've never seen anyone throw it back like you do.'

'That's because you don't labour under the same trials as me.' He wouldn't look at me.

I said softly, 'Yes, I do.'

He didn't pretend to misunderstand me. 'Yes, but you have advantages I don't.' His smile twisted. 'You

281

know what I'm thinking before I've even thought it myself.'

I pointed out he didn't do too badly.

'Really? How do you figure that?'

'You are in possession of the last brownie. An intelligent man would use it to bargain with.'

'Seriously, you'd sell yourself for a brownie?'

'Well, we'll never know will we, because you're being so selfish.'

He cut off a small corner and held out the spoon to me. His colour flared suddenly and the room was filled with golden light.

'Come and get it then. If you think you're brave enough.'

I leaned forwards but couldn't quite reach. I would have to get up. Whether this was what he intended, I don't know. I do know I didn't quite have the same control over my legs that I'd had an hour or so ago, and had to sit, rather suddenly, on his lap.

He closed his eyes. 'You don't make things easy for me, do you?'

His colour enfolded the both of us. I felt warm and comfortable and safe. I rested my head on his shoulder. 'Sorry, I'm not with you.'

He sighed. 'You have many qualities, Cage. You're bright and pretty and I like being with you and you pierce my soul every time you look at me and you're here, now, with me, warm and trusting and very, very drunk.'

'You've had far more to drink than I have. And you're obviously not as clever as you think you are because you haven't noticed that actually, *I'm* taking advantage of you.'

'How do you work that out?'

'From this position, I have easy access to both the brownie and you. Tictacal ... tactical superiority.'

'You can barely say it.'

'Don't have to.' I lifted my head and kissed him, very gently. He tasted of wine and chocolate and coffee. The kiss lasted a long time. The room was very quiet. His colour was a fireworks display.

Eventually, he lifted his head. 'I shouldn't be doing this. I'm not a complete bastard, you know.'

'You're not a bastard at all,' I said, quite indignantly.

He sighed again. 'Yes, unfortunately I am.'

'Not to me.'

'You don't know as much as you think you do.'

'I know as much as I want to.'

He stroked my hair. 'It's too soon.'

'Yes, it is. For both of us. But one day it won't be.'

He kissed my hair. 'I shall look forward to that day.'

'I shall, too.'

One final kiss and then he sat up. 'In the meantime, madam, I must insist you return to your own side of the table and desist from this unseemly behaviour.'

'OK,' I said, standing up and slipping back into my own seat. Making sure I took his brownie with me, of course.

## Chapter Twenty-three

I began Boxing Day in a warm cocoon from which I had no desire to emerge. Being a butterfly is overrated. I would remain a warm, snug, duvet-wrapped caterpillar for the rest of my life. Unfortunately for this ambitious programme, a maniac was banging on the bedroom door. There was no ignoring him. I stifled a groan and shouted, 'What do you want? Leave me alone.'

He barged in, armed with tea and croissants and enthusiasm. 'Morning, Cage. Hung over?'

'No.' I said, surprised. 'I'm not.'

'Why not?'

'I think more to the point, why aren't you?'

'There's paracetamol here if you need them.'

'I don't.'

'Close your eyes.'

'Why?'

'I'm about to open the curtains. Ready?'

He flung back the curtains onto a glittering white world. I gave a cry and fell back on the pillows.

'It must have snowed all night. It's about a foot deep out there. Thank God it's Boxing Day.'

'Why?'

'We've had *snow*, Cage. And in winter too. The country will be at a standstill. Such rail services as still remain to us will be cancelled. Airports will close.

Local councils will order in grit which won't arrive until May. Power lines will fall. The army will be mobilised. Pregnant women will be dangling from helicopters like wind chimes. Trust me, the entire population of Canada will be laughing their socks off at us by lunchtime.'

'Good for them,' I said, slightly muffled by a croissant.

'Tell you what,' he said, turning back from the window. 'When you've finished your breakfast – in about fifteen seconds at the rate you're feeding your face – do you fancy going tobogganing? In the snow.'

It might have been my imagination, but did the day darken slightly?

'You have a toboggan?'

'Course not,' he said, grinning. 'We're going to make one,' and disappeared out of the door.

I thought he was winding me up, but when I took my tray back into the kitchen, he was wrestling a very large cardboard box and half a dozen bin liners. The cardboard box was winning.

'Here,' he said, impatiently. 'Can you hold this?'

'That's a big box.'

'My screen came in this. I've been saving it.'

'What for.'

'I told you. We're going tobogganing.'

'Oh no, we're not.'

'It'll be fun.'

'You can tell me all about it on your return.'

He paused, bin liner in one hand, duct tape in the other. 'Don't you want to come?'

'I have a headache.'

'No, you don't. You were very definite you didn't.'

I groaned. 'Trapped in my own web of deceit.'

'Come on. It'll be fun,' he said, ripping off great lumps of duct tape and doing something technical.

'Where will we go?'

'To the park. There's that hill that runs down to the river. Hold this.'

I held that.

'And this.'

I held that, too.

'And then we'll come back and have hot chocolate and watch James Bond save the world again.'

He grinned at me. I couldn't resist. 'Oh, all right then.'

The glittering snow made my eyes run. The bitter cold made my nose run.

Jones paused outside on the steps and donned a pair of aviator sunglasses, posing in the sunshine. 'Now I look really cool.'

The tragedy was that he really did. We set off. My nose was still running. I sniffed again.

'Could you walk on the other side of the road, Cage. You're not doing my image any good at all.'

I glared at him and he passed me a tissue and an old pair of sunglasses.

I put them on. 'Now I look cool too.'

He patted my shoulder. 'Keep telling yourself that.'

We'd had a frost as well and the snow had a crust on top of it. 'Deep and crisp and even,' said Jones, but it was a beautiful day. The sky was a rich, cloudless blue. Anything that wasn't a rich, cloudless blue was a brilliant white. Even ugly buildings looked beautiful. We paused at the park gates where the big Christmas tree glittered and twinkled in the sunlight. Half of Rushford had obviously had the same idea. There were lots of people with real sledges. I pointed this out to Jones who shrugged dismissively. 'Not one of them will be as good as ours.'

'Ours? You're not involving me in this. I'll wait at the bottom. With bandages.'

The park was full of families, all shouting at the tops of their voices and falling over. 'I've never seen so many children,' said Jones, looking around in bewilderment. 'Where do they all come from?'

'Well, when two people love each other very much ...'

'Don't push your luck, Cage.'

And dogs. There were dogs everywhere, having a wonderful time. Some were running about barking. Some were digging as if their lives depended on it. Several sat on sledges with their owners and were whizzing down the slope, ears and tongues flapping with excitement.

'That will be you,' said Jones, laying his gigantic piece of bin liner covered cardboard on the ground. I distinctly heard someone say, 'Wow, look at that. Cool.'

'It's never going to work,' I said.

'Yes, it will. We've got here just in time. The snow is all compacted. We're going to go like the wind.'

'The river's at the bottom,' I said doubtfully, looking at the wide, winding white Rush with just a narrow dark line of unfrozen water down the middle.

'We'll never get that far,' he said comfortingly. 'Now, you get up front.'

'Why?'

'You're my airbag. I'll sit behind you, hold you on and steer. Come on.'

There was no arguing with him. Very carefully I seated myself at the front.

'Hold tight,' he said.

'To what?'

'Me,' he said, wrapping himself around me. 'Ready?'

'Not really, no.'

Too late. We were off. He was right. We went like the wind.

'It's all the extra weight,' he shouted in my ear. 'That's why I brought you.'

I could hear people cheering us on. From somewhere along the way we'd collected a whole pack of dogs who ran enthusiastically alongside, alternately barking and snapping at the cardboard.

I could see my breath puffing in the bright sunshine and feel the icy wind in my face. We hit a bump that sent us off on a new path, leaving the dogs behind us, and finished the rest of the run backwards, facing up the way we had come. Despite my worst fears, we did not fall in the river but became entangled in some shrubbery instead. I fell off.

'That was brilliant,' shouted Jones, hoisting me to my feet and dusting off the loose snow. 'Let's do it again.'

We struggled back up the hill, which was considerably steeper going up than coming down and did it again. And again. We were challenged by two boys who each had their own tea tray and a few other people joined in. Someone shouted, 'Ready, steady, go,' and off we went again.

'Go on, admit it,' said Jones, picking me up and dusting me off for the umpteenth time. 'You're having a great time.' And actually, I was. 'Do you want to have a go on your own?'

I shook my head. 'No, but you do it.'

There was no chance for him. As soon as he sat down he found himself loaded up with small children. They clambered all over him. I think there was even a cocker spaniel in there somewhere. Either that or a very odd-looking child. Two parents launched them, they spun around and completed the whole trip backwards. They all fell off at the end, including the dog. Everyone was laughing. It was a wonderful afternoon. Jones was almost completely white, except for his face which was flushed with excitement and exertion. His colour roiled around him, such a kaleidoscope of peach, gold, pink and cream that I was astonished no one else could see it.

A burger van turned up and we both had hot dogs. Well, I had one. Jones had three.

There were TV cameras there and at their request, we all lined up at the top of the hill for a spectacular finale to a report on the meteorological phenomenon of snow in winter.

'Three, two, one,' and off we all went. It must have looked like a cavalry charge on cardboard.

'Hold on,' shouted Jones in my ear. 'Try not to fall off this time.'

And I didn't. We reached the bottom in one piece. I stood up and punched the air, shouting, 'Yes!' and two small girls and their mother, careering downhill completely out of control and unable to stop in time, hit me hard, and I crashed backwards onto the ice-hard snow.

Everything went dark but that might just have been Jones's head blocking out the sun.

'Cage, are you all right?'

'Yes,' I said, trying to lift my head.

'No, just lay still for a moment.'

I did as I was told, feeling the icy cold bleed through my clothes. 'No, I'm fine, let me get up.'

He helped me up. 'Are you sure? You look a bit shaken. Did you bang your head?'

'No. Not at all. I fell on my shoulder.'

'I still think I should take you to be checked out.'

'No, really, I'm fine.'

'Well let's get you home anyway. The sun's going down and it's going to snow again.'

He was right. We must have been here for hours because the sun had nearly gone. Ominous clouds were beginning to gather over the horizon. A snowflake drifted down. And then another.

He picked up his by now quite tattered piece of cardboard and offered it around. 'Anyone interested?' There was a storm of 'yes'es and we left them to it.

We were just leaving the park when his phone began to ring.

He cursed, pulled it out, tapped the screen and spoke. 'This had better be good.'

I knew it wasn't. He was silent for a long time which is never good in telephone calls. I stood and watched as his colour contracted around him.

'Can't someone else go?'

Silence.

'Can't it wait? The weather's not looking good.'

More silence.

Finally, he said, 'OK,' and snapped it shut.

'What's up?'

'Cage, I'm sorry, I have to go.'

'Go where?'

'Up north. Well, the Midlands anyway.'

I felt an icy fear that had nothing to do with the current temperatures. 'Not Droitwich?'

He smiled and put his arm around me. 'No. Not Droitwich. Promise.'

'For how long?'

'Tonight definitely, but I should be back by tomorrow lunchtime. I'm sorry about this. Do you want to stay at my place tonight or go back to your own?'

I thought about being alone in that big flat. 'I'll go home, I think.'

'OK. That's probably a better idea. I don't know exactly when I'll be back.'

'But you are coming back.'

'I'm definitely coming back.'

Back at his apartment, we gathered my stuff together which didn't take long and he packed a bag.

I gestured at the snow now beginning to come down quite heavily. 'You're not driving in this, are you?'

'No. I'm being collected.' He said no more and I didn't ask.

I felt quite sad to leave his flat. I'd enjoyed myself here. And there had been that moment ...

He seemed to sense this. 'I am sorry, Cage. It's a

pretty poor host who asks a friend for Christmas and then pushes off and leaves her.'

'It's OK. I understand. And I'll be fine at my place. And this time tomorrow you could be back again.'

He grinned down at me. 'I'd better be.'

We set off back to my house. The streets had emptied and the snow was really beginning to come down hard as we crossed the medieval bridge. We trudged along, heads down.

'Are you really going to travel in this?'

'I'll be fine. I'm more worried about getting you back home safely.'

We passed under the arch and out into Castle Close. I stopped. Even in the fast fading light it was a wonderful sight. The snow completely obscured the very few trappings of modern life that had made it up the hill, and except for the modern streetlights, the scene before us could have come from any time in the last five centuries. The outline of the castle was dark and dramatic against the lowering sky. The uneven roofline of the surrounding houses, with their twisted chimney stacks and brightly lit windows, a comforting contrast. The snow before us was unmarked. It would seem that no one had been out all day.

'Seems a pity to spoil it,' said Jones, 'but I must go and you should be inside.'

'You don't have to come to my door. I do know the way.'

'Certainly not,' he said primly. 'Heroes always see the heroine to her own front door.'

I sighed idiotically. 'My hero.'

'I'd better be. You're certainly my heroine.'

I wasn't quite sure what to make of that, but before I had time to feel embarrassed he picked up my suitcase and we trudged the last few yards, heads down in the whirling snow. As we passed the first streetlight I thought I saw a figure standing beneath it, collar turned up, hands thrust deep into his pockets. I wondered whether he was there waiting for Jones.

Colonel Barton was just drawing his curtains as we passed. He waved. We waved back. I decided I would call in to see them tomorrow and ask how their Christmas had gone.

I opened my front door, and suddenly I was home. I let the warmth and welcome of my little house wash over me. Jones put down my suitcase and handed me a carrier bag. 'I thought I'd better carry this myself since you're not too steady on your feet these days.'

I pulled out my beautiful red bowl and gave it pride of place on the coffee table.

'Very nice', he said approvingly. 'Now I must go.'

We looked at each other.

'See you tomorrow,' I said.

He turned away and then turned back again. 'I think both of us will need to take things very slowly but I want to try. Can we talk about this when I get back?'

'I would like that.'

We looked at each other some more and it suddenly seemed churlish to let him go back out into the snow without a kiss, so I stood on tiptoe and kissed him. He responded with such enthusiasm that I began to have concerns he would be late.

'Go,' I said, pushing him gently towards the door.

He laughed. 'See you tomorrow, Cage. Try to stay

out of trouble until then.'

'Pot,' I said. 'Kettle. Black.'

He ran down the steps and out into the snow. The wind had risen. The whirling snow had ceased to dance. Now it looked ... angry. I shivered. This was not a night on which to be out. I hoped he arrived at his destination safely. Wherever that was. I watched him tramp off out of sight. He marched straight past the figure under the lamppost. As he reached the arch, I thought he turned and waved to me just before he passed out of sight, but the snow was so thick I couldn't tell. I closed the front door, locked it and pulled the curtain across. It was a night for being indoors, snug and warm.

It didn't take me long to unpack my suitcase. I put everything out for washing, kicked the case under the bed and went for the sort of long hot bath you really need after being dumped in a snowdrift ten times in one afternoon. I put on some Mozart and lay back in the fragrant steam while warmth flowed back into my chilled bones. Wild horses could not have shifted me. At some point, I thought I heard the telephone ring, but it sounded so faint and far off that I thought I must be mistaken and I couldn't be bothered to get out and check.

It was hunger that shifted me in the end. It seemed far too much effort to cook anything, but soup and a sandwich in front of the TV sounded good. With luck, I might even catch the end of James and whichever world-ending peril he was saving us all from this year.

I pulled on a thick sweatshirt and jeans and still towelling my hair dry, I wandered across to the bedroom window to look out at the snow. Pulling aside the curtain I peered out into the night. Snow was still falling, white and silent. Jones's footprints had long since been covered over.

Amazingly, the man was still there. Still standing under the lamppost in a tiny circle of light. Except not the first lamppost any longer. He had moved. Now he was standing under the second one.

There are six streetlights in our close. When he reached the third one he would be directly opposite my house. I don't know what put that thought into my head. This was obviously just a man waiting for someone.

'In this weather?' said my common sense. 'And you were in that bath for over half an hour. And he was here when you arrived. And he's getting closer.'

As I pulled the curtain to and turned away, the telephone on my bedside table began to ring, but faintly, as if not enough power was getting through. I stared at it, wondering if the weather was affecting the electricity, although the lights seemed bright enough. No, it wasn't the power, it was more like ... as if the sound was coming from far away. From a great distance. I felt the hairs on the back of my neck lift. To calm myself a little, I took a moment to fold the towel over the radiator and then picked up the receiver.

There was a long-distance crackly noise and then, faint and far away, Ted's voice said, 'I have found you. You are about to die.'

# Chapter Twenty-Four

I panicked.

Slamming down the receiver, I backed away from the phone. As if that would keep me safe. My first thought was – is everything locked up? Can anything get in?

I ran from room to room, checking all the windows were closed and the curtains fully drawn. I switched on every light as I went. For some reason, it was important to flood my house with light. Overhead lights, bedside lights, even the old standard lamp in the corner. I switched on the mirror light in the bathroom and the spotlights in the kitchen. I even turned on the cooker light. I stumbled down the cellar stairs, dragging my fingers down the rough brick walls as I went, and checked the high window was closed. Which it was. In fact, not only was it closed but snow had piled against it. I could see the grey outline through the dirty glass. I left the light on in the cellar as well.

I knew the front door was locked and bolted but I checked again anyway, making sure the bolt was rammed home. And the back door. And the kitchen window. I peered cautiously through the blinds but the snow in my tiny backyard was unmarked. Nothing had been out there. I switched on the outside light. Dark shadows flew away and I could see the big padlock on the back gate was intact.

Everything was locked up and secure. I was as safe as I could be. I stood in the middle of my living room, panting slightly. My heart was hammering and I felt sick. Having no idea from which direction danger would come, I turned slowly, my eyes darting around the room, trying to see everything at once. To be ready. Ready for anything that might come at me. The only sound was my own rapid breathing.

The phone rang again. Louder this time and getting louder all the time. Or getting closer. The sound was strident in the silence. I stared at it. It rang again. And again. On and on and on.

I had a choice. I didn't have to pick it up. I could just leave it to ring and ring for ever. We've all watched those thrillers where someone is receiving threatening telephone calls and you keep thinking 'Don't answer the phone, idiot,' but there's something about a telephone ringing. You just can't help yourself.

I reached out, slowly picked up the receiver and held it to my ear.

Ted's voice was closer. Not so faint now, although the static-filled background was still there. 'Elizabeth. You are about to die. I am coming.'

Suddenly I knew *who* the figure across the street was. Now I needed to know *where* he was. I ran to the window.

He was standing under the third lamppost. The one directly opposite my house. Not twenty feet away, and barely visible through the swirling snow, but he was there. He stood motionless, his hands still in his pockets. His face still concealed by his coat collar, but it was Ted. I knew it was Ted. I whispered his name in disbelief. He couldn't possibly have heard me, but slowly, very slowly, he lifted his head and looked up at me.

My breath caught in my throat. I let the curtain fall and stepped back, panic shortening my breath and making my heart race. I was trapped. I couldn't get out the back way. The gate was locked and I couldn't remember what I'd done with the key. And I certainly couldn't get out the front way. Ted was there. And every time I looked he was that little bit closer. Where would he be the next time I looked? And why was he here? This was Ted. Ted wouldn't hurt me. Ted loved me. I'd loved him. I caught my breath. He'd loved me very much but now I stood on the threshold of a relationship with another man. Nothing much had happened yet, but it would. We both knew it would. Because life moves on and so do people. If they're allowed to. Was that why he was here? I couldn't believe it. I heard his voice in my head. *I have found you*. And then, *you are about to die. I am coming*. Had Ted loved me so much he would kill me if I even considered being with someone else? And most importantly, while I was wasting time thinking about all this, where was he now?

I ran back upstairs, intending to take a peep through the window, but as I burst into the bedroom, the extension began to ring again. I picked it up. I didn't even have to put it to my ear. The voice was speaking even as I lifted the receiver.

'You are about to die. I am coming.'

I slammed it back down, switched out the light so I could see without being seen myself, and ran to the window. He'd gone. Even through the whirling snow I could see the street was empty. Craning my head, I looked up towards the café and down towards the archway. The street was empty. Each streetlight had its own little nimbus of light around which the wild snow danced, but there was no sign of anyone anywhere. There were no footprints in the snow. No nothing.

Except, from here, I couldn't see my own front door. Suppose he was just on the other side. Waiting.

I looked back at the phone, sitting silently on my bedside table. Giving it a wide berth, I crept slowly out of my bedroom and back down the stairs, closing all the doors firmly behind me. I would have locked them, but the keys had been lost years ago. The house was completely quiet. Not a board creaked. Skirting the sofa and the coffee table, I crossed to the front window. The one that looked out over the steps and my front door. The one from which I could see if anyone – anything – was there. I should look. I must know. I told myself there was nothing to fear. He'd gone. And the phone was silent. I was alone. Wasn't I?

I don't know why, but I suddenly remembered the tale of The Monkey's Paw and of the broken thing dragging itself home.

My hands were shaking as I reached out for the curtains. On three. One, two ... I pulled back the curtain.

Ted's face was pressed right up against the window. Level with mine. Familiar brown eyes looked into mine. His hands scrabbled feebly at the window.

I screamed and fell backwards, nearly tripping over the coffee table. There were four steps up from the pavement to the front door. He must be more than six feet off the ground. How? How could he do that?

His lips moved and at the same time the phone began to ring, each ring louder than the last until the shrill sound hurt my ears.

I wrenched the curtains closed with such violence that the pole nearly came down and with that came anger. I would not be terrified in my own home like this. I found the telephone wire, traced it back and ripped the jack out of the wall.

There was a moment's silence – just long enough for me to sigh with relief – and then the phone started up again. Ear-splittingly loud.

Bewildered, I stared, at the jack, still disconnected from the wall. I could hear the extension ringing upstairs as well. In a fit of fear-inspired temper, I knocked the handset to the floor. The receiver fell off the cradle and lay some distance away.

'Let me in. Let me in.'

The voice came from the receiver. And from the voicemail recorder. And from the receiver upstairs still lying on its cradle. All perfectly synchronised.

'Let me in. Let me in. Let me in.'

And now it was coming from the TV as well. And from my laptop lying switched off and unopened on the table. And the little radio in the kitchen.

'You are about to die. You are about to die. You are about to die.'

The words were all around me. No longer weak and distant, as if coming from a long way off. Now they were loud. Demanding. Urgent. Surrounding me with a cacophony of sound. Ted's voice rose to a roar.

'LET. ME. IN.'

And then there was silence. A very long, very loud, white silence.

In the backyard, the outside light flicked on.

And then off again.

And then on again.

And then on and off rapidly, wildly – as if something was repeatedly passing in front of the sensor. Back and forth. Back and forth. He was at the back of the house. Looking for a way in.

I caught a movement in the corner of my eye. Slowly, terrified of what I might see, I dragged my eyes from the back door and turned my head. The wall that divided my house from Colonel Barton's was slowly bulging inwards as if under massive pressure. As if something hideously huge or hideously strong was seeking to push its way through from the other side. An intolerable pressure was building. I felt my ears pop. My jaw ached.

And then the wall exploded.

Thousands and thousands of tiny pieces of wall flew apart in front of my eyes. Like an exploding kaleidoscope. The force knocked me backwards. I sprawled on the floor, winded, staring up at the ceiling and thinking, get up, get up. You must get up. You'll die if you don't get up.

I rolled over, expecting to have to fight my way out from underneath rubble and bricks, and through clouds of choking dust, but there was none of that. Struggling to my feet, I found myself staring at an empty black space where my wall had been. I should have been peering through into Colonel and Mrs Barton's memory-filled sitting room but it wasn't there. Just a thick, black hole where the wall had once been - the entrance to a very long and very dark tunnel and I remembered, when Ted had been dying, the cold empty void in which I'd found myself. From this black tunnel, an icy blast howled. A chill wind cut me to the bone, yet didn't stir a single hair on my head or even move the curtains.

And still Ted's never-ending voice boomed on and on. From the TV, from the telephone, from all around me, rattling the windows and hurting my ears. 'You are about to die you are about to die you are about to die ...'

Something was coming. I could feel it coming. There was something hiding in the darkness. Something was drawing closer with terrifying speed. Oh my God, it was Ted – he was here and he was coming for me.

I struggled to my feet. My first thought was to get to the front door, wrench it open and escape out into the snow, but to where? Where could I possibly go? Who or what could protect me? All I would be doing was dragging the danger with me. I was suddenly conscious of how very alone I was. There was no one in this world to help me. No one *could* help me. No one could protect me from whatever was coming for me. There was no point in running. I had nowhere to run to. I had to stand and face it and I had to do it here, in my home. Where I was strongest.

I took a few steps backwards and set my back against the door to the stairs, feeling it behind me,

solid and strong. My head was full of the old rhyme –
*By the pricking of my thumbs*
*Something evil this way comes.*

Because something evil was definitely coming. I could feel it in the way my skin was crawling and the world was darkening around me. In the same way that once, all those years ago, I'd sensed the beige woman with the black spikes and known to keep my distance from her, here again was something that meant me harm.

I was shivering with cold and shock. And fear. Tears ran down my cheeks. Why me? I'd never wanted any of this. Why was this happening to me?

Never for one moment taking my eyes from the black nothingness in front of me, I felt behind me for the door handle. I couldn't find it and I didn't dare look around, not even for one second, because something in the blackness was moving. Something was growing larger with every second. Something was moving faster than humanly possible, crossing immeasurable distances in no time at all. Something blurred in front of my eyes and then, with heart-stopping suddenness, Ted was here.

Except … he wasn't. The shock stopped my breathing. It wasn't Ted.

I saw a woman, about my own age, slender, taller than me, barefoot and dressed in modern clothes – rumpled jeans and a dirty T-shirt. There was a bloodstained wound over her heart. Her bare arms were badly bruised, especially around the wrists, as if she'd been bound. She'd been beaten, too. One eye was nearly closed and her nose was crusty with blood and snot. A small trail of blood ran sideways from the ugly black hole in the centre of her forehead, as if she had already been lying on the ground when she was shot through the head. An ugly thought. I heard Jones's voice. 'One to the heart and one to the head.' What I could see of her hair was soft and curly except where it was matted with black blood. Most of the back of her head was missing and what remained was just a misshapen hole of grey matter and shards of white bone.

Her face was – or had been – human. It was her mouth that terrified me. Her mouth was wrong. Her mouth belonged to something else. It hung, huge and loose. Her lower jaw didn't seem to be attached to anything and swung as she moved her head. The movement made me feel sick and even as I looked her mouth fell open and dropped right down onto her chest.

I heard Michael Jones's voice. 'She had to write her confession in the end. They'd broken her jaw.'

I thought I'd been afraid when Evelyn Cross climbed onto my bed in the dark. I thought I'd been afraid when Thomas Rookwood took my sight and I'd been right – that had been fear. What I felt now was terror. Sheer, paralysing terror. Terror that took away my thoughts and froze my limbs. I could barely even breathe. Because this time – it was personal. I knew who this was. This was Clare. Or more accurately, this had been Clare once upon a time. And I knew what she wanted. She wanted me. I wasn't sure why she wanted me, but I could hazard a guess. Jealousy. Revenge. The hatred of the living by the dead. The resentment of someone who stood to have what she now never could.

Her lips drew back from jagged, broken teeth and she uttered a long, liquid snarl that went straight to my hind brain. In the same way that I had known, years ago, that the beige spiky woman had meant me harm, I knew now that what was standing here in front of me meant my utter destruction.

I would have screamed. I know I opened my mouth to scream for help. From anyone or anywhere, but no sound came out. I strained and strained, hurting my throat. No sound emerged. Not even a faint whimper. It was like the very worst nightmare come true. I couldn't scream, couldn't move, couldn't do a thing to save myself.

The noise was tremendous. From all over the house, Ted's voice was still shouting for me to let him in. The icy wind still shrieked. Why could no one hear what was happening? An entire wall of my house had disappeared. All around Castle Close, people were eating their evening meals or watching their TVs. Why did no one come to help me?

The answer came unbidden. I had to help myself.

And the thing I thought safely buried inside me, awoke from its long sleep, uncoiled itself and said, 'Fight.'

## Chapter Twenty-Five

I think there comes a place beyond terror. When things are so bad that human emotions simply aren't strong enough to express them. When a person travels through terror and comes out the other side. We hear the phrase – she laughed in the face of danger – and suddenly that made complete sense to me. Not that I was in any danger of laughing, but suddenly I found myself in that place beyond terror and my mind became an oasis of calm and quiet. I could think.

First there had been poor burned Evelyn Cross but she had only ever wanted to help others. And then there had been Margaret Croft. She had only wanted her son. Now there was Clare and she wanted me. The thought sprang into my mind. What would Jones do?

Well, that was easy. I could hear him saying it now. 'Stop screaming, Cage, and start scrapping. If you must go down, then at least let her know she's been in a fight.'

Good advice. I straightened up and we faced each other across my sitting room. Deep inside, I felt again that slow stirring of anger. This was my house. My home. This was supposed to be the place in which I was safe. Enough was enough.

Without any clear idea of what I was doing, I put out my hands, palms outwards in a gesture of denial and said. 'Go back.'

There was no authority in my voice. She sneered at me. I was going to have to do much better than that.

I couldn't understand why she hadn't reached out for me. My house was small. She was no more than five steps away, standing where my wall had been. She could just reach out for me and ... I had a sudden vision of being stuffed, head-first into that enormous mouth. The room swam around me. Desperately I took deep breaths. I couldn't afford to faint. She would be on me in a second. Despite all my best efforts, I swayed. Again, I heard that long, liquid snarl. The one that turned my blood to ice.

The one that made me wake up.

I found I was leaning back against the door – the only thing holding me up at the moment – and nothing had happened. For a few seconds, I was sure I'd been out of it. Not unconscious, but definitely not with it. And yet nothing had happened. I blinked my eyes open and looked at her.

She hadn't moved. She still stood as I'd first seen her. Why hadn't she seized me? I'd been in no position to defend myself. She could have ended things there and then. Was she toying with me? Or ...

She stood on the threshold, thick blackness behind her and with every light in the room shining in her face. Was it possible ... could it be that she didn't like the light? I remembered my instinct to switch on every light in the house. No, surely not. That was far too easy. The forces of darkness held back by the power of light. That couldn't be it. I was convinced it would take more than a few light bulbs from IKEA to hold back this particular force of darkness, but wherever she'd come from, whatever vast distances she had crossed to get here, suppose she couldn't actually step into this world. I'd been fainting, virtually helpless, and she'd failed to take advantage of that. She could just be mocking me, of course, taunting me with the idea that I wasn't completely helpless, but suppose I was right. All I had to do was stay here and there was nothing she could do. Because she couldn't reach me.

I straightened up, thrust my hands forward again, mustered all the conviction I could find, and shouted, 'Go back. Go back to where you came from'

As I spoke, all noise ceased. The wind died away. The phone, the TV, everything fell silent.

Long moments passed. Nothing moved. There was no sound at all and the silence was far more frightening than what had gone before. I suddenly thought, now it really begins.

She drew in a breath. A long slow inhalation that went on and on. She wasn't breathing – she was sucking. I felt an enormous pressure dragging at my chest, sucking the breath from me, pulling me towards her. She was holding out her arms in a welcoming gesture, inviting me into a cruel embrace. An embrace that would lead to my death. Or worse. The destruction of my very soul. The urge to take a step towards her overcame my fears. Unbelievably and without any effort on my part, my right leg lifted.

No! The thought slammed into my brain. No. I wouldn't have that. I remembered again my overwhelming fear when Thomas Rookwood had taken my sight from me. That dreadful feeling of helplessness and panic. That would not happen again. I was me. This body belonged to me. I would not have this.

308

I dragged my foot back again and at the same time, my groping hand finally found the door handle. It felt reassuringly cold and solid under my hand. Something to hang on to. And my escape route. If she couldn't get to me then all I had to do was keep my distance. To run away. I had no idea where to, but anywhere away from Clare seemed a good idea.

The handle wouldn't turn.

The door wasn't locked. There was no lock on this door. The handle just wouldn't turn. Still without taking my eyes from her, I tried turning it the other way. This was an old house. Sometimes things didn't work quite the way they should.

The handle still wouldn't turn.

I felt the pressure dragging at me. Pulling me away from the door.

Instinctively – without thinking about it, I put up my hands again, palms outwards to keep her off and said as forcefully as I could, 'No.'

The pressure eased, fractionally. She seemed puzzled for a moment. And then angry. Her prey was not as helpless as she had supposed.

She snarled again. A long deep note that ran right up my spine and made the hair on my neck rise and once again the thing inside my head hissed and said, 'Fight.'

I did. I summoned all my strength and pushed hard. For a moment – just for a moment – she rocked back on her heels but before I could do anything, she regained her balance and redoubled her strength. Inch by inch I was pulled away from the door. I tried to resist. I tried so hard, but just I wasn't strong enough to push her away. My head ached with the effort.

Whatever was giving her strength – hate, rage, jealousy, the desire to hurt as she had been hurt – she was far too powerful for me.

She was stealing my breath. The very air that I breathed. My chest was heaving with the struggle to drag in enough oxygen. My vision blurred. My heart fluttered like a panicked bird. I couldn't breathe in. I couldn't breathe out. My whole chest felt as if my ribs were in an enormous vice.

Like a giant snake, her blue tongue flickered in and out. Tasting my fear. Savouring it. Nothing I could do could hurt her. I had no way of fighting back. All I could do was fight her every inch of the way and struggle to delay the inevitable.

She was pulling me towards her all the time. My body was leaning at an impossible angle. I could only keep my balance by taking a step forwards. Then another, and another, and each tiny step took me that bit closer to my death. I fought to breathe. I kept telling myself not to panic. Just breathe slowly. Take in a little air. Let it out gently. I dared not take my eyes off her. She pulled. I pushed as hard as I could, but it wasn't enough. It just wasn't enough. She was inexorable. She would reach out, gather me in and consume me. This thing – Clare – would eat my very soul. The pace was quickening. She was winning. I couldn't hold her. I couldn't breathe. I couldn't see. I was fighting for my life and I was losing. I was growing weaker by the moment.

And then, as if I wasn't doing badly enough, I made a fatal mistake. Not daring to take my eyes off her even for an instant, my foot caught in the rug. I stumbled and fell forwards onto my knees.

Almost within touching distance.

Her shriek of triumph froze my blood. Her arms reached out for me. I tried to scrabble backwards but the pressure was bursting my chest. I tried to push her away, but there was nothing to catch hold of. She was as insubstantial as cold, greasy fog.

I was on the floor. I was helpless. She loomed over me. I remember the smell of her. Once, when I was out walking, I had come across the body of a dog. It had been dead for some time and writhing with maggots. The smell made my stomach heave. This was the same. The stench of rotting dog.

I tried to roll away, but none of my limbs would function. I couldn't move.

Her body was lowering itself over mine, her arms held out in some ghastly parody of a fond embrace.

Her mouth grew and grew until it was wider than my head and I knew she would eat me. Now there were no teeth, no tongue, just an unending blackness. A nothingness. My world was filled with a great dark void that would swallow me whole and it was getting closer every second. I would be lost. Lost for ever. No one would ever know what had become of me. I could smell her rotting dog breath. Feel my heart fail.

Her mouth grew wider and wider. Impossible, obscenely wide. Like a snake about to devour its enormous prey, she would devour me.

I tried to hold her back but she was far too strong for me. She had always been too strong. Everything was too strong for me. I realised now how unprepared I was for the world in which I'd found myself since Ted's death. I had something that was possibly a gift, but more probably a curse and I'd

311

tried to ignore it. I'd buried it. I'd run from it and that had been wrong. My dad had been wrong. I should have worked at it, honed it, learned to use it – if only to defend myself. Perhaps I should have let Sorensen have his way. If I'd placed myself under his protection and worked with him, would I be here today?

Her face was in mine. Her breath was on me. My stomach heaved again. I tried to twist my head away but I had no strength left and I was going to die. Her mouth was enormous. Bigger than the world. A nothingness. A great dark void that would swallow me whole. I closed my eyes and waited to die.

She stopped. Everything stopped. I was alone in a world of silence. I couldn't even hear my own heart pounding. It was as if the whole world waited. But for what?

I sucked in a desperate, painful breath, half expecting it to be my last. And then, unbelievably, another one. The pressure eased. I couldn't understand what was happening. Was I already dead? She was pulling back. I could feel her body sliding against mine. The world was so quiet I could hear the rasp of her clothing. The crushing weight lifted from my chest. I sucked in another great breath of air that didn't smell of rotting dog and opened my eyes. The expression on her face was one of puzzlement. For some reason, she was trying to twist away. Trying, it seemed to look back over her own shoulder.

It broke the spell for me. I kicked out at her, although I don't think she even noticed my puny efforts, rolled away, frantic to get as far away from her as I possibly could, and tried to get up.

Ted – my Ted – stood behind her, his arms locked

tightly around her, pinning her arms, holding her close.

She bellowed with fury, flailing her head and body wildly in her efforts to break free. Her monstrous jaw swung sickeningly. But all to no avail. Ted would not let go. She roared again and the sound rippled the air around her head. She was contorting herself in fury, and as I watched, her body exploded in a violent eruption of red and orange flames. I wrapped my arms around my head. The heat was immense. I could feel it radiating off the walls, but never for one moment did Ted release his grip. If anything, he hung on even more tightly as she twisted and turned and roared in impotent rage. My lovely Ted who had done his best to warn me. What strength must it have taken for him to cross that vast distance to come to my aid. Even to utter those few words of warning. I had misunderstood his message. I could see now that he'd been warning me I was going to die. He'd begged me to let him in and I had been too stupid to understand what he was trying to say to me.

I couldn't see his face. She was burning too brightly for me to look at her directly and everything else was just green and purple shadows. I so desperately wanted to see him again – one last time. What pain was he enduring at this moment? For my sake. But he never let go. Slowly he pulled her backwards, away from this world. Now the two of them were enveloped in raging flames. And they were real flames – I could feel their heat and see their dancing reflections on the walls. He was pulling her further away from me with every moment, but still she wouldn't give up. Her burning hands kept reaching out for me, clutching at me. The two of them were smaller now and getting smaller all the time. Her cries grew fainter, as if coming from a great distance. I could still see them, locked together in a fiery ball, tumbling over and over. Back into the black emptiness.

The wall snapped shut and there was nothing but a vast stillness.

Tears ran down my face. He'd saved me. Ted had saved me. At what cost to himself? I couldn't believe I'd ever doubted he loved me. My Ted. My wonderful husband. I couldn't hold it back any longer. Great, uncontrollable sobs hurt my chest and throat. I curled into a ball on the floor and cried for a very long time.

Hours later and I was still shivering from cold and shock. I made myself stop crying, and used the sofa to pull myself to my feet. Apart from the telephone on the floor, everything was as it had been before. I plugged in the jack and picked the handset up off the floor. The receiver sighed and very faintly, almost lost in the static of long distance, I heard the word, 'Elizabeth.'

I swallowed hard, holding the receiver tightly in both hands and whispered, 'Thank you.'

The crackling noise died away to be replaced by the dial tone. He'd gone. Where was he now? I couldn't bear to think of him locked in death with the thing that had been Clare, the two of them burning for eternity. He deserved better. I wasn't worth such a sacrifice.

I left all the lights switched on and spent the rest of the night huddled in a blanket on the sofa, with Ted's

314

photo clutched to my chest, hardly daring even to blink, let alone go to sleep. I couldn't stop shivering. That icy wind had frozen me to my very core.

I couldn't tell when dawn happened. I suppose the sun must have risen but the cloud was too heavy for it to break through. Everything outside was white. Shapes were rounded and unfamiliar. Everything was silent. There was no life anywhere. No birds, no people. Even the ducks and swans had disappeared. The whole world was filled with white silence. I sat on, barely moving. Only when I really, really had to go to the loo did I move, and, even then, I was up and down the stairs as fast as my stiff legs would carry me.

Once I was up, I walked around the house, still wrapped in my blanket, checking the doors and windows and switching off the lights. I made myself some tea, waiting for the water to boil while standing with my back to the worktop, always watchful. Suppose she came back. Suppose, somehow, she managed to break free …

My hands were still shaking as I poured the tea. I hadn't realised I was so thirsty and cold. I gulped the scalding liquid as fast as I could get it down, and then poured myself another. Taking it over to the window seat, I sat and waited for Michael Jones.

315

# Chapter Twenty-Six

I sat for what felt like for ever, straining my eyes to see through the still falling snow, although it was dancing again now, rather than whirling furiously in the wind. There wasn't a sign of anyone anywhere. No one was outside shovelling. No children were building snowmen while their parents cleared the paths. Everyone was staying inside in the warm.

The TV was full of weather warnings. We were warned to brace ourselves for blizzards and freezing conditions. I added Jones not being able to get back today to my quite long list of things to worry about.

I barely moved all day. The TV told me it was only just past noon, but already the lights were coming on again around the close. Seeing them was something of a relief. I was beginning to wonder if I was the only person left in this strange white world.

I pulled my blanket around me and was watching the world grow dark again when the telephone rang, jolting me out of my half-sleep. I stared at it for a few seconds, just to check I had remembered to plug it back in again. Taking two or three deep breaths, I picked up the receiver, gripping it tightly, and waited.

No one spoke. There was complete silence at the other end. Not a sound. My hands were suddenly clammy. Was it all beginning again? My stomach turned over in sick horror because I was certain I had no strength left in me to go through that again.

The receiver crackled. 'Cage? Cage, are you there? Say something.'

Overwhelming relief caused my legs to sag. I had to clutch at the back of the armchair to hold myself up.

'Cage? Can you hear me?'

I nodded, cursed myself for an idiot, cleared my throat and said, 'Yes. I'm here.'

'Look, I can't talk now, but I'm on my way back.'

I managed to say, 'That's good news.'

'I'll be with you in about thirty minutes.'

'I can't wait to see you.'

'Me neither. Thirty minutes.'

Nothing had changed, but for me, suddenly everything was different. Jones was on his way back and the world was a better place.

I sprinted upstairs, showered quickly, threw my clothes into the laundry basket because I never wanted to see them again, dressed again. brushed my hair, and raced back downstairs. I switched on the kettle even though I was pretty sure he'd want a whole St Bernard's worth of brandy after all that snow, and waited by the window, noticing that, at last, the snow had stopped.

I didn't have long to wait because he was here in minutes, appearing through the archway and kicking up the snow like a small boy. His were the first footprints in the virgin snow, spoiling the white perfection. Whatever the reason for his absence, I could see he was happy to be back. He was surrounded by an outline of flickering gold and red, the only colours in today's strange white world. He looked up and saw me waiting at the window and his whole colour jumped in anticipation.

I watched him wave to the Bartons next door. They must be sitting in their window, as I was in mine. I could see the rectangle of light from their window streaming out over the snow.

I opened the front door just as he was coming up the steps, grinning all over his face. I gave him a huge hug, holding on tight.

'Hey, what's this?' he said, giving me a huge, snowy hug back again. 'Everything all right?'

'Yes, but I have something to tell you. Something happened while you were away. Come in.'

I stepped back and closed the door on the icy white silence outside.

He shrugged himself out of his heavy coat, tossed it on the sofa and turned around.

For a moment, he was just Michael Jones – all smiling eagerness – and then ... something happened. I don't know what. I barely had time to register it but his colour disappeared. It just vanished. Completely and instantaneously. There was no gradual fading away. No slow diminishing. I'd never seen anything like it. It just vanished. To be replaced, a heartbeat later, by a glutinous, murky yellowy-brown. The colour of pus, thick, unclean, and reaching out towards me. I stepped back to avoid it and opened my mouth to warn him. I don't know what I thought I was going to say, but it didn't matter because I was never able to say it.

He drew back his arm and slapped me hard. The sound rang around the room. I staggered backwards, bewildered by the unexpectedness and the pain. No one had ever struck me before. Not in my entire life. It had been an open-handed blow but still hard enough to rock me on my feet. I put my hand to my face and backed away from him, wasting valuable seconds while my stupid brain tried to take in what was happening. He followed me, trapping me against the sofa and slapped me again.

Behind me, in the kitchen, the kettle clicked off. Distracted for a moment, he turned his head to trace the sound and I tried to slip past him and head for the door. He grabbed me, pulled me back and threw me against the bookcase. I felt myself fly through the air. Something sharp hurt my back and something else fell on my head.

I had no time to think. It was all happening so quickly that I still wasn't sure what was going on. Surely this couldn't be happening to me. But it was. Instinct left my brain behind and took over. Groping for some means of defence, I snatched up Ted's photo and threw it, left-handed, at him. He dodged it easily and it smashed against the wall. I wondered if Colonel Barton next door would hear the noise and if so, whether he would come to investigate.

In two long steps, Jones was across the room and upon me. There was a frightening lack of expression on his face. He could have been simply reading a newspaper or doing the washing up. He'd never said, and I'd ever asked exactly what his job entailed, but I was seeing it now. He was a professional killer. There was no emotion involved. I was a job he had to do and he was doing it as efficiently as he knew how.

Seizing my arm, he broke it. Quite easily and effortlessly. I heard the snap and felt the pain. I screamed and struggled to get away. It was vital to get some distance between us so I could rip open the front door and shout for help.

Again, he dragged me back. Holding me so I couldn't get away, he clenched his fist and hit me. Several times. Short, sharp punches to the ribs. Each one in exactly the same place. It was agonising. And professional. He knew how to inflict pain. He was standing on my feet so I couldn't get away. I was only aware of blow after blow. After a while, I was unable to distinguish the individual punches. Everything was a solid wall of hurt.

When he finally released me, I fell to the ground and he began to kick me. I felt a huge hot pain in my leg and a small part of my mind wondered if that was broken too.

I was crying and gasping. I couldn't catch my breath. My ribs hurt too much to shout for help. And who would hear me anyway. I still couldn't believe this was happening to me. That it was Michael Jones doing this to me. I curled up and protected myself as best I could. The thing in my head was twisting and spitting but it was as helpless as I was. Pain, shock and disbelief were the only emotions I was capable of at that moment. I wondered if he would kill me.

And then, dimly, I thought I heard something. Hope blossomed. It seemed too good to be true, but over everything that was happening to me, I could hear Colonel Barton banging on the front door.

'Elizabeth? Mrs Cage? Is everything all right in there?'

The kicking paused.

'Mrs Cage? Are you there? Please open the door.'

It was as if the intervention from outside world had jolted Jones to his senses. He stopped, his leg drawn back, his boot level with my face. I could see the snow still clinging to his soles. It filled my entire world. I held my breath. With his strength ... if he let go ... would I ever know anything about it?

I squinted up at him, still sobbing. It hurt so much to cry, but I couldn't stop. I lay helplessly at his feet looking up at him. He lowered his leg and looked around as if suddenly realising where he was. His awful colour wavered, the yellowy-brown colour fought for one moment with the golden peach and then disappeared.

He said, 'Cage?' more in disbelief than recognition, and dropped to his knees at my side.

I heard the rasp of my spare key in the lock and felt the blast of icy air as Colonel Barton opened the door. He limped in, calling 'Mrs Cage, are you here? May I come in?' because we're British and we don't just barge into other people's houses. He took in the scene at a glance. There was no blood – not that I could see, anyway – but there I was in a heap on the floor and it must be very obvious to him what had been happening here.

Jones turned to face him.

Colonel Barton was wonderful. He never hesitated – not for a moment. He thumped the floor with his walking stick. 'Step back, sir. Step back, I say.'

There was a moment when I feared for his safety, too. The colonel was old and frail and probably even less able to defend himself than I was, but his voice had all the authority of one who had commanded a regiment in a war and Jones stepped back. Perhaps he was drilled to respond to that military rasp, I don't know. He disappeared out of my range of vision.

Pausing only to yank off the tablecloth, the colonel knelt stiffly and carefully wrapped it around me.

'You're quite safe now, my dear.'

I heard Jones say something. I couldn't hear what.

'You will keep your distance, sir. If you wish to render assistance, then you may telephone for an ambulance.'

The world was blurring around me. Time distorted. There were people here who had seemingly come from nowhere. There were soft red blankets but nothing could warm me. I remember Colonel Barton telling me he would take care of everything. I remember thinking my life was finished. That there was no coming back from this. And then I closed my eyes. Because nothing was important and I didn't care any longer.

## Chapter Twenty-Seven

I sat cross-legged in a white box in a white, silent world. I was safe. The box encased me completely, protecting me from anything that might be prowling around the outside. It fitted me perfectly because it was my box. I'd created it just for me. My back rested against one wall, my knees touched the sides and my head grazed the top. No one could find me here. Nothing could touch me. I sat unmoving in an unmoving world. Slowly, now that all danger had disappeared, the thing in my head grew quiet and still, until finally, satisfied, it lowered its head and closed its eyes. I knew it hadn't gone. That it was waiting. I'd summoned it from its long sleep and it wasn't ever going away again. I wasn't sure I wanted it to. I'd had enough of being pushed around by the world. Of being betrayed by people who thought I was weak. I'd really had enough of that. I was stronger than I thought. I was stronger than everyone thought. One day, I'd show them.

I sat for a very long time. Long enough to still my mind and regain my composure. There was no pain here. No fear. Just me and the silence. The long, safe silence. I couldn't stay for ever, of course. I knew that, but I could stay for long enough. I leaned back, let my eyes close and just … breathed.

Gradually, very gradually, when I was ready, I began to let the world back in again. First, there was the occasional muted sound in the background. Once, I thought I heard someone speak my name. Voices came and went. And then, one day, I thought, now, and stood up. The fragile box shattered around me, but I was ready to rejoin the world. I opened my eyes.

Not surprisingly, I was in hospital. In a private room, it seemed, which was nice. Without moving my head, I let my eyes wander around.

No, I wasn't in hospital. I was back in my old room in the Sorensen Clinic. Of course I was. Where else would I be? It said much for the levels of sedatives and painkillers that I couldn't even be bothered to care.

A pleasant-faced girl with hazel eyes and freckles whom I remembered from my previous stay, leaned over me and said, 'Hello, Mrs Cage. Awake at last.'

I liked her at once. Her colour, a soft spring green, twirled gently around her.

'My name is Erin. Do you remember me? I'm a nurse on this floor and I've been assigned to you. I'm going to leave you for a moment to fetch the doctor. I won't be a minute.'

When I opened my eyes, Sorensen was standing at the foot of my bed, reading what I assumed to be my notes.

His dirty milk colour seemed remarkable restrained. He was holding himself in tightly. He looked up and smiled.

'Mrs Cage, hello. How are you feeling?'

I wasn't sure how I was feeling and my mouth felt dry and sticky and unpleasant, so I just nodded.

I thought he would come to sit beside me – Erin had put a chair ready, but he remained at the foot of the bed. A safe distance away.

'I'm not going to trouble you with talking about your injuries just at this moment. I shall leave that to Dr Lewis whom I'm sure you will remember. She will be your primary doctor. I want to assure you that I shall not be directly involved in your treatment. You have enough on your plate without having to cope with your dislike of me, but I'm here if you need anything. You have only to ask.'

I nodded again, suddenly tired, and when I next opened my eyes, he was gone.

Dr Lewis was here, however, standing in the doorway talking to someone I couldn't see. I used the opportunity to look around. Apart from the medical equipment, nothing much seemed to have changed although it was obvious this was now a hospital room rather than a bedroom. I looked down at my white hospital gown and the catheter in my hand and sighed. To distract myself I turned my head to look out of the window. The view through the window was equally discouraging. The patch of sky that I could see was grey, full of ominous, dark clouds swollen with snow.

While I was looking out of the window, she had approached the bed. 'Mrs Cage, I can't tell you how sorry I am to see you here. And I don't mean that to sound unwelcoming.'

Still not feeling like speaking, I nodded.

She hesitated and then said, 'Do you want to know the extent of your injuries?

Did I? Did I want to know what Michael Jones

had done to me? I closed my eyes. As if that would shut out my thoughts.

She put a gentle hand on mine. 'Another day then. There's no rush. The important thing you should know is that you're quite safe here, Mrs Cage. There is nothing here that can hurt you. Dr Sorensen has asked me to assure you that we only want you to be well. I know your last visit did not go ... quite as well as we could have wished, but you need have no fears this time. Now ...' she opened the locker next to my bed. 'Here is your handbag. Your keys are inside. Your neighbour, Colonel ... Barton?' She looked at me and I nodded, 'has your other set. He says he will keep an eye on your house for you. Especially in this weather. He telephones every afternoon to tell us everything is well and to ask after you.'

I felt my eyes fill with tears. He was such a lovely man. I saw him again, standing over me, heard him bark defiance at Michael Jones who could probably have snapped him in half without even trying.

I had to know. I forced my mouth open and said, weakly, 'Jones. Where?'

'He's not here,' she said, crisply and I could see she was telling the truth. 'I'm afraid I don't know where he is – they haven't told me and I don't particularly care anyway – but he's absolutely and categorically not in this clinic, Mrs Cage. You need have no fears. You are quite safe here.'

I nodded again, feeling my eyelids growing heavy. She patted my hand and left.

Initially I just slept. And if I wasn't sleeping then I pretended to. I lay in my bed, not thinking about anything and watching the snow pile up on the window sill. One morning it was over six inches deep. How deep must it be outside? I didn't speak much to anyone, but I smiled and nodded in all the right places and gave them no trouble.

'You're in the right place here, Mrs Cage,' said Erin one morning, brushing my hair for me. I'd said I could do it myself and then discovered I barely had the strength to lift the brush. 'It's a nightmare out there. It hasn't stopped snowing for nearly a week. They've had to mobilise the army to take food to the more remote areas and even they can't get through most of the time.' She caught my expression. 'Oh, no need to worry – we'll be all right. We've plenty of food here, and we have our own generator, not like some of the poor souls out there.' She replaced my hairbrush. 'You stick with us, Mrs Cage. Best place to be.'

She was right. We watched the news bulletins together. The weather was getting worse all the time. There were power cuts and food distribution problems. It was rather frightening and all the time the snow never stopped floating down from the sky, day and night. Was this climate change at last? Were we embarking on another ice age? The world seemed so silent and, apart from the snowflakes whirling past the window, so still. There was a feeling of unreality about everything. People were beginning to worry. I could hear the nurses discussing the situation as they worked. They were anxious for their families. Especially Erin whose family farmed in the Lake District.

'They're all right for the time being,' she said one

morning, straightening my bed covers. 'The army's dropping supplies from helicopters now and that'll tide them over for a bit, but there's food shortages everywhere. Nothing's getting through.'

They talked to me about my injuries. Not that there was much need – I could see my injuries. A broken arm, a bruise the size of a dinner plate over my ribs – which were cracked. As was my shinbone, also badly bruised. There was nothing that wouldn't heal. Physically.

I closed my mind to it. All of it. The disbelief. The betrayal. The pain. I would not waste my time in endless replays. I would not wonder what I could possibly have done to make him do such a thing. I would not spend hours trying to concoct plausible scenarios. I would not look for a reason. Or an excuse. I would not seek for something that would make everything all right again. I would wipe it all from my mind and move on.

My recovery was slow. Probably because I wasn't trying particularly hard. Fortunately, there weren't many patients. I remembered Ted telling me they always sent as many people home as possible at Christmas time, so I had three nurses altogether. Erin, my principal nurse, Keira and Beverley.

Surrounded by their protective clucking I began to move around. I had my first bath. They washed my hair for me. I think they fought over me behind my back. There were so few patients that they were desperate for something to do. As I said to them, the service here was superb. They laughed and said they were mostly trying to avoid snow-clearing duties. They were young and light-hearted and for them, this was all a bit of an adventure. I smiled. Compared to them, I felt about a hundred years old.

Dr Sorensen stuck his head around the door just once. He wouldn't come in, he said, but he had messages from Colonel Barton – everything was fine at home and he and Mrs Barton were very well, all things considered.

'I passed on your thanks and best wishes,' he said. 'I thought you would want me to.'

I nodded.

'You must be sick of this room. Get Erin to wheel you around a bit tomorrow. Go and have a poke around the library or have a coffee in the dining room. Nothing too strenuous, mind, but a change of scenery will give you something else to think about.'

I never thought I'd actually say this, but Sorensen was right. It did give me something else to think about.

Erin stuck her head around the door the next morning. 'Dr Sorensen's compliments and would you like to join him for tea this afternoon. He promises not to eat you.'

I looked up. 'Did he say those exact words?'

'He did. And I think he was nearly smiling too.'

'Do you think he's been replaced by an alien?'

'We all certainly hope so. Do you want to go? I can get you a wheelchair.'

I looked out of the window at the grey sky and the still falling snow. Suddenly the thought of looking out of a different window was very inviting.

'Yes, my compliments to Dr Sorensen, I shall be

delighted to join him this afternoon. I promise not to eat *him*.'

'Great. I'll find you a chair.' She disappeared.

We all enjoyed a small girlie flurry that afternoon as they found me a clean gown, did my hair for me and installed me in one of the hospital wheelchairs.

'Here you go,' said Erin, smoothing a blanket over my legs. 'Ready?'

'As I'll ever be.'

She wheeled me along the corridor, past the nurses' station and on towards the lift. Just as we arrived, someone called her name. 'Erin! Telephone call for you. It's your mum.'

She stopped. 'Mrs Cage, do you mind? I must find out how they're coping.'

'Of course,' I said. 'Take as long as you like. I'll just wait here for you.'

'Oh, thank you so much. I'll park you here by the window so you can see out and I'll be as quick as I can. Promise.'

She disappeared.

I was quite horrified at the view from the window. The gardens had completely disappeared under a blanket of white. Rounded humps denoted former trees, bushes and garden ornaments. Everything was just a featureless, undulating white plain. And still the snow came down. I felt a twist of unease. Suppose it never stopped. It would be bad enough when the thaw came – we were all going to be swimming for our lives – but suppose the thaw never came. Suppose this was our weather from now on. They say we have Stone Age DNA within us. My Stone Age DNA was very, very uneasy indeed and urging me to migrate south before it was too late.

I turned away from the window and sat quietly for a few minutes, just looking up and down the corridor. No one was around. I suspected they were all off having tea – as I should be. I sat back in the chair, closed my eyes and let my mind wander.

It was very faint to begin with. So faint that I only became aware very, very gradually. Like a door opening briefly a very long way away. I opened my eyes but nothing had changed. I still sat in a warm corridor, painted in shades of expensively neutral colours, looking out at a snowscape. I closed my eyes again.

Shit!

I jolted in my chair, hurting my arm, my ribs and my leg all at the same time.

Stop. Stay calm. Stay ... calm. Breathe slowly. I stared at my hands. It was very, very important that I stay calm.

Only when I had a reasonable amount of control did I look up. The corridor was still empty, as was the nurses' station behind me. I couldn't even hear Erin's voice on the telephone. The lift was only six feet away. I trundled towards it, careful not to hurt my arm and pressed the button. The doors opened immediately. Once inside, I closed the doors before anyone saw me and studied the controls. Second floor, first floor, ground floor. And the basement.

Taking a deep breath, I pressed 'B'.

The lift slid smoothly downwards.

I found myself in a familiar long corridor. Pipes

still ran along the walls – a little more neatly than they had done seventy years ago, and there were more of them now – but I'm sure I recognised some of them. And there were the doors to the medical supply storerooms, now all with keypad locks in this much less trusting age. Gone was the old furniture and piles of files – too much of a fire hazard, I guessed, but just above me was where the ceiling had come down, blocking our escape. The night we tried to save Evelyn Cross. Me and Michael Jones.

That thought reminded me why I was here. I wheeled myself out of the lift, hurting my arm and hardly noticing because it was just down this corridor here and off to the left ...

There were five doors on the right-hand side and all of them were open. I set off.

The first room was empty. I never found out what was in any of the others because the second was the one I was looking for. I stopped in the doorway.

It was a bare, bleak room. Not dirty – I'm certain that Dr Sorensen – that's Sorensen as in 'that lying bastard Sorensen' – wouldn't permit dirt anywhere in his clinic, but it was a far cry from the comfortable rooms upstairs.

I saw a bed – not against the wall, but at an angle in the middle of the room as if it had just been shoved in here as quickly as possible and left. Abandoned even. Next to the bed was a small wooden cabinet with three drawers. There was no traditional fruit bowl or water glass. The top was empty. On the other side of the bed was a drip of some kind. I had no idea what it was dripping. It was a clear fluid, so not blood, but further than that I couldn't say. A thin transparent tube ran downwards to the bed. And at the end of the tube lay the thing that had been Michael Jones.

## Chapter Twenty-Eight

I was more angry than I could ever remember.

No. Angry wasn't the right word. Anger didn't even begin to cover it. I was ready to explode with rage. Hot and cold waves of fury washed over me. I clenched my fists so hard they hurt. They'd lied to me. They'd all lied to me. Again. And I'd believed them. All of them. Again. Over and over they'd told me I was safe. That Michael Jones wasn't here. That I had nothing to worry about and all this time he'd been here. In the same building as me. He'd been here all the time. I could feel the blood pounding in my head, beating out a rhythm in time to the words. He'd been here all the time.

And running through all that, a cold vein of fear. Because he'd been here and I hadn't known. I had once sensed his distress across an entire town. I should have known he was here. Yes, I was ill and yes, his presence was very weak – I'd had to leave my room to feel it ... but even so ...

No, wait – I hadn't had to leave my room – I'd been invited out of my room. By Sorensen. I'd been taken from my room by Erin in all good faith. She'd certainly believed the telephone call was from her mother. I'd been parked near the lift. And there were cameras everywhere. I was willing to believe Sorensen knew exactly where I was at this moment.

I was clumsy with the chair, but I eventually got myself alongside the bed so I could see him properly. I knew it was Michael Jones because ... well, I just did, but his own mother wouldn't have known him. I could not believe such a change could occur in only one week.

My next thought was that I was too late. That he was already dead and I was looking at his corpse. His face had fallen in. Thin, grey skin was stretched tightly over sharp cheekbones. His nose stood out like a prow on a ship. His hair had mostly fallen out. A few sad wisps lay on the pillow.

No one had bothered to shave him. Patchy grey stubble covered his chin. He looked like an old man. A week ago he'd been – well, he'd been Michael Jones, vigorous and full of life and rolling in the snow – and now he was here, abandoned and cold and dirty and neglected. And dying.

I wondered if that was why I'd been brought here. To say my farewell. Unlikely. I couldn't see Sorensen giving way to a compassionate impulse. I was here so they could see how I reacted. I wasn't aware of it at the time, but I think that was the moment I made the decision.

I was having trouble catching my breath and I knew from experience that coughing was not something my ribs would want me to do, so I sat back in my chair, gripped my cold hands together under the blanket and struggled to be calm. The cold was a help. This room was freezing. Anger raced through me again. There wasn't much of him left and the bastards couldn't even be bothered to keep him warm.

He was, quite literally, a shell of his former self and what was left was diseased and stinking. His stick-like arms lay outside the thin sheet that was all they'd covered him with. His once solid body had caved in on itself. Michael Jones was no longer a big man. Worst of all was the smell. They say smell is the most evocative of all the senses and with just one breath I was back in my living room not a week ago, fighting against the endless void that lies beyond death, and smelling the rancid smell of rotting dog. Here, in this horrible room, I could smell Clare all over again and I knew what she'd done.

She'd used him to strike at me and it had killed him. I suspected Michael Jones had been dead since the moment he walked through my front door. His body had continued to function, powered by whatever malignant thing had been consuming him from the inside, but it had killed him. Eaten him up. He was strong – had been strong – but what lay in front of me now was just a burned-out husk. Her ultimate revenge on both of us. To use him to punish me and then to leave him with just enough awareness to realise what he had done. I remembered his bewilderment. He'd said, 'Cage …?'

My stomach heaved. What was in front of me were the final remains of Michael Jones, used and discarded. Rotting from the inside out. The stench of putrid flesh was overwhelming. I couldn't help it – I gagged, vomiting up my lunch onto the bare concrete floor.

I found a tissue in my pocket, wiped my mouth and threw it away. I would sit here for a moment, regain my composure, then return to my room. And after that … after that, there would be … revenge.

He opened his eyes. Even his eyes were different. A runny, watery blue. Almost colourless. The whites were yellow, shot through with blood where the delicate veins had burst. Like an egg, poached in blood.

He saw me and all at once I saw a little flicker of gold, just over his heart. Just a tiny flicker. Like a match struck in the vastness of a dark night.

I put my hand on his, feeling his cold dry skin beneath my touch.

He made a faint inarticulate sound and tried to pull his hand away. Shame and humiliation very nearly extinguished his little flame. I tightened my grip. 'Michael, it's me. Can you hear me?'

A tear trickled down his cheek.

Now I knew why what I had to do. Ignoring the stench, I leaned forwards.

'Can you hear me?'

He nodded very slightly. Another tear ran down the track of the first one. A glistening trail to be lost in his stubble.

'It wasn't you. Do you understand me? It wasn't you. It was Clare.'

He made another faint sound.

'I don't forgive you because there's nothing to forgive. It wasn't you. She used you, but it's all over now.'

And it was. That tiny flicker was fading fast.

I felt a whisper of wind in the still, cold air. The world blurred – and not because my eyes had filled with tears. I looked up and Evelyn Cross stood on the other side of the bed. She wore her nursing sister's uniform – a dark blue dress, starched cap and apron. I could even make out the upside-down watch pinned to her breast.

She frowned at me. 'I told him to leave this place. That he would die here.'

I stared at her, struggling to remember. What had she said? She had said, 'You should leave this place. You should not stay. You will die here. This place is not good for you.' And she'd been talking to Jones, not me, and neither of us had realised it at the time.

'I thought you were warning *me*.'

Now she looked straight at me. 'I wasn't then, but I am now.'

'What does that mean?' But she was bending over Jones. I heard the starchy rustle of her apron. She put her hand on his forehead. His dreadful struggle for breath eased.

Scalding hot tears ran down my cheeks. I wouldn't change his end – he was going peacefully, but I was full of red hot rage at the cruelty that had been done to him. I tightened my grip on his hand but he no longer knew I was here.

Evelyn Cross took his other hand. He drew one last faltering breath, and then silence. He was gone. Michael Jones was dead.

She straightened up and regarded me across the bed.

I said, 'Why are you warning me?'

'If you tread this path I cannot help you.'

'What path?'

There was a sound behind me. Sorensen stood in the doorway. When I looked back again, Evelyn Cross had disappeared.

He approached the bed. Two male orderlies, silent in their soft white shoes, followed him. He felt for a pulse, found none, and said, 'Time of death 16:23.'

Someone pulled the sheet up over his face and that was it. Michael Jones was gone.

Someone wheeled me back to Dr Sorensen's office. I didn't have the strength or the will to do it myself. It did cross my mind how helpless I was. I had a broken arm, cracked ribs and I still couldn't walk properly. But I wasn't so angry and grief stricken that I couldn't think straight. Because they'd lied to me and I had believed them. But no – I hadn't asked Sorensen, who was probably the only person who did know Jones was downstairs. None of the nurses had known, I was sure of it. Nor Dr Lewis either. Yes, I was angry with them, but I was more angry at myself. I made up my mind, there and then, that I would never be this gullible again. I'd been a good girl and it had got me nowhere. I had a gift. I should use it. I would use it.

His office seemed very warm after the chill in the basement. Someone put a cup of tea by my elbow. Sorensen tried to take my pulse. I jerked my arm away.

Retiring back behind his desk he said, 'I understand your attitude, but you are mistaken. I did not tell you of Mr Jones's presence here because it was vital to your recovery that you felt safe and secure. You were not aware of it but Mr Jones collapsed shortly after he telephoned for the air ambulance and he was brought back with you. I placed you in Dr Lewis' care while I supervised Mr Jones's treatment myself. Let me say that from the outset it was very obvious we could do nothing for him except try to alleviate his pain. We had no idea what was the matter with him. I would have said he was suffering from some kind of unknown and very virulent cancer, but I freely admit I have never seen anything like that. Nothing we did made any difference and so we concentrated all our resources on pain management. To some extent we were successful. You may have remarked on the temperature of his room but I assure you that, whatever was the matter with him, it was at that temperature at which he felt most ... comfortable. Although I'm not sure that's the right word.'

He looked at me again and then pressed something on his desk. Behind me, the door opened and Erin entered.

'Good afternoon, nurse. If you could take Mrs Cage back to her room and stay with her, please. She has had rather a shock. Please ensure she is not left alone at any time.'

And there we were. I was a prisoner again. Only this time there was no Michael Jones to save me. This time I would have to save myself.

If I wanted to.

## Chapter Twenty-Nine

He renewed his invitation to tea the next day and I accepted. It's not as if there was anything else to do. The snow still fell. I could hear the spickley-spackledy of sleet hitting the window.

His study was warm, however, and he was very attentive, placing my tea where I could reach it, ensuring I wasn't sitting in a draught, and several times asking if I was comfortable. His movements, as always were quick and precise. Ostensibly he was everything the attentive host should be, but I could see his colour reaching out for me.

I stirred my tea and waited to see how he would begin. Eventually, after he'd asked me how I was and commented on the weather, he put down his cup.

'I wonder if I might put a proposition to you, Mrs Cage. All I ask is that you hear me out before throwing the furniture at my head. Your attempts at living a "normal" life on your own have not been particularly successful, have they? That business with the Rookwoods, for example. You were lucky not to have been blinded permanently. And then, as it turned out you weren't even safe in your own home.'

I knew what he wanted – and I knew what my response would be – but I saw no reason why I shouldn't make him work for it.

I made my voice strong. 'It was escaping from my

illegal incarceration at this very facility that took me to the Rookwood's in the first place. And it was your man, Michael Jones, who was responsible for my injuries, I think it would be more accurate to state that all the misfortunes that have befallen me since my husband's death can be laid at your door.'

'Well, I do think that might be overstating the case a little ...'

'I don't think so.'

'Might I remind you that you promised to hear me out?'

He paused for a moment in case I wanted to argue some more and then got up to look out of the window.

'I wish to set out a proposition before you and I would like you at least to approach it with an open mind. You are at liberty to say no, but I do ask you to *consider* saying yes, before you reject it out of hand.

'Firstly, let me assure you that you are perfectly safe here. You are in no danger at all. At the moment, all you have to do is take advantage of our facilities and get well. Whatever your answer, our first priority is to get you well again.

'Secondly, when you feel a little more up to it, I would like you to consider working here, with me.' He came and sat back down again. 'And before you ask for details of how that would work, I can give you none. Thanks to the prevarication of both your husband and Mr Jones, I still don't have a clear idea of what you can do. I suspect that because you've been at great pains to conceal your abilities, you don't either. I suggest, therefore, that we sit down one afternoon and discuss your ... range of talents. From that discussion, I would be able to frame an appropriate job offer for you to consider.

'I accept that our relationship did not get off to a good start and for that I think I must bear responsibility. I was too eager. I think I frightened you, didn't I? My apologies for that. I can assure you that once you ... *if* you join my staff here, you will be taken care of. You will never want for anything, ever. Every want, every desire will be fulfilled. You will never have to hide what you are. Or who you are. All I ask is that we work together to discover your full potential. With me behind you there is no limit to the things you can achieve. No – what *we* can achieve. Together. Just say yes, Elizabeth. Say you will work with me. To achieve greatness.'

He sat back, watching me very closely.

I let him wait.

'I'm really not sure what you're talking about, Dr Sorensen. Ever since we met, you've been pursuing me for something I'm not sure I possess.'

'I think we both know that's not true, Mrs Cage.'

Well, he was right there. I did know that wasn't true, but how did he? I remembered the first time we had met. He had known then that there was something different about me. I remembered the way his hungry colour reached for me. How had he known?

Time to find out. 'You don't know that's not true. You don't know anything about me.'

As if he'd been waiting for a cue, he stood up and unlocked a filing cabinet. Pulling out the bottom drawer, he removed a cardboard box which he carried back to his desk. Inside the cardboard box was a brown A4 envelope. He was watching me very carefully. I was able to stare back in unfeigned bewilderment.

He spoke softly. 'When I first arrived here the building was not quite as I could have wished and so I commissioned extensive renovations. During the work in the basement, some strange items were uncovered. They appeared to have been buried for a considerable period of time. Not knowing what to do with them, the builders handed them to me.'

He waited. His colour's resemblance to unhealthy milk was increasing with every second. His face might be calm and inscrutable but inside he was anything but.

I waited too.

Eventually, he said, 'There were two items altogether. I wonder if you can guess what they were?'

I smiled politely and thought I'd play a little. I said, 'Oh, a game. Well, let me see now ...' I paused as if waiting for inspiration to strike. 'A torch ...' And watched his colour leap towards me in anticipation '... or a ... a shoe ... and ... and an umbrella.'

He regarded me steadily. 'No.'

'Oh, what a shame.'

'Although you were partly right.'

'Was I? How gratifying.'

'Don't you want to know what was found buried so deeply?'

'Well, I can see that you very badly want to tell me, so in the interests of our newly harmonious relationship ...'

'First, as you so accurately guessed, we had a

torch. Of a surprisingly modern design, considering it was discovered in a part of the building that had been demolished and rebuilt some seventy years ago.'

'Oh, how clever of me,' I said, pushing my luck and not caring in the slightest.

'Secondly, there was a man's jacket. Easy to see why it had been abandoned – it was quite badly burned in places. And a very modern design. A bit of an anomaly there, don't you think?'

'Yes, indeed. How puzzling. May I see it?'

His colour receded. 'Not just at the moment.'

Well, that was interesting. I wondered why not.

'The jacket contained a wallet. The wallet, again, was of excellent quality and contained some very interesting items. A number of banknotes and coins of unfamiliar design. A strange government ID card identifying the owner as one Michael Jones – a person I must admit I'd never heard of, and a member of a department that didn't exist. Then.'

I tried not to show my surprise. Jones had never said anything to me about losing his wallet.

'And most interesting of all – although I didn't know that at the time, of course – a piece of paper.'

And now I was completely bewildered.

He forged on, his voice quiet and relentless. 'I confess, none of it meant anything to me and I was very busy setting up my clinic, negotiating for government contracts and so on.'

'May I see these strange objects?'

'I'm afraid not, no.'

I wasn't sure whether this was good or bad. 'Well, that's rather the end of the matter then, isn't it?'

'Not really, Mrs Cage. It's the fact that I can't

produce these items that leads me to believe there's something distinctly "cagey" about you.'

He smirked. I had the impression he'd been waiting a long time to make that joke.

I said politely, 'I'm sorry?'

Nothing kills a joke faster than having to explain it. Sadly, he wasn't distracted at all.

'You see, I was more than a little intrigued by these strange finds, so I packed them carefully away. In this very box. And placed them in the bottom drawer of that very filing cabinet. I spent a great deal of time trying to account for them. I examined them regularly, hoping for some clue. And then, one day, I pulled out the box and the torch had – disappeared.'

He waited for me to say something.

I shrugged. 'Petty theft?'

'The seals were unbroken.'

'*Clever* petty theft?'

'Well, perhaps. Except that six months later a new batch of torches turned up here and not only were they of an entirely new design, but they were identical to the one no longer sitting in my bottom drawer. Intrigued, and with the forethought for which I am so renowned, I photographed the remaining contents.'

'The modern jacket, the wallet, and the piece of paper,' I said, trying to give the impression of one labouring to keep up.

'And then, about a year ago, the jacket disappeared as well. I'm sure you can imagine that by now, this was a mystery I was never going to let go.'

Sadly, I could.

He opened the envelope and began to lay photographs on the desk in front of me. Rather like an end-of-the-pier fortune teller slapping down the tarot cards.

I looked at the first one – a torch. I recognised it at once. The one I'd left in the cellar seventy years ago.

'How can you have a picture of a torch that disappeared?'

'That,' he said, 'is a photo of my own torch. Do you recognise it?'

'I don't know. I've never seen your torch.'

He looked at me for a second too long and then let it go.

I picked up the second photo. The one of Jones's jacket. Very scorched. Almost black in places.

The third photo showed the contents of the jacket, all of which were entirely new to me. A wallet, some banknotes and change. And an ID card showing a picture of a slightly younger Michael Jones.

I stared at it for a long time, almost forgetting to say, 'Is that Michael Jones?'

He didn't reply.

I shrugged again. He could wave around as many photos as he liked. Torches, jackets, ID cards … none of this was anything to do with me.

And then, like a poker player with a winning hand, he played his ace. He snapped down a photo of a scrap of paper. A corner torn from a larger sheet. There was a single line of writing. I'd seen Jones scribbling a shopping list. There could be no doubt this was his writing.

*E Cage Rm11.*

It would appear that at some point Jones had discovered my room number and had written it down.

'A piece of paper,' I said politely. 'With Ted's

name on it. Discovered at a place where Ted used to work. I can see how you were unable to contain your excitement.'

He ignored that. 'No, Mrs Cage, a torch and a jacket that vanished from a sealed box.'

'So where did they go?'

'You're asking the wrong question. You should be asking *why* did they go?'

I sighed in irritation. 'All right – why did they go?'

'They returned to their point of origin.'

No need to feign complete and utter bewilderment. 'What?'

'The torch, for example, returned to the date it was manufactured. As did the other objects.'

'Why?'

'Because otherwise there would have been two of them. Really, Mrs Cage, do you never read Science Fiction?'

I answered thoughtfully, remembering the cinema trip with Jones, 'I saw a *Star Trek* film once.'

He dismissed my cautious foray into the world of science fiction and fantasy with a casual wave.

'No object can be in two places at the same time. Once the torch was manufactured, it vanished from my box. It had to. It couldn't be both there and here.'

'So where is it now?'

'I haven't the slightest idea. And before you ask, I assume the same thing happened to the jacket. And the piece of paper written by Jones.'

'Do I understand that has vanished too? I'm sorry, Sorensen, but to lose two objects is a misfortune. To lose three is just carelessness.'

'Mrs Cage, I think you're missing the point.'

I said wearily, 'I wouldn't be at all surprised. Just tell me.'

'Very well. I know these items belonged to Michael Jones. Somehow, they found their way under a pile of rubble some seventy years ago and I'm convinced that somehow you, Mrs Cage, were involved.'

Well, that was true.

He sat back, all set to show me how clever he was. 'I was intrigued by the anomalous aspects of the puzzle. Modern equipment, modern fibres – all discovered – verifiably discovered – years before they could possibly have existed. I had, by this time, built up an excellent – shall we call it "communications network"? – and although I was busy setting up and building my reputation, I put out the word that I was interested in certain anomalies and sat back to see what would transpire.

'And then, into my life, came the man whom we called Michael Jones. The name rang a bell immediately. I checked the photograph and there was no doubt. The man before me was very much younger than the photo, which, in itself, is quite mysterious, don't you think?

'And while I was still thinking about that, I met a man named Edward Cage. I must admit, at first I was excited because I thought he was the E Cage on the sheet of paper there. It soon became apparent that he wasn't, but I was intrigued enough by his name to offer him employment and he accepted. So I had some pieces of the puzzle but not all of them, and by now, of course, I wasn't going to let it go.

He sighed. 'I can't tell you how many blind alleys I wandered down over the years. How much effort I wasted. How difficult it was to convince my supervisors that I wasn't wasting my time. And then, one day, a report crossed my desk. From an educational psychologist, no less. She'd written across the front "Have a look at this." I opened the file of one Elizabeth Ford. And very nearly closed it again when I saw how little there was to go on, but as you have your instincts, Elizabeth, I have mine. I watched you over the next few years. Very discreetly, of course. And before you spring indignantly to your feet, I was watching another half dozen people as well, so don't become completely paranoid about it. Then one day, after yet another difficult session with my manager, when she had made it clear that this particular dead end was to be abandoned, I thought I'd be a little more proactive. I put together a plan and summoned Edward Cage – Ted, as everyone called him. I had an Elizabeth – and he had the name Cage. It was perfect. I found an appropriate operative and an adorable puppy – you remember them, I'm sure – and hatched a plan.'

So that was how he'd known about me. Jones and I had left these things behind us in the fire and they'd come back to bite us seventy years later.

He paused and stared out of the window, smiling slightly. 'And then, having successfully moved mountains, I found I had a fly in my ointment. I cannot tell you how difficult it was to persuade Ted to bring you here to meet me. There was always some problem – some excuse. Do you know, I actually had to invent an entire Open Day and order Ted to bring you along? The same for the Christmas Party. I was becoming quite irritated. But then, of course, Ted died.'

A huge ball of ice sat in my chest. I stared and stared at his colour. He was excited, I could see that. And pleased with himself – I could see that too. I don't know if he had himself under control or whether I just wasn't functioning properly today. In the end, I went old school and just fired the question straight at him.

'Did you have Ted killed?'

He was horrified. I could see that. No, he hadn't had Ted killed. He was innocent of that, at least. Of course he was. I began to feel guilty for even thinking such a thing, and then, being Sorensen, he blew it.

'I won't deny it was a fortunate event, of course, but ...' He suddenly remembered who he was talking to.

Any remaining doubts about what I was about to do fled straight out into the snow. He'd played the long game and, one by one, the different pieces had tumbled into his lap. And when he'd needed an E. Cage – he'd made one. I'd been manipulated. We all had. I felt as if I'd been ... manufactured. He'd played with all our lives. All three of us. And of those three, two were dead.

I felt a stone-cold certainty. I was doing the right thing.

'So, Mrs Cage – I am certain you have something to tell me and I very much wish you would do so.'

I let the silence gather, staring out of the window

across the snow-filled garden. Eventually I sighed, as if coming to a reluctant decision and dropped the words into his world like pebbles into a still pool of water.

I told him what I'd told Jones. 'I can see things. About people. I can see the sort of person they are. I can see what they know. Whether they're lying. Whether they're happy or not. Or ill. Or hiding something. I look at people and I just ... know.'

His colour boiled around him. Like greasy milk again. He swallowed a couple of times and then said hoarsely, 'And the jacket?'

Well, I'd come this far ...

'You have a ghost. She took both of us back to 1940. We saved her from burning. Jones left his jacket and the torch behind in the confusion. That's what the builders found.'

His office was so silent I could hear the snow hissing against the windows. On the other side of the door, I heard a telephone ring far away. It rang twice and then fell silent.

He sat staring at me, his mouth working as he struggled to put the words together. His colour was vibrating with excitement, giving off an unpleasant oily sheen. I could see the turmoil of his emotions. Triumph. Pride. Elation. Satisfaction. Exultation It was the first time I'd ever seen him not in complete control of either himself or the situation.

Eventually he managed to say, 'Does this mean you will consider my offer?'

It wasn't too late. I could still pull back.

No I couldn't. I'd come too far. No turning back. He thought I'd walked into his trap and actually – he'd walked into mine. I had only to slam the door behind him.

I held the silence just long enough for him to begin to worry and then said, 'Yes, it means I will consider your offer.'

He didn't rub his hands together but I had the impression it was only by exercising the greatest restraint. 'Excellent. That's excellent. Now, we mustn't overtax your strength. I shall ring for Erin to take you back to your room and we'll begin tomorrow, shall we?'

We had several sessions together. Something he seemed to look forward to. I was too busy telling him as little as possible to gain any enjoyment from them. I honestly thought I hadn't given him much to go on but he obviously felt he'd heard enough, however, and moved more quickly than I expected, because he startled me one day, saying he'd arranged for some people to come and meet me.

'I thought a small demonstration might be in order. And then once you've impressed them, we should be able to attract some investment and really get moving.'

I had obviously underestimated his desire to justify himself in his boss's eyes. Perhaps I could use that somehow. I regarded him warily. 'What did you have in mind?'

'Oh, I don't know. I'm not sure what they'll be looking for, so we'll just wing it, shall we?'

He was so obviously lying to me that I was easily able to tell my conscience to shut up. I sat quietly, looking at my hands and trying to work through the implications. I hadn't factored other people into my plan. I tried to prise more information from him but he was very cagey and I didn't want to arouse any suspicions, so I changed the subject and he seemed happy to let it go.

I don't know what he'd said, but they came the very next day.

## Chapter Thirty

They came in a military helicopter. I watched it pass out of sight behind a stand of bare trees where, presumably, there was some sort of landing pad. I heard the flurry as they came in through the front door, their voices rising and falling, doors opening as Sorensen took them into his office, and then silence as the doors closed. I wondered what Sorensen was saying about me. What exactly he was telling them. And I wondered how long they would keep me waiting.

Not very long, it would seem. These were busy people. I suspected I was just one appointment among many today. The helicopter was still here, ready to whisk them away to wherever they were scheduled to be next.

I refused lunch. Just for once, I wasn't hungry. Erin called for me as they were taking my tray away. I could probably have walked – I should have walked, it would have done me good, but I wasn't offered the choice.

The sight of her caused a tiny stir in my conscience. I had no idea what was going to happen but none of it was going to be good, so as she pushed me to the lift, I said, 'Not on snow-clearing duties today?'

She laughed. 'You're kidding. I'm not going out there.'

I twisted around to look over her shoulder. 'You should.'

'Should what?'

'Get yourself on snow-clearing today. Outside. You all should.'

'Why?'

Why indeed?

I said, 'Exercise is good for you. Or so you're always telling me.'

We arrived at the lift and she pressed the button, never taking her eyes off me. Moments passed.

'Perhaps I will,' she said slowly.

I had no time to wonder what she knew or even if she knew anything at all. And I couldn't say any more. I nodded. 'A wise decision.'

The lift sped me silently downwards. I wasn't the slightest bit surprised to be decanted into the basement. It seemed to me that everything since my first visit to the Sorensen Clinic had been building up for this moment. For the record, I felt no qualms. No guilt at abandoning the rules under which I had lived my life. I was calm. I was very calm. I was the calm before the storm.

I could sense the disbelief as soon as Erin opened the door. I had to suppress a smile. Had they been expecting Merlin the Magician? What they got was me, battered, arm in a sling, dressed in clinic sweats and with a blanket over my knees like an old woman. Disbelief turned to disappointment. They eyed each other and said nothing.

I saw four people, excluding Sorensen. One woman and three men. The woman was Sorensen's boss, I was sure of it, and they really didn't like each other at all. Her colour was a deep crimson, strong and powerful. The two colours – her red and his milky blue-white battled against each other, each constantly probing the other for weakness. Usually, incompatible colours stay away from each other, but these two were engaged in a real battle of wills. I would have liked some time to observe their struggle, but not today. Not ever, actually. She wore a Cossack-style fur hat and smartly frogged coat. The basement was as chilly as I remembered so I didn't blame her.

Two of the men were in army uniform. One had slightly more medal ribbons than the other so I assumed he was the one in charge. He looked just as I always imagined a high-ranking army officer would look, square-built and with a crew-cut. He looked youngish, but there were lines around his face and mouth. His colour was a grey green, the colour of lavender leaves, and flickered occasionally. He was not as completely confident as he would wish. The other was tall and thin, exquisitely turned out. Not a hair out of place. Even his nails were manicured. Interestingly, his colour was a bright fuchsia pink, shot through with purple. If ever anyone was in the wrong job …

Off to one side sat a smaller man, a civilian, a little older than the others. He had thinning hair grey hair. His pin-striped suit was neat and precise. A notebook lay on the table in front of him. Compared with the other two, he had little physical presence. His colour was a deep, deep blue. Very thick and very controlled.

They sat at tables placed in a U-shaped formation. Sorensen at the table on my left, the civilian on my right, and the other three directly opposite me. A very nervous Erin, conscious that all eyes were on us, helped me into the plain wooden chair that had been set out for me, whispered, 'Good luck,' and then left me taking my wheelchair with her. I wondered if I was supposed to feel as exposed and vulnerable as I did. This was a very adversarial layout and my getaway vehicle had just been wheeled out of the door.

There were no introductions. Presumably they already knew my name and I wasn't important enough to know theirs.

I looked around me. We were in a bare concrete room, harshly lit by three sets of overhead lights. Other than the tables and chairs, there were two grey metal filing cabinets and an old wooden bookcase. I wasn't close enough to read the titles. Spare wooden chairs were arranged around the walls. Tea and coffee-making equipment stood on a table in the corner. No one offered me anything. So much for being an important asset. The red fire extinguisher by the door was the brightest spot colour in the room. I heard a quick exchange of voices outside. The door opened and an armed soldier slipped inside, taking up his position in front of the door. From similar sounds, I assumed another was on the other side. I had no idea whether they were to prevent unauthorised entry by someone else or an even more unauthorised exit by me.

I settled myself comfortably on my creaky wooden chair and smoothed the blanket over my knees. We looked at each other. I think it's fair to say neither side was particularly impressed by the other.

The silence went on but I didn't care. I could wait.

The woman spoke first. Placing a red pencil on the table in front of her, she said, 'Can you move this?'

'Don't be in too much of a hurry to show them what you can do,' said the thing inside my head. 'Have a little fun first. Remember you are stronger than you think.'

She was impatient and abrupt. 'Well, can you?'

No one, apart from Sorensen was even bothering to look at me. Their colours were streaming away from me. I could see they all thought I was just another fake. And if I wasn't a fake then I was a freak.

I said quietly, 'Yes,' and saw Sorensen stir uneasily. His colour had moved towards me and was jumping about all over the place. I wondered if he'd suddenly had some sort of premonition.

She sat back and gestured to the pencil. 'Then do it.'

I threw the blanket aside, stood up creakily, picked up the pencil, moved it six inches to the right and sat back down again.

There was rather a nasty silence, although I thought I saw the civilian bite back a smile.

She sighed. 'I meant – can you move it without touching it?'

Sighing, I got up again and approached. I blew hard and the pencil rolled away across the table. You should have seen their faces. I have to say – that was a really good moment. I was enjoying this. The thought crossed my mind that I should have done this years ago.

Sorensen's boss glared at him across the table. You

didn't have to have any sort of special gift to see what she was thinking. Or whose fault this was all going to turn out to be. He made a placatory gesture.

She picked up a folder and began to leaf through the contents. Ah – this would be Sorensen's legendary file. The one I'd discussed with Michael Jones. Almost a year ago, now. That had been another life.

She began to read aloud. 'Elizabeth Louise Cage. Née Ford. Date of birth unknown. Place of birth unknown. Parents unknown. Adoptive parents Richard James Ford and Sandra Louise Elizabeth Ford of 29 Painswick Avenue, Rushford. Attended Whitewood Infants School and then on to Rushford St Winifred's. Exam results unspectacular. 'A' Levels in English Language, English Literature and History. Employed as a basic records clerk for Rushford Council for six years. No promotions. Married Edward James Cage of 36 The Copse, Whittington, Rushfordshire. Widowed … um … one year ago. No details of hobbies, activities, interests, club memberships or close friends. Current address 13 Castle Close, Rushford. Daily activities appear to consist solely of shopping and visiting the library.'

Her tone of voice stung. As, no doubt, it was intended to.

'Is that it?' said someone. 'Is that all we've got? What about close associates? Holidays? Daily routines?'

She held up the single sheet of paper between her forefinger and thumb and then let it fall contemptuously. 'She's a housewife. Just a bored and boring little housewife trying to make herself interesting.'

I felt the cold ball of anger begin to uncoil itself in my stomach.

'Not yet,' said the thing in my head. 'Not quite yet.'

The civilian closed his notebook and as if that was some sort of signal, the others began to pick up their files.

I let them get as far as standing up. They were stuffing things in briefcases and muttering to each other. No one was looking at me. That was the last time that would ever happen.

The pencil was lying on the table. A good six feet away from me.

'Well, what are you waiting for?' said the thing in my head.

Here goes.

I picked it up with my thoughts and hurled it at the wall with such force that it actually drove itself deep into the plaster, about four inches from the woman's head. She froze with shock. As did everyone else. Including me. I'd never done that before and it had been slightly more ... spectacular ... than I'd intended. But quite enjoyable.

They stared at the pencil, its stump firmly embedded at the centre of a spider's web of cracked plaster. No one moved. No one spoke. Their colours had turned very muddy indeed, shot through with red. Suddenly, they were all very, very afraid. And they were afraid of me.

'Cool,' said the thing in my head. 'But don't stop there.'

The woman sat back down with thud and the room was full of a frightened stillness of which I had

361

no difficulty taking advantage. I closed my eyes and let my mind wander free. Because everyone has secrets. Words, thoughts and images all tumbled through my brain. I saw it all. Just for once, I was on the same side as the thing in my head. We were working together and it was exhilarating.

I opened my eyes and turned to the woman, still staring open-mouthed at the pencil. 'You had a choice. Two paths lay before you. You chose wrongly. You would have been happy. You know it and you know you killed your baby for nothing. He would have been your son. You would have been his mother. You should have given your last breath in his defence, but you just swatted him aside for the benefit of lesser prizes. He's never left you, has he? Do you still feel the touch of his cold hand whenever you're alone?'

She went white to her lips, screamed, 'Bitch,' and shot to her feet, knocking over her chair.

Sorensen restrained her, putting his hand on her arm and whispering urgently in her ear. One of the soldiers picked up her chair. She sat slowly, ashen-faced, but I'd moved on to the crew-cutted man.

'You ran away, didn't you? You took the radio and you ran. They called you a hero – they still do – but you and I both know what a filthy coward you really are.'

He stared for a moment, his expression ugly, and then said, 'This interview is terminated.' Shouldering his aide aside, he made for the door.

My head began to throb. Just as it usually did when I tried this sort of thing for too long. This time, I ignored it, turning to his aide, who was just

362

straightening his immaculate uniform and preparing to follow his boss.

'And you. Using your money to buy your way through life. You paid handsomely to get through university. There's always a bright boy or girl desperate for money and willing to do anything to get it, isn't there? Doesn't it keep you awake at night – the fear that one day you'll find yourself in a place where your money can't save you. Well I have news for you, buster. Today's the day. Isn't it, Colonel?'

I turned to the civilian, sitting still and silent and not missing a thing.

'That was pathetic, Colonel. You thought you'd swap places with your aides to see if I would know. Utterly pathetic – just as you were all those years ago when you failed to save her. I know what you did. I know what you've all done, all of you, you worthless pieces of shit.'

I felt something warm and wet collect on my top lip and wiped it off with my sleeve. My nose was bleeding. Quite badly by the feel of it and my headache was becoming worse by the second. It hurt my eyes to look at the lights.

They were all on their feet now. Sorensen, as frightened as the rest of them, took a step towards me, his hand outstretched, saying, 'Elizabeth, you're not well. Perhaps we should all take a moment ...' and my mind picked up a glass of water and threw it at him. Most of it missed him, but I was learning all the time.

I was surprised to find that despite the pain, I was enjoying myself. No – more than that – I was loving it. I could feel the strength running through me and I gloried in it. There was nothing I couldn't do. I could feed on their fear. Use it to give me strength. For the first time, I tasted the exhilaration of power. No wonder people killed for it. All these years I'd kept so quiet – creeping through my life like a little mouse. Why? Why had I done that when I could do … this.'

I watched the general's notepad wobble and lift itself off the table. That didn't go so well. I needed more emotion to harness. Strong emotion. I needed to be angry. I thought of Michael Jones dying in Sorensen's cold basement. I looked at the uncomfortable wooden chair which was, apparently, all I was worth. I thought of Ted and how he had saved me. I looked at Sorensen and what he'd done to us all.

An empty chair jerked itself slightly and then fell over. I hadn't quite got the hang of this although to be fair, it's not something I could have practised beforehand. Someone screamed a warning. Behind me, I felt a movement. An unseen man shouted, 'Hands in the air. Down on your knees.' No, that wasn't going to happen. Not in a million years. I heard a thunk as his gun hit the ceiling.

Even through the blinding pain, I could feel the exhilaration. It was like the excitement of riding a bike full-speed downhill. No more inching my way cautiously round the bends with the brakes on all the time. Now I careered downhill at breakneck speed, the wind in my face. Flat out. No stopping. Always in control. Sowing the storm and reaping the whirlwind. They were afraid of me. Again, I experienced that heady rush of power. They were afraid of me. All of them.

Slowly at first, I picked things up off the tables. Pens, pencils, notepads, glasses – all small stuff but you have to start somewhere. They wobbled a little at first and then, with a flick of my wrist, I gave them movement. Round and round they flew. Faster and faster as I prepared to bring their world down around their ears.

The more I did, the more it hurt. The pain in my head was beginning to overpower me. My stomach churned. Any minute now I was going to be horribly ill. There's a price to pay for doing this sort of thing. There's always a price to pay, but I was happy to pay it today. There was nothing left for me in this world.

I could hear the door rattling behind me. I had no idea whether people were trying to get in or trying to get out but it didn't matter either way. No one was leaving this room alive. There was shouting on the other side but it was all very far away and of no concern to me and the thing inside my head smiled, stretched luxuriously, and said, 'At last.'

They'd all grouped themselves in the farthest corner where, presumably, they thought they would be safe from the whirling maelstrom of office equipment. Time to give them something else to think about.

I started with the furniture. I concentrated on Sorensen's chair first. There was a moment when I groped clumsily and then I had it. It lurched across the floor. A little bit zig-zaggy at first, while I got the hang of control, but eventually I was able to lift it high and let it smash it into his table. It was a heavy office chair so it didn't shatter, but it didn't do the table any good at all.

Small objects were still spinning around the room. Papers, a stapler, pens, a plastic in-tray hurtled past, scattering its contents in its wake. A low hum filled my ears. The world began to take on a red hue. With every fresh evidence of my power, I felt a huge anger welling up inside me. Fires that had been tamped down for so long all began to explode into life. Power fed on fear which increased the power which made them even more afraid. It was limitless. I could go on for ever. There wasn't anything I couldn't do. I felt a fierce exultation. No longer would I stand in the shadows and hide. No longer would I stay out of the way. This was me. I was here. This was what I could do. It was the world's turn to stay out of *my* way.

Now a table began to move and I was hardly even trying. Pleased with my success, my mind reached for the cabinets, which were much heavier than I expected. I couldn't hold them. One tilted back against the wall and I lost the other one completely. It fell over with a crash. Sorensen and the others were all crouched down in the corner, gazing around them, shielding their heads, terrified. Now, the bookcase lurched. Books tumbled from the shelves and flew around the room, their pages flapping like giant birds. That was quite funny.

I stood in the centre of a vortex. My old wooden chair smashed into a wall and shattered. Jagged lumps of wood, books, pens, all whirled around the room at lethal speeds. A whirlwind of office equipment. Really, it was so funny. Why was no one laughing?

The whirlwind was spinning faster and faster. I saw the civilian hit across the shoulders with the remnants of a chair. He fell to the ground and stayed there. The other two tried to protect their heads. One of them had already been hit by something heavy. Thick red blood was running down his face. Things spun faster. The room was filled with a rushing wind. The woman's hair was streaming out behind her. She clung on to Sorensen, using him as a shield. He crouched, arms wrapped around his head, shouting at me.

The crew-cutted soldier was the first to go, picked up by that old cliché, the unseen hand. I lifted him, screaming, into the air. His feet kicked wildly as I thrust him into the vortex where he was funnelled upwards with every turn. I wondered idly what would happen when he reached the ceiling. The other army man went next, waving his arms and shouting as he rose into the air. He was helpless. It was so funny. I moved my arms and the two of them collided with a very nasty crack – bad steering on my part, but to be fair, it was my first time. At least their shouting stopped. Both hung limply and now there was quite a lot of blood, spraying around the room in great arcs. Every wall looked like a Jackson Pollock painting.

This is fun, said the thing. And it was. I considered crashing the two soldiers together again, just because I could, but the pain in my head was becoming rather severe. I put my hand to my face and it came away thick with red blood but whether it was theirs or mine I didn't know and really, did it matter?

I stood, arms raised, head back, riding the storm as easily as the ice giants ride the glaciers which will one day end our world.

The sound of the vortex had risen to a scream. The speed was such that I could no longer make out the individual components. Or people. Everything was flashing past in a blur. The colours of the world mixed and mingled in a kind of grungy grey. The fire extinguisher was the only bright spot in the room. Speaking of which ... With only the lightest of thoughts, it wrenched itself off the wall, straight at Sorensen, hitting him square in the face, crushing bone and cartilage, and suddenly, everything was red.

The furniture was beginning to disintegrate. Occasionally a table leg or anonymous piece of metal would escape from the maelstrom and thud into the wall, shattering even more plaster which, in turn, was sucked into the whirlwind. I spared a moment to wonder what was happening to the very much softer and squishier people.

I clenched my fists above my head, feeling for all the world like the ringmaster in some sort of bizarre circus and above me, the ceiling cracked like a pistol shot. Dust and plaster joined the maelstrom that had once been an ordinary basement room. I made one, final, huge effort that flashed sick white pain behind my eyes. The entire vortex seemed to blow upwards and then the whole boiling mass whirled up, up and away. I have no idea where it all went.

My head felt as if it was on fire. My eyes were bulging with pain. I couldn't do this any longer. I was losing control. I had lost myself in a red orgy of revenge and destruction and now it was all getting away from me.

And the thing that had lived in my head for so long, turned on me with a gibber of triumph. Something exploded behind my eyes. My world turned red. And purple. And black. Time to end it all. Shrieking words that were lost even to me, I spread my arms and let the wind take me away.

## Chapter Thirty-One

I was a snowflake, floating in a blizzard of white, soft and weightless. Around me were other snowflakes, dancing in the bright light.

And then I hit something cold and hard, knocking all the breath from my body. I lay on my back as the angry snow sought to engulf us all.

'Open your eyes, Elizabeth.'

I did as I was told. Evelyn Cross bent over me. I felt no fear – just a quiet acceptance of my death.

'Have you come for me?'

Her voice was soft and sorrowful. 'I am sorry. I cannot help you.'

I tried to lift my head but the cold snow had me in its grip. 'Why not?'

'You have damned yourself. I cannot help you.'

Cold washed over me. All the iciness of the world was claiming ownership of me.

'You have unleashed something you cannot control.' She gestured at the never-ending angry snow. 'You are doing this. This is you. Your hatred. Your fear. Your rage. Your desire for revenge. You have passed beyond me. I cannot help you now.'

Now I knew real fear. 'Don't leave me here. Please don't leave me.'

Because now I was alone. I knew I was. The thing in my head, unleashed at last, given free reign at last, was gone. That old biblical phrase – gone to seek what it might devour.

'I must.' She bent over me. 'I would help you if I could but I cannot.'

'Don't leave me here.'

'You had a gift. You have used it to hurt people and make them fear you.'

I could feel the cold seeping through into my bones. I knew I would never get up again. I was being slowly buried in my own punishment.

'Goodbye, Elizabeth.'

'Help me.'

'Elizabeth.'

'Don't leave me. Please don't leave me.'

'Cage? Can you hear me?'

What?

'Open your eyes.'

I didn't want to. What would I see?

'Cage.'

I opened my eyes. I was lying on my back on the hard snow, looking up at a sea of faces looking down at me. I stared in bewilderment. The sun was shining brightly. Some of these faces were children. My head hurt. My back hurt. Was I dead? I could feel the cold snow through my clothes. I could hear screaming but these were screams of pleasure. From children. I could smell the delicious smell of hot dogs and frying onions.

I was struggling to understand what was going on when the circle broke up and Jones was there. Right above me.

'Are you all right, Cage? You came an awful cropper. Don't try and move just for the moment.

371

Move up, boys, give the lady some room.'

I lay still, trying to work out what was happening. Jones was alive. I wasn't lying among the ruins of the Sorensen Clinic. No one was dead because of me. The world wasn't disappearing under a blanket of white death.

'Can you get up?'

'Yes, I think so. Nothing's broken.'

He helped me to my feet. I clung to his arm and stared, dazed, trying to understand where I was and what had just happened.

'Do you know if you lost consciousness?'

I couldn't answer him. To have him here again when I thought I had lost him.

I said, stupidly, 'You're not dead.'

'No,' he said cheerfully, 'not yet anyway. Can you remember what happened?'

I shook my head. I knew what hadn't happened. Sorensen. The clinic. Clare. His death. None of that had happened. Had it?

'Are you sure you're all right, Cage? Don't you remember? Someone lost control of their sledge and cannoned straight into you. You went flying. Are you sure you weren't unconscious?'

I said I didn't know, but I must have been, surely. To have dreamed all that. And in such detail. I'd been in another world. One that – at this moment – was more real to me than this one. I could still feel the pain in my head. And the metallic taste of blood. My heart was still pounding with shock, and fear, and the violence of my feelings. My legs were weak and I was shivering.

'I think you're a bit shaken up,' he said and I was.

372

Hugely shaken up. And not just by the fall. I tried to tell him it was all right and that I was fine, but I was shivering so hard the words wouldn't come.

Nearby, two little girls were in tears. Their mother didn't look much better. I gathered they were the ones who had hit me.

'It's all right, sweethearts,' said Jones. 'Not your fault. She stood right in your path.'

I had no knowledge of doing any such thing but nodded anyway. Actually, I had no knowledge of anything. I stared around me as if I'd never seen any of it before. A world that was far less real to me than the one I'd just left.

'Who's a concussed little girl then?' said Jones, supporting me with one arm as we made our way out of the park.

'I don't remember hitting my head,' I said slowly, although it was throbbing.

'Well no, Cage, that's kind of the point when you have concussion. Let's go and get you checked out at the hospital.'

'No,' I said, more out of fear of what they would find than actual stoicism.

I don't know why I bothered. I was talking to myself.

A&E was full of people apparently unable to keep their feet today, but they saw me quite quickly. I answered questions, went off for an X-ray and was admitted for an overnight stay.

'I'm quite all right,' I said, and no one took any notice.

Jones stayed a while, talking to me, and then they brought the evening meal round. He inspected my plate, told me it was a punishment for being too stupid to stand on my own two feet properly, that he would take my stuff back to my own house for me, and collect me in the morning and take me home.

I did sleep a little, but not much and they woke me at regular intervals anyway. Apparently, there was nothing the matter with me because I was released after breakfast with instructions to take it easy for at least the next forty-eight hours. Jones promised I would never be left alone for one moment, cross his heart, and took me home.

We walked slowly through the dirty streets. Far from being the civilisation-ending snowy wilderness I'd dreamed about at the Sorensen clinic, in true British fashion, the snow was rapidly turning to muddy slush. I could hear dripping water everywhere.

I wasn't sure what I would find behind my own front door. I waited anxiously at the bottom of the steps as Jones took my key and opened the door. He stepped back. 'Aren't you coming in?'

I took a deep breath and slowly climbed the steps. Nothing terrible happened. I walked past him through the front door and looked around. Nothing was out of place. Everything looked just as it had the last time I'd been here. My suitcase was by the door and my lovely red bowl stood on the coffee table.

'I brought all your stuff back while you were snoring your head off in hospital. Looks good, doesn't it?'

He meant the bowl.

I pulled myself together. 'It does. Thank you.'

Brilliant sunshine slanted through the window, highlighting the fact I hadn't dusted recently.

'Would you like me to take your suitcase upstairs?'

'Yes, please.'

'Well, take off your coat, sit down and put your feet up. I'll put the kettle on in a minute.'

'I can do that.'

'No, you can't. Just sit down. And don't fall asleep,' he added, as if dropping off in the middle of the morning was something I did all the time.

I felt so tired. I sat down with a sigh. It was still only the day after Boxing Day. I'd only been gone just over two days. It seemed a hell of a lot longer. I could hear Jones moving around upstairs. I closed my eyes for a moment and then opened them again in case I was accused of malicious sleeping.

I looked around. It was good to be home. This was my home – my house, and it welcomed me. My first home had been my parents' house and my second had been Ted's. This was the first house I had ever owned all by myself and I loved it. I looked around at all the familiar landmarks of my life so far. My books sat in orderly rows on the shelves. My beautiful red lacquer bowl sat on the coffee table, brightening the room. My picture of Ted was still on the shelf. His flowers in the vase nearby were drooping. I must go out tomorrow and buy some fresh ones.

I stood up to take the vase into the kitchen and found myself picking up Ted's picture instead. Remembering that other world, I wiped the glass and the frame with my sleeve, and whispered, 'Thank you for what you did,' and whether I was thanking him for our years together or for saving my life, I wasn't really sure. Whichever it was, he deserved my thanks anyway.

My fingers were sticky. As I replaced the picture a tiny snail trail of something hung briefly from the frame. Taking the picture to the window where there was more light, I turned it over for a better look.

A long crack ran across the glass and into the right-hand side of the frame. This picture had been broken. Two small, clear beads of something had oozed from the crack. At some point this picture had been broken and then glued back together again.

Unbidden, that other world came rushing back. A picture came to my mind. A moment of terror and desperation. Of grabbing at the picture and in the same sweeping moment, hurling it at Jones. Of him carelessly batting it away with his arm. In my mind, I heard the crash as it hit the wall. Heard the glass crack. Saw the two pieces of frame fall to the floor.

Someone had mended this.

I scratched at one of the beads of glue. The exterior was hard, but a tiny piece crumbled away. I touched it with my thumb and it was soft.

I stared down at my thumb and then at the picture, my mind racing. I couldn't take it in. The picture had been broken and then repaired again. At some point in the very, very recent past, this picture had been broken. And I knew how. Again, I saw Michael Jones striding towards me, impassive and detached as he beat me. Again, I saw the picture fly through the air. Hit the wall. Fall to the floor. It had happened. It had all happened.

My stomach crawled with fear. There were two worlds. Two versions of events. One was normal and believable. The other apocalyptic and horrifying. Which one was true? Had someone been doing something with drugs? Confusing me. Was that manipulative bastard Sorensen messing with my mind. Was this real? Or was this the dream? Were these my last thoughts as I lay buried in angry snow? Or was everything a lie?

At that moment, I heard Jones stumping back down the stairs again. The door opened and he stood there. He saw me holding the picture and I imagine my face must have given everything away.

We faced each other across the room. I could feel the ache in my head and arm, although whether that had been caused by me hitting the ground or Jones hitting me I couldn't, at that moment, have said.

We stared for what seemed like for ever. I waited for him to say, 'What's the matter?' or 'I told you to sit down, Cage. Don't you ever do as you're told?' but he didn't and now the silence had gone on too long and I knew and he knew I knew.

He said heavily, 'Nothing gets past you, does it?'

I said nothing, but I took a step closer to the front door. Just in case. I held my breath, waiting for him to explode with violence again.

He made no move. 'I can explain. If you'll allow me.'

I found a voice. 'Stay back.'

'What do you think I'm going to do to you?'

'Nothing. You're never going to do anything to me again.'

'Again? What's this all about?'

I held up the picture. 'This.'

He sighed and his shoulders sagged. 'Yes, sorry about that. We tried to get a replacement but the shops were shut over the holidays.'

'We?'

He narrowed his eyes. 'What are you talking about?'

I flourished the picture again. 'I told you. This.'

'Yes, I can see that, but I'm not sure we're talking about the same thing here.'

'I'm talking about how this got broken.'

'So am I – although Sorensen will have my guts for telling you.'

My world was whirling about me, not dissimilar to the way it had swooped and plunged in Sorensen's clinic. Angry snow danced before my eyes. 'Tell me.'

He sighed.

I shouted, 'Tell me,' and something in my head flashed pain. I stamped it down. I'd had my warning. I would never do that again.

'I work for Sorensen.'

'Yes, I know.'

'No, I'm working for him now.'

I stared. Again my head thumped. The thought flashed through my mind. Get out of here. Get away while you still can.

He said quietly, 'You know I told you they wouldn't give me my full security clearance back. Because of the Clare thing.'

I nodded.

He sighed, looked away from me for a moment and then said, 'He made me an offer. Full reinstatement if I got you out of the way so they could search this place from top to bottom. And install some equipment.'

I wasn't sure I was taking it all in.

'I had to get you out of your house for a couple of

days, so ... so I invited you for Christmas. We left by the front door – they came in through the back. Unfortunately, someone was clumsy. The picture was broken. The shops were shut for the holidays so they repaired it as best they could and everyone hoped you wouldn't notice. It would probably have been replaced tomorrow or the day after.'

'By whom?'

There was a long pause. 'By me.'

The silence went on and on. My head thumped again. A warning. Because I was angry and I was struggling. This was my fault. All the warnings had been there and I'd either ignored them or missed them completely. How many times had he said, 'Sweetheart, we are the authorities.' Not, 'Sweetheart, they are the authorities,' but we. Always we.

And worse – had he been working for Sorensen all the time? He said he'd stolen Sorensen's car to get me out of the clinic, but who steals their boss's car? I'd been deceived and lied to. And it wasn't even as if it was for the first time. I'd fallen into Sorensen's trap with Ted and then again into exactly the same trap with Jones. Sorensen had called me a stupid woman and I was. I was the most stupid woman in the world. To be caught twice with the same trick. Self-loathing and disgust and humiliation boiled around inside me. My head thumped again.

And then I suddenly thought – had I always known? Subconsciously, had I known what he was doing? Was that why I dreamed he had turned on me? Had my own mind being trying to tell me something?

'Well,' I said, and even my voice wasn't my own. 'Aren't you going to tell me you didn't have a choice.

That's what men usually say when they're caught doing something despicable they could perfectly easily have said "no" to, but they're too gutless to take that option.'

He said nothing.

'What happened to – you're Ted's wife, I'd never let anything happen to you?'

He said nothing.

'Or – you can trust me?'

Nothing.

His colour had shifted away from me. The golden colour had gone. His face expressionless and detached. For some reason, this made me even more furious.

I said quietly, 'You really are doomed to betray the women you love, aren't you?'

He gave a sharp intake of breath. For one moment, his colour flared around him and then he said, 'Look, we really should sit down and discuss this.'

There was something false there. I could see it in his colour. His eyes shifted to the light fitting and then back to me again. And then he did it again and I suddenly remembered what he'd said about installing equipment. Were we being overheard? Or watched? I had a sudden vision of my every move being scrutinised by a team of Sorensen's people. A cauldron of rage erupted inside my head. This was my house. My own little house. My home. I swear, if, at that moment, I actually did possess the power to bring Sorensen's world down around his ears, then I would have done so.

I cut my eyes back to Jones who was staring at me. He said, 'Let me get your suitcase. There's something in it which will explain everything.'

Without waiting for a reply, he ran back upstairs again, returning a moment later with my suitcase. He crossed the room and placed it by the front door, then returned to his original position across the room. His colour flared towards me. And then away again.

For a moment, I couldn't think what he was doing and then I got it. He was giving me an escape route.

I was going to cry. I couldn't look at him. My hopes, my dreams, my future, even my past. Everything was crashing down around me. It was the end of everything.

He said very quietly, 'Take Ted with you,' and I realised I was still holding the photograph. Then, more loudly, 'No, no, Elizabeth. Don't go.'

I whirled around, snatched up my suitcase, wrenched open the door and ran down the steps. Out and away.

I'd like to say I walked away, because walking away sounds so much better than running away, but I can't. I ran. I ran from everything that had anchored me in this world. My life. My house, Michael Jones. Suitcase in one hand, Ted in the other, I ran.

I had no idea where I could go or how I was to escape this web in which Sorensen had entangled me, but that's the great advantage of losing everything. There's nothing left to lose.

## Acknowledgements

Thanks, as always, to everyone at Accent Press for their help, encouragement and chocolate.

Thanks to everyone at Octavos' Bookshop for their hospitality and their apparent willingness to put up with me at a moment's notice. Thanks especially to Matt for his exceptional American Pancakes with bacon and maple syrup. I feel another Homer Simpson moment coming on.

Thanks to my editor, Rebecca Lloyd, for her unfailing patience and who is, apparently, a bottomless pit of knowledge. Actually, having read that it occurs to me that's not the most flattering thing to say, but she really is.

Thanks to Jan and Mike for their hospitality.

Thanks to Hazel for *he*r hospitality and the eventual provision of Chinese Food. Conversations go like this:

'What do you fancy to eat?'

'I could really murder a Chinese.'

'Jamaican it is then.'

And finally, a massive thanks to my lovely readers,

who have taken everything I've thrown at them over the past four years *and come back for more.* Guys, I salute you!

## *ABOUT THE AUTHOR*

JODI TAYLOR was born in Bristol and educated in Gloucester.

Her last proper job was that of Facilities Manager for the Library Service in North Yorkshire, where she gained enormous experience of everything going wrong at once.

She left to run a hotel in Turkey where she then gained enormous experience of everything going wrong at once, but in a foreign language.

Her early attempts at writing were not well received. Apparently cannibalism is not a suitable subject for a school poetry competition.

All attempts to stop writing have failed. Jodi Taylor is the author of the phenomenally successful Chronicles of St Marys – the story of a group of tea-sodden historians, and the Frogmorton Farm series – the heart warming and frequently hilarious story of a ramshackle farmhouse and its erratic owner.

She currently lives in Gloucestershire.

# The Chronicles of St Mary's

**BOOK ONE**

**BOOK TWO**

**BOOK THREE**

**BOOK FOUR**

**BOOK FIVE**

**BOOK SIX**

**BOOK SEVEN**

**BOOK EIGHT**

**BOOK NINE**

'A carnival ride through laughter and tears'
Publisher's Weekly

# Discover
# The Frogmorton Farm Series

Getting a life isn't always easy. Hanging on to it is even harder...

THE
NOTHING
GIRL

JODI TAYLOR

From the bestselling author of The Chronicles of St Mary's

Jodi Taylor brings all her comic writing skills to this heart-warming tale of self-discovery.

# The Nothing Girl has grown up…

From the bestselling author of The Chronicles of St Mary's

THE SOMETHING GIRL

JODI TAYLOR

It's life as usual at Frogmorton Farm – which is to say that events have passed the merely eccentric and are now galloping headlong towards the completely bizarre…

**_Feisty independent publishing_**

/AccentPressBooks

@AccentPress

@accentpressbooks

www.accentpress.co.uk